Also by Tom Pollock

The City's Son
The Glass Republic

OUR Lady OF THE STREETS

TOM POLLOCK

Jo Fletcher
New York • London

JF

Jo Fletcher Books
An imprint of Quercus
New York • London

ISBN 978-1-68144-381-2

Names: Pollock, Tom, author.
Title: Our lady of the streets / Tom Pollock.
Description: New York : Jo Fletcher Books, 2017. | Series: Skyscraper throne; 3 | Summary: As the city of London sickens, so does Beth Bradley, and when it is revealed that goddess Mater Viae's plans for dominion stretch far beyond the city's borders, Beth must make a choice: flee, or sacrifice her city in order to save it.
Identifiers: LCCN 2016045230 (print) | LCCN 2017001214 (ebook) | ISBN 9781681443812 (paperback) | ISBN 9781681443805 (ebook) | ISBN 9781681443799 (library ebook)
Subjects: | CYAC: Fantasy. | Supernatural–Fiction. | London (England)–Fiction. | England–Fiction. | BISAC: JUVENILE FICTION / Fantasy & Magic. | JUVENILE FICTION / Monsters.
Classification: LCC PZ7.P76813 Ou 2017 (print) | LCC PZ7.P76813 (ebook) | DDC [Fic]–dc23
LC record available at https://lccn.loc.gov/2016045230

Distributed in the United States and Canada by
Hachette Book Group
1290 Avenue of the Americas
New York, NY 10104

Manufactured in the United States

10 9 8 7 6 5 4 3 2 1

www.quercus.com

For my parents, who first introduced me to London

I

THE FEVER STREETS

CHAPTER ONE

A girl hurried barefoot through the streets of what had once been East London.

She stumbled, clumsy in her haste, and caught herself with the iron railing she carried in her right hand. Her skin was covered in scales of tiny terracotta rooftops. A fringe of rubberised cable fell across her forehead from under the hood of her sweatshirt. The hair-fine streets that crisscrossed her back were flooded with oily sweat. As she ran, her shadow loomed and shambled in front of her, stretched by the dawn.

Beth could barely keep her eyes open. Hunger, exhaustion and week after week of pretending to be fine had hollowed her out. She licked her dry lips. She could sense the pulse of the street under her, but instead of slapping her soles flat to the pavement and replenishing herself from that tantalising thrum of energy, she ran on tiptoes like she was trying to avoid broken glass. She looked up at where the houses had used to be and swallowed fearfully. Hungry as she was, she didn't dare feed here.

Brick terraces rose on both sides of her, their façades unbroken but for the zigzag of mortar: no windows, no doors. Gravel paths led through the overgrown front gardens to dead-end against the featureless walls. No one knew exactly when Hackney had fallen to the Blank Streets, or how many people had been trapped in their homes when all the entrances and exits had suddenly vanished. Beth had heard rumours of fat beads of blood rolling down the cracks between bricks like marbles through children's toy mazes, but she'd never witnessed it. All she knew for certain was what everyone knew: the cries for help had fallen silent quickly—far too quickly for those entombed inside to have starved to death.

Oscar, nestled in her hood, growled and curled tighter into her neck.

I hear you, little buddy, she thought. She reached back into her hood and let the little lizard lick her fingertips.

I hear you.

She paused at the end of the street and bent double. Her breath sawed in and out of her lungs, rattling like a troubled engine. *Get a grip*, she ordered herself. She straightened slowly, feeling the steel hinges in her vertebrae click into place.

She heard a noise and froze.

It was very faint, like a shoe-scuff, but the city was all but silent now and such small sounds carried. She felt a brief impulse to open herself up to the street, to push her consciousness into the asphalt and feel what it felt—but she held back, eyeing the windowless walls. On these streets, she didn't know what might push *back* into her. She imagined her eyes, nose, mouth, ears, even her pores, sealing over with the same seamless brick and shuddered.

She inhaled deeply and all the minuscule lights that dotted the city on her skin flared in response to the fresh oxygen.

Thames, she whispered inside her head, *please, dear Christ, let me be in time.*

She turned the corner—and stared.

If her voice had still belonged to her, she would have laughed, but instead she just stood there in silence, her mouth open, while her chest heaved and her jaw ached.

Garner Street, the road where she'd lived all her life until three months ago, had been spared.

She stumped towards number 18 in a relieved daze. Wilting plants and dead bracken blocked the gate from opening more than a few inches, but she knew that gap well and squeezed through it with ease. Chapped paint surrounded a letterbox with so fierce a spring that when she was a kid she'd imagined it was the snapping jaws of a brass wolf.

She smiled to herself. *Back when we had to pretend.*

The place looked the same as always, the same as it had the night she'd fled it: the night Mater Viae returned.

She relived it between eye-blinks: the blue glare from the blazing Sewermanders reflecting off the walls; the stink of burning methane and wet cement; the terrified faces of London's Masonry Men pressing out of the brickwork, their mouths silently shaping pleas for help. The walls had rippled as Mater Viae's clayling soldiers swarmed under them, clamping red hands over those screaming mouths and pulling them back beneath the surface; the Sodiumites had fled their bulbs in bright panic, leaving darkness and silence in their wake when everything passed on.

And the cranes . . .

A spindly shape caught her eye and she looked up. A crane loomed over the tiled roofs at the far end of the street. It was stock-still.

If you're looking for something to be grateful for, Beth, she told herself, *there's always that.*

When Mater Viae first stepped through the mirror, the cranes had started to move. For three days and three nights they'd torn at the flesh of the city, but then, as suddenly as they'd woken, they'd stopped, fallen silent. Not a single crane had moved since. No one knew why, but it was the smallest of small mercies, and Beth wasn't complaining.

She fumbled in the pocket of her hoodie, but came up empty.

You've got to be kidding me. What kind of Street Goddess locks herself out of her own damn house?

Lizard claws pricked their way down her arm and Oscar appeared on her hand, growling at her questioningly. Beth sighed and nodded; the Sewermander rolled an eye and moved towards the lock. There was a faint hiss from inside the house, from the direction of the kitchen. Beth smelled gas.

Oscar's tongue flicked out. Blue flame flared in the keyhole and with a *snap-sizzle* the lock vanished and was replaced by smoke, charred wood and a hole two inches across. Beth stroked the back of Oscar's head and he let out a self-satisfied purr.

Ah, the Sewer Dragon. What self-respecting burglar would be seen without one?

She pushed inside and let her feet settle flat on the carpet. For a moment she swayed in place, stretching her feet, wiggling her toes and relishing the return of her balance as the tension ran out of her insteps. The place smelled of dust and next door's interloping cat.

The house felt smaller than it had when she'd left it, like a three-quarter-scale mock-up for a film set. She hurried up the stairs, passing photos of her mum and dad and herself as a kid. She trailed her tile-clad fingertips across them as she passed, but she didn't look at them.

A cobweb stretched across the doorway to her room and she broke it like a finishing-line tape. A sunbeam shone in through the skylight. Old sketches were strewn all over the floor. She accidentally kicked a mug over, and cold, mould-skinned tea crept over a half-finished flamenco dancer with swirling charcoal galaxies for eyes.

She yanked her wardrobe open, shovelled armfuls of clothes out of the way and pulled out a battered Crayola carry-case. Over the years that yellow plastic box had held her diaries, her love letters (both the ones she'd received and the ones she hadn't had the guts to send; sadly, they were seldom to the same boys), condoms, a handful of razor blades and her first-ever eighth of ganja, still wrapped in cellophane: everything she'd ever been scared of her dad finding.

She snapped the clasps and tipped out the current contents—a round-bottomed chemical flask and a yellowing paperback novel—onto the bed. She picked up the book and turned it over. The cover had fallen off and the pages had the texture of ash. *The Iron Condor Mystery:* she'd locked it away in her box the day after Dad gave it to her. She remembered her mum leafing through it when she was alive, and her dad obsessively doing the same after her death. She ran her thumb delicately along the spine, then pulled her hand back like she'd been burned.

Even after the cranes and the trains and the metal wolves, even after the chemicals had changed her skin to concrete and her sweat to oil, Beth feared the traces this book had left on her heart. She stuffed it into her back pocket and turned to the flask. The liquid inside it glimmered like mercury and reflected the green light of Beth's eyes back at her as it clung to the inside of the glass. A label taped to it read: *Childhood outlooks, proclivities and memories: traumatic and unusual. Dilute as required.*

She pulled the label off and turned it around. The words were written on the back of a sepia photo of a boy with messy hair and a cocky smile.

So here we are, Petrol-Sweat. Beth looked from the photo to the room and back again. *With everything we used to be.*

She lifted the bottle and peered into her reflection in the glass. *And here's what I am now. What you* made *me.* She felt a dull ache set into her forearm from the simple act of holding up the flask. A drop of sweat fell from her brow and stained the duvet black.

But did you know any way to save me from it?

"That him?"

Beth looked up sharply. The skylight was open and a girl in a black headscarf was looking in, her chin resting on folded arms. The scars on her brown skin bracketed her mouth as she smiled, a smile Beth returned with an open-mouthed stare.

"Anyone else, I'd say this was an awkward silence," Pen said. "But since it's you, I'll let it pass." She swung her legs in through the window and dropped into the room.

Recovering herself, Beth rummaged in her pocket for her marker pen and grabbed a scrap of paper from the floor.

Told you to wait back at Withersham, she scrawled on the back of it. Her surprise made the words jagged. *Blank Streets, fever Streets. Not safe here.*

Pen lifted her scarred chin the way she always did when Beth implied she couldn't take care of herself. "Chill, B. I came over the rooftops. The *tiles* aren't deadly yet, far as we know, anyway. Besides, you were taking so long—I got worried." She frowned, puzzled. "What gives? I covered the distance here in forty-five minutes, which means *you* could have run it less than five. But you've been gone more than an hour. What happened?"

Beth swallowed, her rough tongue sticking to the roof of her mouth as she wrote her reply. *Being careful. Masonry Men at junction with Shakespeare Ave. Didn't know whose side they were on.*

She passed the note over, watching Pen carefully. *One advantage of losing your voice*, she thought to herself. *Lies go over easier on paper.*

Pen's frown deepened. She sat on the end of Beth's bed, crossed her legs under her and started drumming her palms against her kneecaps. "Weird being back in this room after all the nights we spent sitting up in it," she said. "You remember the very first time? When we were bitching about Gwen Hardy? I was so worried you'd tell her I could barely get the words out." She laughed and showed the scarred back of her hand to Beth. "It felt like the riskiest thing I'd ever do."

Beth smiled carefully, keeping her church-spire teeth hidden behind her lips. She went to sit beside Pen.

"You miss it?" Pen asked. "Talking like that?" She paused, but Beth made no move towards her paper. Pen started to pick at the cuticles on her hands, peeling the skin back from around her nails like pencil shavings.

Quickly, Beth put a hand over hers to stop that little self-demolition. She mouthed, *What is it?*

Pen looked right into her eyes. Beth could see the green glow from her own gaze fill her friend's eye sockets. "Could you use your other voice, B?" Pen asked quietly. "Your new one? I miss hearing you talk back."

Beth hesitated, but then she opened her hands in front of her. The lines in her palms were streets, dark canyons between miniature rooftops. As she concentrated, tiny lights began to traverse them: the wash of headlights from invisible cars. She heard the growl of their engines and the faint protest of their horns. Water gurgled through turbines on her shoulder. A train rattled over tracks near her heart.

The sounds were faint, but if you knew how to listen, you could hear words in the edges of them where they blended into one another: a precise and literal body language.

"*What's wrong, Pen?*" Beth asked.

Pen sighed. "Glas sent a pigeon," she said. "She found my parents."

Beth started forward in concern. "*Thames! Are they okay? Are they?*"

"They're alive," Pen said. "They're not hurt. They made it to the evacuation helicopter when Dalston fell—they manage to dodge the Sewermanders and get out. They're staying in Birmingham right now—"

"*Pen! That's grea—*"

"—with Aunt Soraya."

Beth sat back. "*Oh.*"

"Yes."

"*Your* favourite *Aunt Soraya? The one whose house I stayed at?*"

"That's the one."

"*The one with pictures of you up all along her hall? The one who named her cat after you?*"

"Yeah. Can't imagine that was awkward when my folks turned up, what with them not even remembering I exist."

"*Pen, I—*"

"I did that to them, B," Pen cut her off, her voice still quiet but stony, matter-of-fact, brooking no argument. She kept her eye on the shred of skin she was flicking on her thumb. "I was the most important thing in their lives and I stole myself from them." Her gaze fell on the bottle of Fil's memories. "Just like that. I thought that what they couldn't remember couldn't hurt them, but damn, it's hurting them now.

"Glas had her bird sit right on the window ledge. It listened in to a whole conversation. You'd be amazed how many words that trash-spirit has to use to say, 'You've made your parents think they're crazy' when she's trying to be nice about it." She sniffed like she'd been crying, though no tears had fallen, and rubbed the sleeve of her jacket across her eyes.

After a moment she continued, "Anyway, Glas just told me, and since we were here anyway, it felt kind of appropriate to tell you here, for old time's sake, you know?"

Beth nodded, but she couldn't hold her friend's gaze so she studied the swallow pattern on her duvet cover instead.

"B?"

Beth didn't look up.

"Is there anything you want to talk about?"

Beth stilled her shaking right hand by making a fist.

For old time's sake, she thought. Her old backpack was tucked under her desk, stuffed with aerosol cans and stencils and markers. The smile she gave Pen was almost shy. "*You feeling inspired, Pen?*"

Pen returned the smile, stood up and stretched. "I think I might have some game, sure."

CHAPTER TWO

Beth gave Pen a boost back out of the skylight, and then dragged herself out after her with a showy chin-up she immediately regretted. She straightened stiffly, all the while feeling Pen's gaze on her. She walked to the edge of the roof and looked out over the eaves.

A blast of hot air hit her in the face and she recoiled. Swearing inwardly, she covered her face with a forearm and edged back over the gable. In the early-morning light she could see little dots glinting on the bricks of the street below: beads of oily sweat. There was a heat distortion in the air over the tarmac, making it shimmer and warp.

"*Pen?*" she called.

"What?"

"*Don't get too close to the edge.*"

"Why not?"

"*We're backed onto a Fever Street.*"

Behind her, Pen instinctively gripped the edge of the skylight. "I thought these were Blank Streets," she protested, "not Fever Streets."

"*Except for the one behind us, looks like. By the feel of it, it's running at about four hundred degrees. Losing your footing would be—*"

"—uncomfortable?" Pen proposed.

"*I was going to go with crispy.*"

A tearing sound echoed through the morning air, and on a hillside a few miles away a twelve-storey tower block erupted through the pavement like a compound fracture breaking skin. There were many more hills in London these days, where muscles of cable and piping and earth had gone into spasm under its surface, rucking the city up on top of it. In some places the buildings leaned at crazy angles; in others, they toppled from decayed roots like rotten teeth.

Ever since Mater Viae had stepped through from London-Under-Glass the city had been sickening. It was racked with fevers and sweats and the strange brick cataracts they called Blank Streets, but the convulsions were the worst. London was twisting like a tortured man away from a knife, putting Ealing in the east and Norwood in the north and splitting the river into oxbow lakes and pipework waterfalls.

Beth folded her arms and eyed her city's new skyline.

Canary Wharf reared up from what was now London's very heart, the only tower still standing true. The Square Mile's skyscrapers had crashed down around it creating a labyrinth of shattered steel and glass. At night, the aircraft-warning beacon still blinked on and off, and Mater Viae's Sewermanders went flapping around it like moths at a light bulb.

"Think she's at home?" Pen asked, following Beth's gaze.

"*Bitch has just got back from a lifetime's exile,*" Beth replied. "*I don't reckon she's ever planning on leaving home again.*"

"Well, she'd better," Pen said, edging cautiously to stand at Beth's shoulder. "I need things back to normal. I'll be damned if

I'm going to put up with Primrose Hill right next door to me—no decent clothes shops and *everyone's* got a bloody baby."

Beth grinned. "*Well, maybe you should explain it to her, just that way.*" She unslung her rucksack and pulled out some chalks and some spray-paints, then knelt and began to sketch on the bricks of the chimneystack. Pen peered over her shoulder, watching the picture emerge. When Beth glanced up, she could see her friend's scarred lips moving as she tried out lines in her head.

The sun climbed steadily behind Beth as she worked. Eventually, she paused and stood back, stretching out the stiffness in her calves. The partially shaded outlines of herself, Pen and her dad stood out on the bricks. There was a fourth outline too, vaguer than the others: a skinny, bare-chested boy holding the same railing that was now thrust under Beth's bag strap. All of them were smiling.

"Those are good, B—bit tame for you, though, no?"

Beth shrugged. "*I'd draw you a couple of monsters, but my stuff can't compete with the real thing.*"

Pen laughed.

"But your picture of *me* can? Thanks."

"*No, 'course not . . . but it's not supposed to be a portrait so much as a . . .*" The city-sounds from her body went silent for a second as she searched for the right words. At last she said, "*It's like a coin in a wishing-well, you know?*"

Pen pursed her lips and stepped up to the picture. Her fingers traced Fil's outline and then drifted wider and sketched a fifth, invisible, figure on the brick.

She snapped the lid off her marker and wrote:

Out of sight, but not of mind: the shapes of those we've left behind

The floors and flaws beneath our feet. The storeys here on our home street.

Beth appraised it slowly. "*Nice.*"

"You too, B. You been practising? The one of Fil's pretty much perfect." It was too. So was the one of Pen. The only one that was a little off, a little hazy, was Beth's own.

"*You know me, Pen. It's how I vent a little—*"

She'd been about to say "pressure" but she was cut off by a human scream.

It came from behind them. It was close, maybe two streets away, and Pen was already running before Beth had even turned around, slipping and sliding on the tiles, throwing out her arms for balance. Beth's heart clamped up in her chest as she tore off after Pen. They crossed the end of a narrow alley, a cul-de-sac where the roofs had a steep rake. Ahead, Pen dropped to all fours and scuttled along the ridge, grasping at it with her hands and feet. It was only then that Beth noticed Pen had shed her shoes and socks for better grip.

Did you learn that trick from your steeplejill? Beth wondered with a pang of mixed jealousy and pride as she followed.

The screaming grew clearer as they crested the peak of the next roof. While Pen scrambled down a drainpipe to the street Beth followed her instinct and jumped—but she landed badly and had to roll. She levered herself up with the spear, careful to avoid putting her hand flat to the pavement. She breathed in as shallowly as she could; the air was burning in her lungs and all her joints felt rusted.

This street was Blank. The walls were unbroken, the houses delineated only by striations of white paint and bare brick. The screaming stopped briefly, breaking into shuddering gasps, and then it began again: high-pitched and young, a girl's voice, coming from the last house in the terrace.

Beth and Pen looked at each other uncertainly. This was the first human sound to emerge from a Blank Street in months. Pen went to the wall and pressed her hands to the bricks.

"It's okay," she called into a crack in the mortar like it was an intercom, "we're here. We'll help you."

If the screamer heard Pen, she gave no sign of it. This wasn't a cry in hope of help, not any more. Now it was just sheer animal terror.

Pen looked back over her shoulder at Beth.

Beth knew what she needed to do. She braced herself and approached the wall, clenching the tiny muscles in her feet to close her pores, to keep the street out of her. Yet again she felt the urge to reach out with her consciousness, to probe for what awaited her there, but she couldn't risk it: she couldn't trust these pavements. She reversed her grip on her spear.

"*If you can, get back from the wall.*" Beth's turbine-growl made the bricks vibrate, but the girl trapped inside the terrace didn't respond.

The first blow almost crippled her. She sucked up the last dregs of energy from her muscles and slammed the base of her spear against the bricks, hard enough to make the whole wall shudder. A hacking cough ripped out of her. Under her feet, the pulse of the street thrummed, enticing her, but she shook her head. She would not feed.

"Beth?" Pen asked in alarm, but Beth had already raised the spear and rammed it down again, spraying mortar and dust everywhere. This time the brick shifted inwards and she hurriedly spun the railing around and jammed its point into the gap, worrying at the mortar, wiggling and scraping, digging and hacking. The scream came louder, then multiplied, becoming a dozen screams from a dozen directions. Beth's arms burned as she levered bits from the wall and smashed at the edges of the hole she'd made to widen it. She felt a breeze as fresh air rushed into the wound in the wall. Next to her, Pen coughed in the dust.

Beth stepped forward, the green wash from her eyes illuminating the darkness inside.

"*Shit.*" Her head swam. The inside of the house was a labyrinth. Passageways opened at bizarre angles onto dusty corridors that stretched for miles into the distance. Stairways looped in mad, tangled curls, climbing beyond the light cast by Beth's eyes, far above where the roof of the terrace should have bounded them. Doors hung open on hinges set into nothingness; windows lay on the floor, their sashes jammed open onto limitless depths. It looked like every exit stolen from this terrace was here, and the same little girl's scream came from every one of them.

Pen came to Beth's shoulder. Beth heard her breath hiss out, then she said, "Beth." She pointed.

Running from the corner of one of the windows, like drool from a mouth, was a trickle of drying blood. Beth gazed around the inside of the blank house: every doorway and window frame had similar obscene markings.

Pen set her hands inside the gap and stiffened, ready to lever herself inside, but Beth stopped her with a hand on the shoulder.

"*No.*"

"We have to help her,"

"*There's no one to help*," Beth countered hurriedly. "*She's already dead.*"

"Beth, I can hear her screaming."

"*The scream's all that's left. It's just coming from a really long way away. Wherever she is, she's gone.*"

"How do you know?"

"*I just do.*"

Beth looked at her best friend and prayed that the strange make-up of her voice would hide how uncertain she was; that Pen wouldn't realise she was only guessing. All she knew for certain was that Pen couldn't go in there. If she did, she would never find her way out.

Pen shook her head stubbornly. "We still have to try."

"*Pen—*" She broke off. The screaming had ceased.

Something glimmered inside the labyrinth: a light that wasn't Beth's own. A smell like burning hair stung her nostrils. She stepped back and looked up. Every single chimney on the terrace had black smoke seeping from it. A roaring sound drew her eyes back to the hole in the wall. Her ears popped as air rushed into the terrace: in every passageway a wall of orange flame stormed up to meet her.

"*Pen—*" Beth said as the ground began to shudder under her, "*run!*"

CHAPTER THREE

Beth relaxed the unseen muscles in her feet and let the city's essence flow up into her. A wave of dizziness struck and she staggered sideways. Bile boiled up into her throat and she gasped past it, but poisoned as it was, it was still energy. Deep under her skin, urbosynthetic cells fired. It took her one step to recover her balance, and then she accelerated hard.

Beth grabbed Pen around the chest, lifted her bodily off the ground and raced back the way they'd come, Oscar screeching angrily inside her hood. The terrace shook, and shuddered. Tiles clattered from gables and cracks zigzagged between Beth's feet, but she didn't break stride. Her breath burned like chemicals in her lungs. Her railing-spear was ready in her right hand; Pen, bundled over her shoulder and shouting incomprehensible obscenities, occupied her left. She looked back as they hit the bottom of the hill and felt something heavy drop into the pit of her gut.

With a low groan, the entire terrace of the Blank Street shook itself free of its foundations and reared up, bunching into coils like a vast, blunt-nosed snake. Chimneystacks rose from its back like dorsal spines, gouting foul black smoke. Fire and rolling smog spumed from the wound Beth had made in its side.

Beth tried to summon more power from the street, more speed, but she was drawing in too many toxins and she staggered. Sweat pricked her brow and a shiver raced under her skin.

Pen was hammering on her back. "Beth, put me *down*!" Beth ignored her; she had to get Pen away. Oscar was still stirring inside her hood, reacting to her fear. The air whipping past her began to twist into strange geometries. A manhole cover leapt into the air and clanged down hard on the pavement as the Sewermander summoned methane from tunnels below.

Beth couldn't breathe. She felt sick. Every step was sapping her. A long, blunt-nose shadow bled over her and she looked up to see the Street-Serpent rearing in the air above her. Nestled amongst the ripped foundations and pipes and clods of earth that clung to its belly she saw a design: tower blocks arranged into the spokes of a crown.

With an angry hiss, Oscar flew from Beth's hood, straight at the beast. He banked hard a moment before he hit the Street-Serpent and Beth saw his metal tongue glint.

Blue fire ignited in the air: a vast gas flame in the shape of a dragon. Oscar's tiny reptilian body was black at the core of the ghostly blue form. The Sewermander beat his methane wings and shot down the length of the Street-Serpent, bathing it in fire. When he reached the end of it, he wheeled around to see his handiwork, but he screeched in dismay: the Serpent was covered in soot, but otherwise Oscar's heat hadn't marked it at all.

A crack split the end of the terrace, right under the peak of the snake's tiled roof. Beth ran and ran, but she couldn't get out from under it. She looked up as the crack widened, following the line of the bricks as it broke open into a massive, blunt-toothed mouth. Inside, for just an instant, Beth glimpsed banks of rolling flame consuming banisters and wardrobes and still-living bodies:

the fuel the Blank Street had been saving up. It was a creature of fire already; it had no cause to fear Oscar's.

As the maw came crashing down over her, a voice out of her memory cried, *For Thames' sake! Get the fuck out of the way!*

Beth danced sideways as the flaming masonry piled into the asphalt beside her and her world shuddered. She stumbled and fell to her knees, levered herself up and staggered on.

A thin trickle of blood was running from Pen's ear but she was still hammering on Beth's arm and shouting, "Let me go, Beth!"

Beth shook her head dumbly. No way was she leaving Pen behind here.

"I'm not suicidal," Pen shouted. "I've got an idea. Just bloody well trust me, all right?"

Startled, Beth released her. Pen reeled a little, but hit the ground running. Beth was shocked to find she didn't have to brake for her friend to keep pace with her.

Christ, she thought, *how slow have I got?*

With a grinding roar, the terrace reared back into the air behind them. Brick scraped deafeningly over stone. The Street-Serpent followed, bending stiffly where its houses joined as it undulated after them in sidewinder coils.

Pen reached out and threaded her fingers between Beth's own. "Follow where I lead," she gasped. She was half a pace ahead now, her head ducked like a greyhound's.

Pen dragged and Beth followed. They jinked left down an alleyway. Beth didn't even see the skip before they were scrambling up over the side of it. They clambered over sodden cardboard and builders' rubble and then out into the street beyond. Pen hared right between abandoned houses. A wooden gate reared up in front of them but she let go of Beth and threw her shoulder at it and the bolt flew off in a spray of splinters. Beth staggered after

her into a garden. Pen dropped to one knee beside the back fence
and held her linked hands out in front of her.

"All those special powers, you didn't think to grow a couple of
inches?" Pen muttered as Beth stepped into the boost. Pen smiled
tightly between the sweat-soaked strands of hair that had escaped
her hijab.

Beth hit the road on the other side, and Pen followed an instant
later. There was a shockingly loud churning sound behind them,
like a garbage compactor filled with rocks. Beth pulled herself far
enough back up the fence to see over. Now she understood.

Pen had led them through narrow gaps into each of three parallel roads, and the Street-Serpent was trying to follow. It hurled
itself sidelong against the buildings in its path, which gave way
with dizzying concussions, but the collapsed masonry was building up against its flanks, slowing it. Beth couldn't be positive,
but it seemed to be moving more sluggishly. She watched as it
gathered itself, preparing to throw itself against the next row of
houses in its path.

"*That's inspired, Pen,*" Beth managed. "*You slowed it down.*"

Pen's reply was a hiss of frustration. "I was kind of hoping to
stop it. Keep running."

They turned and ran on, pelting along the pavement, past abandoned cars and empty houses. A viaduct plunged them briefly into
darkness as they raced under it, then the sun broke over them
again. They came racing up hard on a T-junction. The heat of the
day made the air shimmer over the asphalt in the distance.

"Left at the end," Pen gasped between strides. "There's a
canal—a way into the sewers, we'll . . . lose—*hey—!*"

Beth had snagged Pen's jacket and she reeled back, flailing,
then skidded onto her arse on the pavement. "*Ow!* B! What th—?"

She stopped abruptly, staring as Beth pointed at the glimmering heat distortion on the road in front of them. She picked

herself up and tried to go on, but after a few steps she threw her arm across her face and turned back. Even from where Beth stood, she could feel the radiation from the Fever Street like a hot wind on her face. When the fevers had first flared, months ago, they'd melted cars and incinerated anyone unlucky enough to be caught walking on them, and it didn't feel like they'd cooled any.

Pen cast about them for an escape route, but the houses on either side were unbroken terraces with no ways through and no way to climb over. There was nowhere for them to go.

With a *whummph* of burning wings, Oscar banked and circled over them, calling forlornly to Beth with his quiet fire-crackle voice.

"*Won't work, buddy,*" Beth replied.

"What won't?" Pen asked urgently. The houses were tall enough to block out the sight of the Street-Serpent, but they could hear it and *feel* it through the ground, rumbling towards them. "Because I'm prepared to consider pretty much anything right now."

"*He's saying we should climb on and he'll carry us out of here.*"

"Oh." Pen stared up at the flaming form of the Sewermander. "Not to be all 'me me me' about it," she said tightly, "but I think I might find that a little too toasty."

The grind of masonry on asphalt swelled until Beth thought her eardrums would burst. Behind them, the houses at the far end of the road burst apart in a shower of bricks as the Street-Serpent bulldozed its way through. Its blunt head swayed towards them, just inches from the ground. It slithered down the confined street, wrapped in its own oily smoke.

"Beth?"

"*What?*" Beth didn't take her eyes from the thing; she felt like she couldn't—like the eyeless snake had hypnotised her.

"Oscar's right."

"*What?*"

"Get on him." Pen's voice was quiet, but there was no hesitation in it. "Fly away."

"*Pen?*"

"Yeah."

"*Fuck that.*"

"You have a better idea?"

"*Not yet.*" Beth winced at the thought of what she was about to try to do. "*But I'm working on it.*" She reversed her hold on her spear, took a deep breath, closed her eyes and plunged her consciousness into the street beneath her feet.

It was like swimming in polluted water. She gasped and swallowed the toxins flowing through it and felt nausea bolt through her. She grasped at the substance of the street desperately with her mind, trying to imagine human shapes, to pull the asphalt into them, to fill them with her consciousness, to make them live. With every ounce of her concentration, she fought to summon Masonry Men to aid them, but the beast was too close; its fearful clatter sent waves through the asphalt, breaking Beth's rudimentary forms, shattering her focus. She tried again and again, but it was hopeless.

The serpent writhed towards them with inexorable rhythm, each coil thudding against the ground, over and over, just like a—

Beth snapped her eyes open. She grabbed Pen's wrist and dragged her, stumbling, back the way they'd come, straight towards the onrushing beast.

"Beth! What are you—?"

Trust me. Beth thought it, but she didn't say it. She didn't want those to be the last words Pen heard if she was wrong.

The Street-Serpent closed on them, but Beth didn't look up; she just felt it; she heard its thunder, smelled its smoke. When they got to the viaduct, she snapped, "*Get on my back.*"

Pen stared at her for a moment, then obeyed, grabbing her shoulders and locking her legs round her waist. Beth grunted and jumped at the wall. She skidded down the bricks for an instant, then her hands found holds, the texture of the masonry locking into the grooves of her palms. She scrambled upwards.

Beth felt Pen stiffen a fraction of a second before her own head rose above the bricks. The Street-Serpent was on them—she could feel the heat of its fire on her face as it reared in a jagged coil over the viaduct. It opened its zigzag mouth and black smoke boiled out, filling the air above it like a stormcloud. Beth didn't pause; she barely even looked at it. Something metallic glimmered in the centre of the viaduct—the railway track—and she threw herself down on it.

Sparks sizzled and hissed as Beth hit the live rail, electricity arced, smoke roiled around them, obscuring everything, but the current didn't penetrate her concrete skin. The track shuddered, all of Beth's muscles tensed, but the Street-Serpent hadn't hit them—it hadn't even moved. But a thunderous rhythm still shook the ground . . .

. . . *thrumclatterclatterthrumclatterclatter* . . .

On the tiny tracks that ran over her heart, Beth felt a train answer in its own language.

Full-beam headlights glared through the smoke. Pen was trying to say something, but a scream of steel drowned her voice. The ghostly shape of a train stormed out of the haze towards them.

The Street-Serpent struck.

It felt like Beth's own skeleton was shaking itself apart, like her brain was liquefying inside her skull. She screwed up her eyes and waited for all sensation to cease . . .

. . . but it didn't. Instead the sound gradually quieted, the motion around her became more even. She could still feel the heave of the breath into her lungs. She opened her eyes.

She was sprawled face-down over a control panel, Pen still clinging to her back. Indicator hands whipped round dials next to her eyes. She pushed herself up and Pen slid to the floor. They were inside a train.

The front of the train was misty, insubstantial; when it wavered, Beth could see trees and the edges of the viaduct rushing past. She made her way to a bit of the wall of the carriage where the ghostly chassis looked firmer, gripped it where it became the most solid and leaned out.

The train parted around her like fog and she looked above to see Oscar flying overhead, easily keeping pace. The track curved away behind them, and there, already dwindling into the distance, she could see the collapsed ruin of the viaduct. The Street-Serpent emerged from it in a bunched ruck of rooftops, its smoke slowly dissipating in the breeze.

A steam-whistle cry rose into the air, the Railwraith crowing victoriously, and a grin split Beth's face. She'd heard that cry before. She recognised the graffiti looping along on the outside of the carriages too. Without her even thinking about it, a matching whistle emerged from the railway tracks in her body.

"*You're alive.*" The words emerged exultantly. "*Thank Christ and Thames you made it.*"

She felt a hand on her shoulder and with a touch of reluctance she pulled herself back inside the Railwraith.

"Can you speak to it?" Pen asked her. She was still breathing a little heavily, but otherwise she'd recovered her composure remarkably quickly. "Did you summon it here?"

Beth nodded slowly. "*I called to it. It's . . . a friend of mine.*"

Pen started to laugh. "Just saying," she said, "your friends are pretty cool. You reckon it knows a way to Bond Street?"

"*Only one way to find out,*" Beth said, and the trains rattling over the railways grooved deep into her body clattered out the instruction. The Railwraith brayed in response. It shuddered with pleasure at having passengers aboard as it steamed into the day.

CHAPTER FOUR

In a paradox of topography, the city's contractions made it feel bigger. The roads and rails were broken, the pavements fractured. There were no longer direct ways to navigate the metropolis. The Railwraith could only manage short jumps between the stretches of track that sustained it, the *Bahngeist* equivalent, Pen supposed, of holding your breath under water.

Beth sat slumped against the train's dashboard with her legs crossed and her spear across her lap. Pen would have thought she was asleep if not for the green glow from her eyes that lit up the front of her hoodie.

What's wrong?

For the hundredth time she *almost* asked it aloud. She could feel the question pressing urgently against the inside of her. Didn't she deserve to know?

Let her rest, she told herself, swallowing her indignation. *Whatever she owes you, you owe her that.*

They plunged into a tunnel and the light disappeared. The ghost train rocked under them in the darkness.

It was mid-afternoon by the time they reached Bond Street station, but the roof of slate-grey clouds over the city made it feel later.

Rain speckled Pen's face as she emerged from the tube station. Drops hissed into vapour on the surface of Oxford Circus, six hundred yards away. The Fever Streets had advanced again in the night.

Pen inhaled deeply. The rain smelled of limestone and for a moment she was back on the rooftops of London-Under-Glass, dodging chunks of brick and tile and concrete as they fell from the clouds.

At least the weather here's still safe, she thought, *even if nothing else is.*

Metal rang off metal behind her as Beth climbed the stationary escalators, swinging her spear jauntily, like a dandy's walking cane—but that didn't hide the way she leaned on it every time it hit the floor. Pen offered her an arm, but Beth put on a baffled smile and waved her away.

They crossed the empty expanse of Oxford Street. A statue stood on the steps in front of Selfridges, watching them. Pen didn't recognise the Pavement Priest, but Beth obviously did. She stiffened, and the city-voice that emerged from her body sounded shocked. "*Timon?*"

The air blurred and then the statue was standing on the pavement in front of them. Deep gouges had been dug into the stone of his torso, and Pen thought she could make out fingerprints in the bases of them. Whoever this Timon was, he'd been in a fight. His face had been chipped so badly Pen couldn't read an expression, but his body language was pleading. Inked on his right shoulder, faded but still visible, were four wolf-heads.

"Lady B," Timon said. He sounded desperately relieved. Through the crack in the statue's limestone mouth, Pen glimpsed his flesh lips moving.

"*When did you get here?*" Beth asked. She clapped him on the shoulder. "*Were you at Abney Park when Mater Viae hit it? Where's Al?*"

Timon's voice cracked as he answered, "Al didn't make it. He got reborn."

"*Oh, Thames. Timon—*" Beth sounded stricken. "*I'm sorry.*"

"I don't know where he is," Timon went on. "Been trying to look for him, but the city's ripped up into so many bad zones and I can't travel without tangling with *Her* Masonry Men. I can't—Lady B, I can't stop thinking about him as a little reborn baby, all alone out there, sealed up inside a statue, without no one to look out for him."

The eyeholes in Timon's stone mask were tiny pinpricks, but Pen didn't have to be able to see his eyes to sense the hope as he looked at Beth.

"I came to you 'cause I wanted to ask something," he said quietly. "Lady B, I don't know how many more times he can do this. You hear about fellas going crazy from the rebirthing, from the dark and the claustrophobia. I came because I wanted to beg, Lady B, *please*: give him his mortality back. Let him die for real—let him rest. He's earned it."

Beth's face set. The light from her gaze refracted through the rain to speckle his face. "*Timon—*" She kept her lips pressed tightly together, and when she spoke, her voice was the whisper of tyres on a wet street. "*Timon, I'm so, so sorry, but I can't. I'm not Her, you understand? I know I look like Her, but I'm not. The goddess who took his death—your death and all your brothers' deaths—away from you, She is dead herself. She killed herself with the poison She brewed up from your mortality. She used up all your deaths.*"

Beth spoke gently, but even so, Pen could sense Timon's frail flesh body shrinking inside the statue with every word.

"*If I could give you what you're asking for, you know I would. If I had it, it'd be yours, like it should be. But I don't.*"

The silence that followed was all but unbearable, so Pen broke it. "Timon, right?" she said, putting a hand on his carved sleeve.

"Good meeting you. Petris and Ezekiel are inside. What do you say we talk to them, get a search party organised? I'm sure we can find your friend."

Timon hesitated, considering this, and then nodded, the stone of his neck grinding loudly against itself. Pen gestured for him to follow her inside, but he said, "If it's all right, Lady Khan, I'll stay out here and smoke for a bit. Can I find you later?"

His hand blurred to his mouth and suddenly there was a lit roll-up jammed between his stone lips. The tip flared as he drew on it.

Lady Khan. Pen stiffened slightly. "Call me Pen," she said.

She ushered Beth towards the doors, and this time Beth did lean on her. As they went inside Pen looked over her shoulder. Smoke streamed slowly out between Timon's lips. He was breathing deeply, gathering himself to step back onto the long, exhausting path of searching and hoping. As she watched, he turned his hand over and stared at the inside of his right wrist. The stone had flaked away, and on the pallid skin underneath it was a tattoo of a tower-block crown.

Funny, Pen thought to herself as she surveyed the lower lobby, *when I was a kid I would have killed to live in Selfridges.*

The concession stands thronged with figures, glass, stone and flesh. Shouts echoed off the art deco rafters, threats and bids and promises and insults. Lampfolk argued in flash-bulb semaphores, their voices glimmering from the wires in their glass throats and throwing stark shadows on the walls. The display cases once stocked with expensive perfumes and skin-creams and make-up now were loaded up with wires and batteries and chocolate, carrots and cabbages, old family keepsakes, tins of soup and cans of Coke. In the middle, in the densest part of the crowd, two old men were ladling stew from a massive aluminium saucepan balanced on top of four camping stoves. Men and women jostled and elbowed each other as they waited their turn in what was more a small linear scrum than a queue.

Affrit Candleman stood at one stall, his glass skin shabby with soot. The old Blankleit was haranguing a passing Pavement Priest with hand gestures and semaphores as he pointed to a plastic bag of light bulbs by his foot, but the statue didn't turn around; he wasn't interested in Candleman's particular brand of bespoke nostalgia. Right now, no one needed reminding how good the good times had been.

Selfridges' ground floor was now part market, part soup kitchen and all chaos. Beth pulled her hood up carefully and, with Pen still supporting her, they entered the ruckus.

It had made sense, when the symptoms first struck the city, for those families displaced from their homes to come here. The fevers hadn't touched this place, and there was food and shelter—and even an improbably well-stocked wine cellar for the large numbers of men and women who'd felt the apocalypse would be more appealing if they were blind drunk. As stocks dwindled they'd organised. Rough and ready committees had formed and then almost immediately disintegrated, but enterprising foragers brought in just enough extortionately priced carrots and canned tuna to keep the whole thing going. It was noisy and crowded, with plenty of people coming and going, and in those first weeks it was as good a place as any for Beth to hide.

But then Petris had appeared, his stone monk's habit silhouetted in the doorway. He'd zigzagged across the floor in his stop-motion, Pavement Priest way, growling drunkenly and peering into frightened faces until he'd clapped eyes on Beth.

Even drunk—and he had been *astoundingly* drunk; the vodka sharpness that had risen off him still stung Pen's nostrils—he'd understood the situation. He'd let his gaze slide off Beth and then he'd blurred away.

Later, while the rest of the building slept, he'd met them on the roof. He'd been scared and angry, swigging constantly from an unmarked bottle. *The cemetery had been hit*, he'd said.

"Goddamn clayling popped right out of Stoke Newington High Street," he'd growled. "Asked if we would serve *Her*. I told him to fuck off." Another swig. "I hadn't even closed my mouth and then there were a thousand of them, all identical, all staring at me with those empty fucking eyes. We didn't stand a chance."

He had fifty stoneskins, he'd said, in sore need of a stiff drink, a place to regroup and something to believe in. "We can find the first two somewhere else," he'd grunted at Beth, "but right now, you're the only candidate for the third I don't want to put my fist through."

So, with Pen praying she wouldn't, Beth had let them stay. And then, as Pen had known they would, more stone and bronze figures had appeared at Selfridges' doors. Ezekiel and Bracchion and Templar and Churchill had all limped in at the head of their own decimated bands. Then came little glowing clusters that were the remnants of Sodiumite war-families, their glass skins cracked and their limbs shattered; then the Blankleits had come after them.

It took constant, frantic work to keep Beth's presence quiet. All anyone knew when they arrived was that this was where the others had come. One by one, newcomers were vetted and vouched for before being let in on the secret. Others—whom no one knew or no one trusted—were frozen out until they left to look for another home. For those whom remained, Beth's was the name that lurked unspoken in every room, that hovered dangerously on the lips of sleepers as they mumbled in their dreams.

Beth looked increasingly alarmed as their numbers swelled. Pen knew what she was thinking: these people were all looking for her to lead them against the power of the Mirrored Goddess, but she had not the faintest idea how. More and more, Beth said less and less. She'd withdrawn, losing herself amongst the department store's human population, where her roof-tile scales and street-laced skin were unremarkable: just one more oddity in a world gone insane.

Pen wondered, as she wondered almost every day now, whether it was time to go.

Beth kept her head down and pressed through the crowd, Oscar chirruping quietly under her hood. A thickset man blundered into her and she would have fallen if Pen hadn't caught her.

They called the lift and Beth pressed five. A few seconds later they arrived at the Beds and Bedlinen department. The wooden bedsteads had long since been smashed up and used for firewood, but they'd designated this floor the dormitory regardless, and mattresses were lined up all over the floor, even made up with store stock, thanks to a cheery, middle-aged man from Dalston called Henry. Henry believed in the power of little luxuries like clean sheets to lift people's moods, and he spent most of his time whistling show tunes and hand-washing duvet covers while he waited for the government rescue he was convinced was coming any day now.

Beth dropped onto an unoccupied bed and arched a road-marked eyebrow at Pen. "*What?*"

"What do you mean, what?" Pen countered.

"*You look like you have something on your mind.*"

Pen shrugged. She really wanted to have it out with Beth, but not while she was exhausted. She gestured at the duvet cover, and the beaming cartoon panda dyed on it. "It's just I've been your best friend for almost four years now and I never would have you pegged for a panda girl."

Beth smiled thinly. She looked back towards the front of the building where, for all Pen knew, Timon was still smoking and brooding.

"*Well*," she said, "*I do move in mysterious ways.*" She shuffled down under the duvet. "*You know what? At times like this, I miss the cats. I mean, I know Mater Viae wants to kill me and all, and She's smashing up the city I live in, but did She have to lure away all my sodding cats as well?*"

"That was harsh," Pen agreed. She remembered the morning they'd awakened to find all the stray moggies that'd been following Beth around had slunk away in the night. *Bet they've gone to Her*, Beth had grumbled. *She's probably got a stronger divine musk.*

"Beth?" Pen said.

"*Yes, Pen?*" Beth's eyes were already shut, her voice groggy.

Pen hesitated. "Sleep well."

CHAPTER FIVE

Pen had expected the smell: overripe bananas and rotting meat, sump oil and thick dust: a miasma of decay. What she hadn't expected was the music.

It was very faint, a classical piece: strings and flutes and deep, brassy horns. Pen thought she'd heard it before, but it was off somehow. All the notes were in tune, but there was something indefinably odd about how they sounded. Pen hurried down the steps to the basement, something between eagerness and anxiety pinching at her throat.

In her pocket, she rolled a cold glass marble between her fingers.

A pair of overstuffed bin bags flanked the doors to the kitchen like squat guard towers. As Pen approached, a stinking fountain of garbage erupted and an arm articulated from bits of an old bike frame emerged from the top of the bag on the right. The arm ended in a hammer-head made from old paint cans. It waved threateningly over Pen's head.

The second bin bag split slowly up the middle and a tiny make-shift crossbow crept from the gap on matchstick spider's legs. Pen didn't have to look at the pinkie-sized bolt to know the nail on the end of it was poisoned. She sucked her teeth. It was like being faced down by the Heavy Armaments division of *Blue Peter*.

"Glas," she protested, keeping her voice as mild as she could manage, but never taking her eye from the nail, "it's only me."

With apparent reluctance both the hammer and the crossbow returned to their black-plastic posts, and Pen pushed through the smoked glass double doors. The music swelled and enveloped her. She stared, open-mouthed despite the stench.

Selfridges' kitchen was teeming with hands.

Hands made of old Biros, hands made of sucked lolly-sticks, hands made of broken scissors and bent umbrella spines and used syringes and de-pronged forks, all scrambled hither and thither across the stainless-steel work surfaces born by teams of beetles lashed to their wrists with garden wire. Their improvised fingers held flasks and bottles and cardboard boxes. Yet more hands extended in a chain down the kitchen's rubbish chute, passing hunks of brick and concrete and tea cups of shimmering sewer water from one to the next. The last hand in the line sealed each sample in a plastic pouch and carefully wrote out a label with an expensive-looking fountain pen. Other hands selected previously prepared pouches, dumped their contents into Pyrex beakers and held them over the gas rings of the great industrial cookers until the chemicals inside changed colour to dark blues and bloody reds.

The orchestra occupied the far corner: yet more hands, drawing bows over the strings of violins hammered from broken bed-frames. Punctured footballs sealed with condom lips blew air into flutes carefully fashioned from old curtain rails, producing pure, sweet notes. The music swirled and dipped in the air, making Pen giddy. She put out a hand to steady herself, only to have another passing hand take it in a genteel shake; she couldn't stop herself recoiling from the worms that articulated its braided pipe-cleaner fingers.

A three-dimensional model of the city took up most of the kitchen floor. Juice cartons and ripped-up cardboard boxes stood in for houses, blackened bananas for bridges. Hands spider-picked their way over narrow streets, shifting them into new configurations based on the information from the latest samples, pushing over loo-roll tower blocks or flooding avenues with filthy water, continually mapping the city's transformation. In the centre a mineral water bottle stood stubbornly upright, emerging from a nest of shredded plastic: Canary Wharf.

Wings fluttered by her ear and she ducked instinctively as a petrol-grey pigeon flew past. It circled the room, a pair of broken eggshells clutched in its claws. The pigeon's gyre grew tighter, the music swelled, the hands disintegrated into their component parts and the beetles under them took flight. The air filled with a fever of wings. The pigeon wheeled tighter still, and Pen shied as something buzzed past her ear. As she watched, a cloud of insects, each clasping a fragment of rubbish, whirled into formation under the pigeon and spun faster and faster: a black tornado dancing over the kitchen tiles. Pen squinted as the buzzing mass slowly morphed into a vague human shape.

The pigeon cawed once, then dived into the heart of the cloud. The music crescendoed, then cut out. Every beetle flipped sharply over in the air, dragging their garbage over them. The wings felt silent.

Pen blinked. With a sudden sleight of eye, Gutterglass had a skin.

He wore a tailcoat patched together from dozens of carpet sample squares. His skeletal face was built of split Biro pens. His hands, one also made of Biros, the other of long screws, rested on a mop he held in front of him like a cane. A third—disembodied—hand, the last remaining on its beetle conveyor, scuttled over his shoulder, planted a cigarette between his lips and lit it with a taper before scuttling away again.

Gutterglass drew slowly on the cigarette, and the smoke billowed from the gaps in the plastic frame of his skull. "Miss Khan." His voice still carried the notes of the music. "Always a pleasure."

"Dr. Goutierre." Pen inclined her head respectfully.

"Gutterglass is fine." The trash-spirit waved away the title. "It may be a name She gave me, but I've lived with it for long enough that I think I can call it mine."

There was a wistfulness to the way he said *She* that twisted Pen's heart. "I know exactly what you mean," she said.

Glas smiled. His mouth was full of penny-sweet milk-bottle teeth.

"What's with the arts-and-crafts artillery?" Pen jerked her head at the door and the garbage guard towers.

Gutterglass made an indelicate sound. "In spite of the amnesty very kindly extended to me by Lady Bradley, there still appears to be a certain amount of resentment towards me among the Pavement Priests," he said. "What with our Lady having been a little distracted lately with affairs of incipient Godhood, I thought it only prudent to make arrangements for my own security."

You were their Goddess' closest advisor. You told them She'd flounced off and it was their fault, when She'd actually conned them and killed Herself. When they rumbled you, they were always going to be pretty pissed off, Pen thought, but she didn't say it. She was here for a favour, after all.

"So how goes the diagnosis?"

Gutterglass turned to face the map, the beetles under his skin chittering as they reoriented him.

"Well, analysing the samples and judging by what my pigeons and rats have seen, the last twenty-four hours have brought us five new Tideways." He pointed to a tangle of streets flooded with an inky-grey liquid. "There's a muscle spasm under Victoria"—he indicated a large box with Queen Victoria's head inked on it, now rucked up on a patch of old carpet—"and *eighteen miles* of new Fever Streets."

The spidery hand on his shoulder dropped its taper onto the model. Blue flame licked out along the roadways, tracing the afflicted roadways.

"In my unparalleled medical opinion," Gutterglass said drily, "the city is sick."

"Still no idea what's causing it?" Pen asked.

"Well, since it started the same night that Mater Viae's deranged twin arrived in town, one rather assumes *She* is. But as to *how* She's causing it, on a medical level? I confess I am stumped."

"And we stop it by . . . ?" Pen couldn't hide the hope in her voice.

"If it even can be stopped," Gutterglass murmured, his eggshell eyes intent on the map. "To be honest, I have no idea."

Pen snorted. "Well, aren't you just made of optimism?"

Glas pursed his balloon lips speculatively. "At the present moment? Eighty-seven discarded writing implements, two rusting jerry cans, a pair of football bladders and eleven feet of rubber hose—but no, no optimism, since you ask."

Pen shrugged, suddenly uncomfortable. "I'm just saying, you know, keep a little faith."

Glas rounded on Pen. His tone hardened. "Oh, *faith*, is it? Faith is something I'm all out of, and not freshly, I'm afraid. I am a physician and a scientist, Miss Khan: a realist. Faith was never in the job description. In a hospital, all faith yields is false hope and broken hearts."

Pen was shocked: Gutterglass *never* raised his voice. He controlled himself almost immediately, but Pen still caught the eggshell gaze flickering towards the Evian tower in the centre of the map.

"You weren't any less of a scientist when you believed," she said quietly.

Glas didn't meet her gaze. "My apologies," he said at last. "Working conditions aren't ideal."

"It's all right." Pen hesitated, then put a hand on his mouldering carpet arm. "How's the . . . um . . . the *other* project going?"

Gutterglass raised his head slowly. The white insides of the eggshells looked at her. He reached inside his carpet tailcoat and produced a phial of clear liquid. "I made up the latest batch last night, but I haven't had a chance to test it yet."

Pen eyed the phial. She felt her heart swell in her chest until it threatened to cut off the air to her lungs. "Then let's test it now."

The highly polished side of the stainless-steel oven range made an only-slightly-distorted mirror. Pen looked past her own reflection into London-Under-Glass. She was breathing fast, she realised, anticipating. She braced herself and finally focused on her own scarred face. She remembered cold tiles under her palms and her hands curled. She remembered a dusty mirror in an abandoned bathroom in a school. She remembered her image reflected back at her as the mirror-glass sealed the doorway and shut Espel's face out.

Espel. The memory was a tiny piece of shrapnel, embedded close to her heart, flaring painfully at every beat.

"Ready?" Gutterglass asked softly.

Pen nodded.

The trash-spirit spun the lid off the phial and flung the contents against the side of the oven.

The liquid spattered across the stainless steel and Pen stared into the spreading distortion, willing the metal to disappear and leave only the reflection—willing the doorway to the inverted world to open—but as the chemical dribbled to the floor, the steel stayed as solid as ever.

Pen let out a shuddering breath.

"I'm sorry," Gutterglass murmured. He stood awkwardly for a second, then reversed his grip on his mop and began to prod at the pooling concoction. He mumbled, embarrassed, "I really don't understand what's wrong. The city's sickness—it's denaturing the reactants somehow. I can't get untainted ingredients. I'm trying to work around it, but . . ." He gestured helplessly at the puddle.

Pen nodded. Sudden tiredness weighed down her limbs and her eyelids. Gutterglass was turning back to the model of the city when she asked, "Why are you here?"

The trash-spirit looked around. "I'm sorry?"

"Why are you here," Pen repeated, "with us? Why aren't you with Mater Viae?"

"*Mirror Mater*," he insisted, a little primly. "I am serving the will of my Goddess."

"No, you aren't." Pen contradicted him. "Your Goddess is dead—She has been for decades. She killed herself. You're serving the will of Beth Bradley, who—much as I love her—is an imitation patched up from the scraps your Goddess left behind.

"But *her*?" She jerked her head at the Evian-bottle Canary Wharf. "She's the real deal: an exact copy—just as powerful, just as implacable. Tell me, Glas, with Her around, why *are* you working for the knock-off version I just put to bed under a panda duvet?"

Gutterglass sighed out a fug of sweetly corrupted rubbish. "Well, I guess I'm just a knock-off, patched-up kind of guy." He smiled tightly and affected an accent, but neither accent nor smile held against Pen's gaze.

"I thought She *could* be," he said at last. "I thought the reflected Goddess could be the one. When I heard She'd come through the mirror, I hurried to the Shard, my plastic skirts clutched in both hands, my heart bubbling over with the promise of it, but then I . . . I *saw* Her. I looked into those green eyes . . ."

The piping in his neck flexed as he swallowed. "The first time I met my true mistress, it was like falling in love, and like falling in love, I just *knew*. *This* was who I wanted to spend my life serving, *this* was what I wanted to define me." He licked his lips nervously. "But that night, when I looked at Her mirror-sister, well—you tell me, you've met her—is She a thing to love?"

Pen looked into the eggshell eyes and slowly shook her head.

Gutterglass matched the motion with his skeletal plastic face. "No," he agreed. "Fear—fear is all you can do: fear Her jealousy, fear Her anger, fear Her pain . . . but not love." He shrugged, but his indifference was unconvincing. He went back to mopping the floor. "You just know," he repeated.

Pen stared at the reflection on the side of oven and thought of a blonde girl with a silver seam dividing her perfectly symmetrical face. "You just know," she echoed.

CHAPTER SIX

To most people it would look like graffiti or shadows, a web of darkness cast across the concrete of the distant tower blocks. You had to be in exactly the right place to see the rhino—formed out of the edges of concrete walls and patches of occluded light—charging out at you.

Beth shaded her eyes with one hand and looked up from her street corner. There was a chill breeze and her forearm was puckered in gooseflesh, the hairs glowing like embers in the evening sun. She peered at the rhino on the towers. There was something not quite right about it.

"You're blind." She said it aloud. The city was silent around her, no cars or trains or footsteps or music to break the quiet, and her voice, high and human, carried clear through the air.

Beth pointed at the rhino. "You're blind," she said again. It felt important, though she couldn't have said why.

Her free hand, she was abruptly aware, held an aerosol can. She raised it and sprayed a cloud of fine white paint droplets into the air. The wind picked up, catching the paint spray and bearing it over the gables and peaks of intervening rooftops to settle, at last, against the wall that held the rhino.

Beth felt a satisfaction verging on delight, a sense of the world working with her, for her: now there was a rough oval of white emptiness in the animal silhouette, just where its eye would be, and it was staring straight at her.

That oval of white closed, and then opened again. The rhino snorted.

The sound echoed through the silent city, shaking the towers by their steel and concrete roots. The rhino began to advance. Beth didn't move, but her perspective on the creature shifted somehow and now it was erupting from the shadows of a nearer cluster of towers, and now it was nearer still. Beth's delight froze inside her. The world shuddered under the impact of hooves made of nothing but darkness. Beth threw out her arms, desperately trying to keep her balance.

Another snort, close and deafening; a gust of wet breath hit the back of her neck. Slowly, she turned to face the houses behind her. Their walls were invisible—she couldn't see. Everything was blackness but that one oval eye. She recoiled, teetering backwards on her heels. The pavement spasmed under her once more and as she fell, she screamed the first word that came into her head—

"PEN!"

A pair of scarred, slender hands caught her.

"Beth?"

Beth opened her eyes slowly. Pen was sitting on the edge of her bed, holding her shoulders as though she'd been trying to shake her awake. The light from Beth's eyes highlighted Pen's scars.

"Are you okay?" Pen asked. She pulled her hands off Beth and shook them in the air as if to cool them. "You're *boiling*."

Beth nodded blearily and peeled back the duvet. Her throat was parched and her tongue was stuck to the roof of her mouth. She looked around. Every other bed in the showroom was empty, sheets rumpled as if hurriedly thrown off. She threw a questioning look at Pen.

"That's why I woke you," Pen said. "They're trying again."

Pen usually avoided the electronics department, but it was where many of the human refugees tended to cluster. Voices in a dozen languages blared loudly from the display TVs as trapped tourists fought to keep the news from *their* home countries audible. It wasn't the jaw-clenching decibel level that made Pen steer clear of the place, though; it was the faces of the men and women as they watched the feeds coming in from Beijing and Moscow and New York and Delhi. She'd watched the disbelief, then the anger and then the hurt in their expressions as the rolling twenty-four-hour coverage of the crisis in London had given way to stories about house price rebounds and livestock health scares and a (Pen had to admit, truly terrifying) twelve-year-old boy who had a six-pack like a male stripper. London now rated only a thirty-second segment each night on most overseas stations, if that. The world had got bored of them; it no longer cared about the fates of the people stranded here. They were expendable, and Pen found it too painful to watch them realise it.

Tonight, though, all the screens were black except for the sixty-inch plasma on the back wall. Pen saw Beth fumbling with her hood as though her fingers were numb, and like a mother with a small child, she pulled it up for her. Without a word, the two of them slipped into the edge of the crowd clustering around the one active television.

Above the scrolling BBC News banner was a placid suburban street: semi-detached houses, manicured gardens, branching trees and electricity pylons. The moon was bright and clear, etching every shape in silver and shadow.

The picture went to split-screen, the left side staying on the street while the right cut to a doughy man in an ill-fitting suit, standing on the steps of some town hall and speaking into a collar of microphones.

"*Once again*"—some problem with the Beeb's sound-mixing rendered the man's voice weak and tinny—"*I am calling on the acting Prime Minister to abort this operation now, before it's too late. Too many of our brave servicemen and women have already given their lives in pointless raids."*

Someone behind Pen booed at the telly. Next to her, Beth huddled closer into her hoodie.

"*This is just another sign of a government that is both reckless and out of ideas,*" the doughy man went on, "*and frankly, yet more evidence that the acting Prime Minister's previous position as a junior minister cannot possibly have prepared him for his present responsibility, nor*"—there were spots the colour of raw bacon in his cheeks—"*can the British public be reasonably expected to have ever anticipated his ascension to the leadership of the Conservative Party when they voted for it. The acting government has no legitimacy. We need a general election, and we need one now!*"

"Shut it, tit-face," someone snapped at the TV.

"Call your damn election," said another. "If you come and collect my vote in person, you can have it."

"*Shh!*" Pen put a finger to her lips and hissed. Everyone fell quiet and Beth threw her an impressed look from inside her hoodie. "Just watch."

The picture was back to full-screen again. Bright white halogen lights washed over the suburban street. With a rumble low enough to make the speakers rattle, a battle tank rolled into frame. A soldier in a camouflaged helmet leaned out of the turret aiming a mounted machine gun directly between the genteel houses. A string of armoured vehicles followed behind, their passengers watchful behind the sights of their automatic rifles, engines growling impatiently at their cautious progress. A hissing sound like static, just audible from the TV speakers, underlaid it all.

"Jeez Louise," someone said. "They're coming in heavy this time, aren't they?"

"Where are they?" someone else whispered.

"I dunno—Ealing?"

"Nah, that's Beckenham. My daughter . . . lived there."

"Have they tried there before?"

"No, not yet."

"Come on," someone close to Pen was muttering. She could feel their breath on her ear. "Come on, come on, come on."

Shadow divided the road: a place where the streetlights cut out. From that point on, only moonlight lit the street and everything was spectral and sharp. Pen drew in a breath as the tank approached that line. Radios crackled faintly in the air as the tank rumbled into the shadow . . .

. . . and carried on rumbling.

Pen exhaled. Someone at the back of the crowd whooped. The camera zoomed in on the soldier in the turret. His shoulders relaxed and he reached back and beckoned those behind him onwards. The tank purred up a gear as they followed. Chatter broke out around Pen, voices shaky with relief.

"How far is that from here?" someone was saying eagerly.

"About fifteen miles."

"Do you think they'll make it all the way?"

"What about the hot streets?"

"They must have satellites," another voice said knowingly, "thermal imaging. They'll know what streets to avoid. Maybe they've found a way through!"

"A way through," someone echoed, and the crowd cheered. "A way *out*."

The crowd kept cheering, chanting, "A way out!" It went through them like a wind through rushes. "*A way out, a way out*."

Pen was still watching the soldier in the tank turret. He was tiny now, a long way from the camera: a toy figurine silhouetted by the headlight wash, but he wasn't getting any smaller, she realised. She kept watching. Long seconds passed. The column had stopped advancing. The soldier's silhouette was bent over, his hands braced on the edge of his hatch. He was staring at the road beside the tank.

"Everybody shut up!" Pen yelled over the din in the room. Heads turned irritably towards her, but the cheering cut off. In the silence that followed, soft and distant and mediated by microphone crackle, she could hear the soldier shouting.

The camera zoomed in until he was in close up, pointing and yelling—his voice still surreally quiet; the microphone was as close as it could get. The camera panned downwards in the direction he was pointing and Pen hissed.

The tank tracks were half submerged in the road. The asphalt lapped at the steel wheels like seawater.

"It's a Tideway," she breathed in horror.

The vehicles were sinking. Liquid tarmac was pouring in through the smallest gaps. The soldiers were standing on their seats, already up to their knees in it. They held their discipline, snapping into their radios, but the camera mercilessly homed in on their wide, panicky eyes.

With a groan of metal, the tank tipped backwards. The massive gun barrel stuck up into the air like a flagpole. The soldier was hanging backwards out of the turret, the asphalt licking at his uniform as the tank slid in deeper. The camera zoomed in on his hands as they fumbled with his gun-strap, his helmet. He was getting ready to swim for it.

"No," Pen whispered. "No. Don't. No."

The helmet came free and an instant later he dived into the road. There was barely a splash as the asphalt swallowed him.

Pen stared. They all stared. For silent moments there was nothing, and then . . .

There! He erupted from the surface of the road in a fit of coughing and flailing. He was only a few feet from his stricken vehicle, as far as his leap had taken him, but no further. He windmilled his arms raggedly, trying to drag his body into a front crawl, but he just splashed. He didn't advance a single inch.

A weight settled in Pen's stomach as she watched.

"Why isn't he swimming?" a thickset man in a turban demanded.

"The liquid's not dense enough," Pen answered, trying to keep her voice from shaking. "There's no resistance, nothing for him to push against."

He was sinking. The road was already up to his chin and the tide was pushing it into his mouth. He spat and gasped. His mates were hollering at him to swim, holding out their rifles for him to grab hold of, but they were just out of reach. They swore and revved their vehicles, but though their wheels spun and churned up the road, they went nowhere. There was a commotion in the foreground of the picture: more armed figures, sprinting up the road, but as soon as they reached the line where the streetlights cut out they reeled back. They milled about, toeing the edge of the shadow: the liquid street, lapping up onto dry land.

The soldier wasn't even splashing now. His arms were fully submerged. His head tilted back, desperate for breath.

And then, like sudden thunder came the sound of helicopter blades.

A dark shape swooped into the picture: the chopper, black and angular as an insect, a light flashing on its nose. Pen saw the ripples its rotors threw up in the centre of the road; she watched the soldiers raise their arms in greeting as it came to hover over them, but the *whup whup whup* of its blades drowned out their cheers. It drowned out another sound too, Pen was sure of it. One she'd forgotten and remembered only as it disappeared: the static hiss she'd heard earlier from the TV.

A man emerged from the chopper, his silhouette bulked out by a life jacket. He bobbed on a cable like a cat's toy as he descended towards the sinking soldier.

"Thank Christ for that," someone exhaled.

Pen stirred uneasily and looked at Beth, who shook her head. Something wasn't right, but she couldn't quite—

"The hissing!" she exclaimed suddenly. "Why would static from the TV set get drowned out by a sound *inside* the broadcast?"

It was only then she realised the windows of every house on the street were open.

With a bang like a thunderclap, fire erupted over the road. A pair of dragons, their outlines drawn in blue flame, beat their wings and shot towards the helicopter. Inside Beth's hood, Oscar crooned.

The soldiers babbled in panic and struggled to bring their rifles to bear. The air filled with the rattle-roar of machine-gun fire, but the Sewermanders didn't even flinch. They lifted their talons and bowed their backs like hunting falcons as they crashed one after the other into the side of the helicopter.

Orange flared into blue as their claws found the fuel tank, then, shrouded in filthy smoke, the chopper plummeted towards the ground. The liquid street swallowed it with barely a splash, though the hiss of the extinguished fire carried clearly to the news team's microphones.

The Sewermanders bent their necks as though calling, but they made no sound Pen could hear. They twisted in the air and began to circle the sinking men.

Two more gunshots sounded, then nothing. The soldiers stared upwards, their faces lit blue by the fire.

Pen waited. They all waited. She imagined the gas-drakes swooping down, incinerating their prey with flaming jaws, but they didn't. They just beat the air, riding their own thermals, waiting.

Beth forgot herself and put a street-laced hand over her mouth, but it was the man in the turban who spoke.

"My God. They're just leaving them."

The soldiers splashed and struggled, flailing their arms like children who didn't know how to swim. They were up to their necks now, the vehicles invisible under them. Pen could almost read their lips as they prayed and begged and fought for breath.

Their outstretched fingers less than two feet from the pavement, one by one, they slipped below the surface.

No one spoke. Pen switched off the TV. She turned to Beth, looking for someone to share her horror, but Beth wasn't looking at her. She was bent over, crooked, staring at the floor.

Beth's hand was still clamped across her mouth, but cupped, as though to catch something, and from between her fingers a liquid the colour of asphalt was dripping with a *plack plack plack* sound onto the marble floor.

CHAPTER SEVEN

Steeped in shock, the people in the crowd didn't even notice when the scar-faced Asian girl grabbed her quiet friend by the front of her hoodie and dragged her out onto the fire stairwell.

Pen pushed Beth down onto the steps and squatted in front of her. Ignoring her friend's weak attempts to bat her away, she put a hand behind Beth's head, under the slick rubber cable of her hair and eased her backwards. Then she prised Beth's hand from her face.

The tiny streets that marked the frown-lines at the edge of Beth's mouth were brimming with liquid asphalt; the stuff seeped slowly out of them like blood from scraped open scabs.

"Crap," Pen muttered. She hesitated, then struggled out of her jumper and slapped it against Beth's cheek. "Hold that there. I'm getting Glas."

Beth shook her head weakly, but Pen turned away and was half-way down the first flight of stairs before she heard the city-rumble of her friend's new voice. "*Pen, it's okay. They'll re-clot. They always do.*"

Pen turned back slowly, a prickle crawling across her neck as she climbed back to the landing. "Always?" she said, her voice taut. "What do you mean, '*always,*' B?"

Beth stared up at her from under heavy lids, the jumper still clamped to her face like an icepack. She didn't say anything.

"You know what?" Pen said. "I've had about enough of this sealed-lip stuff. We never used to keep secrets."

Beth's lips curled upwards, but didn't part as she said, "*Once upon a time, you told me we should have.*"

"Yeah, well, I've changed my mind."

"*Why?*"

"Because we're crap at it!" Pen snapped. "B, you've been shambling around looking sicker than my mum did after chemo—what, you think I haven't noticed?" Pen actually put her hands on her hips. "How many doctors am I related to, Beth?"

Beth smiled despite herself. "*About four thousand at last count.*"

"So do I know sick when I see it?"

"*I know you do.*"

"And I know *you* know, which is why I've been trying not to say anything. Because I figured you didn't want to talk about it, but, *but* . . .*" Pen clutched at the air as all her anger and frustration came bubbling up into her chest.

". . . *fuck*, B! How can you *not* want to talk about it? I'm your best friend. You and me—together we've seen—we've, we've *done*—" She gestured helplessly at Beth's street-etched cheeks, and then her hands dropped to her sides. "We always find each other, at the end of the day, you know?"

Beth nodded haltingly.

"B, I've been trying. I've been trying to trust you, to make it your call. You're obviously hurting and I don't want to add to that, but . . . I'm sorry, but I can't, not any more. You have to tell me, B. You have to *talk* to me."

Beth bit her lower lip, and Pen mirrored the gesture, feeling the tougher consistency of the reconstructed skin between her teeth.

"*I'm sick,*" she mumbled. She shrugged, staring at the ground like a grumpy kid.

"That far I'd got. Sick how, B? Sick *why*?"

Beth looked up. The light in her irises was dim. "*Because She made me so.*"

Pen didn't have to ask who "She" was. *She* was Mater Viae—the only other being to ever look at her with eyes like that.

"How?" she said.

"*She infected the streets, and every time I feed from them, a little bit of their sickness seeps into me.*" Beth's mouth twisted into a tight, bitter smile and the voice emerged from her body in a growl of heavy machinery. "*Fever Streets, Tideways, what just happened to those soldiers—who do you think this is all aimed at, Pen?*"

"Glas said he didn't know."

"*He's right. He doesn't.*" Beth exhaled heavily. "*But I do. I can feel Her malice in every brick, every stone, every scrap of concrete. Her mirror-sister ruled this city for centuries and no one was any the wiser, but* She's *only been here five minutes and She's tearing the place apart with the plague—but why?*"

Pen shook her head mutely. She didn't know.

"*She's doing it to* punish *us, Pen.*" The word was a sudden plaintive shriek of train brakes. "*Not attack, punish. It's aimed at me, yes, but more than that, at them, for believing in me: Glas, and Zeke, and Petris, and the Lampies, and everyone else She thinks should be hers.*"

Beth buried her face in her hands, but her voice didn't break. "*The city's been weaponised. She's turned it against us. She is so, so much stronger than me, and we're all out of allies, and now . . .*" Only now did Beth falter. "*Now She knows it.*"

Pen struggled to swallow "What do you mean, 'now'?" she asked.

"*She saw it,*" Beth said. "*Through the eyes of Her Street-Serpent yesterday. Thames, Pen, I could barely run! If She ever works out where we are, She'll come at us with everything She's got.*"

Pen spread her hands in exasperation. She couldn't believe she was having to say this. "Then don't *be* here." She almost laughed at the simplicity of it. "If the city's making you sick, then bloody well leave it!"

"*I can't.*"

"Why not?"

"*BECAUSE I HAVE TO FIND A WAY TO STOP HER!*" Beth's shout had the sudden violence of a car crash.

Pen fell back a step, but then she saw Beth's expression: not angry but desperate, pleading for Pen to understand.

"*Thames and Christ, Pen, you've met Her. You've looked into Her eyes. You really think if I bail tonight it'll all be hugs and cocoa and making up for the rest of 'em tomorrow? You really think She'll forgive them? Pen—they're our friends, and they're trusting me to save them from Her. They've put their faith in me.*"

"Don't lecture me on faith, Beth," Pen snapped. "You never understood it. They're trusting you to save them? You said it yourself: She's stronger. You really think you're keeping faith with them by lying to them about that?"

She took a half-step closer to Beth and the diesel scent of her best friend filled her nostrils. "You're right, Beth," she said. She held Beth's gaze with her own. "I've looked into Her eyes. I've seen what She's capable of, far closer up than you have, and I'm telling you, if this creature's coming for you, you *run.*"

She searched for Beth's hand; took it; threaded her fingers with Beth's. "You run for your dad, and . . ." She hesitated. "You run for your mum. Please, Beth, you run for *me.*"

But Beth wouldn't meet her gaze. "*Pen, I can't. I can't do that to them.*"

"Beth," Pen said in as even a voice as she could, "if you stay, this sickness—will it kill you?"

"*Yes.*"

The determination in that one word chilled Pen. She heard Beth's insistence on staying, her insistence on *dying*, and everything felt unstable. The thought of that loss filled her like a vacuum.

They put their faith in me.

Just like she had.

And just like that, Pen knew what she needed to do. She squeezed Beth's hand, then released it and turned back down the steps.

"Pen, where are you going?"

Even though her voice was made of engines and turbines and smoke, the fear in it was almost palpable. It made Pen's stomach clench. But she had known Beth for a long time and she knew she wouldn't change her mind, not as long as she thought people were depending on her. Whatever other changes the bizarre alchemy moving through her friend had wrought, one thing at least was the same: she was still more afraid of letting people down than she was of getting herself killed.

She looked back over her shoulder. "To see the friends you're waiting on. Maybe they'll be able to talk some sense into you when they know what's happening to you." She took the first two steps slowly, then something broke inside her and she ran, half expecting at every step for Beth's street-laced hand to clamp down on her shoulder before the next.

CHAPTER EIGHT

She was breathless by the time she reached the kitchen. Gutterglass had company. Now a woman, the old trash-spirit was pointing at one of the latest symptoms on the map with a ludicrous fake fingernail stuck to the end of a carrot broken in the places where the knuckles ought to be.

Two statues flanked her. The one carved into the form of a limestone angel was in considerably better repair. Ezekiel's face was turned to Gutterglass in an expression of bored but saintly patience. The second statue was a granite monk with lichen patching him like mould. *His* face was hidden by the jut of his carved hood, but Pen knew his eyes were the first to track her as she burst in.

"Kid"—as ever, Petris' voice sounded like he was gargling rock salt and it was pissing him off—"what do you want?"

"Petris, don't be such an arse." The rebuke came from behind Pen and she jumped as she realised there was a fourth figure in the room.

She turned, and her heart lurched to see Paul Bradley, Beth's dad, smiling his worried smile. His wide cheeks had turned pink in the heat put out by Gutterglass' burners.

"Is everything all right, Parva?" he asked.

Pen felt unbalanced by his presence. She hesitated. She couldn't do this, not in front of him. He was Beth's dad; it would be too cruel. She heard brick-soled feet in the corridor outside and a green glow showed through the bubbled glass in the doors, growing brighter with every step. She felt a sick kind of relief. She'd lost her chance; Beth was here and she'd stop her, and then she would stay and keep her secret and die here, Beth would die and—

"Beth's dying," she blurted just as the door swung open again, framing her best friend. Beth's city-face was etched in a kind of sad resignation.

"W-w-what?" Paul Bradley's lower jaw was trembling, making him stammer. "What do you mean?"

"What's happening to the city," Pen said, "it's happening to her too, in that new skin of hers."

There was a long silence. Petris shifted, his stone feet grinding over the tiles. And now Pen could see his eyes, the way the mica glittered in them as he stared at her. "Urbosynthesis," he grunted.

Then the air blurred and he was suddenly facing Gutterglass. The trash-spirit put a hand to the front of her makeshift dress as Petris demanded, "Why in the fucking River's name didn't you tell us, Glas?"

"Why?" Gutterglass countered mildly. "What precisely would you have done, old man? Vibrate with worry against the inside of that rock suit of yours until you liquefied yourself? The only one of us qualified to act on the information is me, and I am already acting on it. Trust me," she added, with a brittle smile. "I'm a doctor."

Pen stared at her, remembering the frenzied energy with which she'd attacked the diagnosis of the city, the dozens of hands that must have been so exhausting for her to animate, the way she never slept. She remembered, too, that though the two statue-skinned men she stood by were both members of the priest-hood, their zeal had never matched Gutterglass'. She'd lied for her faith and betrayed people for it, and ultimately she had cradled all the scraps of it that were left in her garbage hands and put it all in the girl who was now embracing her shaking father a few feet away.

Most of all, Pen remembered the cold anger in Gutterglass' voice as she'd said, "*Faith I'm all out of, and not freshly, I'm afraid.*"

"You told her." Pen sounded stunned, even to herself, as she turned to face Beth. "Her, but not him"—she nodded at Paul, who tightened his embrace on his daughter—"her, but not me."

Beth stayed within her dad's arms as she said, "*Like she said, Pen, she's a doctor.*"

Pen swallowed. She felt like she was going to be sick. She was panicking. She looked at tearful Paul Bradley and at Beth, and then she turned back to Gutterglass. She'd lost control. There was no making this right; there was only what she'd come down here to do.

"As a doctor then, you have to tell her to go," she demanded. "It's the city that's making her sick—she can't save you, none of you. She needs to leave. Tell her to go, all of you!" she demanded, looking from face to unreadable face. "She needs to hear it from you, so tell her to get out. She won't listen to me," she snarled, "so you have tell her to go!"

That last shout seemed to suck all the noise out of the room and left a heavy silence in its wake. Pen's vision blurred. She felt moisture streak down her face. She tasted salt.

"*I told you, Pen,*" Beth was speaking as gently as she could. "*I can't.*"

"But . . . but why not?" Pen didn't understand. "They know now—they *know*. If you stay, in a few days or weeks or months you'll be dead and then they won't have anyone to protect them anyway. So what are you staying for?"

"*A few days, or weeks, or months,*" Beth said. She left off hugging her dad, but left a hand on his arm. "*You're right, Pen: the city is killing me. Every time I feed on it it makes me sicker—but that doesn't magically mean I can live off anything else. London's become my substance, Pen. If I step off these streets, I starve.*"

Her green eyes reluctantly met Pen's teary gaze. "*That's what I couldn't tell you, Pen. That's what I didn't know how to say—not that I'm sick, but that there's no way for me to get better.*"

Pen stared at her. She lifted a hand towards her, but it felt clumsy, useless, and she let it drop.

"Oh, B," she whispered. "I'm so sorry."

Beth came to her then and wrapped her arms around her. Pen returned the hug fiercely, feeling the warmth of their cheeks next to each other, street to scar. Something bubbled up in her chest and Pen was mortified to find she was laughing and there was nothing she seemed to be able to do about it. "I'm sorry, I just . . . don't know what I . . . I thought I was . . . I—" She managed to fight her breath back under control. "I've really screwed this up, haven't I?"

Beth shook, laughing silently herself. "*Yeah, a little bit. It's okay, Pen.*"

Behind her, Pen heard stone grinding against stone as the Pavement Priests moved. "This doesn't leave the room," Petris was saying. "If it gets out we'll have fifty per cent desertion by sun-up and we'll lose the rest before Monday."

"Gutterglass"—this was Ezekiel's haughty drawl—"does your expertise with chemicals run to a memory solution?"

"A crude one," Glas replied, in a tone that suggested she was making a show of modestly inspecting her nails. "I'm not Johnny Naphtha, but I can manage a little amnesia if pressed."

"Consider yourself pressed," Ezekiel said. "Best prepare several doses, just in case. If word gets out, it would be nice to have at least a chance of containing it."

"Who do you think's going to tell?" Paul Bradley asked.

"I couldn't possibly say, but there are six of us now who know, and that's usually five more than can keep a secret for any length of time. Isn't that right, dear seneschal?" he added to Gutterglass with a waspish snap. "You're our resident expert on secrets."

Pen barely heard all this; she was focused on stalling the tremor in her limbs, focused on breathing in and out, slowly and regularly. "Forgive me?" she whispered to Beth. She was still holding her.

"*Of course, Pen. Always*," Beth answered.

"Okay." Pen looked at Beth's dad. His face looked bruised, swollen with grief, and to her shame she felt herself recoil from it.

"I'm going to leave you and your dad to . . ." She faltered. "I'll be back upstairs afterwards if you want to talk."

"*No*," Beth said in her shushed tyre whisper. "*You won't.*"

"What do you mean?"

"*You have to go, Pen.*"

Pen's heart thudded in her chest. She pulled back against Beth's hug and felt Beth's concrete-textured fingers come away from the back of her neck. "Beth, I'm sorry, I really am. But it's me—you can trust me. Please don't do this."

Beth looked puzzled for a moment, then her eyes widened in appalled sympathy. "*You think I'm punishing you? God, Pen, no! I would never . . . It's just—you were right.*"

Pen shook her head, not understanding. It was like there was a sudden loss of air pressure in the room. Beth sounded muffled; she could barely hear her.

"*If She's coming for you, you run. You said that, and you were right. But we can't.*" The light from Beth's gaze fell on Petris, Ezekiel and Gutterglass in turn. "*We're of the City, all of us. We have nowhere else to go.*" Her gaze came finally back to Pen. "*But you do.*"

"B, please don't do this—"

But Beth's right hand had already dipped into Pen's pocket, quick as smoke, and now she held it out in front of her. Resting in the cross-hatched grey palm was a glass sphere, no larger than an ordinary marble. A ribbon of dark images twisted through the heart of it like a stormcloud. "*Take it to the Chemical Synod and sell it to Johnny Naphtha. Get your parents' memories back. Go to them. It's time to leave us behind.*"

Pen just stood there, blinking and stammering and feeling like a fool and not managing to say anything.

"*Go home, Pen.*"

Pen stared at her, shaking her head, not even in denial, just astonishment. "You are my home," she said at last.

Beth flinched, but didn't look away.

"B, I already made this choice."

"*Make it again.*"

Pen felt sick and heavy, like she'd drunk liquid lead. "If I don't," she asked, "what are you going to do? Have Petris throw me out?"

Beth didn't answer. The muscles in Pen's stomach locked up. She felt humiliated.

"If you do this," she said, "I don't know if I'll ever be able to forgive you."

Beth pursed her lips. She was weighing the threat, taking it perfectly seriously. "*If it will keep you alive,*" she said at last, "*I can live with that.*"

"Screw you, Beth," Pen mumbled around a throat full of tears. "You aren't the one who'll have to." She snatched Goutierre's Eye from Beth's hand and shoved past her to the door. She stumbled on the steps and the glass Eye clacked loudly on the stone as she put her hands out to catch herself. Blurrily, out of the corner of her eye she saw a little pile of cigarette ash and the ground-out dog-end of a roll-up, but she barely registered it. She pushed herself back up and with an angry burst of energy threw herself onwards.

CHAPTER NINE

"Come now, My Lady, just one more time."

Beth concentrated, focusing on the shapes in her mind: the human outlines, clad in a skin of concrete grey. She stretched out her hand towards the floor as though she could physically pull them out of it. The muscles in her arms trembled, beads of sweat stood out on her forehead, the floor under her rippled like a puddle in an earthquake.

Dizziness swept over her and her concentration broke. The rippling stopped. "*I can't.*" She rocked back against the corner of the kitchen counter and slid to the floor, the air aching inside her lungs.

Gutterglass pursed her rubber lips speculatively and poised a pencil-tipped index finger over a small notepad half hidden amongst the morass of her forearm. "What exactly feels like the problem? Describe it as fully as you can."

Beth shook her head. "*I just* can't. *I can see them, hold them in my head, but when I try to make them in the world, they just don't come up.*"

Gutterglass scribbled, then tapped her finger against her cheek. "Hmmm," she murmured in a voice made from the low buzz of beetle wings. "It *could* be a new progression in your pathology. It could be weakness due to your lack of sustenance, or," she mused, "it could simply be stress. Has anything happened recently to cause you any stress, My Lady?"

"*Really?*" Beth said. "*You're doing that joke?*"

Gutterglass shrugged, a complicated manoeuvre involving the scurrying of half a dozen rats under her shoulder blades; it was one of the human gestures she was least accomplished at.

"In my experience, in situations like this one you can't be too picky about where you pick up your laughs, My Lady."

Beth peered at her from under her drooping eyelids. "*You actually have experience of situations like this?*"

"Not exactly like this," Gutterglass admitted, "but over the years you'd be surprised how close I've got."

"*How did they turn out?*"

"Varied," Glas replied, "but I'm still here, aren't I?" She crouched and patted Beth's knee. "There's usually a way out. Just because we haven't seen it yet doesn't mean it's not there."

Beth nodded at the floor beside her. "*Sit down.*"

Gutterglass obeyed by simply allowing her lower body to collapse in a miniature landfill. Her torso emerged from it like some salvage-sculpture bust.

"*Petris and Zeke are pretty pissed off at us.*"

"They are," Gutterglass confirmed.

"*Think we did the right thing, not telling them?*"

"I think that the speed with which they're taking measures to keep the news from their followers implies that *they* think we did, whether they'll admit it or not," Gutterglass said.

"*Yeah—but what about you? Would you have told them? If I hadn't ordered you not to?*"

"Would I have told them that, in our best but by no means expert opinion, we are woefully overmatched in a battle against an Urban Goddess who is an exact copy, except, if possible, slightly *more* callous and sadistic than the one who stole their deaths and condemned them to an eternity under rock? And that the girl on whom all their hopes depend as a challenger to this demonic entity is a rotten apple-skin's thickness from the grave herself?"

Gutterglass considered it. "If I'm honest, I think it might not have been the *best* morale booster I could think of."

"*Still, it might have given them a chance to prepare.*"

"They're soldiers, My Lady. They live prepared." Gutterglass paused. "Mater Viae's mirror-sister is stronger than you," she said, "that I grant, but there is at least this: She is alone. We have three hundred and fifty-nine streetlamp spirits and Pavement Priests and garbage avatars and," she added with a smile, "dying semi-divine graffiti artists."

Beth peered at her through half-closed eyes. Gutterglass' rats covertly counted every non-human resident of the department store in the morning and again in the evening. One body too many, Glas had pointed out, and there could be a spy in their midst. One unaccounted for could be the first sign of a rout.

"*Three hundred and fifty-nine, huh?*" Beth said wearily. That was less than a third of the force she and Fil had led against Reach, and not even the Crane King himself had been a match for the enemy they faced now. "*That's not a lot.*"

"Not a lot," Gutterglass conceded, "but it is something. Three hundred and fifty-nine smart, scared, motivated minds. And maybe, just maybe, one of them will think of something." She paused. "As long as we can keep their faith alive." She turned her eggshell eyes towards the counter. Lined up under the spice rack in plastic bottles were a dozen carefully measured draughts of a dark metallic liquid.

"*And if keeping their faith means stealing their memories,*" Beth said, "*then that's what we'll do, huh? No, Glas. I'm not crossing that line.*"

"My Lady, it is wise to have contingency plans. Petris and Eze-kiel both feel—"

"*I don't care. Destroy it.*"

She thought about the conical flask in her rucksack upstairs, about the memories that churned and crawled under the glass. The pang in her chest was like a broken rib.

Gutterglass bowed in acquiescence. "Shall we go again?" she asked. "Try for only one Masonry Man this time?"

Beth shook her head. "*Later. There's someone I want to see.*"

In a bay in the lowest level of the car park lay a hunk of rock bleached by strip-lighting. It might once have been human-shaped, but it had been heavily eroded by rain and wind and whittled by knife-point graffiti. A muffled crying came from inside the stone.

Beth tapped the worn statue with the butt of her railing, and it crumbled. The crying grew louder for a moment and then stopped altogether. A pudgy baby with slate-grey skin and storm-grey eyes regarded her seriously from his crevice inside the stone. He always looked at her like this, Beth thought, no matter how much she changed, no matter that her eyes were full of lights and her skin scaled with tiny roofs and speckled with little sodium lamps, he always recognised her.

"*You're growing, Petrol-Sweat,*" she said to him, and he gurgled delightedly at the urban sounds that made up her voice. "*It'll be getting cramped in there in a bit.*" In truth, the space inside the statue grew along with him. This was normal for a Pavement Priest, Petris had told her.

When they'd brought him here, Beth had insisted on trying to take him out of the statue, to have him with her in the dormi-tory, despite the monk's protestations, but over the course of four hours the stone had grown back, out of him and around him like fast-swelling tumours. He'd shrieked and shrieked, and though

Beth had sat with him the whole time, there'd been nothing she could do.

This, Petris had assured her, was also normal.

"*Not growing fast enough*," Beth thought ruefully. She showed him the conical flask and he gurgled and reached for it.

"*Whoa there!*" She pulled it out of his reach and he made a disgruntled little fist. "*Not until you're older.*" She thought of the memories pent up in the flask: the rangy teenager with brick dust in his hair who'd raced Railwraiths and fought against the Crane King. She felt a flush of heat through the subways under her cheeks as she remembered the texture of his hands under the trees of Battersea Park.

"*A lot older,*" she repeated. She sighed. There was more than her embarrassment to think about. Gutterglass didn't know what would happen if you fed seventeen-year-old memories to a six-month-old child, but in the words of the trash-spirit: "*I wouldn't anticipate anything good.*"

So Beth waited, and waited some more, and prayed she could last out the days of the war and still be here when the Son of the Streets' reborn body caught up with his bottled dreams.

"*I did a bad thing today,*" she said. "*I hurt a friend. I did it on purpose. I'm telling myself it's because her safety's more important than her feelings and that's true as far as it goes. Only, I can't help remembering that you told me to go home so many times, to keep me safe, and I never went. And even if I'd known then about what would happen to me, about all this . . .*"

She turned her tiled hand over, inspecting it in the light of her gaze. "*I still would have killed you, Filius Viae, if you'd tried to make me leave.*"

She stopped talking then, pierced through by loneliness and the bone-deep knowledge that the girl she'd just pushed out of her life was utterly irreplaceable. She felt it go through her like a needle pulling thread, tightening and drawing her in on herself. Worst of all, she knew that Pen was hurting this exact same way, and Beth had done it to her, and she'd done it on purpose and there was nothing she could do to fix it. She trembled as she breathed. Her eyes fell on the flask and the label that read *Childhood outlooks, proclivities and memories.*

The child gurgled impatiently and reached for the flask. For a second, for even the glimmer of a chance, Beth was tempted to risk it. She popped the rubber stopper from the flask.

"Lady Bradley!"

Wings fluttered somewhere in the darkness. A white plastic bin bag ghosted in under the strip lights, borne by a pigeon. It billowed and folded into the shape of a swollen skull, with eggshells in the eye sockets. Beth hurriedly crammed the stopper back into the bottle and pushed the bottle into her hoodie pocket, but it wasn't her Gutterglass was worried about.

"Lady Bradley, we have a problem."

"*What problem?*"

Gutterglass hesitated, eggshells blinking stupidly. Beth started to ask again when he blurted out, "Three hundred and fifty-eight."

"*Do we know who?*"

"The stoneskins are checking now."

They were back in the kitchen—Gutterglass' paranoid sentries made it the perfect place to confer when they didn't want to be overheard. The white bin bag had been settled on the shoulders of a makeshift body, but the hasty construction showed none of Glas' usual attention to detail. He shed out-of-circulation coins and gelatinous bits of pasta as he fidgeted around the room.

"*Maybe you miscounted?*"

"I didn't."

"*Maybe whoever it is just slipped out for something to eat . . .*"

Glas didn't answer. He began chewing on a bacon-rind cuticle and accidentally pulled it free of his hand. He stood there for a moment with it dangling from his mouth, then spat it out like a cat with a dead mouse.

"*Maybe . . .*" Beth began again, but she heard the rusty squeak of the hammer arm outside extending and retracting, and then the door was shoved open. Petris appeared framed in the doorway, then disappeared, then reappeared again a foot from Beth's face.

"We have a name," the granite monk said.

"*Who?*"

"Timon. He didn't tell anyone where he was going and no one's seen him all afternoon."

"Do they know why you were asking?" Gutterglass asked, but Petris' only answer was a stare and a withering, "*Please.*"

"Timon?" Gutterglass sounded puzzled. "He's only just arrived. Why would he suddenly just up and go again now that he's reached us?"

"Maybe he didn't like what he saw," Petris grunted with a spray of stony dust. "Not sure I blame him. Our first desertion. Still, it could be a lot worse; no one seems to have any idea why he's gone, so if he's running scared he's kept it to himself. We don't have a crisis, not yet."

Beth slumped back against the countertop. "*Sure we do,*" she muttered, certain she was right.

Gutterglass looked at her sharply. "My Lady?"

"*It's not a desertion,*" she said, "*it's a* defection. *He's going to Her.*"

Gutterglass straightened in alarm and Beth felt the sudden shift of attention from inside the statue as Petris turned his gaze on her.

"How can you possibly know that?" Glas demanded.

Beth thought of the limestone-robed kid smoking miserably in the rain.

Lady B, please: give him his mortality back. Let him die for real—let him rest. He's earned it.

He hadn't even asked for himself, just for Al. She bit her lip and then said, "*Because there's nothing he wouldn't do for his best friend.*"

CHAPTER TEN

Brackish, clay-coloured water splashed onto Pen's face and washed the dirt from between her fingers as she climbed. There was grit in her mouth and grit lodged in the folds of her eyelids. Her arms and hips and back ached. The city's convulsions had broken the river and her destination was now perched on top of a five-hundred-foot escarpment. The only climbable side was, lamentably, the one with a torrent running down it. The waterfall wasn't steep, mercifully, but it was slippery, a jagged façade of packed earth and tree roots and broken pipework. Pen placed each hand and foot with painstaking slowness, feeling the space underneath her like a vacuum in her gut.

To try to take her mind off it, she played a game. She pretended to herself that Espel was climbing beside her, with that oh-so-casual scramble she used on London-Under-Glass's rooftops, her blonde hair plastered to her symmetrical forehead by the river water.

"*Come on, Countess,*" Pen imagined her saying. "*Left foot here, right hand on that pipe there—see, it's easy. Tell you what, make it up another ten feet and . . .*"

"*I can have a rest?*" Head bent against the flow of water, Pen's lips moved to fill in her half of the conversation.

"You wish, Countess. But you can have a kiss, and then we go another ten feet."

"What do I get then?"

"Another kiss." The steeplejill beamed an imaginary smile. *"I am prepared to be very generous with my kisses."*

Pen made it the ten feet, and the ten feet after that, and claimed her prizes. They were, she had to admit, pretty disappointing compared to her memories of the real thing.

When she finally reached the top, she turned and sat herself on the edge. She was sodden—she'd climbed the whole way in the river's full flow. She blew water off her nose. The old dye factory crouched on the river bend behind her like the husk of a giant insect, but she didn't want to look at it yet. Instead, she gazed out over the broken city.

In the middle distance, the spokes of the London Eye emerged from the river at crazy angles, its passenger pods dangling like clods of earth from a bicycle wheel. The spasms of the earth had split the Thames and its tributaries, glimmered in silver veins that zigzagged between those buildings still standing. Here and there, Pen could see rolling banks of fog where the river water encountered Fever Streets and erupted into sudden vapour.

A breeze picked up, piercing her wet headscarf and freezing her ears. With a creaking sound that carried across the skyline, a cluster of satellite dishes tore themselves free from the roof of the old MI6 headquarters and were caught by the wind; it bore the dishes up and away as if they were as insubstantial as autumn leaves, scattering and swirling them across the sky. A flock of seagulls cawed and banked to avoid them. Pen eyed the dishes as they drifted over the rooftops. There was a rumour that Mater Viae could hear through those receivers, and far too many rumours like that had turned out to be true.

Warily she watched the dishes bob up over the Olympic Stadium, gathered in from the east in the same contortions that had shattered the city and elevated Canary Wharf to its new hill-top. The stadium sat on the banked-up rubble of the houses it had crushed on its way in. Forces Pen couldn't begin to guess at had twisted it into an infinity loop filled with dust and earth, spines snapped, glass teeth jutting from every window frame, cables flapping in the breeze.

The wind blew stronger, shifting to the east, and the dishes scattered. The one Pen had her eye on gusted back towards her and she stiffened, ready to run if it reached her, but it dipped over the edge of the glittering thatch of broken steel and glass that covered the hill Canary Wharf now stood on. Then, buoyed up on a sudden thermal, it rose over a ridge of houses before catching on a protruding spire.

Pen felt her throat dry as she focused on the building that had snared the dish. The spire led down into the broad sweep of a dome and then the bulk of a familiar white stone edifice that shone blinding in the spring sun.

St. Paul's, it seemed, had survived the city's convulsions rela-tively untouched. Even the cranes still reared over it, spindly dor-mant sentinels.

Pen stared for a moment, then almost as a reflex, for *anything* else to look at, she jammed her fingers into her jeans pocket and wangled out the little glass sphere that had brought her here. Her heart snagged on the sight of the black stormcloud twisting through it.

For the millionth time, she lifted the marble to her eye and tried to separate the minuscule images as they rushed through the glass. She closed her left eye and peered with her right until she felt it twitching in its socket, but it did no good: the pictures were too small and moved too fast for her to track them, and even if they hadn't been, there were millions upon millions of them, each showing her a different reflection from inside London-Under-Glass: reflections from the inverted city's mirrors and windows and puddles and falling raindrops. Even if she could see each frame with perfect clarity, she could sit here for a decade and she'd probably still never see Espel in any of them.

Espel.

Pen's stomach flipped over at the memory of what the Mirrorstocracy had done to her steeplejill: the awakening of her id, the terrible, blameless passenger consciousness inside her, how it had fought Espel for possession of her own body, her primal and most intimate home. And then, as always, the nausea gave way to a fierce burst of pride as Pen remembered the painful, faltering, *incredible* steps Es had taken in collaboration with that id, doing what no one had ever believed possible: making a truce with the second mind nesting in her skull.

And then, as always, that pride shivered into icy fear as Pen relived the mirror-glass closing behind her, sealing out Espel's face as Mater Viae's gaunt, clay-skinned soldier advanced on her with predatory steps.

For three months now, whenever Pen had woken up sweating and clawing at the duvet, she'd barely had to choke out a syllable before Beth was there, holding her, the light from her green eyes warding off the dark. Pen had clung to her. She hadn't felt weak. She hadn't felt ashamed. Now she did. Now she felt like a damned fool.

She wiped her eyes with the back of her hand, straightened her back, and then stood. There was nothing about this she'd chosen, nothing that was fair. All there was now was one foot in front of the other.

"It's no use to you, Pen," she whispered to herself. "You can't use it." She closed her fingers tightly around the marble. "You can give it up. You *can* give it up." She had to concentrate to make sure she said *it* instead of *her.*

The doorway to the factory creaked, but unlike the last time Pen had been there, the space beyond wasn't flooded with darkness.

Beams of cold spring light skewered the building through holes in the roof. Pen stood on the threshold for a moment and let a shiver pass through her. She took in the bare brick walls and the vast red stains of lichen and the vats and pipes and distilling columns. The place felt small; the darkness that had once made it seem infinite had been banished, but a residue of fear still clung to it. It was like a washed-out poison bottle with the skull label still stuck on.

"Hello?" she called. "Johnny?"

Only echoes answered her. She advanced, the scuff and scratch of her trainers keeping her company.

"Johnny?" she called. She bit her reconstructed lip and then said, "I've got something for you. Something from the other side of the mirror—unique, like we agreed, remember? I want to trade . . ."

No answer again. Pen felt a lump rise into her throat, because Johnny Naphtha ignoring an invitation to trade was like a buzzard ignoring a buffalo corpse.

"Hello?"

A scuffling sound came from behind a thicket of pipes, then it stopped abruptly, almost guiltily.

Pen faltered. That sound hadn't come from any oil-soaked brogue. "Who's there?" she demanded.

No answer.

She stopped still and listened. Very faintly, she thought she could hear the distinctly un-synod sound of someone trying not to hyperventilate. She eyed the pipes.

Someone's hiding from me, she thought, *someone scared.*

She stifled the urge to run over and look. Instead, she sat on the ground and crossed her legs. She slipped Goutierre's Eye back into her pocket and laid both hands open and palm-up at her sides.

"I'm just here," she announced, clearly and calmly. "I'm not coming any closer, but I'm not going away, either."

She didn't say *I'm not going to hurt you* because if someone felt the need to state that it was usually a sign it wasn't true.

"Come out if you want to talk," she said. "Or stay back there if you want. I'm in no rush." She sighed and looked at the walls. "Doesn't look like the guys I came to see are here, which means I have to go home without what I came here for." She paused. "*That's* a trip I can put off pretty much for ever," she added fervently.

"Did . . . did you get sent out for milk?" It was a high-pitched voice: a boy's childish treble.

"My dad sent me out for milk once, but I lost the money he gave me. He shouted at me for like half an hour, then he didn't speak to me for a week, like he'd used it all up with the shouting."

A small grubby hand emerged from behind the pipework, fol-lowed by a bony forearm and then a shock of tangled, dusty hair. Then the boy's whole head popped out and he blinked at Pen. He couldn't have been more than eight. He didn't smile, and Pen didn't smile either. She knew better than to try to persuade him to trust her. She just sat there, with her hands open and empty, letting him see her, letting him make up his mind.

"Was it milk?" he asked again. "Or a paper? Or cigarettes? My dad sent me out for cigarettes once. He's pretty dumb. The corner-shop man was never going to sell them to me. I knew I was going to get yelled at. Maybe he did too. You afraid your folks are going to shout at you?" he asked. "For not getting what you were supposed to get?"

Pen shook her head, but solemnly, to indicate that even though she wasn't, that would have been a wholly reasonable thing to be afraid of.

The boy came wholly out from behind the pipes and stood, swivelling from his hips, his arms flapping by his sides. He was the kind of bony that made him look like he had too many joints. He scratched the top of his head. "Didn't mean to take your spot," he said. "I didn't know it was yours."

"It's not," Pen said, shrugging. The boy shrugged too. He walked to within ten feet of her, frowned, and then, apparently judging this to be a safe distance, he sat down opposite her on the dusty floor. She watched him begin to cross his legs to mimic hers, then hesitate as he realised that tangling his legs like that would make it that much harder to escape if she turned out to be hostile, and the fact that Pen's legs were crossed in turn made him marginally safer from her. Maybe he knew she'd done that on purpose, maybe not. He drew his knees up under his chin instead, put his hands palm-down on the ground. He looked like a frog ready to jump.

"What happened?" Pen asked after a long silence.

"Got lost," he said, simply.

"Your parents left you?"

He shook his head.

"Got *lost*," he emphasised, and scowled at her for not listening. "Not *parents*, neither," he corrected her. "Mum. Our street got hot and melted our car, but we weren't in it. We ran instead, but I got left behind. She told me to hold onto her hand but the ground shook and I couldn't." He sighed, a big, demonstratively adult, sigh. "I tried, but I bet she won't believe me. Bet the first thing she does when I see her is yell at me for not holding onto her hand."

"Parents, huh?" Pen said, rolling her eyes and smiling and trying very, very hard to swallow.

The boy considered this for a while. "Yeah," he said. He frowned at her. "What happened to your face?"

Pen ran a finger over the ridge of one of her scars. "Got into a fight."

"Cool," the kid whispered, impressed. "Bad one?"

"Yep."

The kid beamed. "Was it a monster?" he asked.

Pen didn't ask what monsters he'd seen that might have made him jump to that conclusion. "Yes, it was."

"Did you kill it?"

Pen hesitated and glanced over her shoulder. As luck had it, she could see St. Paul's framed in the doorway, still standing, its dome shining hazily in the sun. "Actually? I don't know if I did."

The boy pondered this. "I could help you kill it," he said after a while. "And then you could help me find my mum."

The outlandish balance of this proposal struck Pen so hard that for a second she wondered if the kid was Johnny Naphtha in disguise. Then she laughed. "It's okay," she said. "My friend and I put it out of action pretty good. I can try and help you find your mum anyway, though," she offered. She probably could, too, if the woman was still alive. There were only a handful of unin-fected places where London's trapped residents gravitated to, and she knew them all: the big Asda in Clapham Junction, the shop-ping centre in Liverpool Street Station, or maybe she'd been at Selfridges the whole time, though Pen shrivelled inwardly at the thought of going back there and being thrown out again.

The boy looked suspicious.

"Why?" he asked.

Pen shrugged.

"It's what friends do, I guess."

"Are we friends now?" the boy frowned again, but not suspi-cious any more, only puzzled. Then he beamed at her. "I have lots of friends."

"Oh yeah? What are they like?"

He looked at her critically. "Not as tall as you."

Pen snorted. "Yeah, well, I suppose I would be freakishly lanky for an eight-year-old."

"Me too," said the boy. "I'm the tallest in my—"

He broke off as a pair of clay-grey hands breached the floor under him like water and seized his ankles. Pen started hard. She saw the boy's skin go white around the Masonry Man's grip, and then he vanished, dragged under like the ground was a riptide. He didn't even have time to cry out.

Pen tried to lunge forward, but her crossed legs were too long and awkward and she couldn't get them untangled quickly enough. She sprawled forward onto her face. A second later she was up on her knees, her hands pattering over the floor where the boy had been sitting, but they just left handprints in the dust on the solid concrete.

Pen screamed.

She screamed her throat raw and hammered on the floor. She shoved herself to her feet and cast about wildly, looking for any sign of the boy at all.

But there was nothing: no tell tale ripple in the earth, no four-limbed ghosting shape under the floor. The Masonry Man had taken him deep.

Pen ran at one wall and with another savage scream slammed her hand into the bricks. The pain flared, making her gasp, and she started breathing again. She stood bent over with her hands on her knees, sucking in air as the seconds came and went. Dimly she heard herself snarling for the clayling creature to come back, to come back for her, even though she had no means to fight it. She thought of the boy, darkness and earth pressing in on him, desperately straining at air that wasn't there. Would the clayling breach again to let him breathe, or leave him buried?

No. Pen was all but sure that the kid would live, at least for a little while. This wasn't a kill; it was a kidnap. She'd seen Mater Viae's creatures do it before.

"There's nothing you can do here," she told herself. "Run—run before it comes back." But she didn't move. Absurdly, even though she knew there was nothing she could do to help the kid, it felt like abandoning him. "*Run*," she snarled at herself, and finally the muscles in her legs answered her.

She stumbled out into the light of day, running before she even knew where she was going. She shook her head like she was dazed. She couldn't work out what to do.

Beth, she thought at last. *I have to tell Beth.*

"*She's so much stronger than me*," B had said. And Mater Viae wasn't done yet. She was kidnapping people, and the only reason She'd do that, Pen knew, was if they had something the Lady of the Streets needed. This was important. This was *bad*.

But then she slowed.

Warn her—and then what? a desperate, lonely voice in her was demanding.

"*. . . she's so much stronger than me*," she remembered Beth saying.

"*We're out of allies, and she's so much stronger than me . . .*"

"*. . . we're out of allies . . .*"

Shading her eyes from the sun, she looked up. St. Paul's blazed huge and white before her on the crest of the next hill. The cranes attending it looked thin and black as burned matchsticks in the glare.

"*. . . we're out of allies . . .*"

She cast around, but her gaze kept coming back, again and again, to the cathedral. Her hand went unconsciously to the sphere in her pocket.

"*Was it a monster?*"

"*Yes.*"

"*Did you kill it?*"

"*I'm not sure.*"

Muscle memory guided Pen's steps as she entered the tunnels under the cathedral. As she crossed the threshold, she looked up fearfully at the black metal cross-beams of the cranes. But if they were not dead, merely sleeping, then they didn't stir.

The cool air of the tunnel rushed into her nostrils as she left the day behind. The shadows were so dense she could barely see, but that didn't matter; she could walk this path in total darkness. She would never forget it. It was etched far more deeply in her than the scars on her face.

The closer she came, the heavier her feet felt. Her legs were numb, resisting her.

"All there is," she said aloud, even though her jaw muscles were tight too, "is one foot after another."

She counted fifty paces and then turned left off the main passage into the labyrinth. She could barely breathe. She put a hand to the wall and slowed to grope along it, but she didn't stop.

At long last, light glimmered around a corner. She turned it and saw a small pyramidal chamber where all the walls looked like they were collapsing against one another. It was pierced by a cat's cradle of interwoven sunbeams. Something undulated in the dust.

Her strides became stiffer, even more awkward, her body fighting her harder as she entered the chamber. She thought of Espel, walking like she'd just learned how, thinking each step through and working with the second mind in her skull to take it, each step a negotiation, a sacrifice that made her stronger, a choice.

Every single step was a choice.

"Please," she whispered. "*Please.*"

In the dust beneath her, strands of barbed wire twitched and crawled like inchworms. Dismembered like this, stranded and hostless, the creature had been too weak even to leave this room.

Pen closed her eyes. Behind her lids, images played: of steel tendrils and blood and churning water. She felt herself flinch, and stilled it. Her scars tingled. One of the wire worms paused in its path, one barbed tip waving in the air like it could smell her.

Pen breathed out, long and slow, and let the memories emerge through her. The tingles on her skin became deeper, darker, with remembered pain of metal thorns inside her elbows, behind her knees, constricting her chest. Her eyes still closed, she tasted the acid of the panic, and the paralysis—

—and the power.

We're out of allies.

Pen opened her eyes.

She lowered herself to a crouch. She felt like every cell in her skin was rebelling, but she did it. All the wire strands had stopped moving now. The closest one hesitated in the air, and then recoiled from her.

"You remember me," Pen breathed. "You're *afraid* of me."

Her hand didn't shake as she held it out towards the wire. The wire shivered in the air, then, very slowly, lowered itself towards her skin. Pen didn't flinch as the barbs bit.

Now, she thought, knowing the Wire Mistress could hear her, *I have a proposition for you.*

CHAPTER ELEVEN

"He's barely moving." Gutterglass' body was completely motion-less as she spoke. Two egg-carton sockets sat empty where her eyes ought to have been. The pigeon that was seeing for her soared overhead, a black hyphen against the sun. "He's still half a mile ahead of us, but he's slowed right down."

"He's tired," Ezekiel said. Beth could hear the hunter's grim smile in his voice as he talked about their quarry. "He used all his energy to get himself into the labyrinth as fast as he could. He has barely anything left."

He's not the only one, Beth thought. Her muscles felt like wet sandbags. She held herself stiffly upright, though, keen not to show any sign of weakness. She could feel the team they'd assem-bled watching her, their expectancy weighing her down.

There were twenty-two in all, as skilled and loyal a crew as Zeke and Petris had been able to round up in the panicked twenty minutes after they'd realised Timon was gone. The five Sodiumite sisters and five Blankleit brothers had to march blindfolded, their vestigial glass eyelids unable to keep out the glare of the sun, but they moved with astonishing dexterity, even in their blindness. Dust-devils and small stones went whirling in front of them as they groped their way with their fields, their metal veins glowing

like embers under their transparent skins. Behind them, twelve
Pavement Priests ground their way up what was left of the road.
The Heavy Brigade, Gutterglass called them: veterans all, their
stone and bronze armour scored with knife-point graffiti: battle-
baptistery mottos and tattoos listing Scaffwolf kills. Despite Petris'
gruff protestations, Ezekiel had insisted on leading the detachment himself.

"*Timon's one of my boys.*" The angel's tone had been harder than
his limestone punishment skin. "*I'll do the necessary.*"

Escarpments of shattered skyscraper reared either side of them
and they picked their way between fangs of glass twenty feet high.
It's like walking into the mouth of a giant shark, Beth thought.

The silence was broken only by the grind of the Pavement
Priests' passage over the rubble, and the occasional chime of a
Sodiumite foot on a scaffolding strut. Save for the muttered coun-
sels of Gutterglass and Ezekiel, nobody spoke. They were all intent,
ready. Even so, every now and then one of them would smile shyly
at Beth. *Nothing bad can happen to me*, their eager gazes said. *I am
watched over.* Beth sweated and smiled back and tried to keep her
spine straight. She felt just as stalked as Timon.

I am watched over, she thought sourly, and looked up at Canary
Wharf. It reared very close now, its malignant little light still
blinking. Beth knew full well how far and how clearly the creature
squatting at the tower's apex could see.

Gutterglass raised a worm-riddled hand and they stopped.
"There's a bend ahead of him," she said. "The labyrinth doubles
back on itself. If Timon follows it, he'll be within about a hundred
yards of us for a few minutes." Her eyeless head turned eerily to
face the Sodiumite detachment. "Is that close enough?" she asked.

Beth relayed the question with a torch pressed against the
blindfold of the Sodiumite captain. The heavy-shouldered glass-
skinned woman nodded impatiently.

"Very well then," Gutterglass said. "Now we wait."

The Sodiumites stretched and set themselves for the first steps of their dance. The Blankleits arrayed themselves behind, back-up in case the Amberglow sisters couldn't get the job done. Beth saw a couple of disgruntled flickers from them, not happy at being second string, but nothing outright racist. They must be on their best behaviour—and all because of her.

"Remember," Ezekiel was saying, "we'll have a few seconds, no more. Timon will be thrashing around like a landed fish and we'll have to get a grip on him before the Lampies lose theirs."

Beth was intensely aware of her own breath: the swell of her lungs, the length of each exhalation. The spiked railing hissed against its leather harness as she pulled it free and she felt the pavement-calluses on her palms fit into the rough texture of the iron. She stared at the wall of glass and crumpled metal in front of her. Her reflection was razor-sharp in the midday sun. The statues flanked her like an honour guard. She could feel them watching her expectantly.

Something prickled over her forearm—a chill, a memory of more vulnerable flesh—and she looked up. Gutterglass' pigeon was a dot now, wheeling against the blue; it wavered, hesitating in the sky, then suddenly, it was dropping like a stone towards them and Beth could make out its grey and blue feathers, and its claws clutching the eggshells with their white staring innards, and Ezekiel was shouting at his troops to get ready.

The air filled with chiming as the streetlamp sisters started to dance.

Veins blazed orange under their skin as they skipped and turned, whirling faster and faster. Their feet blurred under them. The air thickened with sudden charge and Beth felt sparks leap between her church-spire teeth.

"*Got him!*" they semaphored joyously as one, their minds as well as bodies linked by their fields.

Ezekiel barked, "Now! Now! *Now!*" and like a horizontal avalanche, the Pavement Priests surged directly at the labyrinth wall.

The glass dissolved into sleet as they hit it and Beth threw up a hand up to cover her eyes as she charged with them. Shards tinkled harmlessly off her architecture skin. She peered through the glittering blizzard, squinting and blinking until she could make out a familiar limestone figure: Timon, flickering and struggling, held tight by invisible force.

There was a close, deep *crack* of air and a winged shape shot over Beth's head and smacked hard into Timon's chest. The two figures blurred together, wrestling for a split second, and then the other priests piled on. An instant later the blur resolved: Timon was on his knees. Ezekiel stood over him, stone wings spread tauntingly. With one hand he gripped the back of Timon's neck, dragging him painfully back on himself. The other statues stood back in a half-circle, watching coldly.

"Timon Alexandrine." The angel-skinned priest spat the name into his quarry's face. "For the crimes of blasphemy and treason you are hereby sentenced to immediate reincarnation, and"—he bent close to Timon's ear, but Beth still heard his furious hiss—"if I ever happen across the treacherous child you're about to become, I'll fucking blind it."

He curled his stone fist and drew it back in front of Timon's face, but Timon didn't even look. The expression on his mask was slack with misery; his eyes were dull inside the eyeholes.

"Al," he muttered softly, "Al, mate, I'm sorry."

"*STOP!*"

The shout was so loud—a sound of train-brakes and car crashes and pile-drivers—that for a moment it sounded like London itself had woken to amplify Beth's voice.

Ezekiel hesitated, his fist still raised.

"*We can't.*" Beth stumbled as she reached them; she was wheezing and she wanted to retch. "*Not like this.*" She looked down at the kneeling statue.

"*Timon,*" she said. "*What are you doing?*"

Timon said nothing, but there was a fearful *crack* as Ezekiel's gauntlet tightened and fissures split the back of his limestone neck.

"Answer her," Ezekiel barked. "It's the only reason I'm still letting you put air in your lungs."

Timon didn't look at her. He seemed to lack the energy to move the stone. His voice was flat. "Going to Her," he said, then respectfully added, "Milady."

"*Why?*"

"'Cause Al needs me to."

Beth sighed and the air in front of her discoloured with turbine-steam. She dropped to a crouch in front of him. "*She can't help you, Timon,*" she whispered, low, so only he could hear. "*She can't help Al: She's just a* copy *of the Goddess who took your deaths away from you, just like I am. And She can't give those deaths back to you any more than I can.*"

"I'm sorry, Lady B—"

Beth heard the stubbornness in his voice. She knew he was clinging to that stubbornness; that no logic, nothing she could say, would change his mind, and she understood exactly why.

"—but you don't know that."

"I do," she said. She stood up. "*Bring him,*" she said to Ezekiel. "*We're taking him back with us.*"

"To do what?" Ezekiel spluttered. "We can't spare the men to guard him—he's confessed his treason, right in front of you!"

"*And I've decided to be lenient.*" Beth stared at him, letting the green light from her gaze pour right into his eyes until he had to look away. "*You heard what I told you to do, Stonewing. The question is,*

*are you going to obey? Make up your mind quickly, because I've only got
so much leniency in me today."*

For a moment she thought the angel-skinned zealot was sizing
her up, the way he had months back, before she'd fully trans-
formed, before his uncertainty collapsed into his need to believe
in her. Beth's fist tightened on the shaft of her spear as she wondered how strong that need still was. The tight-shut pores on the
soles of her feet tingled, ready to let the street in.

Ezekiel's stone neck creaked as he bowed his head. "Yes, My—"
he began, but he never finished his sentence.

Beth followed his gaze. The surface of the ground they stood on
was rippling like a pond in a breeze. Ezekiel sucked in his breath,
even as the ground began to shudder.

"CLAYLINGS!"

A pair of sinewy grey arms burst up from the ground and
seized the hem of Ezekiel's robes, the liquid street dripping from
them like water. The old Pavement Priest flickered; there was a
rush of air and suddenly the Masonry Man's arms were gouting
stumps and Ezekiel was crouched, his stone right wing slick with
asphalt-coloured blood.

Soft detonations echoed behind Beth and she spun around to
see hollow-cheeked Masonry Men standing amongst them, their
mouths puckered in soundless howls. One of them erupted from
the floor in front of her; its shadow bled over her for a second
before she slashed it from the air with her spear. Her ears filled
with the grinding of stone as the Pavement Priests engaged.

Statues blurred into stop-motion speed, dis- and re-appearing,
their gauntlets ripping into clayling skin, exposing grey ribs and
veins and pulsing organs. Masonry Men screamed softly and fell,
but as they perished even more emerged, teeming from the earth
like termites from rotting wood. Beth dropped her weight a few
inches and relaxed, opening herself to the street. The city's force

surged up into her. She tasted the toxins in the back of her throat. She shuddered and gagged and seized on the energy like a drowning woman onto air.

She surged into the mêlée, sliding swift and smooth on the city air, slashing and stabbing, goading her burning muscles. She slammed her spear into a grey throat and *shrieked* her fury into the blank face of the Masonry Man as she cut him down.

"Lady, help me!"

Beth staggered backwards, blinking, casting about for the source of the voice. A bronze-armoured priest was sunk waist-high in the pavement and a dozen slick grey hands were dragging him down. He gaped down at himself, then back at her. She could feel his astonishment and his sense of betrayal that she'd let this happen to him.

"My La—" His voice cut off as they pulled him under.

Beth lurched forward, spear raised, but it was too late. Her ears filled with more implosions—more enemies arriving. Gutterglass was swearing filthily, lashing out with tentacles of plastic and rotting rubber hose. Stoneskins were screaming and yelling; Lampfolk were blazing and dancing furiously. From the corners of her eyes she could see them crack and gutter into darkness.

"Lady Bradley!"

It was Ezekiel's voice.

Beth's heart lurched as she turned. Her eyes found the stone angel; he was on one knee, sheltering under the sweep of his wings, clay figures dragging at him with their talons, but whatever he was screaming for, it wasn't help. His stone arm was extended, pointing.

Fifty yards from where she stood, Timon was being hauled under the earth. He wasn't struggling. His eyes were open, his carven muscles slack. They were bearing him slowly, carefully under, cradling his neck where Ezekiel had fractured it. They were taking him alive.

"Lady Bradley!" Ezekiel roared again, and Beth knew what he was demanding. She drew her spear back above her shoulder, but the muscle locked, rebelling.

Only Timon's chest and head were above ground now, the wolf-heads she'd drawn on his shoulder level with the pavement. He looked at her with a dreadful pleading. *I have to help Al*, she could see him thinking. And he would, if she let him—by running to Mater Viae with all their secrets.

Ezekiel was staring at her too, so were other Pavement Priests. Even the blindfolded Lampfolk were twitching their heads in her direction.

We're watched over, Beth thought.

Timon slid down until his chin was touching the earth.

"BETH!" Ezekiel screamed.

She didn't think.

The spear point smashed through Timon's mask and the limestone imploded around it. The grey hands holding him slipped away, leaving his impaled head resting on the surface. Blood ran red as shock down his chin and dripped into the dust.

Beth slumped onto her knees, head bowed, heaving ragged breaths. Stone bodies and shattered glass surrounded her.

"*Oscar*," she whispered; a wall of blue flame filled her vision from edge to edge and a concussive wave of air smacked her back as the Sewermander exploded from her hood. He soared into the air for an instant, and then dived straight back into the battlefield.

"*GET DOWN!*" Ezekiel roared.

All the Pavement Priests and lamp spirits threw themselves to the floor. Gutterglass dissolved into a carpet of garbage. The clayling soldiers arced their spines to dive after them, but they were a fraction too slow and Oscar engulfed them like a cloud. With breathtaking precision, the Sewermander broke his dive a foot from the ground. For an instant he hovered there, blazing so hot even Beth had to turn her gaze away. Then he was banking and soaring upwards again, his fire now just a distortion against the blue of the sky.

The exposed Masonry Men stood like statues in his wake, multiplied into an army by the walls of the glass labyrinth. Their clay hides were darkened to a matte finish, baked solid as though in a kiln. Smoke coiled from the scorch marks.

Pavement Priests and Lampfolk lifted themselves to their feet. Oscar had pulled up before his fire could touch them, but they weren't unhurt. The stoneskins' backs had been scorched black by the radiated heat and they hissed with pain through the slits between their stone mouths. A few yards from where Beth knelt, a young Sodiumite girl whimpered in dull flickers; her shoulder blades had fused together.

A priest in a stone toga, roaring in pain and rage, smashed his fist into one of the immobile Masonry Men and the figure exploded into a shower of terracotta gravel. Beth didn't look round. She couldn't take her eyes off Timon's head where it stuck out of the ground, skewered by her spear. She could still feel the weapon's texture on her palm.

Ezekiel gathered himself first. He shook soot off his wings and tested them until he was satisfied by the range of movement. He eyed the carnage wordlessly for a moment, then said curtly, "We got what came for." He flickered and vanished.

Beth was sure that she was the only one who noticed the tiny pause as he whispered in her ear, "Right choice."

He reappeared a dozen feet away, facing back the way they'd come. "Let's go"—he jerked his head at one of the fire-hardened Masonry Men—"before any more of them show up."

Beth shook herself, trying to ward off the dizziness. She sealed herself back off from the poisoned street as best she could.

"*All right.*" The voice she managed was barely more than a whisper now. "*Let's—*"

There was a ratcheting click and a cold circle pressed itself against the tiles on her temple. "Please don't move, Lady Bradley. If you resist, I have instructions to kill you all." The voice was clipped, assured, upper class, and right beside her ear. Beth swivelled her eyes to look, but there was no one in the space where the voice was coming from. There was nothing there at all but empty air, despite the fact that she could *feel* the pressure of the narrow metal circle digging into her skin.

And then she looked past that space and into the glass jags of the labyrinth walls and all the air went out of her. In the crystal-clear reflection of the glass she saw them: dozens of human figures, mixed in amongst her burned and battered band. The Mirrorstocrats wore flak jackets strapped over their suits and they held heavy, fat-barrelled rifles like they knew how to use them. Every Pavement Priest, Blankleit and Sodiumite reflection had a gun to its head.

Beth let her awareness seep back into the street, but no matter how she groped through its murk, she couldn't *feel* the Mirrorstocrats. London's reflection was a different city and she was confined to this side of the glass. With a twinge in her heart, she finally understood why Mater Viae had encircled Her throne with the glazed wreckage.

Very, very slowly, Beth turned until she was looking straight into the reflection. The Mirrorstocrat who'd spoken to her was a dark-haired young woman wearing a striped blouse and chinos under her bulletproof vest. She spoke not to Beth's reflection but directly out of the mirror at her. "I am sorry about this, Milady," she said. It was neither sincere, nor especially sarcastic, just a formality, courteously observed.

"*You look familiar,*" Beth grunted.

"I served with you under the young prince at Chelsea Bridge last year—Tonge," she introduced herself, and actually saluted with her spare hand. "Daphne Tonge, Fourteenth Marchioness of Tooting."

"*You aren't Chevaliers.*"

"Oh, Lord Mago, no!" She sounded appalled by the idea. "We're not police—we're military, albeit irregulars."

"*The Officer Class?*" Beth said with a curl of her closed lips.

"Well, not to put too fine a point on it, yes," Daphne Tonge conceded.

"*Why?*" Beth demanded. "*Why fight for Her? She held your city hostage, kidnapped and killed your people—*"

"Why?" Tonge echoed, and an angry edge entered her sardonic voice. "Because your use of the past tense is a trifle premature."

Beth fought to think, but her brain was a fug of pain and poison and no clarity came. She played for time. "*So what now?*"

"That rather depends on you. You can cooperate, in which case I'll let your followers leave, or you can resist, in which case I won't."

"*If I come quietly, you'll let them go?*"

Daphne Tonge sighed. "Not quite. You *stand* there quietly while I try every means I can think of to kill you, and then I'll let them go. My instructions, I'm afraid, are expressly against bringing you in alive." The Mirrorstocrat lowered her gun with a slightly embarrassed air. "To tell you the truth, I'm not sure this will do it, but we have a considerable arsenal here to play with, and plenty of time."

Beth hesitated. Oscar crackled and hissed mournfully overhead, feeling her uncertainty. She licked her lips. She was so tired. She could feel the faith of every Pavement Priest and Lampie radiating out at her like physical heat: *We are watched over.* She could barely lift her head to look at them, though whether it was shame or exhaustion sapping her, she couldn't tell.

I don't know what to do.

She peered blearily into the reflection, trying to count the enemy. They outnumbered her two to one, even if Beth's soldiers could manage to coordinate themselves to fight a force they could only see in the mirror. It was hopeless. There was even a reserve detachment of Mirrorstocrats clustered a little way off, their guns held up at rest—no, not at rest, she realised, *poised*. She could see the tension in their muscles; they were aiming, but at something she couldn't see. A man in a grey suit suddenly whacked the empty air with the butt of his rifle; there was a puff of dust as though something—or someone—invisible had just hit the ground heavily in front of him.

"Do try and keep the prisoners in line, Stephan," Daphne Tonge called back over her shoulder at him without taking her eyes from Beth.

Prisoners, Beth thought frantically. *There are prisoners.* There must be something she could do with that information—something clever? *Come on, think.* But she couldn't see a way to use it. Acid frustration bubbled up in her and she choked as she stared into the mirror. She couldn't see a way out.

"Well, Lady Bradley," Daphne Tonge said, pressing the gun back to her head. "What do you say? Shall we give this little thing a try for starters?"

There was a whip-crack of air in Beth's ear. For a heart-stopping sliver of an instant she thought the gun had gone off, then a tendril of something black snapped past her head and the mirror shivered into splinters.

More whip-cracks, more tendrils of darkness, more shattering glass.

The labyrinth dissolved around them. Beth heard a gunshot—this time she was certain it was a gun—but when she cast about, nobody on her side of the mirror had fallen.

Muffled, confused shouts came from the mess of broken glass under their feet. The snapping tendrils slowed, just a fraction, but enough to see one, clearly silhouetted against the sun: a strand of wire threaded with cruel barbs.

Beth's heart clamped up in her chest.

No—oh dear God and Thames, no—

Every muscle in her rebelled against looking, but somehow her eyes still followed the length of that strand, tracing it back to its source: a figure, standing in a haze of dust, wires snapping and coiling around it like angry snakes.

Beth faltered. She tried to speak but the engines of her voice wouldn't respond.

Pen said nothing. Wire was corded tight around her mouth, like a metal bandana, but there was no blood—the barbs weren't biting, Beth realised; every one of them faced outwards. There was no fear in Pen's eyes, only a dreadful concentration.

Wires splayed out suddenly in front of her and planted themselves into the earth. With ferocious power, the Wire Mistress bore Pen forward.

II

THE STEEL BENEATH THE SKIN

CHAPTER TWELVE

Pen raced over the shattered glass, borne on strands of wire like insect feet. It was frightening how quickly the motion came back to her: she could feel the wire's instincts in her, dripping through its barbs into her nerves, its muscle memory overlaying her own. She swept past Beth—barely registering the horror on her friend's face—and dropped to a crouch amidst the shattered glass. She grasped desperately at a chunk the size of a car window, but her fingers were numb where the wire bound them and she couldn't get under the edges of it. She snarled at the consciousness she could feel lurking at the base of her skull to loosen its grip.

Its grip. In its grip. In the grip of the wire, wire binding her tight, wire constricting her breath, wire carrying her away, wire stopping her mouth as she screams . . .

She fought the panic back down, forced the memories away. *Forced* herself to feel past the dreadful power in the metal strands and find the weak spots, the fissures in the steel: where Beth's spear had severed it, the places where it had to cling to itself to hold itself together. In these places the Wire Mistress was vulnerable and she knew it.

"Ease up." She snarled it low in the hollow of her throat.

The pressure on her fingers eased and she finally got a grip on the fragment of glass.

"*Pen—*" Beth found her voice at last. "*Pen, what did you. What did?*" She was hovering over her, her spear wavering in her grip like she was about to try to cut the Mistress off her back.

Without looking around, Pen uncoiled a strand from her back and slapped the weapon down. "There were prisoners," she snapped. "I heard him say there were *prisoners.*"

Beth shook her head, not understanding. "*Pen, what are?*"

Muffled gunshots cut her off, the sound echoing through the glass on the ground. Pen scrabbled and finally managed to lift the fragment of broken glass to her face. She stared into the reflection. She straightened. Her heart skittered at the sight of herself, bound and bandoliered in wire, but she stayed in control. She looked past her own image into the makeshift window. She started to step in a slow circle, one foot across the other, tilting the glass this way and that, trying to get a view of the city on the other side.

Bodies in black flak jackets lay strewn over the floor, their expensive collars sticky with the gore that was leaking from their head wounds. Pen gaped at the carnage. *How?* How could they have—?

"*Countess.*"

Pen froze.

"Countess Khan."

Pen took one more step to the left and Daphne Tonge came into view in the mirror. She sat upright on the ground, hands limp in her lap, legs splayed out in front of her. She looked like she was sitting against something, but Pen couldn't see what was supporting her. She kept her head very still as she spoke, but her eyes kept darting to the left and right as though she wanted to look behind her.

"I bring you greetings from the Faceless."

Pen stared at her in astonishment. "You expect me to believe you're Faceless?" she said.

Tonge licked her lips nervously and Pen could hear how taut her voice was. "I'm most certainly not," she said, "but the young lady who currently has a blade pressed to my jugular is."

Daphne's eyes darted to her right again and this time Pen's followed them. She focused on the empty space above her shoulder, on the girl holding the Mirrorstocrat, the girl she couldn't see but knew was there. The vast majority of London-Under-Glass' residents lacked enough richness in their own image to cast reflections, so they were not visible from this side of the mirror. Pen thought back to that reflected city, to another labyrinth and to rank upon rank of figures standing silent, their faces hidden under black hoods and behind black bandanas, agents of an invisible insurgency: the Faceless.

"This Faceless girl, she's speaking through you?"

"She is," Daphne sniffed, "and I wish you'd let her get on it, because she doesn't smell any better than she looksaaaah!" Her head tilted back a fraction of an inch as a fine red line appeared on the skin of her neck.

Pen flicked her gaze back to her.

"If I were you I wouldn't editorialise," Pen said. "I know scars are in right now, but trust me, there's only so many you can live with." She returned her attention to the invisible presence behind the Mirrorstocrat. "You were their prisoners?"

"Yes," Tonge confirmed hoarsely.

"You overcame them?"

"Yes."

"How?" Pen snapped, more harshly than she meant to. "There were loads of them." She could feel the Mistress coiling and bridling in her mind, suspicious that this was somehow a trap.

"There are more of us, and the posh—" Tonge broke off, then said, "Oh, come on, I'm not going to say *that*—aaah! All right, all right!" She recoiled as far as she could from the invisible knife. Her lip curled as she spoke. "The posh shits are an unadulterated shambles, a disgrace to the name 'soldier,' and"—she ground her teeth and then exhaled through them—"they don't fight any better than they look."

Pen's lip quirked, but she felt the wire tug at it and lost her smile. "And?"

"And they fell apart when you showed up and in the confusion, we grabbed a couple of their guns." Tonge swallowed, her gaze travelling, and Pen realised she was surveying all the bodies on her side of the mirror, the bodies of those she'd led.

"We didn't hesitate," she croaked.

"So what do the Faceless want with me?"

"Simply to pass on the regards of their leader," Tonge said. "Cray says hello."

"*Cray?*" Pen started as another image flashed into her mind; she remembered backing away from the hulking insurgent boss on unwilling feet, leaving him in the back alleys of London-Under-Glass while the city's black armoured police closed on him. She remembered his mutilated, symmetrical face: his makeshift razor-slash mouth and above it the ice-blue eyes that begged her to do right by the unconscious girl draped across her shoulders.

"C-Cray's alive?" she stammered hopefully. "He *survived*? What about Jack? Jack Wingborough? Did he get out too?"

"Ah . . ." There was no disguising the satisfaction in the Mirrorstocrat's voice as she delivered the news. "I'm afraid you misunderstood me: both Lord Wingborough and Garrison Cray were killed by Simularchy forces on Draw Night. The leadership of the Faceless has been taken over by his sister, a steeplejill called—"

"—Espel."

Pen whispered the name at the same time as Tonge did, and her legs would have gone out from under her had the wire strands not been holding her up. She felt gelatinous, unstable. Without her asking, more wires uncoiled and bound themselves around the edges of the mirror, holding it up for her. She pressed both her hands to the glass.

"Espel," she said again, breathing the name. "Where is she? Is she here?"

Tonge snorted. "You think if we'd had the leader of the Faceless in our custody all day we'd have been stuck around on sentry duty? No, she's not here."

"But she's alive." Pen's heart suddenly felt about five times too big for her chest. She drew in a long, shivering breath. "She's leading the Faceless and she's alive. Could you . . . ?"

She stopped and directed her gaze back at the space above Tonge's shoulder. "Could *you* bring her here?"

"*Pen, no.*" A voice, a burr of motors, buzzed in her ear: Beth's voice. Pen had all but forgotten she was there. She looked down. Beth's architecture-clad hand was resting on her wrist. "*We have to get out of here.*"

Pen shook her head doggedly. "Espel's alive," she stammered. "She's alive. She could come—we could talk. Es is *alive.*"

"*But you won't be,*" Beth said, "*not if you stay here.*"

Reluctantly, Pen followed her best friend's gaze upwards. Oscar was wheeling and crackling frantically over their heads.

"*Sewermanders are coming,*" Beth said, "*five of them. He can feel them drawing from the gas mains.*"

"But—but—" Pen felt a twist of pain in her chest. She shot another look at the glass, and the promise of contact. She couldn't bear to walk away from it knowing she might never get another chance. "I can't—I can't just—"

Beth took her hand, threaded her rough fingers through Pen's own. "*You want to stay, I'll stay. Okay? But I can't ask them to.*" She looked over at the Pavement Priests and Lampfolk, who were already retreating.

Gutterglass was beckoning to them in alarm, calling, "Lady Bradley! Miss Khan, come! *Please.*"

Pen swallowed hard, still hesitating. Beth squeezed her hand, but didn't pull away. Pen turned her gaze back onto the mirror and looked straight at the space where she knew the Faceless stood.

"There's a bathroom," she said, "in a school—your boss will know which one. If she . . ." She hesitated. "If she feels the way I feel, tell her to be there the night after next."

Tonge twitched away from the invisible knife. "She says she'll deliver the message."

Pen felt the strength drain out of her. She let Beth's arm turn her and guide her away. A twitch in her own muscles echoed the movement of the wire coils as they unwound from the mirror and let it fall to shatter in the dust.

CHAPTER THIRTEEN

Beth walked the streets of her dreams alone.

She could feel the rhino behind her, staring down from tower-block walls and billboards. Its acrylic-white eyes burned into her back, but she didn't look round. A breeze picked up. It penetrated the fabric of her hoodie and made the hairs on her arms stand up. She hugged herself and hurried onwards.

The buildings were taller here than she remembered, and closer together, hemming her in. She heard a snort behind her and she started to run, taking turnings at random: left, now right, now right again. She could feel the beast behind her, the hammer of its hooves not quite drowning the hammer of her pulse. The wind picked up, blowing harder down the narrow concrete ravines, pressing against her face and chest. She bent her head and forced her way onwards. The wind redoubled again. She ducked into another side street to try to get out of it, but no matter which way she turned it was always blowing right into her face, so hard it snatched the air from in front of her lips. She heard another snort, this time in front of her, and the breathy spray of aerosol-paint spattered over her clothes and into her hair. She knew the wind was the rhino's breath; that the animal was somehow in front of her as well as behind. The gale shrieked full into her, burning her skin, making her eyes water and sting.

Every step was slower than the last, like pushing through dense, invisible bracken, until she could no longer force herself onwards. She stood for a second, knees bent, leaning into the wind's fury. The effort of resisting seared the muscles in her calves and her back. Then, slowly, she began to slip backwards.

Her heart sped up, and so did the sound of the rhino's hooves. She could feel it stampeding up behind her. Her feet skidded on streets slippery with wet paint. Her stomach lurched and she was blown backwards, tumbling like a leaf towards the beast. Her heart seemed to stop altogether . . .

. . . and then sputtered back to life as her fingers snagged a doorway. The door was open, dark, inviting shelter. Her fingers gouged the wood of the frame, pushing splinters under her nails, and she hissed with pain as, drawing on her last strength, she pulled herself in.

At first the darkness inside seemed absolute, then Beth became aware of a single bulb recessed into an oval fitting in the ceiling, shining with a dim green light. She blinked the tears from her wind-stung eyes. The light strobed off and on again and she saw that she wasn't alone.

Dark figures lined the walls of the room. They didn't move as she approached them. They stood stiffly to attention: figurines, life-sized clay models of men and women, lovingly detailed, with brick-red veins protruding from clay skin, strands of clay spittle stretched between motionless clay lips.

She knew them, she realised. She knew them all. She hurried around the room, putting her hands to their cheeks as she examined them. This was the one she'd tried to summon when the Street-Serpent had attacked, and this one and this one: this squat one here who looked a bit like her dad was exactly who she'd pictured and fought futilely to shape from the kitchen floor at Selfridges. They were all here, she realised, every single avatar she'd ever tried and failed to conjure.

And then, with sudden, startling clarity, she knew more—that every thought she'd ever had and believed she'd forgotten was somewhere in the streets of this city.

Something moved in the dust, a coiling, snapping thing, and Beth jumped, suddenly aware of the vulnerability of her soft bare feet. The thing on the floor flickered like a snake's tongue, but it didn't come for her; instead it wound its way around the leg of the nearest body, its barbs leaving sidewinder track-marks in the clay.

Beth stared at the wire, hypnotised by its motion. When it gained the figure's face, it began, as carefully and methodically as an artist's pencil, to mark out scars on the clay features, scars that Beth knew as well as her own face. The clay eyes just stared at her, dead. The wire snaked and coiled around the figure's limbs, hooking itself into joints and pores.

"Beth—" Her name came as a hissing rattle, metal over clay, metal over skin. "Bethhhhh."

With sinuous speed, a clay hand flashed out and grabbed her throat.

Beth's eyes snapped open. She gasped for air that wouldn't come. She tried to scream, but no sound came out. There was something on her throat, something sharp. She swatted at it and it tumbled onto the floor with a static crackle. Beth leaned over the edge of the bed after it.

A spider the colour of fibreglass stared up at her with eight coal-black eyes. Its mandibles were coated in brick dust. Beth put her hand to her throat and felt two tiny holes either side of her larynx.

"*Deal's a deal,*" the spider said. Its voice was hijacked from a TV game show host, bracketed with static. "*One human voice, harvested free-range, in the wild. That's what you promised, that's what you pay.*"

Beth fought to recover her breath before she answered it. "*I know,*" she said. "*I'm sorry. Bad dreams.*"

"*No problem,*" the spider replied in its breezy American accent. "*Got what I needed anyway.*" It scuttled across the floor to a strand of hanging silk and scrambled up it. The silk raced up behind it like a disappearing fuse, faster and faster until both spider and web vanished in a crackle of bad reception.

Beth exhaled and collapsed back on her bed. She stared at the patch of green light her eyes cast on the ceiling; it was dimmed and refracted through dirty tears. The dorm around her was dark, and quiet but for the gentle snoring of a man opposite. She thought back to before all this, when she didn't know how strange the world really was. How many exchanges like that had *she* slept through? she wondered, and then decided it didn't really matter.

All that mattered was that she wasn't sleeping now.

She forced herself to count her breaths until she felt back under control, then she let herself rise. The sheet pulled tackily away from her back as she sat up, and when she turned around she smelled tar. There was a black sticky patch on the sheet, and her T-shirt was gummed to her skin with half-dried tarmac.

No wonder she felt so dizzy: her scars had opened in the night.

She looked around furtively, but everyone else was still asleep, so she struggled out of her T-shirt, yelping despite herself when it pulled at the still-healing scabs. Then she tugged on her hoodie and went looking for Pen.

She found her on the roof, staring out at Canary Wharf. Her chin was resting against her arms where they lay folded on a gargoyle's head. The moonlight made the steel coils on her neck and back glimmer and Beth felt a little hitch in her chest at the sight of them. Part of her had believed she'd get to leave that thing in the dream.

She stepped cautiously out from the fire escape, making her footsteps as noisy as she could. "*That's some pretty serious bling you've got going on there, Pen,*" she ventured. "*To be honest, I'm not sure it suits you.*"

Pen didn't look round. The light wash from a Sodiumite encampment on the street below showed her breath fogging as she sighed. "Yeah," she said, "and since you *did* work as a professional style icon in the most image-obsessed city in the universe,

I suppose I'd better listen to—Oh no, wait—that was me, wasn't it? So hush."

Beth came to stand beside her. "*Pen, that was for less than two weeks.*"

"So?"

"*It was under false pretences—they thought you were your mirror-sister!*"

"Even so." Under her barbed exo-skeleton, Pen sucked her scarred lip. "It's a better track record than your concrete skincare routine, so . . ." She gestured.

"*Hush?*"

"Precisely."

Beth fell silent. She saw the way the veins of silver wire mimicked the twist of muscles as they snaked over Pen's back and shoulders and slipped in below her headscarf. It wasn't all one length of wire, she realised; the metal web encasing her best friend was made of dozens of strands, carefully plaited together.

As if she had anticipated the question, Pen reached back and lifted the hem of her hijab. There, to her appalled fascination, Beth saw four barbs, resting in neat, red-rimmed puncture wounds at the base of Pen's neck. The wire flexed gently in a steady rhythm, like it was breathing.

"It's the only place she's under the skin," Pen said quietly. "Unless I need her to lend my muscles more power; in that case she can latch into them too."

Beth started to speak, but before the voice could rise off her skin, Pen cut her off, her voice hard. "I know what you're about to say, B, and don't you dare." Behind the wire cage, her eyes swivelled to look at Beth. "Don't you dare judge me. You gave your voice to the spiders and your life to the street, so think very carefully about your next few words, okay?"

Beth swallowed and nodded. "*Okay, Pen.*"

"Okay. So what do you want to know?"

Beth floundered, unsure where to even begin. "*Does it* hurt?"

The wry quirk of Pen's lip was just visible under the metal. "Why? Does it look like it hurts?"

"*Yeah, Pen. It* looks *like you have a load of barbed wire wrapped round you.*"

"Then let's assume it hurts. Next question."

Beth blinked at Pen's abruptness. "*Can you control it?*"

"No, but on the plus side, she can't control me either. We weakened her at St. Paul's, badly. She hasn't recovered. I can . . . *negotiate* with her."

"*Negotiate?*" Beth was appalled.

"Sure," Pen said calmly. "Our current deal is: she comes with me where I say, and I let her use me to keep herself alive. You said we were out of allies, B. I found us another one."

Beth gaped at her. "*Pen, you didn't have to do this for me!*"

"I didn't, Beth," Pen said flatly. "I did it for *us.* I did it so *we* could win, not just you. Learn the difference, would you?"

"*Pen, please, I'm only trying to—*"

"Oh, I know you are, B, but frankly, I'm mad as hell at you. I'm trying not to be because you're all"—she flapped her hands irritably—"*dying* and everything, and I feel like a terrible bloody person, really I do, but there's nothing I can do about it."

She looked right at Beth. "Beth, you cannot ever, *ever* try and throw me out again. Do you understand?"

Beth nodded, her lips tightly shut.

"If I get killed next to you, you're just going to have to live with that. And if you die next to me, I'll have to live with that too. You can't protect me from it. That's who we are. That's what *this* means." Pen held her gaze. "That whole 'dying alone' thing? You don't get to do that."

Beth closed her eyes and felt a shudder in her chest. She nodded again, more decisively.

"Good." Pen exhaled explosively, then choked out a laugh. "That's settled then."

It was only when she heard Pen sniff her tears back that Beth saw the streaks of wet mascara running out from under the wire mesh on her face.

"Now all I have to worry about is whether my invisible girlfriend will turn up tomorrow night."

Beth smiled at that. "*Tell me about her*," she said.

"I've told you about her loads of times already—"

"*You've told me about the last time you saw her loads of times already*," Beth corrected her. "*Tell me about* her."

"She's . . ." Pen hesitated, then sucked her teeth and gave Beth a wary, sidelong glance. "She's like you."

"*Me?*"

"Yeah."

"*Parva Khan, we're seriously going to have to talk about your taste in women.*"

"I know, right?"

Beth saw a flash of a smile under the metal as Pen said, "It's tragic."

"*You're meeting her in the Frostfield bathroom?*"

"Yep."

"*Then we're also going to have to talk about your choice of date.*"

Pen laughed, and a knot in Beth's stomach relaxed at the sound. They fell silent for a moment, side by side, looking out over the altered city. The night air was cold, but the heat coming off a nearby Fever Street touched their faces like a bonfire.

"You think she'll come?" Pen asked eventually.

"*'Course she will, Pen.*"

"Why? It's not guaranteed. For all I know, she hates me—I left her in pretty much the lurchiest lurch imaginable. Besides, she's head of the Faceless now. She might be busy—I don't know, blowing something up."

Beth snorted.

"I'm just saying," Pen fretted, "even if she wants to come, I don't know if she'll be able to get there."

"*She'll find a way.*"

"How do you know?"

Beth looked up at Pen. Even under the wire cage the shape was still utterly, recognisably her.

"*Because she's like me. And it's you.*"

Pen looked at her then, and Beth knew she was utterly vulnerable to that gaze.

"B, what happened with Timon—you know you had to, right?"

Beth felt something stir in her gut. She thought of Timon's pleading face the moment before her spear slammed into it. "*Yeah,*" she said quietly.

"You okay?"

"*Yeah.*"

"You're lying to me right now, aren't you?"

"*Yeah.*"

"Ah—there you are!"

Beth looked around sharply as her dad appeared ruddy-faced in the fire-escape doorway. He carried a tray laden down with three mugs and a teapot with a coil of steam writhing from the spout.

"Somehow I knew," he said as he ambled over, balanced the tray on the gargoyle's head and wiped his hands on his trousers, "that given the best opportunity we've had in ages to get some sleep, the two of you would be up somewhere nattering."

He poured tea into two of the mugs and Beth and Pen accepted them gratefully. He hesitated over the third, and Beth sighed and took the pot from him, filled the final mug and thrust it into his hands.

"Only if you're sure," he mumbled. "Don't want to intrude."

"*Don't worry*," Beth said. "*We were only talking about what Pen's going to get up to on her date tomorrow night.*"

"Oh, right." He grinned. "Where are you taking the young lady?"

"A bathroom in Frostfield High that was condemned for asbestos," Pen said drily. "Romantic, huh?"

Paul Bradley pursed his lips, considering it. "Positively upmarket compared to some of the dives in Deptford Beth's mum dragged me to when we first met," he said finally. "She had this thing for punk bands."

"*Things we do for love, eh?*" Beth smiled around the little dull thorn she always felt in her heart when her dad mentioned her mum.

"B." There was a tightness in Pen's voice that pulled the smile from Beth's lips. "There's something else we need to talk about."

CHAPTER FOURTEEN

"What's going on?" Pen asked as the three of them descended the stationary escalators that zigzagged through the men's wear and women's wear floors. Trash hands were crawling like spiders over the pillars, prising the mirrored glass from the walls and bearing it away past the mannequin's blank gazes.

"*I told Glas to get rid of all the mirrors,*" Beth replied. "*If Mater Viae's still holding the Mirrorstocracy's leash, then it's probably a good idea not to give them a hundred ways to look into our house uninvited.*" She winced. "*'Course, it would have been an even better idea not to set up in a dress shop packed out with half of London's reflective surfaces—but hey, we live and learn.*"

They reached the fourth floor and shouldered through the doors into the electronics section. The most hardcore half-dozen of Selfridges' stranded tourists sat crosslegged on the floor, gazing despondently at the TV screens.

"Excuse me," Pen said. "Sorry, but we need to borrow the room."

None of them looked round.

"Hey!" she shouted. A pouchy, middle-aged man put his finger to his lips and shushed her, but he didn't take his eyes from the TV.

Pen sighed. She felt the decision—her *suggestion* to the Wire Mistress—like a nerve twitch at the base of her neck. Six wire tendrils unfurled from around her and twisted slowly through the air. She closed her eyes briefly, but she could still feel them. Their barbs shivered in the breeze like they were hairs on her arms.

Perfectly synchronised, the six wire strands found the power switches for the TV screens. The room became instantly silent.

When Pen reopened her eyes, the six men were staring at her in open-mouthed horror.

Their fear sparked something in the back of Pen's mind; her pulse quickened. She felt the wires curl slightly, one in front of each of their faces, tensing to strike—

She stamped down on the urge. That hot metallic taste at the back of her throat didn't belong to her. She'd felt this urge to kill before and she knew it wasn't hers, even if it felt like it was—even if, in that moment, it felt like it was her dearest wish to end these frightened men, to discharge the violence and the anger pent up in her into their fragile flesh.

It's not me.

The wire whined, high and quiet, like an insect in her ear, but the steel tendrils relaxed. Pen stood very still and pressed her nails hard into the palms of her hands until the urge subsided.

Behind her shoulder, engines and generators and nightclub bass surged together into a threatening growl. "*Get out.*"

The six men fled.

Beth came to her shoulder. "*You okay?*" she asked.

"I'm fine," Pen replied, unclenching her fists and letting the blood tingle back into her palms. "I'm just adjusting."

She walked over to the bank of TVs and one by one flicked them back on, then picked up the remotes and held down the channel scroll buttons until they were showing the BBC, ITV and Sky news channels.

Beth stood in front of the screens. She pulled her hood down and her sleeves up. From this little distance, the tiny tiles that covered her skin looked like reptile scales. Her dad stood beside her, a protective hand on her shoulder.

"*What are we looking at, Pen?*" Beth asked.

"It's more what we *aren't* looking at," she replied. "What haven't we seen at all?"

They went back to watching the screens. One of them showed a satellite image of London, a red line demarcating the affected area. A government phone number was scrolling continuously across the bottom of the screen. Another showed the acting Prime Minister barking something; the volume was too low to let them hear it clearly. The third replayed the footage from the previous night's disaster. Pen's gut twisted as she watched the Sewermanders fly into the helicopter again and again in slow motion.

Beth shook her head slowly. "*Still not getting—*" she began, but Paul Bradley interrupted her.

"Refugees," he murmured.

Pen snapped her fingers and pointed at him. "Right?" she asked him. "I mean, look at that map." She pointed to the leftmost TV screen. "Something like fifteen per cent of the country used to live inside that red line. The streets are empty now. I know some people died in the symptoms, but we're not exactly hip-deep in corpses, are we? So"—she spread her arms—"where did everybody go? They can't all be hiding out in the Clapham Junction Asda."

"*They got evacuated,*" Beth said. "*Like your mum and dad. They got out.*"

"Then like your dad says, where are the refugees? It ought to be bloody *chaos* out there, B. We should be seeing pictures of tents and trucks and food shortages and who knows what else. When that hurricane hit New Orleans a few years back, they ran out of food, water, medicine—the works. They were living in stadiums. It was bedlam. Do you know how many people lived in New Orleans back then?"

"*No—*"

"Me neither, but I bet it's a hell of a lot less than the eight million who used to live here." Pen was pacing, buzzing with energy as she talked it out. She waved her hands agitatedly, and it was only when she saw the wild way that they were looking at her that she realised the wire strands trailing from her back were mimicking the motion. She dropped her hands back to her sides.

"It's been bugging me for ages, but it wasn't until I saw what I saw yesterday that I put my finger on it."

Beth looked at her sharply. "*Until you saw what, yesterday, Pen?*"

"At the synod's factory—one of Mater Viae's Masonry soldiers took a child."

"*A child? I don't understand.*"

"The synod must have abandoned the place because there was this kid hiding out there. A clayling reached right out of the floor and dragged him back under. At first I thought it had killed him, but it hadn't. It took him *alive*, Beth—the way I've seen them take people before."

And with that, she was back in that huge dark room beneath the palace in London-Under-Glass, her feet crunching the broken bottles strewn over the floor and knowing that for every bottle there was a victim: a scared, lonely human, kidnapped, their memories stolen and their body executed, weighted and dumped in the river.

She couldn't keep the shiver out of her voice as she said, "I think I know where the missing people went." She walked to the wavy, frosted window and opened it out onto the night. Canary Wharf pierced the darkness in the distance, the only tower in London where the lights were still burning.

"She took them."

For a long time, no one spoke.

"*I don't know, Pen,*" Beth said at last. "*There's a lot of assumptions there.*"

Pen nodded slowly. "Yeah, there are," she admitted, "and maybe they're wrong, but they fit, and I don't know what else does. And what if they're *right?*"

She felt the hum in the barbs over her diaphragm as urgency entered her voice. "I *know* Her, B—I've seen Her do this before. People aren't *people* to Her. She doesn't care about them. She wouldn't be taking them if She didn't plan to use them. And there are thousands, and thousands missing, so—" She hesitated, licked her lips. "So whatever that use is . . ."

". . . *it's big.*" Beth finished the sentence for her.

"We have to find out what she's up to. And if I'm right—if she does have them, we have to help those people—we have to try at least. B, there's"—Pen spread her hands and a helpless laugh burst out of her—"there's no one else who *can.*"

Beth stood motionless for a second, arms folded. The green light from her eyes spread over the floor. She looked troubled. "*Maybe there's no one who can at all.*"

She met Pen's gaze then, and Pen shrank away, shriven by how sick her friend looked, how tired. Beth's folded arms suddenly didn't look defiant but like they were all that was holding her together.

"*You saw what happened when we went after Timon,*" she said. "*We could barely handle one of their patrols. We would have been swamped by the Sewermanders and reinforcement Masonry Men if we'd hung around any longer.*" The city-voice sounded parched and weary, and Pen began to understand just how much yesterday's battle had taken from her.

"*I'm sorry, Pen. I believe you, and I want to help, I really do. But we won't even get close.*"

Pen held her gaze, but Beth's green eyes burned sadly in front of her until she let her head drop.

Pen turned and pulled the window shut.

"There . . . there might still be a way." Paul Bradley's voice was shaking.

Pen looked around, startled.

"W-w-w—" he started, then he stopped, wet his lips and tried again. "We can't get in through force; Beth's right about that, but there might be another way?" His eyes, very wide, darted between the two girls' faces before settling finally on Pen's.

"They're . . . they're taking people, you said. Taking humans. Well . . ." He smiled nervously and gestured to himself in a bashful *Ta-dah!*

"*Oh, for God's sake,*" Beth snapped, rolling her eyes.

"It might work, Beth," he insisted. He spoke very fast, his words running into each other, as though afraid that if he paused for too long he might lose the courage to speak. "It might be the only way. Humans, right? We don't have many, and it can't be you"—he gestured to Pen, who was staring at him. "She knows you—you said that. She'd spot you straight away. But she doesn't know me. It *has* to be me." The truth of the words seemed to dawn on him even as he spoke them. "It's like Parva said: there's no one else."

"*This. Is. Ridiculous,*" Beth snapped harshly. "*Even if I was willing to consider it, which I'm not, how would you get back to us, genius? How would you get the word out? In case you hadn't noticed, there's kind of a shortage of people coming back* out *of Canary Wharf with stories to tell. Now, I don't know why that is, but if they're in there I doubt it's 'cause they're having too much fun!*"

He flinched, but he didn't look away from the architecture of his daughter's face. Then he said what Pen had been afraid he was going to say from the moment he opened his mouth. "Maybe I don't need to come back."

"*What?*" Beth demanded bluntly.

"Gutterglass," he answered, "Gutterglass could give me a—a rat, or a beetle or a Ribena carton or something to carry with me. She could watch, listen through it . . . I don't know, but that way if I—even if I don't . . ." He tailed off and then muttered, "Well, either way, you'd know."

But Beth was already shaking her head. "*Glas doesn't have that kind of range,*" she said.

He frowned at this immediate dismissal. "You could at least ask her. How do you know?"

"*I. JUST. KNOW.*"

Beth's shout was like a building collapsing, and Pen wondered if somewhere in the miniaturised architecture of her body, some tower had given way to generate it. Beth slumped, breathing heavily. "*Let's just drop it,*" she muttered.

Pen eyed her. She wanted so badly to do what Beth said. She wanted to tell Paul his plan was brave but unworkable. She wanted to forget she'd ever brought it up.

But the serious face of the little boy at the synod's factory stared at her from her memory, and in her ears she heard the crunching of glass beneath her feet.

She met Beth's gaze, but only for an instant. *I'm sorry, B*, she thought. "There might be another way," she said.

"*What?*" Beth's voice was deadly quiet.

"There might be another way," Pen repeated, "even without Glas: there might be a way to do what your dad's talking about."

Beth didn't say anything, but Pen really believed that that was hope in his voice as he said, "What?"

"Hold out your hand."

He obeyed with a puzzled frown. Pen took his hand in both of hers and turned it gently over so the palm was towards the floor. She plucked a half-inch-long piece of wire with two barbs, one at either end, from the back of her own hand. It writhed and twisted in the air like a worm.

Paul's eyes widened. "Will it hurt?" he whispered.

Pen shook her head and smiled as best she could. "Like a jab at the doctor's," she reassured him. "No worse than that."

He swallowed hard, screwed his eyes closed and nodded. Avoiding her best friend's burning green gaze, Pen laid the strand gently on his skin. The wire coiled, flopped restlessly, and then the barbs bit.

Pen felt a jolt. A shiver ran through her. In its wake another layer of sensation overlaid her skin, dulled as if by morphine but there. She felt the prickle of two-day stubble on her neck, the drag of an extra three stone of stomach around her waist. She smelled the anxious fug of his sweat, suddenly close, as if it were coming from her own pores.

"Mr. B," she said, her voice a little unsteady, "open your eyes."

She *felt* the reluctance in her own eyelids as he obeyed.

Pen blinked and inhaled sharply. It was vague, a hazy extra layer just beyond her own sight, but she could focus on it if she tried. Blurred by Paul Bradley's frightened tears, she saw her own face.

CHAPTER FIFTEEN

With her back to the sunset, Pen clambered across the broken city. Dust and fumes had soaked into her clothes. Every fold of her skin felt gritty, the dirt cemented onto her with her own sweat. The city's convulsions had shattered Southwark; its warehouses and viaducts lay in tumbles of brick and sheared-away iron. Pen scrambled up the dunes on all fours, wary of slipping masonry and the blade-like stubs of shorn girders that lurked like traps beneath them. The air was parched. She paused, panting for breath, and then pressed on. It was still a long, long way back to Frostfield.

An alien thought burst into her head, a voice that sounded like her.

Uncoil! Uncoil! Ease your toil!

The Wire Mistress had latched on to the bit of her brain where her poetry lived, speaking to her in half-nonsensical rhymes. There was something about the tangled, twisting language that bent back on itself that the steel creature seemed to recognise.

"Shut up, would you?" Pen muttered.

She knew what she wanted; she could feel the Wire Mistress, itchy and impatient, dripping the urges into her through the back of her neck. The cramps in her coils were aches in Pen's own muscles and she couldn't stop herself from thinking how good it would feel to let the wire stretch out and bear her up on spindly legs, to luxuriate in the cool night air far above the surface of the city.

But even as she imagined it, her heart stuttered and memory assaulted her: barbs burning in her nerves, her skin sticky with her own drying blood as she was carried away, with no way to know where—no way, and no say: no say at all.

"No," she said, "not yet. Not again. I'm not ready."

The wire whined, but she felt it coil back up quietly in her skull.

"Just as well B and her dad aren't here. Talking to you out loud like this would freak them out no end."

She'd left them arguing: Mr. B adamant that he could help, that he *had* to help, Beth just stubbornly shaking her head. Nothing would be done, she insisted, until they had a plan to get him back. Pen hadn't contributed much. The face of the boy in the factory had hovered in front of her, needling her to speak, but every time she'd opened her mouth, Beth's expression, frantic with the premonition of bereavement, had shut it for her.

Brick shale slid from under her foot. Her breath stalled, restarted. She found a new footing and reached for another handhold. She crested the masonry ridge and looked over.

Heat slammed into her like an invisible wall.

"Crap," she muttered.

A Fever Street cut through the sprawl below her like a lava flow. Black smoking stains on the surface of the asphalt marked where *something* unfortunate had fallen onto its surface. She scanned left and right, anxiously looking for a break or crossing, but all she could see was shimmering tarmac. She had no way of knowing how far the pyrexia stretched.

Behind her, the sun was already low and bloody.

"Pick and play, pick and play, bear you on your tick-tock way,
Up across the burning street, oh so many dainty feet."

"Yeah," she muttered, her stomach swimming. "Right."

She exhaled and closed her eyes.

It was like stretching a limb she'd been sitting on for hours: she felt pins and needles ripple through the wire strands as the Mistress' magnetic muscles flexed, unrolling a tendril and sliding it down into a hollow in the brickwork. Another followed it, then a third, and then more, until seven strands connected Pen to the earth.

Sweat spotted her hijab where it lay against her forehead. She felt sick. "Me," she whispered through gritted teeth. "*I'll* do it. Let me."

She concentrated, trying to feel the shape of the wire, the weight of it where it lay wrapped around her torso. She traced it in her mind: how each severed strand connected to the next until, finally, they punctured her neck, plugging into her.

At her command, and with an ease that astonished her, another wire tendril unravelled, wavered in the air, then planted itself into the bricks.

Direct control, she thought. She had direct control. The swimming in her stomach calmed a little. *It can't be that easy, can it?* The Wire Mistress coiled in the back of her mind, purring, too damned quiescent. Pen didn't trust her, but the creature put up no resistance as she pushed her consciousness back along the metal, groping again for the wounds in it, reassuring herself with the Mistress' weakness.

She was tentative at first. She leaned forward into the cage of wires across her chest, then, very slowly, straightened the tendrils underneath her. Her toes dragged in the dust as they came off the floor.

She hung there for a moment: a barbed-wire spider on eight legs of twisted steel burnished by the sunset. For a single dreadful instant, she couldn't breathe, and couldn't stop the thought that the wire had been lying in wait for just this moment to crush her.

You're just panicking, she scolded herself. *Breathe, Pen. Breathe. Stop fighting it. You don't need to fight it—*

—not now.

She tried to slow her lungs, tried to breathe normally, and found she could. She burst out in a laugh so loud it shocked her.

She waited, but the Mistress didn't move, though Pen could feel her savouring the stretch, the feeling of her weight in her strands. She sat quietly, in abeyance, not even talking to her as the coils gently contracted and expanded in time with her breathing.

With an unsteady kind of awe, Pen realised the Mistress was waiting for her to take the first step.

She focused on the foremost strand, lifted and planted it on the far side of the Fever Street. It reached easily across the hot tarmac, shuddered a little bit, but held firm. She planted another next to it. When her front four legs were firmly planted she pushed off hard with her hind ones and sailed over the Fever Street like a pole vaulter, its heat briefly stroking her face.

Her arc carried her too far and she overbalanced; her stomach flipped over and she screwed up her eyes. The rubble on the far side rushed up fast—

Pen bounced, but not as hard as she had expected. She opened her eyes again and saw in astonishment that the wire was *cradling* her; it had balled up around her in a cage, flexing and absorbing the impact. They rolled to a stop at the bottom of the hill and there they lay while the Mistress waited for Pen to make the first move.

"Okay, then," she muttered.

A few moments later, they were up again and crossing the city with a swaying gait, unsteady as a baby giraffe at first. Her confidence grew with each step and soon the bricks began to flow away in a blur under her. The Mistress began to drip in quiet, unspoken suggestions; Pen could feel her, like a stabilising hand, guiding but never pushing her influence. The air flowed faster and faster past her face and secretly, behind her mask of wire, Pen let herself smile a little.

Is this how it was for you, Es? she wondered, the smile tugging a little wider. *What will you make of me?*

Something snagged her attention.

She stopped sharply. Her new legs bent, and slowly flexed back as she lost momentum. She frowned. They'd passed something significant; she'd felt it. She focused, groping for the sensation. She felt more pins and needles: the sense of another wire limb waking up—but this one wasn't attached to her. It was Out There.

In the night.

Pen gasped. Her eyes stretched wide and the lashes tickled wire strands as she realised the scale of what she was connected to. She concentrated harder. She felt the distant wire in her mind, focused on it and felt it flex in response: a remote limb. The more she shifted it, the more the magnetism flowed, the more she felt, sensing its shape, and where it lay on the ground.

The Mistress purred contentedly in her mind.

She coiled and flexed the wire until she had all of it, then to her astonished delight, she felt her awareness jump to another strand close to that one, then another followed, then another. Her proprioception raced along fence-top coils and bales of razor-wire and tendrils buried under hillsides. She was almost screaming with the electric sensation of it, just on the border of pain.

Dark shapes formed in her mind: streets and cellars and empty courtyards, like the half-images she got in her head when she listened to the radio. The wire could feel the form of the city that surrounded it, and the echoes vibrated in its barbs. Pen's awareness raced up over rooftops and along railway tracks. She sensed the electromagnetic thrum of neon and steered towards it. A hulking square black building emerged out of the night—a warehouse or a supermarket, lights were blazing against it. A figure slouched towards those lights across an empty car park, a figure, a man, who looked familiar somehow. Curious, she moved the wire closer towards him—

"Oh." Pen uttered a little shocked breath. Ice crept into her gut and up into her throat. The wire mewled around her, wanting to know what was wrong, why she'd stopped.

"It can't be," she whispered. "I mean, it *can't*—"

Tentatively, almost unwillingly, she reached back out to the supermarket car park and the barbed-wire tendrils that guarded its high brick wall from alighting pigeons. She unwound one tendril and sent it snaking silently after the figure. The closer it got, the more of a sense Pen got of him. He lurched like a man exhausted, and he was thin—far thinner than she'd ever seen him. His beard was a mat of darkness on his hollow cheeks, but Pen knew him. She could never not have known him, no matter how badly she wanted to forget him.

Dr. Julian Salt stumbled towards the building where he'd made his makeshift home, and behind him, Pen coiled the wire to strike.

She held it there for an unbearable time. Her mind was full of his voice, the grate of his stubble on her cheek, his callused fingers sliding up under her clothes, stroking her spine. She felt a snarl build in the back of her throat.

"*It'll be our secret*," she spat, and the wire barbs around her mouth clenched like a second jaw. A metal voice sang in her mind.

> *He stole, he stole*
> *End it now, take your toll.*
> *Fear and doubt, fear and doubt,*
> *End it now. Snuff him out.*

But still she hesitated. The wire remained curled, a scorpion's sting, but her eagerness faltered. Was this her, she wondered, or was it the wire? Could it really *be* her, deciding to kill a man? A nervous thrill ran through her at the thought, at the *freedom* it hinted at. She could choose, and take all his choices away.

She'd waited almost too long. Salt had pressed forward and now he was just a wavering charcoal shape on the edge of her perception. Steel tendrils lashed the air around her in frustration.

> *Now! Before he gets away.*
> *Don't lose this chance, don't let him stray.*

"Stop pushing me!" Pen snapped, and the wires recoiled from her face but then crowded back in, metal hissing over metal. Her eyes darted back and forth, trying to track them all, but they were as tangled and impossible to follow as her own thoughts.

The Mistress made another suggestion in her sing-song voice, and this one stopped Pen cold.

> *Perhaps you're right, we should not kill,*
> *For that won't let us take our fill.*
> *If a human spy is what we lack,*
> *Perhaps then we should take him back.*

Suddenly Paul Bradley was staring out at her from her memory with his earnest, short-sighted eyes, saying, "*It has to be me. There's no one else. Maybe I don't have to come back.*"

Mr. B, Beth's dad, who was willing to walk eyes-open into the trap that had claimed half a city. Who she'd all but cornered into volunteering, and who now, maybe, didn't have to.

Pen felt her resistance wavering. Out across the night, her wire fingers stretched out towards Salt to claim him. For Paul's sake.

For Beth's sake. Salt shivered as a barb brushed a hair on the back of his neck.

The wire hummed inside Pen's mind. "*And maybe,* he *won't have to come back.*"

No.

It was instinctive rebellion. She recoiled, her consciousness rushing back down the wires to where she stood. She blinked, suddenly seeing once more the tumbled brick beneath her, the stars burning coldly above. A breeze cut into her sweat-soaked skin and she shivered. She flexed her hand. These were her fingers, these flesh and blood digits; the metal ones belonged to the Mistress.

We're not the same, she told herself desperately. *We're not the same.*

"*I* will decide." She was shaking, and she spoke aloud to the creature that encased her. "*I* will decide what I want from him—for me. Not for you, not even for B or her dad, for *me.*"

He voice was full of resolve she didn't feel. She didn't know what to do. Her head was a mess of half-made decisions and shreds of purpose. Bloodlust was sharp in her veins: her own, or the wire's or a mix of both. She didn't know how to tell the difference any more.

She steadied herself on the bricks and cast around, but she barely saw anything until she looked back up at the sky.

Clouds were racing in, obscuring the stars, promising storms, and she thought, *Espel.*

She hesitated, her anger still smoking inside her, but then she pictured Espel, pushing her blonde hair out of her eyes and sitting anxiously on the cold bathroom tiles, waiting for her.

What if she leaves? What if she thinks I'm not coming?

Now, she urged herself, echoing the Mistress' words, *before she gets away.*

Don't lose this chance, don't let her stray.

The thought was like a door opening in her mind: a clear direction away from the poisonous turmoil surrounding Salt, and she fled towards it. The wire bridled as Pen's urgency trickled through to her, but the link between them went both ways and she could feel it becoming the Mistress' urgency too. A gust of wind picked up and she swayed for a moment. Then the spindly steel legs uncoiled and bore her onwards.

CHAPTER SIXTEEN

The bathroom was like a cave, cool and dank. The barbs on Pen's feet scratched the lino as she walked in.

"Espel? Es?" She groped for a switch and the neon tubes on the ceiling hummed to life. Pen stared into the long, frameless sheet of mirror-glass screwed to the wall above the sinks. Her face blinked back at her from its nest of wire. Other than her reflection, the room was empty.

For one sick moment she thought she was too late, but then she remembered that half-faces like Espel didn't cast reflections—the steeplejill could be an inch from the glass on the other side and shouting her head off and Pen would neither see nor hear her.

"Es?" she called again. She could feel her pulse, beating at the base of her throat like a trapped bird. "If you're there, slam a door or something—find a way to show me."

She stared at the row of cubicles in the reflection, but none of the doors moved.

Disappointment filled her stomach like concrete. Her gaze roved over the reflection's empty lino floor. *Stupid*, she thought, *of course she's not there—she never was. Even if that Mirrorstocrat was telling the truth, she's leading the Faceless now, why would she make time for you?*

Her head weighed heavy. Her eyes ached. She turned reluctantly towards the door.

Only then did she notice the patch of mirror—just to the right of the middle sink—that had steamed up.

She stared at it. A rough oval of fog was growing on the glass, as though someone was breathing on it. Pen felt her own breath catch in the back of her throat as a clear space appeared in the middle of the condensation: the perfect print of a right hand.

She ran to the mirror and pressed her own hand against it. The glass felt almost cold enough to blister, but Pen tried to imagine that a little of the warmth from Espel's hand was bleeding through from the reflected world to hers.

Questions bubbled up in her: how had Espel escaped the Masonry Man? Had she found a way to put her id back to sleep? What must she *think* of her, standing here all wrapped up in wire? But when she opened her mouth, Pen didn't have the heart to speak. She didn't want to hear her lonely voice echoing off the tiles. And what did the answers matter anyway? Es was here. Es was *here.* That was what counted.

She let her forehead fall against the glass and watched tears she couldn't feel run down her nose and trickle down the mirror.

She didn't know how long she stood like that, overcome with relief, only that it was blissful and she hated the sounds and images that, black and insistent as oil in water, drifted back to the surface of her mind: a vagrant shadow crossing a car park; a voice in her ear . . .

Something must have shown on her face because the glass above her hand fogged again and a question mark cut itself into the condensation, the line of it as thick as a finger.

Pen imagined Espel mouthing on the other side of the glass: *What's wrong, Countess?*

"I . . ." Pen's mouth was startlingly dry. "Nothing. I just . . ." But she tailed off.

The question mark remained, unimpressed by her denial.

"I have a friend," she said at last. "He's going to do something awful to himself, something that will almost certainly kill him, and it was me who gave him the means."

The invisible finger inscribed a capital Y next to the question mark.

"Because it's necessary—because somebody has to, and there wasn't anyone else."

An unseen palm obliterated the writing. Fresh fog clouded the glass and ghostly letters inscribed and underlined themselves.

Wasn't?

Pen laughed humourlessly. "Yeah, well: that's the point." She looked at her reflection and the strands of barbed shadow that obscured her eyes. She tried to imagine she looked predatory, dangerous, but she didn't really; she just looked like her.

"Now there's someone else—someone I *want* to hurt"—the words came up out of her, vicious and true—"and I'm pretty sure that I have the power to make him do it instead."

For the first time, she let the idea fully crystallise in her mind. She imagined snatching Salt in his sleep with her steel tendrils, sending the barbs burrowing under his skin before she shoved him out of some doorway to wait for the claylings to come through the floor.

She tested herself, like prodding a mouth ulcer with her tongue to see when the pain would come. She waited for the revulsion, the pity and the horror at what she was thinking of doing to him. None came. There was no satisfaction either, no eagerness, just a dreadful anger, rolling through her like a forest fire, and the vague sense that this might feed it, if only for a moment.

She met her own brown eyes and imagined Espel's blue ones looking back.

"You'd tell me I shouldn't, right?" she said. "That it's not my choice to make?"

Pen felt a ripple of surprise as she read the message that came back to her.

Sounds like you're the only one who can make it.

And underneath,

Whatever you choose, Countess, I'm here.

Without hesitating, Pen leaned forward and put her lips gently to the glass, then rested her forehead against it and closed her eyes. "Thank you," she whispered, then straightened and, reluctantly, she took her hand from the mirror.

"I have to go," she said. "Knowing Beth, she'll send out a search party if I'm not back by daybreak, and I have a detour to make. Could you . . . could you be back here in three days?"

If I'm breathing, I'm here.

The mist faded slowly from the mirror until all that was left inscribed was *If.*

Pen nodded ruefully, lifted her chin and walked away.

CHAPTER SEVENTEEN

It probably shouldn't have surprised Pen that Salt snored.

He lay wedged at the end of the cereal aisle, curled into a heap of T-shirts and jumpers he must have salvaged from the clothing section. Even hanging right over him, Pen could barely see him. A pair of hollow-eyed women were tending a campfire in the stripped-bare crisps and snacks aisle next door, but the weak light it threw out didn't reach Salt's face. If it hadn't been for his breath, rasping in and out of his throat like a struggling lawn mower, it would have been easy to pretend he wasn't there at all, that his shape was just a trick of the light, another Salt-shadow, thrown across the floor by her mind.

Another snore ripped out of him; he scratched himself and shifted onto his back and his face rolled into the light. Pen thought she saw his eyelids flicker and her heart almost stopped. She imagined his eyes snapping open, fixing on her; she imagined him smiling that old, coldly certain smile.

She was shivering, she realised. Barbs scraped lightly over the backs of her hands as they trembled. She was breathing fast, but whether from fear or eagerness, she couldn't tell. Everything about her body felt very distant to her; the wire was more real than her own arms or legs. A detached calm flooded her mind.

In the next aisle, the two women chattered low over their crackling fire. One of them laughed softly.

Pen bit down hard on her lip. From the edge of her field of vision, black barbed strands curled down towards Salt's sleeping form, but when her tendrils reached him, they flinched away. She could feel their tips, hovering a fraction of an inch from his skin, but it was almost more than she could bear to make them touch him.

Steeling herself, she threaded the wires under him, very gently, so as not to wake him. With the barbs carefully turned outwards she painstakingly laced them around and between his legs and behind his back. His arms were clutching some dream-treasure to his chest and she bound them there, letting her ligatures flex with the movement of his lungs. She wrapped the wire around his neck, and then, finally, with sudden violence, she lashed it around his mouth.

He woke instantly, eyes bulging in his head, blinking desperately and searching for whoever was doing this to him. A scream was stifled deep in his throat. He looked over Pen without seeing her; the shadows in the ceiling were too deep for his eyes to penetrate. Pen watched him curiously. It was no effort at all to hold him. It was incredibly strange to feel his muscles straining so violently against her wires but unable to stir even a hair's breadth.

She marvelled at her own dispassion. She kept expecting her calm to crack, but it held and held, even as her heart beat faster and harder.

She shortened the slack in the wire between them an inch at a time. Gradually, he rose up off the floor towards her.

A line of shadow crossed his face as he was hoisted above the level of the shelves that lined the aisles. Suddenly she could see the sweat glimmering under his nose and latticing his forehead. She could see his teary eyes, pale and round; like tiny moons reflected in puddles.

Feeling only mild curiosity, Pen twisted one of the strands which bound him and buried its barbs into the side of his neck.

The pain echoed; she could feel it in her own skin, but dully. His panic raced through her veins, but left her untouched. Her calm held. She saw his sight wavering in front of her own and now she could see herself through his eyes—she came slowly into view, pressed flat to the ceiling like a giant insect, clinging onto the ceiling with hundreds of barbs.

She drew him up until he was six inches below her face, then let him dangle parallel to her. She could feel the muscles in his jaw working frantically. She thought about unbinding his mouth, but she had no real interest in hearing him speak. She breathed in, and the harsh scent of his aftershave scraped her sinuses.

The smell was like a white-hot knife in her head, shattering her calm around her. She blinked and shuddered. She was back in her body and she was panicking. All the anger and the fright and the maddening, maddening *helplessness* unravelled violently in her stomach.

Oh—suddenly, she was frantic—*Help! How can it feel like this*, she thought furiously, *still?* After all she'd been through, after everything she'd seen and done, even with the wire wrapped around her like armour, even with him hanging helpless as a doll under her?

How can he possibly still make me feel like this?

And it did still feel exactly the way it had before, when she was standing alone with him in an empty classroom with no one to see, and no one to tell, with his stubble scraping along her cheek.

Our secret . . .

The sheer *unfairness* in those two words still felt like it was ripping her open from the inside out. The wire whispered to her,

It feels the same, it always will,
Unless you have the strength to kill.

She drew in a breath to scream at him, but she hesitated. The fire in the next aisle danced in the corner of her eye. The women there still hadn't noticed her.

I am so sick of secrets, she thought.

"FUCK YOU!"

It was the loudest she'd ever heard her own voice, and Salt flinched violently. The women in the next aisle over looked around, then up, startled, and then bolted, screaming.

Pen didn't even watch them go. "I'm sick of pretending," she snapped at the man dangling beneath her. "I'm sick of hiding, sick of sneaking and telling half-truths. I'm sick of my own deepest secrets. All because of *you*."

You, she thought, eyeing him furiously. *You, who I had to bury inside myself, bundled up with everything that was most private, everything that was most mine, until all of me felt tainted by it. You, who made me feel like I had no choice, who made me feel like I was nothing. You, who left me nothing in myself to turn to.*

"It was *you*," she said again, and now she saw his eyes widen as he recognised her voice.

And just like that, looking into his tear-streaked, terrified face, she finally knew what she wanted, and it wasn't this—this scrambling over ceilings like a spider in the night.

Someone I want to hurt, she'd said to Espel, and that was a part of the truth, but only part.

What she wanted, what she *craved*, was to see him *broken*, his *secret* broken. That secret was the chain he'd bound her with, and she wanted it shattered in pieces on the floor. She wanted it out in public, where everyone who knew her and everyone who knew him could hear. She wanted to see their eyes turn from him in disgust as he crumpled under the shame of what he'd done.

And nothing, she realised with a clarity that felt like elation, *nothing else* would satisfy her. She understood then just how hard and how deeply she'd been clinging to the idea of his trial, even as the world had broken around her. She needed that verdict, that vindication, and the thought of giving it up just so he could die in secret, even if it was at her hands, even—she swallowed—to spare Mr. B—No, that was too much to sacrifice.

"*I'll decide what I want from him*," she'd told the wire. No one else had the claim on him that she had.

She met his gaze.

"You remember," she said. It wasn't a question.

He stared up at her.

"You remember," she repeated, her voice as cold as the barbs that held him. She slackened her grip on his neck, just enough for him to nod.

"I could have killed you in your sleep," she said. "I could do worse than kill you now."

He tried to close his eyes, but she brushed a barb across the lids and they snapped back open. A fresh wave of his terror drenched her; she smelled him piss himself.

"I'll be back for you," she promised. She uncoiled her wires and he plummeted back onto the heap of soiled clothes.

Pen retracted her barbs from the ceiling and dropped after him, the wires wrapped around her softening her landing. For a moment she stood and looked down at him from her own height. He gaped up at her in mute terror. She opened her palm and dropped a two-barb link of wire at his feet, where it burrowed into the clothes he slumped on. He scrambled back, his eyes frantic, his jaw gibbering, but no sound coming out. In the base of her mind, Pen suggested to the Mistress that it might like to keep the wire close to this man, and she assented without demur.

Pen turned and walked away without looking back.

A dawn light was promising itself in the open doorway. Behind her, Dr. Julian Salt finally found his breath and began to scream.

CHAPTER EIGHTEEN

"I thought I might find you down here."

Beth looked up and pressed her palms together to hide the little puddle of oily tears that had collected in her cupped hands before surreptitiously wiping them dry on her jeans. At least, she reflected, her new complexion meant there was no red-eye, and her new voice was never exactly going to sound choked up.

"*What gave you that idea?*" she asked in a neutral rumble of traffic.

Her dad smiled as he looked around the bare concrete of the boiler room and made a show of wiping his forehead. "Because it's so bloody hot down here, no sane person would come in here to look for you."

He was barely through the door and dark continents of sweat were already appearing on his blue shirt.

"*Which makes you . . . ?*" Beth left it hanging.

He shrugged. "When you're a parent, sanity is basically whatever your kids need it to be."

Beth uttered a little "Oh," and stiffened. Up to that point in her life, she hadn't given five seconds' thought to kids, but realising that she'd never get the chance to even decide if she wanted them still hurt.

Her dad read her expression and grimaced. "Crap," he muttered. "Sorry. Proverbial bull in a tact shop, me."

" *'S'okay*," Beth muttered. "*I'm a bundle of nerves, nothing you could have said that wouldn't have touched at least one of them.*"

He popped himself up on the ledge beside her. "Want to talk about it?"

"*No. Is Pen back yet?*"

He shook his head. "Look, Beth—"

"*I said I didn't want to talk about it.*"

He nodded solemnly. The heat had stained his cheeks wino-crimson. "Guess I'll just sit here and sweat, then." He clasped his big hands in his lap, studying his thumbnails. Beads of perspiration collected and rolled off his nose, ticking off the seconds like a water clock.

Beth thought about ordering him out. She thought about getting up and leaving herself. In the end she just sat there, her stomach roiling inside her as her anger swelled. A couple of times he looked like he was going to speak, then he thought better of it and went back to examining his thumbs.

Finally, he stood up—and she shoved him back into his seat.

"Wha—?" he protested.

"*You wanted to sweat,*" she muttered, "*so sweat.*"

"Okay . . ." He massaged the knuckles of his left hand with the palm of his right. It was something he only did when he was anxious.

"*What did you think you were doing?*" She stared straight ahead as she spoke; she didn't have to look at him to know he'd be wearing his "wounded innocence" face right about now.

"I—I don't—" he protested.

"*Yes, you do.*"

She glanced sidelong at him as his shoulders slumped.

"I wanted to help."

"*By leaving me?*" She almost added *again* but she caught herself; he'd probably have no idea what she was talking about.

He looked at her then and his expression was stricken. His hand twitched to take hers, but then stopped, as though her not letting him hold it would be more than he could bear. "I . . . I . . ." He was stammering again. She could always make him stammer, she thought; she just wished she could bring out something more useful in him.

"I just thought—from what Parva was saying . . . Half the people in the city are missing, and . . . well, it's obviously pretty bad. I just . . . Well, someone has to go."

"*Someone does,*" Beth said flatly.

"And it didn't seem like there was anyone else but me."

"*There isn't.*"

"Then why—?"

"*Of COURSE it has to be you!*" she shouted at him. "*Why do you think I'm down here fucking well crying? Because once you said it, what the hell else could we do?*"

He gaped at her. "Crying?"

"*Yeah.*" She pointed at her face. "*Tear ducts. Still got 'em. Who knew?*"

"I just thought"—he was shaking his head—"I thought this was something I could do. At last, something *I* could do."

"*You want something to do?*" Beth demanded incredulously. "*How about waiting around for your daughter to actually snuff it before you run off to play martyr? How about being a dad? Do you not get that I'm dying? Do you not get that I had to bloody well fall down the last flight of steps to this basement because I need to save the energy it takes to walk for the times when people are looking at me?*"

She glared at him, wounded.

"*It's* my *job to care about half the people in the city, Dad. It's* your *job to care about* me. *Do you not understand that? Or*"—she flinched as she spoke, but her words had their own momentum now—"*or maybe you get it fine—maybe that's what you were running away from.*"

He looked horrified. "Beth," he protested, "I would never—You didn't even *tell* me about this until two days ago—it's taking some getting used to."

"*I didn't tell anyone, and you bloody well know why.*" Church-spire teeth scraped together in her mouth as she ground them. "*Know what Pen said to me?* '*That whole "dying alone" thing? You don't get to do that.*' *But I never* wanted *to. You were always going to be there, at the . . .*"

She broke off, suddenly feeling very cold, right in the core of her. She drew her knees into her chest and hugged them. After a moment, a warm, pudgy hand crept into hers and she let it stay there.

"*I'm so scared, Dad,*" she said. "*I'm scared of the pain, and I'm scared of the whole . . . nothingness thing, and I am so, so bloody scared of being alone.*"

For a long time there was silence, and when he finally spoke she was startled to hear tears in his voice.

"I know, Beth." He squeezed her hand. "But you won't be alone: I promise you that. I'll be wherever you want me. I'm not going anywhere."

Beth drew in a deep breath and heaved a silent sigh. "*Yes, you are,*" she said. "*You have to.*"

He shook his head. "It doesn't matter. Like I said, sanity is—"

"—*whatever your kids need it to be,*" Beth finished. "*Not whatever they* want *it to be.*"

Outside, feet clattered down the metal steps. A moment later the door swung open. Pen was breathing heavily, the wire wrapped tightly around her. Somehow it looked more natural on her now, like stripes on a tiger.

"Here you are," she said, gasping at the muggy air. "What's with the sauna? What are you talking about?"

"*Nothing*," Beth replied before her dad could speak. "*Was Espel there?*"

Pen nodded.

"*And . . . ?*"

"We had a nice chat."

Beth blinked. "*Is that all? You look pretty shaken up.*"

"No," Pen said, "that's not all," but she wasn't looking at Beth any more, she'd turned to Beth's dad, "I think I have a way to bring you back."

CHAPTER NINETEEN

"*How's he doing?*" It was the sixth time Beth had asked since they'd got back to Selfridges twenty minutes ago. She was perched up on the edge of the kitchen counter, worrying at the cuticle on her thumb with one lead-flashed thumbnail. A little mound of brick dust had collected on the tiles between her feet.

"He's fine." Gutterglass sounded distracted, but betrayed no loss of patience. The trash-spirit stood very still, her back against the side of the fridge. The kitchen lights filled her stained-newspaper eye sockets with shadows; her eggshell eyes were several miles away, staring down from the claws of a pigeon wheeling high over Greenwich. It was Glas' job to keep watch for Sewermanders and make sure that Beth's dad fell prey only to the intended monster.

"He's just waiting," Glas said calmly. "He seems perfectly comfortable."

Pen decided not to contradict her. She didn't know how much of the acid swilling around her stomach was down to her own nerves and how much down to his and how much down to the fact that he'd spent the whole time gnawing anxiously on tri-angles of a giant Toblerone he'd nabbed from the department store's stock. He was onto his second bar now. Pen could feel the ghost of all that chocolate pitching to and fro in her belly like a stormy sea.

Beth shoved herself off the counter and began to pace again. After a few lengths of the kitchen she wheeled towards Pen. "*And his . . . his escape route. It's in place?*" It wasn't the first time she'd asked this either, but once again Pen just nodded.

"*How close?*" Beth asked. "*How close did you get it to the wharf?*"

"About a half a mile."

Beth started to chew her cuticle. Her iron church-spire teeth grated horribly over brick. "*That's not close enough,*" she fretted.

"It is," Pen reassured her again.

"*Get them closer.*" Beth's order was probably more peremptory than she'd meant it to be.

Patient as an imam, Pen went back over the plan. "B, the wires are as close as I can safely get them. We have no idea how long they're going to need to lie there undetected. Any closer in, they'd hit the labyrinth, and that means the patrols. If some Masonry Man or Mirrorstocrat stumbles over a bale of barbed wire fifteen feet from their queen's throne and realises it wasn't there yesterday, the whole game's up."

Beth's green gaze lingered on Pen for a second more than was comfortable. "*Half a mile's a lot of ground to cover in a hurry.*"

"I know, but I can do it." Pen fervently hoped that she was right. She closed her eyes, and looked only through Paul's. Without her own vision to distract her, the bright light and sharp shadows of the dye factory came into focus. The concrete floor of the factory was covered in dust and small stones. The sky, seen though great rents in the roof, was a fathomless blue. When he looked up (which Pen, paranoid that he was going to give the game away, wished he would stop doing) she could see Gutterglass' pigeon: a tiny dot, circling overhead.

"Nothing for miles," Gutterglass intoned, in response to yet another question from Beth that Pen hadn't caught. "It's a desert, basically. Nothing's moving."

And again, before she could stifle it, Pen felt a little traitorous rush of hope: maybe no one was coming. Maybe, having swept through this area less than a week before, Mater Viae's hunters would think it empty and not bother to return. Maybe Mr. B would just sit on his rock in the middle of the factory nibbling until he ran out of Toblerone, and then he could just pick up and come home.

I have to tell you, Parva, You're not the only one sort of hoping that.

It wasn't Paul's voice, exactly, sounding inside her head: his manner, yes, and his inflection, but the voice was the one Pen heard whenever she read a book, the same one she heard when the wire spoke to her.

Crap—sorry, Mr. B, she thought back to him, *that just slipped out.* She hesitated. *I really can get you back, you know.*

I don't doubt it.

It touched Pen deeply that that seemed to be true.

As best as she was able, Pen had taught him to hide his thoughts from her, making him practise for hours on end. He had to hold an idea in his mind and concentrate on it until it drowned out everything he wanted to keep secret. It had added three days to their prep time, but Pen had insisted. A connection this intimate to her dad already felt like a betrayal of Beth. It would have felt *unutterably* wrong that his mind should be naked to hers; that, in what might turn out to be his most desperate moments, he should have no choice over what he showed her.

Still, Mr. B wasn't inclined to hide. She could feel his emotions, solid and strong: his love and his worry and his unswerving faith in Beth, his anxiety that he might screw this up, his impatient resignation that there was nothing he could do to prepare for it so he might as well stop fretting, and then his frustration at his inability to stop fretting, and so on. She could even feel a hunk of rock under his left thigh as if it were pressing into her own skin, and she hoped he'd decide to move off it soon.

And of course, she could also sense the ocean of fear in his mind. She stood beside him on the shore of it while it raged and swelled, threatening to drown him, and all the while he resolutely ignored it.

I'm not ignoring it, he corrected her with a kind of taut amusement.

No? she asked.

What do you think the chocolate's about? I'm feeding the fear so it doesn't eat me. It's like a tribute.

You eat when you're nervous?

That, and I'm tempting Fate—hoping it'll let me stick around long enough to have to deal with the diabetes.

Her eyes still closed, Pen felt her mouth curl into a smile. He might just be putting a brave face on it, but she figured that was more than brave enough.

He looked around the factory and she looked with him, saw dust devils twisting in a morning breeze, heard the hush and slither of the river outside, felt the slow swell of his breathing.

What are we doing? The thought rose in her mind and she was powerless to stop it. *Why are we here?* Suddenly this laughable excuse for a plan seemed as flimsy and transparent as Clingfilm. What would happen to Mr. B once he was taken—even assuming he was taken at all? What if they just left him under the ground? What if whatever Mater Viae was doing with her prisoners required summary execution first? What if she was just pushing them off the top of Canada Tower while cackling maniacally like a pantomime villain?

Parva, do you mind thinking about something else? She could feel his mental wince.

Sorry.

It's all right. She felt him hesitate, and then, *The answer, by the way? To all those "what ifs"?*

Yeah?

Is that it'll be okay: you'll be okay, and so will Beth. You get that, right? Tell me you get that, Parva.

She could feel how important this was to him. *I get it, Mr. B.* She projected the thought with as much conviction as she could muster and his fear instantly lessened.

You'll look out for her?

I always do. And call me Pen.

Call me Paul.

Okay. She sucked in a sharp breath. *Paul?*

Yes, Pen?

Get ready. They're coming.

The factory floor started to tremble. Tiny stones rattled over the surface. A tide of dust billowed an inch up from the ground. For a second the ocean of fear in Paul's mind threw up a tidal wave that dwarfed them both, but with an effort of will that awed Pen he held on to his calm. His grip tightened on the half-eaten Toblerone. He raised it uselessly over his head like a club.

"Paul," Pen snapped—she said it aloud too—"*your feet!*"

They looked down together: the concrete in front of his feet was churning like a boiling liquid. Pen felt a spasm in her chest and didn't know whose heart it was. Grey fingertips breached the floor, then grey knuckles. Greedy grey hands lurched forward, grasping blindly. With a cry of fright, Paul screwed his eyes shut and plunged them into darkness.

"I've lost him," Gutterglass reported clinically. "Miss Khan, it's with you now."

Pen barely heard. She couldn't answer. She couldn't breathe. Solid rock was on all sides of her, flowing over her skin, under her arms, into her pores and her eye sockets, in between every strand of her hair, pushing down and up and in on her with the weight of a mountain. There was no air. No light. No air. *No air.* Her pulse was like a jackhammer in her skull, threatening to break it apart—no, not *her* pulse, *their* pulse, hers and Paul's. They were one, and they were dying. Panic burst from her chest and swarmed her under.

Seconds thudded past. She felt lightheaded, but she didn't pass out. The pain in her heart and her skull didn't diminish, but it didn't grow any worse either. There was a pressure more solid than the rest across her chest, across *Paul's* chest: an arm, pulling him through the liquid earth. A hand was pressed over his mouth and somewhere in the darkness above him another arm was stretched upwards, the fingertips trailing through the surface of the city and into the light. Air rushed into the pores on the Masonry Man's skin, through the tiny cavities in his ceramic body and flowed into the vacuum that clawed at Pen's lungs—at *Paul's* lungs—not filling them, nowhere near filling them, but providing enough, just barely enough, for him to breathe . . .

"I've . . . I've got him," Pen gasped.

"*Where is he?*" Almost palpable relief bled through the engines and speakers and car-horns of Beth's voice.

"Underground." The stone was flowing from right to left across his body. She could feel it tugging at the hairs on his skin. She fought to remember the orientation of his body before the clay-ling had dragged him under. "Heading east."

"He's on his way," Gutterglass murmured with satisfaction.

Paul? Pen thought urgently, *Paul, are you still with me?* She could feel him there, concentrating hard on something, but she couldn't tell what.

At last he responded, *Here.*

You okay? She felt absurd even asking the question.

No.

What's wrong?

Can't breathe. Trying not to vomit—don't think it would be good in this little space. Too much bloody Toblerone. A little weak humour bled into her sense of him and it filled her with relief. *Picked a really good time to find out I'm claustrophobic, huh?*

Your timing's impeccable, she agreed. She could feel the tide of nausea sloshing at the base of her own throat and she swallowed it down. His panic crawled like pins and needles up the inside of her skin.

An idea struck her. *I'm going to try something.*

She returned her attention to her own body, safe in the kitchen under Selfridges.

Don't leave me! Paul's anguished cry almost buckled her knees.

I'm not, she reassured him. *I'm not, I promise. I'm still here. Stick with me. Concentrate on the feeling of me breathing—there: can you feel that?*

He flailed, not understanding what she meant—they hadn't practised this. She could feel his mind thrashing around for something to hold and she reached out to him, guiding him gently to her sense of her own body, the sensation of air filling her lungs, of oxygen rushing through her. He clung to it greedily and she felt his panic and nausea subside. She knew he was feeling the ghost of her breath in his lungs and pretending it was his.

Just stay with me. She reached across herself and squeezed her own hand. *I'm here.*

It was all she could offer him: that she was with him in the dark.

And then, quite suddenly and shockingly, the dark was gone. Light hammered painfully on his screwed-up eyelids. The pressure on his body slacked off and chilly air burst over him. His feet discovered solid ground under them and he managed a couple of steps before collapsing onto it. His cheek slammed into something with the texture of pavement, and Pen tasted metal as he spat blood.

He curled into a foetal ball and lay there, his body tensed as though anticipating a kick. A roaring torrent filled his ears, like millions of gallons of rushing water. A smell as sour as death and as close as a blackout hood rushed down his throat and punched Pen in the gut.

Okay, Paul. Pen swallowed against her rising fear. *Open your eyes.*

He didn't answer her.

Paul? She opened herself up a little more to him, but all she got back was a mess of impressions and an airless, crushing dark—he was reliving the passage.

It's okay, she said, trying to soothe him. *I'm there with you. You made it. But you have to open your eyes now.*

His refusal was like a slap, felt rather than heard: a primal wordless shriek:—*can't*—

Paul . . .

He pulled his knees tighter into his chest. He was shaking terribly. The cold deepened as the sunlight was blocked from his skin: a figure was bending over him. The asthmatic rasp of a Masonry Man breathing was loud in his ear.

Paul, please open your eyes.

Thin fingers closed on his upper arm, but Paul stayed mute as he was hauled onto his feet, his eyes still tightly shut. His head shuddered back and forth in denial. He was too afraid to look.

Blindfolded by Paul's eyelids, Pen fought to listen. At first the roar of the water seemed to be all around her, but then she managed to get a fix on it: it was directly in front of Paul, a few dozen feet away. Gradually she discerned other sounds, footsteps crunching gravel, a clink like glass on stone. Everything echoed in the space around her in a way that put her in mind of a chasm: a vast, steep-sided space. A voice was speaking, the words muffled by the torrent. There was something familiar about it and she fought to make it out, but the water was too loud.

Paul, please . . .

The grip on Paul's arm tightened. She felt him dragged sideways, felt his eyelids squeeze together. He must have been pulled into the lee of some object because the water sound was sharply deadened and now she could make out the voice.

". . . sssolution hasss become insssipid. The sssun hasss denatured the sssequenssing agent fassster than antissipated . . ."

Paul! Pen all but shrieked his name inside her head. Just below Paul's collar, the barbed worm bit deeper, and at last his eyelids flickered open.

". . . sssix, sssseven more at the mosst, then reblending will be required," Johnny Naphtha concluded. He stood twenty feet away, on the edge of a pool that had been sunk into a pit of ripped-up concrete. He was holding up a test tube in his oil-slicked fingers and peering into it with one oil-slicked eye. The four other members of the Chemical Synod flanked him with their inkblot symmetry. Crude oil smoothed every line of their immaculately fitted suits.

Johnny Naphtha lowered the test tube and stared directly at Paul. There were rings of petroleum-rainbow where his irises ought to have been. His black-toothed grin was nightmarish. He held Paul's gaze thoughtfully.

Paul was paralysed and a dozen miles away, Pen was paralysed too, reliving his memory along with him:

The wreckage of the Demolition Fields at St. Paul's on the day the Crane King fell. Scaffwolves snapping and baying; Pavement Priests fighting and dying, and Filius Viae's concrete-coloured body lying broken in the rubble. The synod stalk calmly through the chaos, and just for a heartbeat, for a fleeting instant, the ever-smiling Johnny Naphtha catches Paul Bradley's eye.

"Come now, Naphtha," the oil-soaked man all but purred it to himself, "you ssssubssisst on your recollectionss."

Pen held her breath as Paul sucked air in frantically through his nose, his jaw clenched in a petrified rictus. Five pairs of petrol-coated eyes studied him. Then, as one, they shrugged, their shoulders rising a little too high around their heads, so that for a moment they resembled hunching crows.

Paul's abductor seemed to take this as a signal. It seized his collar and yanked him backwards. Paul's feet went from under him and his heels trailed in the dust. He looked around him like a man coming out of a trance. The ruined hulks of buildings rose on all sides, casting long, broken shadows across a desolate space.

Paul let his eyes travel up the length of the one tower that had been spared the destruction and now reared up behind the Chemical Synod and their pool. Even as Pen recognised Canada Tower, and even though she knew what lay at the apex, she still gasped when she saw the high-backed throne carved into the skyscraper's pyramidal roof.

A figure, human-sized and all-but-human-shaped, sat gripping the arms of that throne. The eyes that glimmered in the shadowed face were a shockingly familiar shade of green. The spokes of Her crown glittered like a city skyline at night. The Estuary-waters of Her skirts poured in an endless torrent down the sheer side of the tower that enthroned Her and crashed into the pool at its base.

Above Her, a pair of Sewermanders circled, the flames of their flapping wings barely visible in the daylight.

Paul was dragged further back and more of what was left of Canada Square came into view. It was a ravaged mess. Voices filtered across to him from missing windowpanes—*human* voices. *People*, Pen thought. Paul let his head loll back and she saw them through his eyes, peeking at him from behind twisted girders, their clothes and skin covered in dust. Great rents gaped in the fabric of the tower where they hunched, and Pen could see daylight coming through from the other side. None of these openings were guarded. Paul was dragged close by a doorway to one of the buildings and a sour, dead smell wafted out, strong enough to make Pen's stomach flip over.

Why aren't you running? she wondered.

Something on the floor caught the light: broken glass, presumably from the missing windows; it had been scattered in a glittering field in front of the doorway. Pen glimpsed a woman just inside. She wore a dusty pinstripe suit, but no shoes. *Perhaps they were all barefoot inside*, Pen thought, *but that couldn't be all that was keeping them there, could it? A little broken glass?*

Paul let his head sag across his neck as though in a gesture of defeat. The slow arc of his gaze showed Pen the entire site.

What am I looking for, Parva? he thought to her. The thought was ragged but coherent and Pen felt a bolt of relief. He was back with her.

I'm not sure. I'm hoping I'll know it when we see it. It's so empty, she marvelled. *Where are all Her claylings? Her soldiers?*

Underground, Paul thought back to her. *Look at this one.* He tilted his head slowly back to look up at the gaunt, grey-skinned face of his captor. It was squinting and wincing at the sunlight. *Doesn't look too happy to be topside, does he?*

Paul! Pen's startled thought had the force of a snap. There was *something*—something she'd seen as he'd tilted his head back. *There*, she directed, *straight ahead and a little right.*

He looked where she told him. The angle of their path across the square had shifted their perspective on the main skyscraper and now she could see them: a long queue of people stretching back around the corner of Canada Tower and into the distance. The queue began just yards from the synod and their pool.

And this lot in the queue *were* guarded: predatory grey figures stalked up and down the line like hyenas, looking for the weakest to pick off. Pen was trying to puzzle out the significance of this when the synod beckoned peremptorily and a Masonry Man grabbed the man who was first in line. He didn't struggle as he was pulled towards the pool, and the woman behind him stepped forward to take his place with an eerie placidity. Pen wondered if the synod had brewed up something to make them docile.

The man was walked towards the waiting grins of the synod, and when he reached the pool the Masonry Man escorting him put an arm around his shoulder, like they were old friends. It walked with him down the slope towards the water, its head crooked as though whispering into the man's ear.

When the man entered the pool, Pen felt herself tense, expecting him to explode or transform into a flock of bats or simply fall down dead, but he just waded in up to his armpits and stood there beside his clayling minder. Above them, the Sewermanders beat their wings and Mater Viae gazed down from Her throne.

After a few seconds, the man was walked out of the other side of the pool. Pen thought he was a little paler, walking a little less steadily, but at this distance it was hard to be sure. He leaned on the Masonry Man for support as they approached the broken building on the square's east side. When they reached the layer of broken glass, the clayling put an arm around his waist and lifted him bodily, its feet crunching the glass into even smaller bits, and disappeared with him inside the hulk. It emerged a few seconds later with the man's shoes in its hands.

The synod gestured to the woman who was next in the queue, and another Masonry Man stepped forward and seized her.

It's a production line, Pen thought, *like a factory. We have to find out what's in that pool. Hey, wait a—*

Pen lost her view as Paul twisted around, looking back over his shoulder. Finally she saw where he was being dragged to: the old supermarket on the south side of the square. Figures were visible through its windows. It was some sort of holding area.

Pen felt the anxiety in Paul deepen, and the thoughts flickered through his head almost too fast to follow.

A holding area. He had no idea what was in there, or how long he'd be in there with it. "Sssseven more," Johnny Naphtha had said. Seven more and they'd need to recess. For what—for reblending? How long might that take? *I have to get out of here. Seven more. We have to find out what's in that pool. What if Naphtha remembers me? Seven. I have to get out . . .*

Seven, and they're on number three.

He let his right hand drop and palmed a pebble as they passed it.

Paul? Pen thought urgently. *What are you doing?*

Trust me, he thought back. Then he twisted sharply and threw the stone right at the Masonry Man's face.

Pen heard a *plink* as the rock bounced harmlessly off the clayling's stony skin, but Paul got what he wanted. The thing flinched, and for a fraction of a second its grip loosened. Paul erupted from its hands like a greyhound from a trap, huffing as he hauled his middle-aged bulk across the square.

"Look where I'm going." He muttered it aloud, and Pen knew he wasn't talking to her but to the clayling. "Don't come after me, don't follow; no need to come after me, just look."

Pen felt herself tense as she waited moment by moment for the concrete hand to slap down on Paul's shoulder, but it never came. When Paul looked up, she saw why: he was heading straight for the front of the queue by the synod's pool. The oil-slicked figures watched him curiously, then, perfectly synchronised, they each held up their right hand to forestall Paul's captor.

The thunder of the waterfall grew louder with every step.

"Stephanie!" Paul roared, wrapping the startled woman who headed the line-up in a bear-hug. "I was so worried about you!" The woman, a black lady in a cream jacket looked at him like he was mad, which was wholly understandable since Paul had never clapped eyes on her in his life.

"It's my old friend Stephanie," he shouted at the Masonry Men guarding the queue. "In all the hullabaloo recently I'd completely lost track of her."

The claylings eyed him with total disinterest, but now Paul was standing at the head of the queue and none of them were moving to pull him away from it again. It wasn't that they'd been taken in by his little cabaret act, Pen realised; just that they didn't care. This was an assembly line, and he was as a good a component as anyone else.

You wanted a closer look at the pool, he thought to her. *Well, this is as close as we're going to get.*

The synod's symmetrical hands gestured him forward. A Masonry Man took him by the arm and walked him around the corner.

Pen made a decision, Paul. I'm getting you out.

Not until we get what we came for, he retorted.

You cannot get into that water—we have no idea what it'll do to you.

Well, there's one way to find out.

Paul!

The synod stood spread before him on the far side of the pool like a welcome committee. A gentle slope led down into the water and this close, Pen could see the oily sheen on the surface. Pipes and cables burst in ragged profusion from the broken earth at its edge and spilled down into the pool, drinking from it like thirsty roots.

Pen shook herself. She tried to ease her attention away from Paul's mind.

Don't you dare leave me, Pen.

She could feel the fright and the determination crashing through him in alternating waves.

I have to get to the wires ready.

Wait! he ordered.

She felt an arm come around Paul's shoulder, heavy as concrete. A voice as dry as brick dust whispered in his ear, "Don't cry out." The Masonry Man hissed it in a flat monotone, reciting a script it didn't appear to understand. "It will hurt, but you'll survive it. But if you scream I will break your neck."

Paul—

Wait!

And God help her, she waited.

He was on the downslope now. There was something almost hungry in the way the water lapped towards him. He walked down to it with big, confident strides that Pen knew were utterly at odds with the terror in his heart. She could feel that fear like a spike in her own chest.

The roar of the waterfall drowned out any sound he made as he broke the surface.

Pen felt the cold seep in and close around his foot. His shoe grew suddenly heavy with liquid. Pen flinched, an instinctive hesitation, but Paul couldn't pause; the weight of the Masonry Man behind his shoulders already bearing him forward.

He splashed into the water and stood, immersed to his armpits, his arms floating slightly away from his body. He was stiff with cold and fright. Miles away, buried in Selfridges' kitchen, Pen mimicked his pose. They waited for pain; for a searing burn, a bolt of sickness or a flash of hallucinatory glee. Pen felt their heartbeats fall into rhythm. Their lips shivered at the same frequency.

Nothing happened.

Pen furrowed her brow, puzzled but relieved. *Paul? Are you okay?*

Yeah. I'm—

The thought broke off.

Paul?

There was a moment's total blankness in his mind: an instant where he wasn't thinking anything at all.

Pen's breath stalled. *Paul?*

She got no reply, heartbeats passed, and then—

PARVA!

Paul's psychic shriek nearly split her head apart. Nauseous waves of fear rocked her and every muscle in her body clenched in spasm. She gritted her teeth as mindless panic flooded Paul's mind and she reeled as she felt his sense of sudden, terrible loss. She fought to get a grip, to understand, but she couldn't—she couldn't tell what was wrong.

What's happening? She threw the question into the teeth of the gale coming out of his mind, but he didn't answer; he just kept screaming her name, over and over again.

PARVA! PARVA! PARVA!

Pen recoiled and flung her consciousness outwards from the basement kitchen, sending it leaping and sparking between wire strands like electric current. Her mind raced across miles and miles of desolate city in the fraction of a beat of a heart, to the outskirts of the labyrinth that cradled Canary Wharf, and found what she had left there.

A pair of steel tendrils exploded up from the thin shale of rubble that had hidden them. They shot into the air like striking snakes, barbed tips pointed straight at Canada Tower.

PARVA!

The two wires seared upwards for hundreds of yards, accelerating all the while, and all the while Paul's silent screams tore through Pen's head. The Wire Mistress sensed her pain and her urgency and exhorted the wires to even greater speed. The labyrinth blurred away beneath them and she felt the blistering cold air rush over the steel. They slowed as their trajectories levelled out, then they speared downwards.

Pen saw them through Paul's terrified eyes as they entered the square, twisting to avoid the tower tops, steel calligraphy against the pale blue sky. They sped towards him, the distance collapsing impossibly fast, and Pen felt, or imagined she felt, the chill tip of the lead wire brushing Paul's chest.

She jerked the wire sideways at the last moment, coiling it back on itself. She wove a blurring metal helix around Paul, never touching him but churning the surface of the pool to foam. With a wheezing growl, the Masonry Man reached for Paul, but Pen lashed her consciousness and the wire lashed with it. The clayling's hand exploded into concrete dust under the barbed tip.

Pen concentrated, sweat blotching through her headscarf. The vortex of wire shrank around Paul. It was maddeningly slow, but it had to be; if she squeezed too hard she'd cut him in half. The other Masonry Men abandoned the line of gaping humans, flexed their grey spines and dived into the ground. Pen breathed out just once before they breached the earth at the edge of the pool, their thin fingers grasping for Paul's shivering skin.

Pen's second wire flashed in among them like a metal thunderbolt. It slashed one of the claylings from shoulder to hip and the creature collapsed. The other claylings fell back. The wire was still caked in grey blood as Pen dragged it back and lashed at another, then set it coiling and hissing through the air in an impenetrable blur between Paul and their outstretched hands.

All the while she was focusing on the first wire: the rescue strand. The spinning cocoon finally closed around Paul's chest and she felt a spark of shock as the two vessels of her mind came into contact like a closing circuit. She remembered at the last second to flip the wire's barbs outwards so they didn't break the shivering man's skin.

Paul was staring glassily upwards. Above him, Mater Viae's Sewermanders crackled, spat sparks, and dived.

"Glas!" Pen's lips were so dry they split as she shouted, "Help!"

A clamour of wings drowned out the waterfall. Like a storm cloud suddenly coalescing, thousands upon thousands of madly flapping dark bodies rose up from the labyrinth. Pen felt the cold as Gutterglass' pigeons blotted out the sun. She watched through Paul's astonished eyes as they flocked into a narrow bank and surged to intercept the Sewermanders. At the head of their formation, she could just make out a pair of tiny white flecks that might have been eggshells.

The Sewermanders ignored the birds and swooped down. Pen could already feel the fire of them, drying Paul's skin, heating the wire to just below painful. The pigeon formation stabbed up to meet the gas-drakes. The lead bird was only a few feet from the lead Sewermander's nose when it broke hard right. The birds behind it followed, a perfectly synchronised flock, as the lead bird, with Glas' eyes flashing in its claws, led its fellows looping in a fast, tight spiral, around and around the diving Sewermanders. Their wings were loud as a machine-gun battle, and Pen felt the wind of them pummel Paul's skin.

Come on, she prayed, even as she lifted him out of the water, *come* on!

The Sewermanders' descent slowed. They struggled and snapped, but the tornado of the pigeons' wings held them up. Their fiery outlines guttered and warped in the air.

Come on, Glas.

The pigeons flew in ever-tighter spirals, bringing their wings closer and closer to the Sewermanders. The gas-drakes screamed quietly, their flames tracking the air currents, stretching too thin, rolling and twisting all out of shape.

Then, one after another, without a sound, they went out.

Back in the kitchen, Gutterglass barked, "Now, Ms. Khan!"

The pigeons scattered, and Pen yanked Paul's body into a suddenly clear sky. He was alive, she knew that much. She could feel his heartbeat coursing through him, hammering against the metal cocoon that held him. He rose fifty feet, a hundred, a hundred and fifty. Pen could feel the air pushing his skin as he accelerated. The Masonry Men watched him go, helpless behind the arc woven by the lashing second wire. A breath Pen didn't know she was holding burst up from her chest. Finally, truly, she started to believe.

It was only a flicker of movement—a blur within a blur, glimpsed from the corner of Paul's eye as he shot upwards. It took Pen an instant to make sense of it—

Mater Viae had jumped from the tower top.

Paul's head turned to track Her. Pen watched Her dark shape plummet through the waterfall, and all the pent-up hope turned to ice in her chest. Her reflexes felt horribly sluggish as she tried to reel in the second tendril of wire, still lagging behind them.

Mater Viae breached the surface of the pool like a hunting shark. Lights glittered on Her street-riddled hand as it closed around the wire.

Pen panicked. She tried desperately to tug the strand free, but the Goddess' grasp was like steel girders, like stone foundations, like gravity itself. As the Lady of the Streets tightened Her grip, Pen felt most of the barbs bend under Her architecture-skin, but one found a soil-filled crevice at the edge of the Goddess' palm and forced its way in.

Mater Viae's consciousness surged back up the wire.

The scream made Pen's teeth vibrate. Everything shuddered and lost definition. In a fuddled, hazy moment of pain, she recognised the scream as her own. She screwed up her eyes; behind them she was spinning, tumbling down through a vertical warren of streets. She was racked by the electricity of rail-tracks; the horrendous discord of factory pistons filled her skull. It felt like her head would burst. The city was too complex. She couldn't parse its systems. She couldn't cope. She couldn't *think*. She felt the vast remorseless weight of the city poised over her own mind, ready to crush it.

Something sparked at the base of Pen's skull and the metal strand went limp in Mater Viae's hand. The Wire Mistress had let it go.

Pen gasped, shaking, as she found herself on her hands and knees. The weight was gone from her mind, but there was a sour smell in the room and her throat was burning: she'd puked onto the kitchen floor and never even realised it. Her eyes were open, but they were watering badly. Blurrily she saw Beth, crouching in front of her, asking her if she was all right. Pen didn't answer; she looked past Beth and through to what Paul was seeing: Canada Square was vanishing into the distance below his feet. Mater Viae was tiny, toy-like, the wire strand still slack in Her fist.

As Pen watched, the Lady of the Streets dragged the wire back over Her shoulder and cracked it like a vast steel whip.

The wire bent back on itself and then snapped forward, fast. A sine-wave ripped through its length, faster and faster as it shot through the air, its barbs lashing straight at Paul's face.

Pen shrieked and yanked Paul hard sideways. The wire flashed next to his eye. Pen felt hot blood on her face, but when she put her hand to it, her fingers came up dry. The room around her *flexed*; the lights were suddenly too bright. She could feel Paul's pulse thundering through him.

The world slipped away.

"*Pen! PEN!*" Beth hollered as loud as she could. Even her lungs were straining, though her vocal chords could add nothing to the booming city-voice.

But when the echoes of the pistons and car-horns had faded from the kitchen walls, Pen remained on the floor, very still.

"*Glas?*" Beth swept around to face Gutterglass. "*Help her!*"

The trash-spirit shook her eyeless head. "I can't do anything until I can see."

"*Glas!*"

"I've got some beetles bringing some spare eyes to me," Glas said. "They'll be here in a few minutes. Put her on her side—is she breathing?"

Beth pulled Pen over onto her right shoulder and tilted her head back gently. She'd practised this with Pen, she realised, just this way, in the first-aid lessons at school, what felt like a hundred lifetimes ago.

Pen's eyes were closed. Her chest rose and fell slowly, the wire flexing gently around it.

"*Yes.*"

"That's something at least, but—" Gutterglass broke off.

"*But what? Spit it out, Glas!*"

When Gutterglass answered, her voice was carefully, self-consciously calm. "Miss Khan got your father clear, I saw that much before he left my field of vision, but if she's unconscious now, then either he fell, or . . ."

"*Or the wire has him.*" Beth finished the sentence for her.

Another host, weakened by whatever that pool had done to him, at the Wire Mistress' mercy. Beth closed her eyes, but when she opened them again she was still in that neon-lit kitchen, facing the same dreadful fact. Dizziness swept over her and she almost lost her balance. She caught herself on the countertop. On reflex she looked outwards towards the city, but the direction was a guess; the wire could have him anywhere by now.

Insect wings buzzed in the doorway and a pair of beetles flew in, each carrying a cracked half-eggshell clamped between their mandibles. They deposited them on Glas' face, the trash-spirit blinked like she'd just put in new contact lenses and then dropped immediately to her bin-bag covered knees beside Pen. She put a pair of Biro-fingers to Pen's neck.

"*How is she?*" Beth asked.

"Her pulse is steady, her breathing strong. I think she just fainted. I suppose one can't blame her." Glas opened her carpet-coat and pulled out a test tube, which she held under Pen's nose. Almost immediately, Pen started to splutter and wheeze.

Beth started pacing, her feet scraping on the tiles. The coils of her hair felt greasy as she ran her hand through them. "*When she wakes,*" she murmured, almost feverishly, "*we'll ask her—maybe she can contact it—maybe she knows where it . . .*" She tailed off, knowing that was a hope born of pure desperation. She sucked in a deep breath, ready to vent all her anger and guilt in one axel-shearing, glass-shattering scream—

But the scream never left her. There was a sound outside on the stair—a tap-tap-tapping like the cane of a blind man.

Both Beth and Gutterglass looked at the door as it opened. A slender wire leg crossed the threshold, then another, steel-tipped feet tapping daintily on the tiles. They bore a man-sized, wire-wrapped bundle into the kitchen. Beth's mouth slipped open. She watched her father's face enter the green light of her gaze. His eyes were open.

The wire set the bundle feet-first on the ground and carefully unwrapped him, then fell to the floor and slithered over to Pen's side. Beth's dad swayed, but kept his feet. He blinked slowly, then he spread his arms.

Beth ran to him and wrapped him up tight in a hug. "*I thought you were gone,*" she whispered. "*I thought you were gone. I thought . . .*"

There was something wet on his cheek where it touched her forehead. She wiped it off him and her fingers came away red. "*You're bleeding,*" she said in alarm.

"It's only a scratch . . ." His voice was hoarse. To Beth's surprise a huge, genuine smile broke over his face. "Thanks to Parva's expert steering." He looked over Beth's shoulder and saw Pen for the first time. "Good lord—is she all right?"

It was Gutterglass who answered, "She's perfectly fine, but for the fussing. She just needs air."

With her hands still on his shoulders, Beth bowed her head and breathed out. She looked back into her father's eyes. "*Did you get what you went for?*"

He pursed his lips, then shook his head regretfully. "I don't know what that pool was. I just—It felt so *wrong*, being in it."

"*Like it was poisoned?*" Beth asked, suddenly alarmed.

"No—it's difficult to put into words. More like something coming out than going *in*." He shook his head again, helplessly, looked at his hands and barked a short laugh. "Two arms, ten fingers. Could have been a lot worse. It's not a total loss on the reconnaissance front either," he ventured. "At least we know Johnny Naphtha and his crew are there, even if we don't know exactly what for."

"*Yeah.*" She stood on tiptoes and kissed his cheek. "*Thanks, Dad.*" She could taste the sweat and the grime and the blood from his cheek. "*You're right: it could be a lot worse.*"

"It's worse." Pen's voice sounded like her throat had been scraped raw. She sat slumped forward, her arms over her knees. The wires had spread wide to give Gutterglass room to tend her.

"B," she croaked. Her eyes were hollow above her scars. Beth was shocked by the dread in them. "B, we have to get ready. She . . . She was in my head. When She grabbed the wire. She could see everything. She knows we're here.

"They're coming."

CHAPTER TWENTY

"*Glas,*" Beth snapped, "*get Petris, get Zeke. Go and wake the Lampies up and get them moving. Tell them to meet us at the south exit. We need to evacuate.*"

"Where are we going to go?" Gutterglass protested, her egg-shells lingering forlornly on the diorama of the city in the centre of the room.

"*Anywhere's better than here. You want to stick around and arm-wrestle a Masonry Man over who gets your lab, go for it—but give everyone else the choice first, okay?*"

Glas gave her a startled look, and then dissolved; flies, beetles, mice and rats all scurried about their tasks. The last beetle to leave the room dropped a sticking plaster into Beth's dad's hand. He eyed it unsteadily, then opened it and slapped it over his cut.

"*Can you walk?*" Beth asked Pen, who nodded. The wire tightened around her, supporting her like a brace as she got to her feet. "*Then let's move.*"

They pounded up the stairs. Beth was knackered after five of them, but she leaned on her spear and swore at herself to keep going. Pen and her dad both looked exhausted, but they easily kept pace with her.

"*They just went toe-to-toe with a Goddess and you can't even climb some stairs? Get over yourself, Bradley,*" she muttered to herself. And then louder, to Pen, "*How long do you think we've got?*"

Pen spread her hands helplessly. She was climbing the steps on the four legs the wire lent her, as well as her own.

Instead, it was Beth's dad who answered. "The speed that thing carried me under the ground? Not long."

They emerged onto the ground floor. The sun was low outside, making silhouettes of the bronze and stone figures crowding the lobby. The glass-skinned Lampfolk, refracting rainbow shadows on the floor in front of them, were still stifling yawns. As Beth approached, Gutterglass coalesced in front of them, now armoured in panels from a scrapped car. She'd worked fast, and now everyone congregated at the edges of the chamber, not yet knowing whether they should be staring or running.

"*We're leaving,*" Beth shouted at them as she ran past, and they flinched from the traffic-thunder of her voice. "*I strongly suggest you do likewise.*"

She didn't break stride, but dropped her voice as she reached Petris. "*Glas told you?*"

"She did."

"*Then let's go.*"

She reached the exit and stuck out her hand to push the door open—but her palm sizzled as it touched the brass. The stench of hot tar filled the air and she recoiled, staring at the door. The metal was glowing like an ember, and it was radiating heat like a stove.

"*Shit! EVERYONE GET BACK,*" she yelled.

The crowd behind her obeyed, looking at her uncertainly. She shoved the door open and the air broke over her in a hot wave. It shimmered above the pavement.

"*Street's burning up,*" she called back.

"This one too," Pen called from the Duke Street exit. She was holding out a wire-wrapped hand towards the door.

"*Glas?*"

But pigeons were already fluttering through the building. Glas' face went strangely blank for a moment, then she confirmed, "We're surrounded. The fevers must just have broken out."

Beth slammed a fist into the door in frustration. Another bout of dizziness made the room blur in front of her, but when the moment passed, the floor still looked like it was trembling.

"B . . ." Pen said uncertainly.

Everyone was looking at her. She looked around at the frightened, confused faces, human and otherwise. "*Down,*" she gasped. "*The car park—one of the walls runs close to the tube station. Maybe we can break through there.*"

They ran for the fire stairs, the Pavement Priests covering the space fastest in their stop-motion way. Winded, Beth looked back over her shoulder. A patch in the centre of the floor was seething like boiling water. The humans cowered behind the display counters, peeking over them as a slender grey figure burst elegantly upwards.

Beads of liquid tile dripped off its predatory jaw. Its head swayed to and fro on its uncannily long, muscular neck, taking in the frightened gazes fixed on it. It locked eyes with one lanky middle-aged man and began to stalk towards him. The man squeaked, but didn't run. He was transfixed. He didn't understand. He had no idea what was about to happen to him.

Beth hesitated in the doorway of the stairwell and felt a bolt of anger at her hesitation. She looked back down the stairs. Her friends were already lost to sight, hurrying down to the bowels of the building, but the Sodiumites' glass footsteps echoed up to her. They were looking to her to save them; *they* were the ones she was responsible for. They were also, a treacherous little voice reminded her, the only ones with half a chance in this fight.

She bit her lip, and chose. "*Oi, Asphalt-Arse!*" she yelled. "*Over here!*"

The Masonry Man froze, and then turned. It looked at her with eyes too deeply shadowed to see, then arched like a dolphin and dived. Beth didn't wait to watch the floor seal over; she haired off down the stairwell.

It was a harum-scarum tumble, half sprint, half fall. She tripped over steps and bounced off walls. Her balance was shot, her vision doubled, but somehow she managed to keep her feet under her. She was panting, and oily spit dribbled from the corner of her mouth.

Concrete fingers burst from the wall and she slashed at them with her railing-spear, slicing them off at the knuckle. Hot liquid spattered onto her cheeks as she crashed past. Inside Beth's hood, Oscar hissed and snapped in frustration; the stairwell was too cramped for him to fly.

A head broke through the step beneath her and a mouth full of rubble-teeth snapped at her foot. She stamped as hard as she could on the bridge of the thing's nose, but a pair of arms breached beside the head and tripped her legs. Acid rose up her throat as she flew headlong down the stairs. She ploughed into the next landing face-first, and the impact juddered her spine. Her face felt hot and puffy, flayed by the friction. She tried to rise, but she was muggy and confused; she couldn't work out where up was. She twisted, looking out from under her own armpit as another hand burst through the floor just an inch from her, its fingers crooked like claws. Beth's breath stalled. The tower-block crown on the inside of the thing's grey wrist filled her whole world.

"Beth!"

The crown mark exploded from the inside out and dust and blood and fragments of bone sprayed everywhere. A flickering wire, snake-tongue fast, skimmed the water on Beth's eyeball, then recoiled, lashed around her ankle and dragged her down the stairs.

Three seconds and two flights later she hit the floor amidst a mess of running legs. Hands dragged her bodily to her feet and shoved her onwards.

"Go!" It was Pen's voice, frantic, but somehow Beth couldn't see her; she couldn't see anything except a jumble of mossy stone shoulders and the backs of glass heads. Every joint and every muscle was screaming at her, but somehow she managed to shove her way to the front.

She ran.

The light ahead of her dimmed; the walls thronged with too many shadows. Dozens of soft explosions blotted out all other sound as the claylings crawled from the ceiling, the walls, the ground beneath their feet. Grey limbs choked the narrow space like spiderweb strands and they hacked and shoved their way through them. A Sodiumite girl next to Beth slowed slightly, trying to coordinate her feet in a dance, but as she took the second step, a grey hand seized her fibre-optic hair and swung her bodily at the wall. She flared a brief, brilliant, terrified white and then shattered into razor-edged shrapnel.

Beth slashed and head-butted and spat. Wires lashed from behind her in angry tentacles, but missed as much as they hit. Beth glanced back and glimpsed Pen between the bodies, her scarred face haggard. Her dad was supporting her as she ran. A Masonry Man burst full-bodied from the wall ahead, eager hands poised to grab them, but Beth jumped and ploughed right into it, pinning it to the wall. She felt it convulse on her spear, its clay skin hot beside her cheek. Her dad and Pen blew past her, gasping.

She dragged the railing free and tore after them.

The stairwell was a heaving tunnel of grey skin. She felt the panic build in her chest. They were hopelessly outnumbered. She almost relaxed the muscles in the soles of her feet, to try one last time to summon claylings of her own to even the odds, but the memory of the heat from Oxford Street hit like a hammer and she stopped. These were Fever Streets now, and they'd kill her instantly.

"Lady!"

A familiar voice, a cry from behind her. An angel-winged statue was the only figure not in motion. He stood with his wings half furled, the stricken shape of his body utterly at odds with his serenely carved face. A dripping grey arm emerged from the wall and plunged seamlessly into Ezekiel's chest.

"La—"

The tendons flexed beneath the grey skin like piano wires and Ezekiel's voice choked off.

Beth's heart clenched, but she didn't stop. To stop was to die.

She choked on clayling dust and fragments of bone. She tried to close her ears and her nose to the sounds and the smells in that charnel trench, and she ran, down and down. An eternity of seconds passed until a sign with a green running man above it materialised like a miracle on her right.

She barrelled through the exit shoulder-first, stumbled and fell, pushed herself up off the floor and staggered onwards. In the dim light of the sub-basement she could make out a handful of stone and bronze figures flickering as they threw themselves against the far wall. The impact of their bodies thudded through the space. Beth searched frantically, and relief surged through her as she caught sight of wire coiling in the air. She rounded a corner and there they were, Pen and her dad, almost hidden by the dust cloud the Pavement Priests were raising. Her dad had his hand clapped to his head and he was squinting at her like he couldn't see properly. Something glistened on his neck.

"Beth?" he yelped. "Beth!"

"*Dad—*"

A sound like a chainsaw made her look back in time to see Gutterglass bursting through from the stairwell amidst a buzzing cloud of beetles. She'd sprouted six extra pairs of arms and was using them to shelter the two glass figures who ran, hunched over, beside her. Beth kept looking as the seconds stretched out long and lonely around her, but no matter how hard she stared at the doorway, no one else came through it.

"My Lady. Gutterglass." Petris' rough bark emerged from the cluster of labouring stoneskins. "A little help would be *fantastic* right now."

Beth turned and ran over to him, Glas on her heels. The Pavement Priests were attacking a section of wall between a blue car and a graffiti'd emergency phone. Their stone shoulders had succeeded in buckling the wall, hammering a six-foot crater, but there was no hole into the tube tunnels—no way out. Gutterglass swarmed and morphed into a giant garbage fist and began to punch into the wall again and again. Beth threw herself forward too, gouging with her spear. She looked to her left, and then to her right, disbelief making her nauseous. Eight Pavement Priests, two Lampfolk, Glas, Pen, her dad—was that all? Could that really be *everyone*?

"*Zeke*," she gasped as she worked, but Petris didn't reply; it was obvious in every inch of the heavyset stone monk that he already knew.

The floor below them began to tremble. Beth seized the Sodiumite girl and the Blankleit boy by their glass shoulders and spun them around to face her. She blinked frantically at them, semaphoring with the lights in her eyes. They didn't waste time nodding their understanding; they just took each other's arms and began to dance, turning faster and faster, whirling each other with total abandon. They blazed as they orbited one another, bright as quasar stars.

The tiny cable hairs on the back of Beth's neck pricked up.

As they finished the last steps of their dance and collapsed onto the floor, Beth could feel the charge they'd built up shudder through the ground beneath them. With a sound like a building being torn in half, a crack opened up in the concrete: a twelve-foot-wide trench that ran from wall to wall, bisecting the car park. On the side where Beth and the others stood, the tremor subsided.

Spindly figures burst up from the ground on the far side, casting long shadows in the low light. Beth gazed, appalled by their numbers, as more and more emerged, rank upon rank of them. Oscar chittered and Beth could feel him straining to attack. Desperately, she tried to calm him—the ceiling was still too low, the front rank of claylings already too close. If the little Sewermander panicked and ignited in here, the explosion would swallow them all.

Clayling figures toed the trench, but it seemed to baffle them. Then, to Beth's utter horror, one of them just stepped over the edge.

She glimpsed its grin an instant before it passed into shadow. For long seconds there was no sound, then she heard the smack of its impact echoing up from below. Another clayling jumped, then another, each one utterly silent. Beth could trace their progress by the muffled thuds as their falls broke, and by the way those thuds drew *closer*. For every grey figure that jumped, another clawed its way out of the earth on the far side of the trench to replace him. Beth watched the concrete dripping off their tower-block-crown scars, then she gazed at the one on her own wrist. She thought of the face of the Goddess that sign belonged to and her heart shrank.

Dear Thames—dear God . . . how powerful are You?

Wire strands whined like flies through the air, slashing down clayling after clayling. They slipped and slid on the cement blood of their fellows, but there were always more. The two Lampfolk were on their knees beside Beth, exhausted, their filaments dull.

Now when the Masonry Men jumped into the trench there was all but no pause until she heard them land. Beth stared as a grey hand crept up over the edge. She slashed straight through the fingers with her spear. Her heart pounded hard in her ears and she was shivering, though she was drenched in sweat. Out of the corner of her eye she saw more fingers curling over the lip of the trench. She saw them brace to pull their owners up and she tried to turn, to get there, but her feet went from under her and her spear clanged loud in her ears as she dropped it. The air was thick, the world slow. Petris was yelling instructions to his stoneskins, but Beth couldn't make out the words. Pen was shouting. Her dad was calling to her. But she had no idea what anyone was saying. Gaunt silhouettes pulled themselves up over the edge.

They were out of time.

She tried to stand, but failed. Her muscles wouldn't respond. As she shifted, something in her pocket clinked and numbly she fumbled for it. A glass flask sat in her palm.

Childhood outlooks, proclivities and memories.

She looked up, searching for Pen, but she couldn't see anything but dark grey bodies. *I'm so sorry, Pen—*she forgot herself and tried to say it with her mouth, but no sound came out.

Claw-like fingers reached for her in the half-light. She batted at them weakly, but they slapped her hand away. She reached for her spear, but it was too far away. She twisted onto her back. Hands clasped her ankles and her elbows and tugged at her clothes. Grey figures leaned over her, pushing her down, and grey figures below her pulled her in. The ground softened like mud under her back—she could feel it pooling in the folds of her clothes; feel the weight that was about to bear her under. The flask was cold in her hand. She didn't want to die alone.

She jerked and thrashed her head and managed to tilt it upwards. She bit the stopper, yanked it out and spat it away, then closed her eyes and tipped the flask to her lips. The glass rattled on her church-spire teeth. The liquid that flowed into her mouth was freezing. She swallowed and it burned all the way down.

CHAPTER TWENTY-ONE

I can't see.

I can't breathe.

I can't open my eyes.

There's a weight on my chest and hands on my throat.

Where in Thames' name is *Naphtha*?

. . . there's something . . .

My dreamless sleep clings to me like river mud. I panic, pulling against it, desperately fighting to wake up. My spear is in my hand and I lash out on instinct, laying about myself with it, not caring what I hit.

. . . there's something else . . .

The floor smells of concrete, but I can't feel it. I reach out for it to sense its pulse, but I'm sealed off from it somehow. My spearpoint connects with something solid and I can feel it grating along bone. The hands gripping me come loose and I lever myself to my feet, gasping.

Why can't I open my eyes? My eyelids won't answer me, won't respond to my brain. There's something else—some . . . other *influence* . . . It's holding them shut. My skin feels wrong, like my whole body's too small and too *heavy*. The rhythm of my pulse is too complex . . .

There's something else in my head, I think.

I reach for it, trying to remember, but it flees me like the memory of a dream.

At last my eyes flicker open. I gape around me at carnage.

There are Masonry Men everywhere, squirming and bleeding at my feet, swarming over flickering statues and glass-skinned bodies—I can see the glow is ebbing from their filaments. I stare but I can't make sense of it . . .

The Masonry Men are *attacking* us.

I don't understand. I can taste the panic in the back of my throat. I hold my hands in front of my face and they're riddled with streets and scaled in rooftops; they're washed in green light.

In the stories, this was how my Mother's hands looked.

Screams jar the air and someone's bellowing frantic instructions. My ears find a familiar sound in the cacophony: Petris' voice.

"My Lady!" he's calling. "Lady Bradley!"

Beth? Her sullen face under messy hair fills my mind. Is she here? I cast around, but I can't see her. I see the squirming, scrapping mass of clayling bodies on the floor and my heart clenches at the thought of her suffocating under them.

Beth! I yell, in case she can hear me. *Beth! Beth!*—but no sound comes out. My lips are shaping the syllable; I can feel the air moving past my teeth, but no voice emerges.

There's something else in my head . . .

I can feel it on the edge of my consciousness, a knot of memory. I touch it, and it unravels inside my mind.

For an instant, I reel, nauseous and terrified—I have no sense of who or where I am—and then my awareness rushes into all the little crevices of memory like water flooding a cave and I remember—

—I remember where and how and *whose* body this is.

There's something else in my head.

*No, some*one.

I can feel Beth in here with me. I can remember everything she remembers; I know everything she knows. I hear myself counting to three and never getting there. A surge of regretful longing fills me, but there's no time. I can't let myself think. Instead, I move on instinct, my legs feeling numb underneath me as I force them into motion. They're sick—*I'm* sick. The effort of the first few steps makes me dizzy. This body is exhausted and it responds sluggishly, but it does still respond. Beth's consciousness gives way to mine in a way that terrifies me, but I run. I can still *run*. There's a concrete wall in front of me, a blue car to my left and a bashed-up phone to my right, and I remember . . .

I remember why I have no voice.

I seize the handset and almost yank the flex out of the box in my haste. Grey hands tug almost pleadingly at me.

Please, I pray, *please*.

A dial tone fills my ear. I hear clicks and buzzing static.

Somewhere in the manifold streets of this body, a phone exchange clicks in response.

I hear a crunch and a scream as a Pavement Priest falls somewhere to my left. From behind me, there's a soft thud and a gust of decaying scent—Gutterglass? It must be.

And then a polite voice comes out of the receiver. *Hello?* Hissing and static. *Hello?* Other voices join it, a buzzing chorus, getting louder and louder and closer and closer, rushing towards us at the speed of electricity. *We're coming do you hear us hold tight we're coming—*

We love you.

I feel them before I see them. A prickling sensation ripples over the hands that are holding the receiver, and then, spilling from the mouthpiece and down onto the floor, fizzing like static and glittering like fibreglass, run thousands and thousands of tiny spiders.

We love you we love you . . .

They pour into the gaps between clayling bodies. The Masonry Men swat at them but there are far too many of them. I see Petris, an instant before his stone monk's habit is obscured by thousands of arachnid bodies. The spiders are crawling over a stocky man—Beth's dad? What's he doing here?—and tracking through the blood that cakes his face. They crawl over Pen and her eye widens as it catches mine; has some instinct told her that it's not her best friend looking back her? There is motion behind me and in the corner of my eye I see Gutterglass. Minuscule spiders are spilling from her eggshells.

It's like a punch in the chest, remembering for the first time how she lied to me.

The buzzing in the air rises to fever pitch and then the next instant it cuts out. I blink. The spiders have vanished, and so has everyone who was in contact with their needle-pointed feet.

The Masonry Men turn towards me: they've been robbed of their quarry. I can hear their dry, rasping breath, and one of them snarls and runs at me, his teeth bared. Another wave of dizziness hits me. The green light ahead of me flickers and darkness creeps in at the edges of my vision. I can't even lift my spear. The muscles in the clayling's legs tense as he prepares to spring.

We love you, a voice whispers in my ear, and then the world dissolves in static.

CHAPTER TWENTY-TWO

"Beth, up here."

Beth climbed the fire escape onto the roof and there he was, sitting cross-legged on the slabs. He leaned forward, his elbows resting on his knees so that shadows filled the arched hollows of his ribcage. He smiled at her and pushed his dusty fringe out of his eyes. Behind him, the rhino etched in shadows and black paint loomed out of the side of a warehouse, its blank eyes watchful.

Beth crossed the roof to him. Her feet felt like they'd give way and pitch her over at any moment, and her hands were shaking as she reached out to take his face in them. He stilled her trembling fingers with his own. The concrete-and-rain smell of him rose up to her. She was almost crying.

"Is it really you?" she asked.

His smile didn't change. It was only from this angle, with his face tilted up at her, that she realised how sad he looked. He stood and kissed her fiercely, one hand on the small of her back, the wiry strength of him pulling her in.

Her lips opened under his. He tasted the way she remembered, exactly that way. She could have been kissing her own memory of him.

Eventually he let her go and took a step backwards. "No," he said. "Not really."

"Fil?"

He turned away and sat on the lip of the building, his legs dangling over the side. There was something angry in the way his shoulders were hunched up. "Gutterglass told me once that all we are is memories," he said. He spoke so quietly that she could barely hear him. His voice turned as hard and brittle as slate. "She lied—just like she lied about everything else."

Beth slid down and sat beside him, kicking her feet out over empty air. Cautiously, she slipped an arm around his shoulders. He leaned into her, but kept staring at the horizon. He didn't blink, and none of the tension left his frame.

"Johnny Naphtha said he took a complete copy of your mind—your memories, your beliefs, what you liked and what you didn't," Beth said.

"He did."

"So it is you then. It must be—what else is there?"

Fil's laugh was quick and harsh. "What else is there? Everything!" He looked at her and she saw with a shock that there were tears in his eyes, clouded with limestone dust.

"Sight and scent and sound, the texture of the world on my skin, the feeling of my friends in my heart, you, for Thames' sake . . . My future, Beth, that's what else: my whole future."

Beth fell back a pace at the ferocity in his voice. "I don't understand," she said.

He looked at her, and his gaze softened, but his tone didn't. "Right now," he said, "your body's sleeping and your mind—that bit of you that's still human—is walking the quiet streets of your brain with me. But when you wake, you'll be back out there, in the world, changing things and making things. And me? I'll still be in here, because this is all I am now. I'm a passenger. I have no body of my own, no way to interact with the world, no way to be in it. I've got no eyes to see new things, nor ears to hear them, no brain to form new synapses. I'll never learn anything, ever again, except through you. I'll never see anything new, ever again, except how you see it. A body is a future, Beth—don't you get that? I'm frozen. I'm all memory. I'm the past."

He looked around at the immaculate empty buildings and the empty grey sky. "Your body is a city now, Beth. Your heart, lungs, skin, bone and brain are all riddled with streets. Your consciousness is a citizen of that city, but mine? Mine is just a refugee."

He cocked his head and then very quietly he said, "I have no home."

Beth didn't know what to say.

"You remember the first time we kissed?" he asked her. "On Canary Wharf, sitting on the Skyscraper Throne."

Beth smiled. "Of course I do."

"I don't."

Beth started to protest, "That doesn't make sense. How do you?"

"I know about it because you remember it—but it's your memory, not mine. I know what it was like for you, but not for me. Know what the last thing I remember is?"

Beth shook her head.

"Standing in the synod's factory with that recording substrate washing past my lips, looking down the length of the bottle at you and praying to my Mother you got out of that pool alive. Then I woke up in that car park, with no idea who I was, where I was or what I was doing."

"You worked it out fast." Beth kicked her legs. "Smart move with the Pylon Spiders, by the way. I never thought of calling them."

He snorted, and it echoed off the towers in a way that made Beth look back at the rhino.

"You're their only food-source now. Free-range voice? They've never had it so good. They were never going to risk losing you."

"Put like that, I feel like a right plank for not thinking of it."

"Ah well, don't beat yourself up. I've known them a lot longer than you have."

"Fil, you said you're just a passenger," Beth started, a little nervously, thinking of Pen and the Wire Mistress riding her, "but back in the car park—well, it felt a lot like you were driving."

"Yeah," he sighed. "Sorry about gate-crashing back there. It was all on instinct. If it makes you feel better, you were always in control."

"I was?"

"You could have shoved me off with a flick of a synapse—they've been your muscles for seventeen years. Who do you think you're going to listen to, me or you?"

Beth thought back to the moment his mind had surged into hers; that desperate moment when their consciousnesses had touched and she hadn't known whether she was Beth Bradley or Filius Viae or both. He was right: it had been her decision, even then. It might have been made on instinct, a split-second choice, but it had been her choice nevertheless, to scramble to the back of her own skull and let him pilot her, because she trusted him, because unbelievably, there'd been hope again—

"My body," she said.

"Yours," he confirmed, "and it could never be anyone else's. They're your eyes, your ears, your taste buds; everything is filtered through you." His tone twisted through wistfulness into something bleaker.

"It's why I'll never be alive again, not really. You need to grow to be alive, and you need a body to grow. And that's where I come up empty."

"You do have a body," Beth said, softly.

"You mean the kid in the statue?" He smiled at his lap, not at her. "I'm sure he's a lovely fella. Maybe—if the claylings didn't snatch or throttle him, which they almost certainly did—he'll grow up big and strong; maybe he'll even grow up into just the boy I remember being. Or maybe not—either way, it means nothing for me because I'm just a copy, a photo gathering dust on a shelf. Or at least I was until you happened along."

Beth looked at him sharply. Just a photo? The Fil she knew would never have used that metaphor. He hadn't even heard of Hobnobs until she introduced him to them.

That phrase had come from her.

To never learn anything else, to never change at all except through her . . . She tried to get her head around that level of dependency, but she couldn't. Maybe he was right: maybe he wasn't really alive at all.

The wind picked up, the way it always seemed to when they were up there. She heard it rushing down between the buildings beneath their feet. It moaned hollowly and carried the sounds of distant construction: diesel-powered diggers and creaking cranes and rumbling dumper trucks, all overlaid with the roar of traffic, the music of car-horns. The wind gusted and grew stronger and stronger, louder and louder, Beth strained to listen to it, the way it rattled the windows and hissed in the leaves; it was intelligible, it was a voice.

"Beth," it said.

She looked back at Fil. If this was a dream, she didn't want to wake up. She didn't want to leave him, not with that look in his eyes.

"It's okay," he said. "I'll be here when you get back." His lip twisted. "Where else can I go?"

"Beth—"

Beth's eyes flickered open. She was lying on her back. Grass tickled the back of her neck; cool air drifted across her face. Metal gantries crossed her vision like spiderweb strands, stretching up away into the night. Somewhere in the distance above her a light was blinking. It took her a handful of muddy seconds to recognise the place. She was lying directly under the Crystal Palace radio mast.

Something tickled the skin of her throat. A glittering little spider scurried off her neck and across to her ear where it let itself down by a thread from her earlobe, whispering, "*I love you,*" to her as it passed.

"*Yeah,*" she muttered back, "*for getting us out of that I think I love you too.*"

"Beth." Pen's voice. The familiar, scarred, anxious face pushed into her field of vision.

"*How long was I out?*" Beth creaked up into a sitting position.

"Only about five minutes, at first. Glas said to let you sleep. She said we were safe for now, and you needed the rest—"

"*She had a point,*" Beth grumbled. "*I feel like I've been hit by a lava flow. I must have picked up another dose of that fever from the streets outside. Next time, maybe listen to the doc's advice and let me snooze?*"

"But—but I couldn't." Pen's eyes were huge in the darkness.

Beth frowned. "*Christ, Pen. I was kidding, I wasn't really having a go—*"

"No, B." Pen put a hand on her arm to silence her. "It's your dad."

He was sitting propped up against one of the tower's metal feet with Gutterglass bending over him. Beth could see his splayed legs, his lolling feet, but everything from his waist up was obscured by a blur of frantically darting trash-arms.

"*Dad!*" She ducked in next to Glas, feeling the warmth of decaying rubbish radiating through the carpet-coat, and stopped dead. Her dad's hands, clasped together on his stomach, were fish-belly white, his knuckles trembling. The left side of his face was as pale as his hands; the right side was a bright glistening red. His hair was soaked with still-wet blood.

Even then, it wasn't the sight of her father that gave her the deepest chill, but Gutterglass' fretful muttering as she worked. "I didn't know—I didn't know . . . I didn't think to check—I didn't see—I didn't *know.* Stupid, Gutterglass, *stupid.*"

"*What? What didn't you know—what? Glas?*" Beth lifted her hands and put them down again. Her fingers felt thick and clumsy in her lap. "*Did a Masonry Man do this?*"

"No." One pair of trash-hands was pressing down hard on the skin of her dad's forehead. Glas' rubber-hose thumb and forefinger were clamped in a ring around the nick just above his right eyebrow, the one Mater Viae had given him—the nick that Gutterglass had already stitched with tight loops of black thread, and yet fresh red blood was still seeping out of the seam. A blood-soaked plaster lay curled on the grass beside him.

Gutterglass' own brow was stained with sour-milk sweat. Her four remaining arms frantically mixed and stirred phials of cloudy liquid; she briefly glanced at each and hissed in disgust before continuing to stir the next.

"Come on, come on," she muttered, and then snarled in frustration, "These are *useless*. Where are those brick-fucking pigeons?"

"*Pigeons?*" Beth shook her head, not understanding. She laced her slate-covered fingers into her dad's, trying to ease the trembling. He felt dreadfully cold.

"Glas sent out pigeons for some kind of ingredient," Pen replied, her voice tight.

"I'm trying to blend a dermal adhesive," Glas snapped, "but there's nothing here that'll set fast enough. You could have told me he was a haemophiliac!"

Beth gaped at her dad. One eye was matted shut with blood; the other didn't even seem to see her.

"*He's not.*"

"Well, I don't know what else to call it when someone's blood doesn't clot."

"*It's just a scratch—*"

"I know it's just a scratch!" Gutterglass spat. "It's like he doesn't have any platelets, not a single damned one." The anger ebbed out of her voice, leaving her fear, naked, in its wake. "It just kept bleeding. In the fight—I didn't see, and he was two and half pints down before I realised. Shit!"

She threw the flasks against a tower strut in fury and they shattered. Liquid oozed down the metal. Then she barked, "Stand back!" and reached into her carpet-coat. She pulled out a short metal rod. A squat gas lighter appeared in another hand and she ignited it; the flame above it looked like a blue arrowhead. She lowered the metal into the flame and after a few seconds it began to glow, first red, then white-hot.

"*Glas*—" Beth started to protest, but the trash-spirit ignored her and pressed the incandescent metal against her dad's skin.

He shuddered hard under her hands; his mouth opened, but no scream came out, only a gurgle that broke off too quickly. Beth's nostrils filled with the scent of burned blood and seared skin.

Gutterglass pulled her branding iron away. The skin over the cut was charred black, giving off little wisps of steam and darker curls of smoke.

Beth stared, and Glas stared too, all the while keeping her fingers on her father's skin. The blood kept coming.

"I don't understand," Gutterglass murmured. She sounded utterly lost, and Beth felt herself lost along with her. "That at least should have cauterised the wound. I—His blood vessels—It's like his cells aren't responding at all. His—" The eggshell eyes flickered sideways, shifted focus.

"His *hair's* not growing," she whispered. "Nor his nails."

Beth stared at her in astonishment. "*You can see that?*"

"There's not even the tiniest bit of growth—his hair, his skin—nothing's renewing, nothing's dividing. He's not growing at *all*."

"The glass," Pen said in a stricken voice behind her. "The broken glass on the floor—I didn't think . . . I didn't *know*—"

"*Glass? What 'glass'? What about his hair?*" Beth looked desperately from one to other of them, desperate for someone to explain, to make sense of this, to tell her what she should do. "*What are you two talking about?*"

Neither of them elaborated.

After too long, Pen began to speak again. "He's not healing," she said. "Oh God, I'm so sorry, Beth—it was the synod's pool. He said it felt like something had been taken out of him—"

Beth gripped her dad's hands and looked into eyes that didn't look back. She felt horrifyingly useless: second by second, heartbeat by heartbeat, she could feel herself failing him. She wanted to speak to him, but she had no idea what to say. She started to form some platitude, to tell him it would be all right, but another gurgle in his throat stopped her.

"N—" he managed, and then, just audibly, "not alone."

To Beth, it sounded like a plea. "*No, Dad,*" she said. "*We're here.*"

She squeezed his hands tighter, but it wasn't his *hands* that were leaving. She looked back at his face. His eyes had closed. His chest rose and sank shallowly.

She barely heard the pigeons flap in behind her. Glas shunted her out of the way and lunged at the cut, a tiny tube of superglue pinched in her Biro-fingers. Beth watched the pulse in her dad's neck as the glue dried over the cut and the blood finally stopped. A few minutes later, Glas took her fingers away from the wound and got a cloth to mop up the blood. Beth just kept watching that pulse, watching her dad's chest rise and fall and rise again, each time just that little bit more shallowly.

She put a hand beside her dad's ear, and let the city in it whisper to him, "*Not alone. You're not alone. We're here. I'm here.*"

If he heard her, he gave no sign of it.

Beth had no sense if minutes or hours passed, but dew formed under her knees. Pen came and sat beside her and held her hand but didn't say anything.

Once, Gutterglass tried to speak to her. "Lady Bradley. He's alive, but—please understand, I've no wish to distress you—but if his cells aren't dividing . . . he won't be able to replace that lost blood . . ."

Beth didn't answer her, and Gutterglass didn't speak again. She stood with her arms crossed and her chin dipped into her chest while Beth just knelt beside her dad and told him that she was with him and that she loved him. With eyes that felt as empty as his, she stared at the weak tic of a pulse on the side of his neck.

Later, when the night had grown colder and fiery cramp had set in behind her knees, the pulse stopped.

CHAPTER TWENTY-THREE

"It's strange—"

Pen looked around, but didn't leave off leaning against the tree. The bark was comfortingly rough and solid against her shoulder. Gutterglass stood a few yards back up the hill, the radio mast a black shadow spike behind her. Fastidious as ever, the trash-spirit had had her rats scavenge new pieces of garbage to replace the bloodstained ones and now wore a stylishly cut dress of plastic bin-liners. Smoke curled up from a lit cigarette clenched between twisted coat-hanger fingers. Pen felt a stab of almost lunatic anger at her neatness, at her *collectedness*. Just how cold did you need to be to play tailor on a night like this? She said nothing, but the tips of the wire tendrils beside her face twitched.

"—I mean," Gutterglass went on, "I'm a doctor, but I'm an epidemiologist, not a shrink, so I'm hardly an expert, but still . . ." She paused and drew on her cigarette. The smoke billowed out from all the gaps in the framework of her skeletal head as she tilted it to one side to consider Pen. "I would have thought that when your best friend has been bereaved, it might be helpful to stay within earshot."

The glare Pen gave her was one of Beth's specials: *You're not funny*, it said, *you're not scary, and you're not welcome. Piss off.*

Gutterglass didn't flinch.

Pen sighed and turned to put her back flat against the tree. "You came out here just to be passive-aggressive at me?"

"You're packing sixty feet of spiked steel whip, and there's a shade under six tons of garbage in the vicinity I could mobilise at a push," Gutterglass observed.

"What's your point?"

"That you can't blame me for wanting to keep any aggression between us as passive as possible."

Pen heard footsteps through damp grass. She didn't look back, but the strengthening scent of mouldy vegetable peelings told her Gutterglass had come to stand just behind her.

"Go to her," the trash-spirit said, her sickly-sweet breath gusting past Pen's ear.

"I can't."

From up here on the hill, Pen could see over the treeline; beyond it was an ocean of darkness. In the distance, the lights of Canary Wharf burned bright: a solitary tower, illuminating the streets around it like a bonfire.

"You can," Gutterglass insisted. "Go to her."

"And say what?" Wires uncurled from Pen's back and shivered their barbs like rattlesnakes, but her tone didn't change. "I sent him there, Glas. I put the idea in his head. I gave him the means. I told him I could get him out—and I believed it too . . ." She faltered, and then recovered herself. "Even the weapon that killed him was mine: 'a spiked steel whip' that I bloody well *dropped.*"

She closed her eyes for a moment and the memory of Canada Square rose up in front of her. The mind that she'd been so immersed in was gone. It was incomprehensible. She'd seen Paul's personality from the inside; it was too big, too *complex*, to have just vanished like that. It was like hearing that the Atlantic Ocean had dried up. It was absurd.

"I saw the broken glass and I *knew* something wasn't right, but I just ignored it."

Gutterglass walked around until she was standing directly in front of Pen, her eggshells just inches from Pen's eyes.

"You asked me the wrong question." The statement came on a gust of rubbish-scent.

"What?"

"The other day, in the kitchen: you asked me why I was following Lady Bradley, but the question *should* have been, 'Why does she *let* me?' After all, Her Ladyship did genuinely love the young prince, for all it was a brief time that she knew him, and he died in a conflict I sent him into under a—well, a *massaged* pretext." The woven drinking-straw muscles in Gutterglass' face contorted to show how awkward that was.

Pen snorted. "You conned Fil into attacking Reach before he was ready, and you sent *Beth* into the Crane King's lair with a weapon that didn't work: that about the size of it?"

"Approximately," Glas conceded.

"Yeah, Beth told me about that." She sighed. "She also told me that when Fil died, he knew what he was doing, that it was his decision, and however much she hated him for it, in the end, he was *right*."

She pressed her lips together in an expression that wasn't quite a smile. "One phrase about you sticks in the memory. I quote: 'I trust that devious crap-mannequin about as much as a fairground coconut shy, but every lie she's ever told seems to be based on faith, and it looks like her faith's in me now.' And besides, *Doctor*"—Pen shrugged—"you're the only one who understands her symptoms. She needs—"

"She needs *you*!" The snapped interruption, coming from Gutterglass' still smiling face, was like a crocodile surging out of calm water.

Pen felt all the air rush out of her lungs.

"Paul Bradley knew what he was doing when he volunteered too, Miss Khan," Gutterglass continued, calm but relentless. "And it was *his* decision. You weren't the only one who saw that broken glass, nor the only one who gave him the means to be there. We all played our part. Your guilt is your problem; deal with it in your own time. Right now, Our Lady has just lost her father, so you give her what she *needs* to keep functioning.

"*What do you say to her?*" Gutterglass' voice was incredulous. "You're her best friend, Miss Khan, for Thames' sake, what do you *think* you damned well say? You say you love her. You say you love her, and that you're there for her, and that with your help she'll get through this, and every other damned cliché that's saved from being a banal platitude purely by the fact that it happens to be true!"

Her eyes were ghostly white under the shadows of the trees. "And even if it isn't true, you say it anyway, because *she* is all we've got. And if she falls now because you didn't hold her up, all the barbed wire in the world won't protect you from me."

Pen eyed her for a long time. "You think I'm afraid of you?" she asked at last.

"I sincerely hope you don't have to be."

Pen didn't answer but turned and hurried back up the hill towards the tower.

Gutterglass' voice carried across the night to her. "Miss Khan?"

Pen paused.

"I'll be here when you're done. There's something I think you should see."

Beth sat with her legs dangling over the side of the gantry. Her head rested against one of the tower struts and the steel was mercifully cool on her fevered cheek. She was facing away from Canary Wharf and the night-time city was a blanket of textured darkness spread out before her. Inch by inch, street by street, the rising sun drew that blanket back, steady as a mortuary nurse, revealing the city's scars.

Beth watched and felt . . . nothing at all. She didn't know how that was possible, but she didn't. She slumped down a little further. She'd forced herself to climb up here, even though her muscles felt like strings of cooked mozzarella and her hands and feet were slippery with sweat. She'd hoped that the sight of her devastated home might do something to shift the emptiness in her.

Dad just died. She kept thinking it, over and over. She jabbed herself with it like it was a needle. *Dad just died.* He was gone, forever, shouldn't she be crying or something? But she couldn't. Her heart felt flat and grey as slate. She looked desolately inside herself and found nothing but a chill.

She was an imposter. She was doing everything wrong. She even—and she knew this thought was nonsensical but she couldn't shift it—thought she was letting him down.

A frightening idea occurred to her: maybe she was broken. *Permanently* broken. Maybe her emotions had snapped like overstretched elastic. Maybe she'd never cry again, or *maybe. . .*? Her lumpen pulse quickened for a moment. Maybe her instincts were telling her something else. Maybe he wasn't really gone forever; maybe there was a way back for him, under the rules of this asylum she'd helped usher into her world. Maybe her body knew something her exhausted mind didn't and *that* was why the plumbing in her face was being so uncooperative.

She held onto that hope for a moment that felt like a thousand years, and then she let it go.

Somewhere, crammed down in her chest there was . . . *something*, a pressure. Maybe tears, maybe screams, maybe laughter; whatever it was, it was buried too deep for her to tell. She tried physically straining her muscles, but she couldn't bring it up into her throat where she could voice it.

A clanking sound brought her back to the present. A head wrapped in a black hijab and a wreath of steel wire appeared between her feet, leaning out from the gantry below.

"Hey!" Pen called up.

"*Hey.*"

More clanking, and then Pen settled herself in beside her.

"*Took your time,*" Beth said.

"It's quite the climb," Pen replied.

Beth waved one overheated hand at her. "*If the girl dying of non-specific urban fever can manage it, you can. What really kept you?*"

Pen chewed her lower lip for a second. "I thought you might want some time alone with your dad."

"*You mean the body?*"

"Yes."

"*It's at the bottom of the tower.*" She looked at Pen. "*I don't know why people do that.*"

"Do what?"

"*Confuse people with their bodies. I mean, look at me. My body's changed beyond all recognition. It's brick and slate and asphalt now. Am I those things? Am I brick, Pen?*" She felt a ferocity enter her gaze. The something in her chest shivered for a second, but then was still again.

"No," Pen said quietly.

Beth nodded. "*You think I blame you.*" It wasn't a question.

"It wouldn't be unreasonable."

"*No, it wouldn't.*"

"So do you?"

Beth paused, then she ran a tile-clad finger through the air above Pen's face, tracing the scars that discoloured her skin.

"*Do you blame me for these?*"

Pen hesitated.

"*Truthfully, Pen.*"

"No. A bit, once, maybe. I honestly don't know."

Beth shrugged. "*Me too.*"

Pen relaxed slightly, as if in acceptance. She opened her mouth, but it was still several seconds before she spoke again. "This is probably the dumbest question in the history of the universe, but how do you feel?"

Beth snorted, and car exhaust fumes blew out of her nostrils. "*Like my dad just died. I mean, I assume. Having no previous experience, maybe this is just how every Wednesday morning feels when you have a city for a body, but I really, really hope not.*"

Pen didn't say anything, but she put her hand into Beth's and her arm around Beth's shoulders and Beth let her.

"*He wasn't ready, Pen,*" Beth said. "*He was so scared. You saw the way he put away that chocolate. He used to do that at home all the time when he was nervous. You could judge his mood by how happy the guy who ran the sweetshop on the corner looked.*"

"I know," Pen said.

"*I feel like I'll never go home again,*" Beth said suddenly. She didn't know what had put those words in her mouth. For an instant the emptiness inside was replaced by sheer, paralysing fear. She felt very fragile, and very small.

"You will," Pen said. "You *are* home, B. Home's with me."

Beth tightened her grip on her best friend's hand and then moved closer. "*What am I going to do, Pen?*"

"Bury him."

"*And then?*"

Pen didn't answer.

Beth looked up, and her green eyes lit up the painful sympathy in Pen's face. "*Carry on, right? Just carry on—because whatever happens, we only ever have two choices: carry on, or stop. And you can't stop. You can never stop, because they have another name for that.*"

"Yes," Pen said simply.

"*Tell you the truth?*" Beth said. The fear had ebbed away. The emptiness was back. "*The truth is, I don't think I feel anything at all.*"

"It's okay, B," Pen whispered too, matching Beth, but there was none of Beth's doubt in her voice. "I'll still be here when you do."

Without letting go of Pen's hand, Beth shifted until she could put her head into her lap. She shut her eyes and concentrated on her breathing. She concentrated on the way that feel of Pen's hand and Pen's pulse and Pen's familiar smell were all telling her this place—halfway up a radio mast above a shattered city—this place was safe and indestructible. She didn't know if she managed to convince herself, but she closed her eyes, and with the gentle weight of Pen's hand on the back of her neck, she let exhaustion claim her.

The sun was high in the sky by the time Pen descended the tower again. She trudged back towards the wood feeling wrung out but alert.

"How is she?" Gutterglass asked the moment Pen stepped into shadow of the trees.

The air in the wood smelled of spring, and Pen took a moment to fill her lungs with it before she answered, "Angry, but I don't think she knows it yet."

The trash-spirit stepped forward. In the dappled light from the foliage she looked like some kind of nymph from an old story. "If she doesn't know it yet, how do you?"

"She's Beth Bradley. You bet on angry, you never lose." Pen sighed. "She's asleep, Glas, and given everything that's happened in the last few days, I don't think I can hold that against her. Now, what did you need to talk to me about?"

Gutterglass inclined her head and stepped to one side, revealing something that flashed in the green-filtered light.

Pen swallowed hard.

A mirror, or at least a large fragment of one, was propped up against the base of a tree. Without another word, Gutterglass produced a test tube, crouched down, tilted her wrist and tipped a clear liquid onto the glass.

The liquid trickled and ran over the surface of the mirror, but slowly, like oil rather than water. Pen watched the edge of the liquid advance. And behind that edge, with a suddenness that was like a trick of the eye, the glass itself disappeared.

Pen crouched down in front of the mirror. She saw grass and trees, but no reflection of herself. She held out a hand, and a spring breeze from another city stirred the hairs on her skin.

She looked up at Gutterglass, who smiled shyly around her bottle-cap teeth.

"I finally cracked it," she said.

CHAPTER TWENTY-FOUR

Later that day, Pen and Gutterglass, Astral the Blankleit and Ixia the Sodiumite, Petris and his clutch of battered Pavement Priests—all that remained of their little band—stood in a rough circle beneath the radio mast and watched while Beth dug.

Pen had asked her five times if she could help. She and Gutterglass pleaded and argued with her—they'd pointed out she was too sick, she was in shock, she wasn't up to it—but Beth held firm. So they watched as she struggled with the rusting spade that Glas' rats had scavenged for her. Beads of oily sweat zigzagged through the tiny streets on her forehead and dripped into her eyes. Once she dropped the spade and Ixia levitated it up for her, but Beth bared her teeth so suddenly and hostilely that the Sodiumite girl dropped it again. Beth dragged it from the dirt and dug on. She worked for three hours while the sun sank towards the horizon. The two Lampfolk's filaments were dim as embers and the sun's last rays refracted through their skins to wash in rainbows over the grave.

No one said anything until the very end, when Beth turned the last spade of earth back in on top of her father's body. She bent, gathered a handful of soil and then, because there was nothing else to do with it, let it run back through her fingers onto the mound.

"*Goodbye.*" The word came so softly that Pen barely heard it. Beth closed her eyes and every light in every window in the city of her face went out. For a full minute she stood there, a black silhouette of a girl with the wind billowing her hoodie and tugging at her hair, then she turned and staggered out of the circle. Her gait was so unsteady Pen scrambled forward to help her, but Beth stopped her with an outstretched hand.

"*I'm okay, Pen. I can handle myself. Besides, you've got a date,*" she spoke in a steam-pipe whisper. Pen could see her lips pulling as she tried to smile. "*You'd better go.*"

She shambled over to one of the tower's legs, broke out her markers and began to draw. Astral knelt behind her to give her light. Pen knew that by the time the sun rose Paul Bradley's image would smile out from the steel, better than any eulogy.

Gutterglass walked over, but seemed to hesitate before offering Pen the glass phial. "As I showed you, Miss Khan," she murmured. "Don't waste it, and make sure—" She broke off, and Pen looked up at her.

"Make sure what?"

"Nothing," Gutterglass said, still watching the phial. "Nothing you need to be told, I'm sure."

Make sure I come back? she wondered. *Was that what you were going to tell me? Do you really think I'm ready to jump ship, Glas?*

Pen curled her fingers around the doorway drug. *Carry on, or stop. That's all you can do. And you can't stop. They have a name for that.*

The Mistress' wires uncurled under her and bore her upwards. First grass and trees and then roads and rooftops flowed away under her as she stalked across the city. Behind her, the radio mast, now the world's tallest gravestone, reared black against a sepia sky. At first she felt dry and airless. She passed through London in a kind of stupor. If she'd been attacked, she would have been all but helpless; her mind was locked back in the moment the falling earth had blotted out Paul's face.

In the back of her head, though, in the quiet, a voice was whispering to her. At first she didn't listen, but it kept on, over and over, and eventually she let herself hear it.

> Crack the window and beyond the sill
> Stands a certain steeplejill.

It felt like a betrayal of Beth, but she couldn't stifle the excitement building in her chest. *Espel.* She squeezed the phial in her right hand; she'd held it all the way here, too scared of it breaking to put it in her pocket. *Espel.* She even felt a smile tug at the corner of her mouth: a real smile—one to welcome the world in, not a shield to keep it out.

She was going to see Espel.

She reached Frostfield a little after midnight. She hurried inside, her pulse loud in her ears. When she walked through the bathroom door and saw a fog of breath already on the mirror, a handprint marked out inside it, it took all her self-control not to just hurl the phial to shatter against the glass. Instead, she carefully unscrewed the cap and, just as Glas had instructed her, stopped the phial with each of her trembling fingers in turn, barely wetting the tips with the doorway drug. This concoction was highly concentrated; she needed only a tiny bit. She had to make it last if she wanted to keep the way open.

Pen swallowed. She felt like there were fireworks going off inside her ears. Her world shrank until it was just that mirror, and then just that handprint. She laid her own hand against it. The glass tingled against her fingertips where they touched it and then faded to cold mist. Pen closed her eyes, took a breath and pushed her hand forward.

Warm fingertips met her own.

The breath held in her throat bubbled out into a delighted laugh and she opened her eyes. The mirrored surface was shrinking away from her palm like water evaporating in a hot pan. Beyond it, in an exact inversion of the Frostfield bathroom, stood a lean blonde girl with tattooed cheeks, a crooked smile and a silver seam stitched in and out of the skin down the very centre of her utterly symmetrical face.

Pen slipped her fingers through Espel's and pulled her into her arms. She squeezed her as tightly as she could, breathing in her soap-and-slate smell, cherishing the warmth of her narrow body and the feel of her hair against her cheek.

They stood like that for a long time, poised on the threshold between the city and its reflection.

Eventually Espel whispered in her ear, "I'm happy to see you too, Countess, and the wire looks great, but the barbs are kind of killing the mood."

"Oh! Sorry!" Pen let her go, searching anxiously for signs of broken skin, but she couldn't see any. Espel pushed her fringe out of her eyes with her left hand. She wore the black hoodie and bandana that was the Faceless' de facto uniform, and a broad grin. She looked really, really good.

"Wow," Espel said slowly, taking Pen in. "So that story about how you got your scars was really true, huh?"

Pen shrugged. She was painfully aware that when their romance had started, she hadn't been packing sixty feet of barbed-wire accessories.

"What is it?" Espel asked.

"Nothing—I'm just hoping you're looking past the wire."

"No need to worry, Countess, I'm looking past the *clothes*."

"*Es!*" Pen grinned despite herself, but it faltered on her face. Espel's words hung in the air around her. They were a little too slow, spoken with a fraction too much effort.

Pen looked closer. There was something a little strange about Espel's smile too: it was asymmetrical—startlingly so in the perfect symmetry of Espel's face. The left side of it was stretched fractionally wider than the right.

Es saw her staring and her smile twisted a little further. "Yes, Countess, there are still two of me."

Pen gaped at her and stuttered, "But—But . . . they said you were leading the Faceless now. I just assumed—"

"Assumed what?" Espel's tone hardened. "That the other half of me had gone back for her beauty sleep? Sorry, honey, we're both wide awake in here."

"But, how . . . ?" Pen couldn't get over her shock. "How do you talk, how do you even *walk* when you're . . ."

For a moment there was no sound but the dripping of a pipe somewhere inside the walls. Espel's smile was like granite now, and Pen was starting to think she'd somehow screwed this up *already.*

Then, both to her awe and utter relief, Espel laughed. "Split in two?" The blonde girl knocked gently on her left temple. "Sharing my head? We compromise, Parva. We work together, we adapt."

She made a steeple with the fingers of both hands. "We both know what the other's thinking, so motor skills and coordination aren't as hard as you'd think, not now we're not trying to kill each other, at least. Half the time I don't even think of us as 'us' any more. It's not so different to how it used to be."

She caught Pen's sceptical look, and her expression turned a little wry. "All right, it's different," she conceded calmly. "It's harder—a lot harder, but so what? How many voices do you have to make peace with when you get out of bed every day?"

Pen held her—*their*—gaze for a moment, then nodded slowly. "More than I used to," she admitted.

"Well then," Espel said as if that settled it. Both her winter-blue eyes were bright, and her smile returned. "It helps that both of us want the same things," she added.

"Oh? And what might those be?"

"A roof to climb, a storm to sculpt, mac and cheese like my bro used to make it, and you."

"In that order?" Pen asked archly.

Es shook her head and twirled a finger in the air. "Reverse it," she said.

Pen looked straight into Espel's eyes. There were two minds looking back at her, she knew, one for each half of that symmetrical face: one belonged to the girl she'd fallen for, the first girl she'd ever kissed, and the other to the living mirrored prosthetic that had been stitched onto the right side of her face at birth. That second mind—her inverse depictor, her intimate devil, her id—had been awakened from what should have been its lifelong slumber only a few months earlier and now it was taking up half the space inside Espel's head. And *somehow*, they were able to deal with each other.

How many voices do you have to make peace with when you get out of bed every day? The voice that spoke in the back of her mind could almost have been her own.

> *Interleaved and intertwined*
> *With the fibres of your mind.*

"Shhh," she muttered.

"I didn't say anything," Espel protested.

"I know," Pen said.

"So why shush me?"

"I wasn't, I'm just making peace." She put her hand onto Espel's neck and pushed it upwards into her hair.

Both sides of Espel beamed at her.

The hell with it, Pen thought, and kissed them both.

Espel exhaled hard when they broke off. "Wow."

"What?" Pen asked. "What are you thinking?"

"That that kiss was even better than I remember."

"How do you know that wasn't that third mind at work?" Pen countered.

"Good point." Espel cocked her left eyebrow. "Want to get together for a threesome?"

"*Es!*" Pen felt the tips of her ears catch fire.

"What?" Espel's face was all innocence. "I'm just saying, there are bold new adventures ahead here, Countess. I'm not knocking the kissing, you understand. Far from it. I just don't think we should knock the, uh—"

"Knocking either?" Pen suggested.

"I would *never* be so crude," Espel said.

Pen guessed she was trying to assume a pious face, the effect of which was only slightly ruined by the fact that the two sides of her clearly had different ideas of what "pious" meant.

"Expression not working for me?" she asked Pen after a moment.

"You just look like you're trying to do really hard sums."

They both laughed. "Okay, so what's new in the old city, Countess?" Espel indicated the tips of the Mistress' coils, which were twitching a little restlessly on Pen's shoulders. "What's with the retro fashion statement?"

Pen felt the laughter dry up in her throat. She moistened her fingertips with the doorway drug and brushed back the mirror's edge where it was trying to creep back in. "Well," she said, "that's quite a story . . ."

And she told Espel the tale, all of it: from Mater Viae's demolition of London, her return to the Wire Mistress, their botched intelligence grab, the decimation of their little resistance band, to Paul's death.

Espel listened in silence and when Pen was done, the steeple-jill sucked her teeth as though appraising the situation. "Shit," she said.

"As one-syllable summaries go, that about nails it." Pen leaned forward with her elbows on the edge of a sink, stretching out her back. "We're screwed, Es. No army, no home, and I think B's ready to drop any minute. I don't know what we're going to do. I don't even know if there's anything we *can* do."

Espel licked her lips. She did it strangely, in two distinct halves, her tongue ran first anti-clockwise round the top and bottom of the left-hand side, then vanished back into her mouth before re-emerging to go clockwise round the top and bottom of the right. "You could come through to me," she said.

Pen looked up at her and Espel bent forward until their eyes were level. Her expression was wistful, hopeful, and a little ashamed. "You could do some real good over here, Countess. This place is right on the edge of open revolt against the Mirrorstocracy. The three-quarters of the Chevalier regiments who are half-faces have finally worked out their bosses aren't doing anything for them and most of them fight for us now. We've got more and more people joining up every day, Half-faced and Mirrorstocrat both. It was *you* who did that, the Looking Glass Lottery's own face speaking out against it." She sounded like she could still barely believe it had happened. "If you came back now, you could put us over the top."

She paused as though musing, then said, "Also: the kissing. The kissing could continue, which I for one find very persuasive all by itself."

Pen smiled, but only to cover the fact that her heart was going double-time in her chest as she thought about it. In the future, assuming she had one, she knew she'd look back on this moment and wonder if she'd got this right. She was tempted—there was no point pretending she wasn't. The fact that Espel was almost certainly right and she *could* do far more good in London-Under-Glass only made it worse.

And yes, there was the kissing, and those bold new adventures to be had.

"I can't," she said at last. "There's someone I need to be here for. A promise I can't break."

Es sighed, and then said, "Sorry. I shouldn't have asked."

"It's okay, I'm glad you did. And for what it's worth, the kissing *was* very persuasive. Oh, hey!" Pen said it like she'd just thought of it. "You could always come through here. I know I must have really sold it to you with all the gloom and doom earlier—"

"You did actually," Espel said. "I'm a sucker for a desperate last stand. Only I'm kinda tied up here leading my aesthetic terror insurgency."

"Must be hectic," Pen said with a mock-sympathetic shrug. "Sounds like it's going well at least?"

Espel's expression soured and the humour left her voice. "*Recruitment's* going well, but the crackdown is more vicious than anything I've ever seen. Case is replacing her lost Chevs with battalions recruited solely from the Mirrorstocracy."

"I've met them," Pen said.

"Lucky you," Espel said drily. "They're clumsy and they're badly trained, but they're hired for brutality and in that they *excel*. They just go round to the neighbourhoods of suspected Faceless and shoot everyone. They don't even pretend to ask questions. Even then we could probably take care of them if it wasn't for the claylings."

"Claylings?"

"Didn't you know? That Goddess who's taking a wrecking ball to your city left a whole fragging garrison in mine. Nominally they're under Case's command, but I wouldn't be surprised if the orders were actually going the other way." Something set hard behind Espel's eyes. "It was bad enough when the secret police used to knock on your door in the middle of the night. It's a lot worse now they come up through the floor."

Pen looked up sharply. "They're taking people? *Still?* Like they did before?"

"Yeah."

"Do you know why? It can't be to feed Mater Viae any more—She's here now."

Espel spread her hands. "We assumed it was just out of a general commitment to the repressive government cliché, only"—she frowned—"only there's the new districts."

"*What* new districts?"

"That's the thing: they don't even have names yet. About three months ago, right around the time the kidnappings got going again, new boroughs in the city opened up to the north."

"I don't follow."

"London-Under-Glass is a reflected city: it exists only as a mirror to the old place. It's why we build upwards, and why we have to grow all our food in greenhouses with soil dug out of the parks. Beyond our city limits, where *your* mirrors stop, it's barren grey dust and a barren grey ocean all the way to Mirrorkech."

"So?"

"So it's *growing*, Countess. There are new roads and buildings and post offices and parks, and for all I know sewers to the north. No one lives in them; no one's building them; they just appear. You can see them from the tops of the taller precipitecture towers in Kenneltown."

Pen felt her throat dry. There was a hollow roaring sound in her ears. She tried to swallow three times, but couldn't. "What did you say?"

"You can see them from the taller—"

"No, before that: no one's building them. So they're growing?" Espel nodded.

"You sure? Have you sent anyone to check them out?"

Espel's face darkened. A furrow appeared either side of her face. "Alexei," she said shortly.

"What happened?"

"He didn't come back."

Dizziness hit Pen in a wave. She leaned back slowly from the sink.

"Parva?" Espel asked. "What is it?"

But Pen wasn't looking at her. Her thoughts were back with Paul Bradley as he stepped into a pool in Canada Square, a pool that he said felt like it had *taken* something from him. She blinked, and there was Gutterglass, crouching over him as the blood they couldn't stop poured from the small cut on his forehead. She heard the trash-spirit's voice as clearly as if she was standing in the dusty bathroom with them, saying, "*His hair's not growing.*"

"Parva! What is it?"

Pen blinked and then focused back on Espel. She'd climbed halfway through the mirror, which was twitching and threatening to seal back around her. Her face was furrowed with worry around her silver seam.

Pen's throat felt full of dust as she answered.

"Mater Viae—I know what She's up to."

CHAPTER TWENTY-FIVE

Beth hadn't slept. The picture of her dad had taken shape over the course of the night and it felt desperately urgent that she finish it *now.* Everything felt more urgent now; there wasn't enough time for anything.

The sun had just risen and she was weighing up the merits of adding colour versus keeping it black and white when she felt a tap on her shoulder. She turned around and her stomach clenched.

Pen was breathless, little licks of sweat-slicked hair were coming loose around the edges of her hijab. Her expression was tense as she gasped, "Up . . ." She pointed to the top of the tower. "We need to *check—*"

Beth didn't know what lay behind Pen's frantic instruction, but she'd spent a sizeable chunk of the last five years reading her friend's face and right now it said: *Don't ask, just do. Trust me.*

Beth capped her marker and dropped it into the grass, dusted off her hands, turned to the tower leg and started to climb. Her muscles were searing under her skin before they reached the first gantry.

Remember this, Petrol-Sweat? she thought, to take her mind off the climb. *Remember the first time we came here: the steel, and the spiders, and the dark? I damn near chucked myself off the top of it.*

Fil's voice muttered wryly back to her, *I remember. Fun times. Mind you, if you spent a little less time reminiscing about the good old days and paid attention to your hand-holds, you might not be about to slip off that . . . WATCH IT!*

The steel was suddenly frictionless under her fingers and then it slid out from under them. Beth grabbed for a hanging cable, but her reflexes were slow and she grasped only air. She fell.

Wire closed around her, as gently as the silk strands of a moth's cocoon. Her descent slowed, and then moments later, she started to rise again.

"*Nice catch, Pen. Now put me back on the tower,*" she called, and when Pen ignored her, "*Pen, put me back on the bloody tower! I can do my own climbing!*"

Pen didn't seem inclined to take the chance.

"*This is your fault, you know,*" she muttered, her cheeks burning with embarrassment as well as fever.

Inside her skull, Fil's voice wasn't having any of it. *Me? You're the one who's driving, Beth. I'm just the comic relief on the car stereo.*

Beth endured the rest of their ascent in huffy silence. When they reached the highest platform, the wires unwound themselves and deposited her on the steel. Tiny spiders swarmed around Beth's feet, winking in and out of existence, their static voices lost in the wind. The cold air up here pierced her hoodie, finding every chink and crack in her street-laced skin. She clung to the struts of a satellite dish and tried not to let her teeth chatter. Her fever must have flipped.

Pen stood next to her, lashed to the mast itself with strands of barbed wire. Insects scrambled past them, heading for the pinnacle of the tower, with bits of garbage clamped in their mandibles.

A moment later, Gutterglass leaned out from the mast above them, silhouetted against the half-light, his bin-bag coat streaming out behind him. A pigeon shot by in a flutter of wings, bearing his eggshell eyes higher still.

"Thames preserve us." Gutterglass had to shout over the wind. Beth was shaken by the awe in the trash-spirit's voice. "I can't see the end of it."

"*What?*" she asked, and Glas pointed a garden-wire finger.

Beyond the twisted wreck of the Wembley Arch, where the dense crosshatch of architecture thinned and gave way to fields, a spur of dirty grey concrete and reddish roof tile stretched to the horizon. Beth didn't need an *A-to-Z* to know those buildings hadn't been there a couple of months before.

Glas' voice turned grim. "I can see terraces without windows," he said. "Those streets are infected."

"Mater Viae did this?" Pen's voice was hollow with fright. "But why? It could be halfway to Birmingham by now—what's it all for? I don't get it."

But Beth did. The understanding that came was sudden, but coldly unshakeable. She looked down at the cross-weaving metal struts of the tower, remembering.

"*The cranes.*" She spoke so quietly the words were almost lost in the wind. "*The Lady of the Streets and the King of the Cranes.*"

"What?" Pen looked at her.

"*It's what She does, Pen. It's what She's always done. It's what She wants, and who She is. She's a mother, and the City is Her child—She wants to see it grow. That's all Reach was, in the beginning: he became a force of demolition, yes, but he was a force of construction first. He just got out of hand.*"

She swallowed out of reflex, even though the voice she was speaking with would never parch her throat. "*For three days and nights, when She first came through, the cranes came awake—She woke them. But the cranes are unpredictable and dangerous. So I guess She had a better idea—Her time behind the mirror* gave *Her a better idea. She'd already learned how to separate people from their memories, so why not take something else too? So She made a deal with the Chemical Synod: She started to steal the growth She wanted for the city straight from the people who lived in it. She put the cranes back to sleep, before they ever properly woke up in the first place. And we were too busy thanking our lucky stars for small mercies to ask why."*

"An organic city," Gutterglass murmured, "capable of growing hundreds of miles in only a few weeks—and bringing its sickness to everything it touches."

"B . . ." Pen took her hand, her voice suddenly urgent. "What can we do? We have to do something. We have to stop Her somehow. If it just keeps growing . . ." She tailed off and an angry lash of barbed wire slammed into the tower hard enough to make it lurch alarmingly.

"We have to *stop* Her!" she said again, and this time there were tears in her eyes. She turned to Gutterglass. "She could just keep on, couldn't She? Taking more land, more people, more growth, and so more land—where would it stop?"

"In principle?" Gutterglass shook his head. "I don't know. I don't think it would have to."

"The whole country?" Pen pressed. "Would it spread over the ocean floor? Could it cover the whole world?"

It sounded ridiculous: *The World.* Like a supervillain's boast from a Saturday morning cartoon. But Gutterglass couldn't contradict it, and anyway, Beth knew it wasn't the world that Pen was really worried about.

It could be halfway to Birmingham by now. She could see in Pen's brown eyes that she was picturing her parents tucked up in her Aunt Soraya's house, with thousand-degree Fever Streets heading their way.

"What can we do?" Pen demanded again.

Her cuticles were bleeding now where she'd worried away at them, and Beth couldn't help noticing that the barbs on the wire were drawing tighter into her, the more agitated her voice became. "We have to do something. What can we do?"

Beth was about to admit she didn't know when she sensed an idea at the back of her head—an idea so strange, so unlikely, that she wasn't sure it had really come from her at all. She recoiled from it, appalled that she'd even thought it, but then she looked back at Pen, hesitated and went to speak.

Don't say it, Beth. Fil's voice sounded in her mind. *Once you've said it, you can't take it back. You'll get her hopes up and you don't know it's even possible.*

It could be though, couldn't it? she countered silently. *You thought of the cranes at the same time I did. It was you who put that idea in my head.* She looked at her street-scored hands. *If Mater Viae did it, maybe I could do it too.*

She's healthy. You're sick.

I know.

Beth, you're dying.

There's enough left in me for this. She said it to herself with more confidence than she felt.

Have you totally lost it? Fil's voice demanded. *Have you forgotten what it cost us to put him down the first time?*

Beth pictured a railing-spear, its point scratching a bloody star in Fil's chest as her hand trembled. *I haven't forgotten. I won't ever forget.*

Beth, please. When he's done with a place, there's no life, no energy—he'll leave nothing to sustain you. You know that. If you do this, if he gives you what you want, you'll die.

Like you said, Fil, I'm dying anyway.

"Beth?" Beth met Pen's eyes; she saw the anxiety there, the need and the desperate hope that, somehow, Beth could help her. "You . . . you looked like you were going to say something?"

Beth, please, Fil started, but the churn of gears and turbines and the growl of cars from Beth's body drowned him out as she started to speak. "*There's one thing we could try,*" she said. "*It's risky, but we don't have an army and we don't have much time, so I guess this is the only idea on the table.*"

"What is it?" Pen asked.

"*London's sick,*" Beth said. "*The city is killing its inhabitants, infecting everything it touches—and it's growing, right?*"

"Right."

"*The only way to stop it growing is to kill it. So we kill it. We need someone who can do that, who can demolish an entire city. Tell me,*" she said, "*does that sound like anyone we know?*"

CHAPTER TWENTY-SIX

Pen led the way through the labyrinth. Of all of them, she knew the way the best. Beth followed close behind her, looking over her shoulder, her eyes washing the narrow passages through the collapsed masonry in traffic-light green.

It was three hours since they'd stood on the radio mast. Pen had gaped at Beth as she'd explained what passed for her plan, and her jaw had virtually unhinged itself when Beth had insisted they execute it that very day.

"Why?" she'd said. "Why are we rushing into it? Can't we at least take a *day* to think of something"—she'd groped—"a little less batshit?"

Beth had shaken her head.

"Why not?"

Beth had held up her arm so Pen could see the rough streaks of newly clotted Tideway where her veins had once been. "*Because tomorrow I might not be well enough any more.*"

So now here she was, crawling behind Pen, elbow over elbow through the wreckage around St. Paul's, with Gutterglass behind her, and Petris laboriously bringing up the rear. Beth had tried to order the granite monk to stay behind, but he'd replied with a curt, "Fuck off, My Lady," and that had been that. None of the others had been allowed to come, though, not Ixia nor Astral nor the rest of the stoneskins. If she failed, Beth wanted them to have a chance to run.

Run where? Fil's voice asked bitterly. *You're about to give their home to His cranes.*

Beth took another step. She relaxed the muscles in her feet, but nothing came through. This was a Demolition Field, the city's scar tissue. There were no symptoms here, and no life either.

No life, Fil picked up the thought, *no energy to feed off. No Urbosynthesis, not ever. If you get what you want—make all of London like this—you'll starve.* He was silent for a moment in her head, and then, in a tone of realisation said, *You're giving up.*

Beth felt a shiver run down her spine. She gave a tight shake of her head. *I'm not*, she thought back. Inside her hood, Oscar curled into her neck crooning unhappily, but Beth told herself it was just the confined space that frightened him.

You are. Fil's voice was shocked. *Glas might still come through with a treatment, but you don't care. You're giving up.*

Beth's lip curled into a sour half-smile. *I'm saving the world.*

London is the world, Fil snapped.

For us, Beth thought, her gaze flashing off the steel that bound Pen. *Not for her.*

The tunnel widened and natural light seeped through cracks in the ceiling, making tiny waterfalls of dust glow. They emerged into a pyramid-shaped chamber. Beth felt a thrill of recognition and tightened her grip on her spear. Ahead of her, Pen didn't so much as break step, but Beth thought she saw the barbs on the coils that wrapped the back of her neck prick up as though they sensed something.

When they finally emerged, coughing and blinking, back into the daylight, Beth was jarred by the silence. In her memory, this place was full of glare and clamour: sunlight springing sharp from newly built skyscrapers, the shriek of machine gears and the footsteps of steel giants.

Now though, the clouds stifled the sun and the cranes that loomed over the building site were motionless. Two half-built towers reared up, one to the north and one to the east. The scaffolding that sheathed them was piebald with rust.

Pen hugged herself against the cold as Beth stomped forward. From where she stood, the undulations of the rubble-strewn ground looked random, but she remembered hanging over it from the yard-arm of a crane. She knew that, from above, these crags and hillocks would become the eyes and chin and cheeks of the Demolition God, hewn from London's bedrock. The dust covered Him like a funeral shroud.

So, Fil, she thought, *how do I do this?*

What, you want me to help now? the voice in her head grumbled. *Piss off.*

She should, she reflected, probably have expected that. She closed her eyes. Now her mind was a city made of shadows, and she filled it with the dark, malevolent shapes of cranes; she imagined them as the fingers of a vast entity, hewn into the bedrock of the city. She took in a deep breath, leaned heavily on her spear and tried to pour the idea into the dead earth under her.

Stop! Even in her head, Fil sounded incredulous. *What in the name of my Mother's tiled left tit are you doing?*

Beth's concentration dissolved. Her eyes flickered open. *What does it look like I'm doing? I'm raising Reach.*

Well, for Thames' sake, don't do it that way! You couldn't even turn out a couple of Pavement Priests a couple of days ago—if you try and recreate the Crane King from scratch out of your own bleedin' head you'll die of exhaustion before you've got one flywheel turning.

If you've got any advice, I'm all ears, Beth shot back. *Well, actually, I'm all roads and houses and satellite dishes, but you know what I mean.*

Fil called her a name so vile that Beth was genuinely impressed. He went on swearing for a good half-minute before saying, *All right, kneel down.*

Beth obeyed, her knees knocking up little scuffs of concrete dust where they hit the floor. She could feel the others' anxiety as they watched her.

Plant both hands palms flat to the floor. Spread your fingers. The Crane King already exists, Beth; River knows we don't need a second one. He's here somewhere, in this machinery, this concrete and clay. We just need to wake Him up.

Even with her palms pressed firmly against the ground, Beth still had a fleeting impression of a grey-skinned hand gently taking hers.

Ready? Fil's voice asked her. *Go.*

She closed her eyes and her mind sank into the city beneath her. For a second she was swimming below the surface, baffled by the darkness, her fevered mind too slow to let go of the senses that had brought her this far. Gradually though, her awareness uncurled in the lightless, airless subcutaneous city, and she began to sense its structure: pipes, cables, layers of sediment, electric fields, all interwoven like muscle fibres, with wires like nerve-endings. She brushed them gently with her mind, but felt nothing from them. They were dead.

Fil led her deeper; she could feel him tugging further down, into the bedrock beneath the clay. Beth felt an ache and at first couldn't work out where; at last she realised it was in her skull. She was concentrating so hard it was hurting. Her attention almost snapped back to her body on the surface, but she wrestled it under control.

She sensed something—a whisper of motion from a cracked pipe or a hissing of sparks from a mains cable behind her. Her mind flitted back to it, but in the instant it had taken her to find and focus on it, it had fallen silent.

Further down, Fil urged, *and further out. Try to sense the whole site at once.*

Beth tried, but it was like trying to wrap her arms around a cathedral. She stretched and strained. The pain in her head flared, but she was only vaguely aware of it. Gradually, like rainwater, her consciousness soaked further and further into the porous rock.

With a rill of horror she realised she was filtering through corpses: Masonry Men and Women in the Walls: civilians, not soldiers in any war. The splinters of a shattered Sodiumite needled her and she almost fled back to the site above.

Steady, Fil whispered. *They're already dead. You can't hurt them. They can't hurt you. It's okay, Beth, take your time. Try to get a sense of the place as a whole.*

Other motions reached her, other scraps of almost-sound: a sigh of concrete expanding with the heat, a drip of groundwater. She strained her mind further and became aware that, on the surface, she'd gritted her church-spire teeth. She felt the whole site poised above her. She was spread so thin she was afraid she would break up. She was trembling. She was too tired, too sick. She couldn't hold it . . .

. . . I will . . .

Beth froze. It was the barest of vibrations, hardly even a sound at all. It began with some sand shifting in the wake of a worm on the east side and finished with a spark discharging on the west. You had to be spread the whole way under the site to make sense of it.

Her mind screaming with the effort, Beth waited.

I will . . .

There it came again: a whisper dying before it was even spoken, like a breath exhaled in sleep. Ten more seconds, and it came again: *I will . . .*

Wait for it to come round again, Beth. You know what to do.

She did, instinctively, she knew. The part of her that had once been a Goddess remembered this. She began to scavenge from all the little forces acting in her city-body, from the turbines in the power stations in her stomach and the foundations straining under the buildings in her knees, from the lights in her eyes and the cranes in her fingers, she sucked up what little energy she could spare and held it thrumming in the core of her body far above.

. . . I will . . .

Beth sprang.

She let her power discharge down through her palms and in the vaults of her mind she heard Fil's voice join with hers as she yelled, "*BE!*"

The site shuddered and Beth's grip slipped. Her mind flew back into her body and she knelt on the rubble shivering and coughing and hacking.

And then, past the sound of her own wheezing, she heard gears start to whine.

Petrol engines coughed into life. Vast drills lowered themselves to the ground and their steel teeth shrieked into the concrete.

Beth's gasps were drowned out by the thunderous noise. The earth shook under the diggers. Crane-mounted hooks slammed into wreckage. Concrete dust billowed like stormclouds. The ground lurched and shifted, shale subsided and a crater opened up under her head. She stared down into it. Recessed into the vast socket was a rough orb—a stone eyeball. The hollow pupil that had been gouged from it was fathomless.

I AM REACH, the machines sang together. *I AM REACH.*

Inside her mind, Beth felt Fil shrink from that voice. A shadow passed over her and she looked up. A crane-arm reared in skeletal silhouette. Its cable whirred as it wound back its hook and Beth could do nothing but watch.

I WILL BE.

Pen screamed.

Beth's heart lurched in her chest.

It was a shriek of agony, so loud it carried clear over the frantic song of Reach's engines. Beth tried to push herself up, but her muscles were exhausted and she fell painfully back onto her face.

Pen screamed again and again, over and over. Beth felt like her heart was cracking under the sound of it. As the dust cleared, Beth saw her: arched backwards, impossibly balanced on tiptoes with her arms thrown back above her head. It was the wire—the wire held her, bound tourniquet-tight around her abdomen, her chest, her legs. Beth could see Pen's clothes darkening as blood soaked them; droplets spilled onto the ground from the curve of her spine.

An umbilical of steel strained into the air from Pen's stomach, twisting and snapping, reaching for the tip of the nearest crane. Her toes skidded sharply through the dust as it dragged her forwards a foot.

Beth stared helplessly, remembering.

Reach has a priestess too. The Wire Mistress, we call her, the Demolition clergy.

They'd brought the cursed thing home.

"Miss Khan!" Petris roared in his gravel voice. He surged towards her in a blur of granite. The wire lashed almost contemptuously and the Pavement Priest crashed heavily to the floor. His stone monk's form flickered and shuddered amidst the rubble, but he failed to rise.

Again Beth tried to push herself up; again she slipped back. Acid filled her mouth. She'd poured everything she had into Reach; she had nothing left.

Pen screamed on. Gutterglass ran towards her. Beth could see the fear in his eggshell eyes. He dissolved into a chaotic tangle of scrap metal and pigeon wings and plastic and then suddenly he was a tiger, baring rusty-nail fangs and crouching to spring. Pen's scream changed; it took on a shape, resolving in the air until it was a single word:

"Wait!"

Pen's eyes were wide in her head, her neck corded, but her voice had authority. "Wait!" she cried again.

Gutterglass growled but didn't move, except for swishing his hosepipe tail.

With sudden violence, Pen swung her hand around and seized the wire that stretched from her abdomen. The metal hissed angrily.

Pen's lips were moving, and Beth could just make out the words amidst Reach's clamour: "We *will* understand one another, you and I."

Blood ran between her fingers where she gripped the wire, but she wasn't screaming any more. "Put. Me. *Down*."

Slowly, Pen's heels descended towards the ground. The Mistress coiled and lashed almost piteously, but it couldn't move even an inch closer to the crane it so longed for. Beth watched, awestruck, as Pen held it for five more seconds, and then, very softly said, "Go."

She cracked the wire in her hand like it was a whip, and the steel tendril shot out and lashed around the steel struts at the top of the crane.

I WILL BE, Reach shrieked.

"Only if you listen," Pen said clearly. Her eyes were closed now. "If you don't, you will never wake again."

The wire stretched between her fist and the crane shivered like a steel guitar string, modulating its frequency as she spoke.

Beth gaped, but in her head it was Fil who spoke. *She's speaking to him through the Mistress.* His voice mirrored her astonishment. *Steel speaking to steel.*

"We woke you," Pen continued. "We have a common enemy. You have to listen to us."

I WILL BE!

Reach is a child, Beth thought; *he's a baby—how can he possibly understand her?*

His mind is a child's mind. Fil sounded awestruck. *But she's not talking to his mind. She's talking to the* system *of him, the cranes, the scaffolding, the Scaffwolves, the dirt, the whole fucking mechanism of him: it understands what will keep him alive. That must be how the Mistress always talked to him—not to what he thinks, but what he* is. *It's a metal language. It's like she's talking to his DNA.*

I WILL BE!

The cranes and diggers shook in their rage, and the ground shook with them. Pen stumbled, and for a second she looked uncertain. "Please," she gasped, but she didn't seem to know what else to say.

Beth, Fil's voice whispered, suddenly full of urgency, *go to her.*

Using her spear as a lever, Beth managed to get to her feet. She swayed over to Pen's side. *Now*, Fil muttered to her, *say what I say, and tell Pen to repeat it.*

Fil, I—

Just trust me.

"*Pen*," Beth swallowed hard, "*repeat after me.*"

And the message was relayed from Fil's voice to Beth to Pen and finally up the Mistress' taut-drawn wire, and of all of those voices, only Pen's rose clearly above the clamour.

"The Lady of the Streets silenced you, and She will do it again if you don't help us. She doesn't need you any more. The city She's wrought will grow by itself. It has no use for a Construction God."

I WILL BE!

"Only if you help—only if you stop the sickened city in its tracks. Only if you do what we tell you. We will help you. We will protect you from Her."

The next sentence made Beth flinch before she repeated it, but Pen spoke it clearly and without hesitation, "Your Mother has moved beyond you, Son of the Streets. Have you moved beyond Her?"

Abruptly, every machine in the site stopped dead. Beth looked around frantically as the echoes faded, but there was no sign that Reach was even still alive.

"Well?" Pen's voice sounded suddenly very lonely in the silence. "What is your answer?"

What is your answer, brother? Fil whispered.

With a squeal and a spray of rust, a scaffolding strut on the nearest tower started to spin. It slid back from its socket and the joints holding it rotated. All over the site, the steel bars started rearticulated themselves, sliding from their buildings like a controlled metal avalanche.

Beth stiffened as struts slotted together to form steel paws and steel haunches and socketed hinges lined up along a low s-curved spine. A skeletal metal muzzle formed, with hackles of rusting chains running from the head. Foot-long brass screws protruded like fangs from the jaw. Beth tightened her grip on her spear, even though, right then, she felt barely strong enough to lift it.

The Scaffwolf watched them with blank-socket eyes. It was bigger than a horse. Dozens more of its kind assembled themselves behind it, then prowled towards them. Beth felt herself shrink slightly. She'd never seen so many of them in one place.

The lead wolf dipped its head and folded its forelegs under it. It bent its neck in front of Pen.

Pen's jaw was locked tight as she opened her hand. Coils of barbed wire lashed themselves to the wolf's neck like barbed reins.

Stiffly, like she was calling on some long-buried muscle memory, Pen stepped onto one of the struts in the wolf's flank and threw her leg over its back. She tugged at her reins and the wolf padded obediently aside. Another of the beasts approached and crouched in front of Beth. Her green gaze flashed off its teeth. She steeled herself and dragged her aching body up and onto its back. Oscar was up on all fours on her shoulder, hissing around his forked tongue, and Beth stroked a finger along his spine to calm him. Gutterglass' trash-tiger scattered and reformed in a man's shape, but he could not disguise the look of distaste as he clambered astride a third Scaffwolf.

"Petris?" Pen asked.

"Fuck. And indeed, no." Petris' voice was measured as he eyed the steel animals. "The day I can't keep up with a Scaffpack is the day I become dinner for one."

Pen tugged at her reins and her wolf bounded agilely up the rubble that closed in the building site. Gutterglass' and Beth's mounts followed suit, their hollow feet ringing off the shattered concrete. Behind them, the woken cranes and diggers and drills laboured and sang on.

I am Reach.

I am Reach.

Ahead of them, Pen looked back. It might have been exhaustion clouding her eyes, but Beth could have sworn she saw her friend's lips move in time to the Crane King's words:

I Will Be.

III

WIELDING THE KNIFE

CHAPTER TWENTY-SEVEN

They returned to Crystal Palace just after nightfall.

The statues were crouched around a brazier, the grooves of their knife-whittled tattoos catching the light from the flames. They muttered in low voices and smoked cigarettes they'd scrounged from God only knew where. Ixia and Astral were missing, but flickering orange and white light from the woods suggested they were having fun. Despite herself, Pen smiled a little. It felt good after the nervous grimace she'd worn the whole way here, shuddering at every clanking paw-fall as they threaded their way on wolf-back through the deserted streets. She'd stared at the bare pavement around them until her eyes ached, watching for the telltale tremor of a Masonry Man, but none emerged.

She let herself relax a little as they climbed up the hill. A knot between her shoulders loosened and she no longer felt like she was liable to throw up at any second. After the chaos and noise of the demolition field, she felt . . . safer. She looked down at the metal wolf under her and then back at the warped and twisted city behind them and laughed.

Glas and Beth looked sharply at her, and she smiled.

Everything's relative, I guess.

I am Reach. I am Reach. I will be. I will be. The words were a constant song inside her head; the Crane King's only two thoughts thrummed over and over through the wire lashed to the wolf's neck. The scaffolding was as much a part of Reach as the cranes were, and she was plugged in. She could feel his longing. He wanted to pour through the city's foundations like a flood, to possess the cranes and drills that hung silent in forgotten Demolition Fields and once again tear at London, reshaping it to his blueprint as he had before.

Soon, she begged him, her thoughts shivering down the wire. *Soon—but not yet.*

Reach was a child; his mind could grasp only two thoughts, but he understood instinctively what it took to keep him alive.

I will be.

Everything hinged on persuading him that his survival depended on holding back.

"Petris?" A Pavement Priest flickered towards them as they reached the foot of the radio mast. His eyes were wide inside his weathered onyx armour. "What the hell, man?"

"I know," the Stone Monk growled, "believe me, Billy. I know. We'll just have to trust Lady Bradley knows what she's doing, because I sure as shit don't."

But Beth wasn't exactly a sight to inspire confidence. She was sagging halfway out of her saddle and her left foot trembled where it hung beside the wolf's metal flank. She slipped suddenly, alarmingly, but Gutterglass dismounted in a flap of rubbish and between them he and Beth managed to turn her fall into something approximating an orderly dismount. Even so, the trash-spirit had to surreptitiously support Beth every step of the way to the far side of the tower, where they'd thrown a couple of beds together from scavenged tarpaulins and cardboard boxes. The priests stared after their limping Goddess, then turned their nervous gazes on the

wolves she'd brought with her. The iron animals sniffed the air
and then prowled into the gathering shade, taking up defensive
positions around the tower.

Pen swung herself down from her mount.

Please wait, she urged Reach once more. The Mistress snarled a
sing-song doggerel in her mind:

> *The one who reigns over the cranes*
> *Doesn't take orders from human brains.*

Pen tightened her grip on the wire, feeling the barbs bite.

*He will if it will keep him alive, which, if I'm not very much mistaken,
is what you want too. So* tell *him.*

The wire shivered as it obeyed, then uncoiled itself from under
the wolf's rusted hackles and wound around her wrist.

A gust of garbage-smell touched her nostrils and she felt a presence behind her. "What is it, Glas?" she said without looking.

"Her Ladyship is . . . not herself," the trash-spirit whispered
through mouldy-hose lips, so that only Pen could hear. As casually
as she could she walked away from the campfire, putting as much
distance as she could between them and the Pavement Priests.

"Oh?"

"She called me a worm-riddled tower of uh, excrement—which
is far from accurate, let me assure you—and told me to get her
hands off her."

"Sounds like her so far. Then what happened?"

"I obeyed. She fell down. When I picked her back up off the
floor she didn't say anything else. But her scabs have opened again
and . . ."

He stopped and glanced back to check they really were alone.
"I'm fairly sure the reason she didn't want me touching her was
that she didn't want me to feel how high her fever's climbed." He

looked down at his fingers and Pen looked with him: the tips of the twisted pipe-cleaners were singed.

"She's very ill, Miss Khan."

Pen crossed her arms and bent her head forward as though she were walking into a stubborn wind. "Glas," she said, "have I done something recently to make you think I'm blind?"

"No—"

"Or stupid?" She spoke with a cold, brittle brightness.

"No—"

"So why are you telling me things I already know? How about telling me something useful, like what can we bloody well *do about* it?"

Gutterglass spread his hands. "At this point? We can wait, and we can hope." His tone hardened slightly. "And put the gift she gave us to best possible use, because I have to tell you, Miss Khan, I really do think that little exercise back at St. Paul's cost her more than she could afford to give."

Pen stopped walking and turned to face him. She flinched instinctively; she hadn't realised how tall his new avatar was.

"What are you getting at?"

A pipe-cleaner index finger pointed upwards and Pen's gaze followed it to where a black dot wheeled against the clouds.

"I have a pigeon up there now. When she lands, I suspect she'll report that Reach has somehow *not* spread into the Demolition Fields of the city and is *not* now wreaking his merry havoc on the mirror-creature, as Lady Bradley had intended he do. Instead, I suspect she'll tell me he is restraining himself for some mysterious reason."

The eggshell gaze was direct. "Some mysterious reason which, given the slightly tortuous way in which we are compelled to communicate with the Crane King, I suspect has rather a lot to do with *you*."

Pen bit her lip. "Glas—" she began.

"It was her *will*." Gutterglass all but snarled the words. "It was her *express will*, and she all but died to make it happen. How dare you countermand it?" His paper nostrils were flared, his pipe-cleaner fingers twitching angrily.

Pen remembered Beth's words. "*It looks like her faith is in me now.*" She stifled an urge to fall back a step. "It'll be a bloodbath," she said at last, in as clear and confident a voice as she could manage. "There are still thousands of people, holed up all over the city. If we don't get them somewhere safe before the fighting starts, it'll be a total massacre—"

Glas tried to interject, but Pen raised her voice and spoke over him. "I know in the past you haven't been that averse to causing massacres, Glas, and maybe you still aren't, but I am. And"—She held up a hand to stop him interrupting—"and so is the Goddess whose will you're apparently so concerned about. If Beth was well enough and together enough to think about it, she'd be telling me to do exactly what I'm doing. *Trust me.* I've known her a lot longer than you have." Pen's voice was measured, and she felt an icy satisfaction as the trash-spirit withered before it.

Gutterglass' expression soured and he started to turn away, but Pen wasn't done with him yet. "She still hates you, by the way," she said. "Beth holds grudges, and lying to her boyfriend and getting him killed? That's a *keeper*. If you want her to forgive you, you'd better go and tend to your patient, and you had better do it damn well."

The eggshell eyes dropped, and Pen felt a faint ripple of surprise. She couldn't remember the proud trash-spirit ever not being able to keep eye contact with anyone.

"We are still badly overmatched," he muttered. "The only element in our favour is surprise, and the longer we wait, the more at risk we place it."

"Again I'm forced to ask why you think I'm stupid."

"I *don't*, Miss Khan," Gutterglass spat the words out with droplets of spoiled milk. "I do, however, think you are exhausted, under acute stress, and carrying around a parasitic barbed-wire demon that, lest we forget, got pretty spectacularly away from you back there."

Pen flinched, and regretted it instantly when Gutterglass' lip curled. "Oh, you didn't think we'd noticed? Have I done something to make you think I'm blind?" He matched her brittle sarcasm exactly. "Now I'm no medical expert, but—oh no, wait, I *am* a medical expert, so forgive me if I observe that the condition you're in is not exactly *ideal* for optimal decision-making."

Pen lifted her chin obstinately. She didn't say anything.

"Do I have to remind you that the longer we wait, the closer the fever gets to Birmingham?"

"Yeah," Pen said flatly, "*that's* what you need to remind me of." She felt a tremor run through her, but she stilled it. The thrash and hammer of Reach's machines was echoing loudly in her mind. She imagined the bloody chaos that would ensue when Mater Viae's forces engaged. She pictured the stocky man in the turban they'd left in Selfridges, and the two girls whispering over their fire in Clapham Junction, and the boy snatched from the Chemical Synod's factory and carried off to Canary Wharf. She pictured them one by one, fixing on their faces and their voices in their mind. She couldn't just let them be collateral damage. She had to *try*.

The faces of her parents swam into her mind and she forced them back out again.

There's time. She willed that to be true. *There's time.*

"Very well, then," Gutterglass muttered. "If you must go, then go quickly, go quietly and go *now.*"

"No kidding," Pen said drily. "The people—I'll need to tell them somewhere to go."

"Oh, for Thames' sake," Gutterglass snapped. "Send them here. I'll scavenge up *something* for them to eat, but it won't be pretty."

The trash-spirit turned away and began to stump back towards the tower and the flickering firelight. A gust of wind rippled his mouldy carpet-coat and blew a smell like rotting carrots into Pen's nostrils.

He paused. "Oh, Miss Khan? That wire demon—she is back under control now, isn't she?"

Pen rubbed her thumb over her palm. It was sticky with drying blood. "Sure," she said, her throat dry. "Where are you going?"

"To tend my patient." Gutterglass' tone softened a little as he echoed Pen, and Pen even smiled a little.

"Do it damn well," she said softly.

"I always do, Miss Khan. I can probably even keep her alive until you get back—but do hurry, eh?"

Pen waited until she'd disappeared out of sight before she slumped, and then sat down hard on the grass. Tendrils of wire uncoiled and thrashed in a buzzing cloud around her. The chaos of it filled her mind, making her feel blurry at the edges.

Now! Now! Now! Attack! Attack!

she snarled.

> *Tighten the coil and take the slack,*
> *Pluck the Mother's church-spire teeth*
> *And kill Her human-poisoned streets.*

"Not yet."

A wire strand snaked back towards the wolves, eager to bring Reach the news that it was time; that he could strike. Pen gritted her teeth and concentrated on bringing the strand lashing and snapping to heel.

"You can't do anything without me," she muttered under her breath, comforted by how much louder and more solid her words sounded compared to what the Mistress was whispering inside her head. "And I won't go until I'm ready, so calm down. I wasn't kidding back there at St. Paul's: you want to keep me as host, we do this my way."

She thought back to the bite of the barbed-wire thorns at the building site. The pain had flared just the way it did in her memories, and for a second Pen had panicked. The Mistress' loyalty to her God had surged back and Pen had felt helpless before her certainty. Her pulse tripped at the memory, knowing that for a second she'd come close to surrendering to the wire. As her toes had skidded through the rubble, she'd almost lost control.

It was only in the final heartbeat that she'd regained her grip, when she'd remembered the weakness Beth's spear had cut into the wire.

"You can't force me," she whispered. "You can't force anyone, not any more. That's why you came back to me when I passed out, wasn't it? That's why you brought Paul back, even though you had him in your grip? Because I am *willing*, and you need that. You can't force me, for all your strength. You can only kill me, and if you do that you'll go back to being a scattering of metal maggots in the dust."

The wire bridled and shivered her barbs an inch from Pen's eye, but she didn't blink.

"You want to give your old boss the all-clear, and I want to get as many people as possible out from under his claws first. The two needs are compatible, so what do you say we work together? Either that or you squeeze me into purée right now—but good luck finding another human host willing to carry you."

She felt her heart drumming as she waited for either a rhyming retort or the cinching of steel coils as the Mistress rejected her pitch. Instead, she felt her feet leave the ground as the wire extended steel stilts under her and turned her towards the north.

One more night, the Mistress hissed to her, suddenly meek and eager as a child, *and then we fight?*

"Yes." Pen swallowed, her throat parched. Finally she let the faces of her parents into her mind. "Then we fight."

CHAPTER TWENTY-EIGHT

The cranes hooked the clouds on the horizon: stiff and lifeless as the legs of a dead insect, the same shape and pose as Beth had imagined them at the building site. Was he a permanent fixture now, she wondered, this God of Demolition, stillborn against the grey sky of her mind?

The scrawny boy leaned on the brick parapet next to her, his head turned towards her, resting on his folded arms.

"No point staring at them now," he said. The concrete dust in his hair had got wet somehow and his fringe was matted against his forehead. "It's done."

"I know it's done," Beth said. Her human voice sounded strange to her now, even in her dreams. Was she remembering it right? she wondered. What if she'd never really sounded like this? "I did it."

The grey boy didn't answer, but his silence suggested he wasn't impressed.

She exhaled slowly and a gust of wind howled down the street below. She stretched, and the bones in her spine popped. "Look," she tried, "there could be something . . . Pen can talk to Reach—maybe she can rein him in."

"For how long?" the grey boy asked. "A night and a day? Long enough for her to warn whichever humans she wants to warn, maybe, but it doesn't make any difference to us, does it? In the end the whole city's going to be

one big Demolition Field, nothing but lifeless rubble. London will be dead."
He paused. His head was still pillowed on his arms, but his eyes were as
hard as the promise of a winter sky. "That's your plan, after all."

Beth ran her tongue against the inside of her teeth. They felt too big,
too blocky in her mouth. "It was dying anyway," she managed

"There might have been a way to save it."

"There was no time," Beth shot back. "It was spreading—everyone, everything was in danger. I had to help—"

She broke off as he arched a dusty eyebrow.

"You did this for everyone and everything, did you?" he asked scepti-
cally. "Go on, finish your sentence. You 'had to help—?'"

She just stared at him.

"It's okay, Beth. Thames knows you can say her name, here of all places.
Her face is graffiti'd fifty feet high on most of the walls."

"Pen." Beth swallowed. "I had to help Pen." Why was she so shy of saying that out loud? Was it because she knew that if helping Pen had meant
giving this whole wretched island to the Crane King's claws, she would
have done that too?

The grey boy kept looking at her. "And that's why you woke Reach, was
it? And in such a hurry, too."

"There was no time—"

"You have no idea how much time there was." His voice was flat, and
hard as concrete.

"No."

"Answer me," he said quietly. "Is helping Pen the reason you woke
Reach?"

"Of course it is, Fil."

He frowned and pursed his lips: a pantomime of puzzlement, then
he straightened and pushed himself up onto the parapet. He tiptoed up
and down the edge of the bricks with his arms thrown out, like he was a
tightrope artist.

"Does it make you feel better," he asked, "calling me that?"

She glared at him. "What else am I supposed to call you?"

"Oh, I don't know," He lifted one leg up straight and pirouetted to face her, perfect as a music-box ballerina. "Childhood outlookss, proclivitiesss and memoriesss?"

The face remained his, but the voice was Johnny Naphtha's. He straightened an imaginary tie at his naked throat.

"Bit of a mouthful. I'll stick with Fil."

"You can call me whatever you like. Your skull, your rules." He squinted up at the clouds. "But we both know I'm not Filius Viae. I'm as much as could be saved of him, maybe, but that's not remotely the same thing." His mouth twisted like there was something unpleasant in it. "Trust me. I remember the difference."

He jumped back down, and his feet crunched in the roof's flat gravel. "So, does calling me that make you feel better?" he asked again.

"About what?"

"About the spear you wielded, about the life you took. About killing Filius Viae."

Beth stared at him, open-mouthed. "You TOLD me to—"

"He told you," he corrected. "And what possible difference would that make? Does it make you feel better, calling me Fil?"

"Yes!" she snapped at him. "A bit. Maybe. Are you happy now?"

He made a little noise in the back of his throat and turned back to look at the cranes.

"What was that noise about?" Beth demanded.

"What noise?"

"That little 'hmmm-that-was-interesting' noise."

"Nothing," he said. "I'm just spotting a pattern."

Beth had had enough of this. "Oh, you can piss off right now."

"Where to?" He gestured to the blocky grey towers that rose around them and smiled, but there was no humour in it. "Why did you wake Reach?"

Beth glared at him. She felt a blank anger rising in her. She hugged herself, as though that could keep it in. Across the skyline, lights flickered.

"To protect the rest of the country."

"Why did you wake Reach?" he asked again, his voice not changing at all.

"To help Pen."

"Why did you wake Reach?"

"I had no choice—"

"Why did you—?"

"BECAUSE WHY THE FUCK NOT?" She screamed it at him so hard it ripped her throat raw, so hard the earth under them shuddered and the clouds above them turned black. On the building behind her, the rhino snorted and strained at the bricks that held it.

Because the city was killing her, and it was in the palm of her hand. Why not squeeze? Finally, after months of feeling so weak, so helpless, just for an instant she'd felt powerful again. Because she was lonely, and it hurt. And yes, it did make her feel better calling this grey-skinned memory by Fil's name—but not nearly enough to make up for the fact that it wasn't really him.

She remembered his warning, whispered inside her skull: don't say it. Once you say it you can't take it back. And so she'd said it, safe in the knowledge that after that it would be too late.

"And so," Fil went on. His voice carried on seamlessly from the voice inside her. "And so the city dies, and you get to wake up the next morning, and the next, and if you're lucky, maybe one or two more after that, until, starved of the city's energy, you die too. And you never have to say to anyone—not to Pen or Glas or me or even yourself—that you did it on purpose."

His gaze bored into her. "Because you gave up," he said.

"Yes," she said quietly.

He pursed his lips, then looked thoughtful.

"Okay," he said.

Beth blinked. "What?"

"I said okay." He propped himself up onto the ledge. "It's no big deal."

"It's not?"

"Nah." He dismissed it with a wave. "You just have to un-give up."

She gaped at him, her breath taken away by the unfairness—by the presumption—of that statement. "I don't know if I can do that, Fil," she said testily.

He shrugged, as if to say that was up to her.

She leaned against the parapet next to him, but only, she told herself, because he was warm. He put his arm around her, and she let him. Yes, there was the heat she remembered: like a coal-fired furnace radiating from his ribs.

She shivered in spite of it. "Doesn't the sun ever come out here?" she wondered, peering at the clouds. The strange grey light that filtered through them made her eyes hurt.

"Dunno," he said. "Want me to wait with you and find out?"

She snorted. "Generous bloody offer. Where else would you go?"

He looked behind them, down at the crisscrossing streets. "This is your mind, right? All those red-hot fantasies you've been dreaming up about me must be around here in one of these buildings. I thought I'd take a look."

"If you can find them," Beth remarked drily, "let me know. I'll burn the place down. Also, you're a dick. Also, yes."

"Yes?"

She pushed tighter into him and settled her head against his collarbone. "Wait with me."

CHAPTER TWENTY-NINE

The dawn light entered the sky over London like sand in an hourglass, and Pen raced against it.

She worked as fast and methodically as she could. She knew she'd never get everywhere, so she limited herself to those places where she'd heard of people gathering in large numbers and which bordered the sickness-stricken streets that were about to become a battleground; that left her twelve destinations to cover and almost no time.

She worked her way anti-clockwise through the city, starting at a shattered bus garage in Lewisham, then moving north to Liverpool Street Station, and then northwest to an old Kosher store in Finchley where the same old couple who had run it for the past twenty years were still brewing up soup for the gaunt-faced people camped outside.

The people she met were, almost without exception, terrified of her. *In fairness*, she supposed, *I am pretty terrifying*: a scar-faced metal Medusa, barbed wire coiling around her head like ophidian hair.

She felt a brief glimmer of satisfaction at how off-balance they looked when the first word out of her mouth was, "*Please.*"

She knew by how they reacted to that first syllable whether she had them or not. If they looked puzzled by her plea, it meant they weren't so scared they weren't listening, and if they were *listening*, they were usually prepared to believe.

After all, she reasoned, if she were them and a girl cocooned in barbed-wire stilt-walked up to *her* and told her she'd come to save her life, she'd figure the normal standards of scepticism had pretty much gone out of the window too.

Breathlessly, she gave directions and instructions to get to Crystal Palace by the morning. *You've got a few hours*, she told them, *eight at the most, before this place becomes a killing ground. Head for the radio tower—it's still standing. You can make it. Go now.*

You can make it . . .

For some—the old folks from Finchley and the sweating man from Lewisham who'd seared his foot to uselessness on a Fever Street—that was almost certainly a lie.

"*Come with us*," a black girl with cornrows had asked her. It was her tone that stuck with Pen; she wasn't begging or demanding, just solemn and certain. "*If you're serious about helping, then show us the way. I don't think we can make it by ourselves.*" She'd spoken softly so the three younger brothers she'd been getting ready to go wouldn't hear. She'd thrown Pen's tactical "*Please*" back at her: "*Please, show us the way.*"

She couldn't have been more than thirteen, but there was no time. Pen had apologised, over and over, as she'd backed out of the dusty storeroom, for the first time feeling like the monster she looked.

The moon was already waning in the sky as she spider-picked her way towards Victoria. Two stops left—and she dreaded arriving at the final one almost as much as she feared running out of time. The last hour of the night stretched around her, and her passage through it felt impossibly slow. The sensation was familiar, but it took her a moment to put her finger on why; when she did, she almost laughed. It was just like the night she'd not been able to sleep before her Maths GCSE, dreading the dawn, while at the same time desperate for the wait to be over.

Cranes punctured the skyline and at the base of them a supermarket took up the corner of the junction. Back before everything had kicked off, this Sainsbury's was the poshest place she'd ever set foot in where you could buy a raw turnip. She remembered joking with Beth as they'd walked through the aisles, pretending to guess which of the shoppers were somebody's butler and whispering in bad fake RP accents about how they'd take that Camembert back to the mansion and let Alfred prepare it for the children. For some reason they'd found the range on offer in the cheese section particularly hilarious.

Now the windows were shattered and black tentacles of cable dangled from behind the giant neon letters of the shop sign. Voices whispered from inside. Pen hesitated, then picked her way over the broken glass, and started her spiel. "Please," she announced to the gloomy interior, "my name is Parva Khan and I've come to warn you that you're in terrible danger. Tomorrow this place will be a battlefield, and you all—"

She faltered as her brain caught up with her eyes. There was no *all*: the aisles stood empty; the shelves had been stripped bare. Even the strip-light covers flapped open, their bulbs salvaged for heaven knew what reason. Pen could only see by the light that washed in through the saw-toothed remains of the windows by the entrance. She walked slowly past row after row of empty shelves. The place was deserted.

Until she reached the last aisle on the right.

The woman sat stiff-backed and cross-legged on a pile of cushions at the end of what Pen thought might have been the kitchenware section. A TV set flickered on the floor in front of her, plugged into an extension lead that snaked away behind the shelves. The voices Pen had heard crackled from its speakers. The shelves around her were full of objects, but from where she stood, Pen couldn't make out what they were.

She paced slowly up the length of the aisle, making sure her steel-bound feet rang on the tiles. If the woman wasn't deaf—and the TV was set to a normal volume, suggesting she wasn't—she had to have heard Pen. The woman looked about seventy, South Asian, with sharp cheekbones and a sharper jaw. Her greying hair was scraped back into a bun. She wore an immaculately pressed dark green jacket and was sipping occasionally from a steaming glass. The medicinal scent of herbal tea hit Pen's nostrils.

"Er, excuse me?" Pen said.

"Yes?" The woman glanced up at her and smiled politely. If the cut-glass accent was anything to go by, she might have been royalty. "Can I help you?"

"I—I thought there would be more people here."

"There were." The woman said, and sipped her tea thoughtfully.

"Er—okay, well, could you tell me what happened to them? There's something they need to hear."

"They left. One of those glowing blue dragon things flew down this road one evening, and a few of them got cold feet and departed. That put the wind up a few others, and soon everyone but me had run off." She frowned as though this was incomprehensible behaviour. "Honestly, it's not as though the bloody thing actually came *in* here."

"Oh—okay," Pen said uncertainly. "Well, you should probably get ready to go. There's a battle—"

"A battle coming. Yes, I heard you the first time. Parva, was it? Thank you for your concern, but I'm afraid it's quite out of the question." She stood, straightened out her jacket and busied herself arranging the objects on her shelves. "Would you like some tea? Only chamomile, I'm afraid; it's all they left behind."

Pen stared at her. "You heard me say *battle*, right?" she asked. "A big one. If I tell you that the people fighting are the ones who control the glowing blue dragons, not to mention twelve-foot-long wolves made out of scaffolding, you . . ." She almost laughed. "You still won't have any idea of how big it's going to be. Seriously, they'll tear this place apart, and you with it, if you stay."

"That's a pity," the woman said amiably, and sipped her tea. She winced slightly. "Ghastly stuff," she murmured.

Pen stared at her. "I'm not kidding, lady," she said. "You really can't stay here."

"I don't think you are kidding, Parva, but I really can."

"What are you so attached to it for? It's a ransacked bloody Sainsbury's!" Pen almost shouted it at her.

"Is it?" The woman blinked at her, her mouth an "O" of mock surprise. She looked at the white-painted shelves surrounding the little den she'd made for herself. "So it is. Have that cup of tea, why don't you? The water's still hot, and I must say it's very nice to have a visitor, even if her manners leave a little to be desired."

Pen glanced back towards the door. The light coming through it had a definite bluish tinge now: the day was coming on fast. But this place was the second-to-last on her list, and the final one was . . .

"A quick one," she said, wondering if, for some reason, the woman might find her more convincing with a cup of pointless floral water in her hand.

The woman brightened considerably. She fumbled behind her for a kettle and poured steaming water into a small saucepan, into which she dumped a yellow-tagged teabag. She prodded at it with a wooden spoon for a few seconds, then decanted the contents into a second novelty glass and handed it to Pen.

"Ghastly stuff," she said again with a smile.

"Thanks," Pen said. And then, "But seriously, why won't you—?"

She broke off because for the first time she'd seen what the objects on the shelves actually were: two silver-framed photos, brightly polished, showing the woman in her younger days, standing with a man in a hat and smiling, an alarm clock, a string of pearls, a few rings, and a small wooden statuette of the sort that might have been whittled for a little girl by a father who was good with his hands. Pen's throat was suddenly dry.

"I had to leave my home, you see," the woman said. Her voice was quiet and even. "The street outside it became so unbearably hot, and Amjad—" She broke off, frowned a little and gave a small shake of her head, like there was something she didn't understand.

"I took what I could—even these cushions are from my sofa—and I left. I thought there might be food here, so here I came and tried to set up again." Again, that puzzled frown. "I've done my best, I really think I have, but it didn't work. I don't expect it would work any better somewhere else."

She smiled almost apologetically at Pen, like she was inconveniencing her. "It was just the two of us, you see. We never had any children, so it was just us."

Pen swallowed hard. She sat beside the old woman, her tea clasped in both hands. "I understand."

"I do hope not." The woman's smile didn't waver. "Girl your age—I mean, I really do hope not." She cocked her head slightly. "Where are your family from, dear?"

"Pakistan. My mum and dad are from Karachi."

"Ah." The woman smiled happily. "I grew up in Lahore—have you ever been to Lahore?"

Pen shook her head.

"Shame; you should go if you can. Parva—that's an unusual name. I don't think I've ever met anyone called that."

Pen ran the hot edge of the glass under her lower lip. "My full name is Parveen, but no one calls me that any more."

"Oh really?" The woman raised her eyebrows. "Why ever not? Didn't you like it?"

"I liked it fine."

"So why?"

Pen paused. It occurred to her that this was an odd thing to be telling a stranger, but somehow she felt like she owed this woman a story in exchange for her own. "My mum, she had cancer when I was a kid—in her breast to start with, but it spread to her mouth. She had chemotherapy and it went into remission, but for a couple of months she . . . couldn't talk very well."

The old woman's gaze was sharp. "She couldn't pronounce your name?"

Pen nodded slowly, remembering. "Something about the wide mouth shape for the 'e.' 'Parva' was as close as she could get. She tried not make a big deal out of it, but you could see how much it upset her, so—"

"—so you changed it."

"Dad and I started saying Parva too."

"So she wouldn't be wrong any more."

Pen sipped her tea and didn't answer.

"Was that your idea, or your father's?" the woman asked.

"Does it matter?" Pen asked sharply.

"Yes, I think it does."

"It was mine." She looked into the woman's eyes, feeling almost belligerent. *So what of it?*

The old woman tapped her fingertips on her glass for a few seconds. "So now people call you Parva."

"Some people do. Some people call me Countess—really, don't ask—and some people, well, one person in particular at least, calls me Pen. I like Pen best, I think."

"Well, then, I should like to call you Pen," the woman said, and added courteously, "if it's not imposing on that one person in particular."

Pen smiled. "It's not. And I think I'd like that too."

"And I'm Nabila." She extended a hand and Pen shook it; the grip was gentle, but warm.

"Would you like some more tea?"

"No, thanks," Pen said reluctantly. "I still have one more place to get to and I think it's time for me to go." The hot tea sat in her stomach, settling her.

"I understand," the woman said.

"We're gathering at Crystal Palace. Gutter—A friend of mine is organising food and shelter, and he can get pretty much anything, anywhere. Are you sure you won't come? I really believe you'd make it."

Nabila smiled and shook her head. She didn't look at the photos on the mantelpiece, but she did clasp her hands together and squeeze until the knuckles paled. "I believe I would too," she said. "But I'll stay."

"Thank you for the tea." Pen drained her glass, stood and, a little absurdly, looked around for somewhere she could wash it up. Failing to find anywhere, she put it on the shelf next to the carving.

For some reason Nabila nodded approvingly. "Thank you for the visit, Pen."

Pen blew through the Clapham Junction Asda in about three minutes flat. The two dozen or so men and women camped out there listened in silence, their eyes as wide as ten-pence pieces, as she explained to them what was going on. Then they got up and left; whether they were making for Crystal Palace or just trying to get as far away as possible from the barbed-wire-wrapped girl, Pen didn't know, nor did she have the time to care. The light of sunrise was already showing through the windows.

She'd turned back towards the doors, ready to head for home, when she felt a twitch through the wire.

"Oh for mercy's sake!" she yelled at the empty shelves. Her instincts told her to just keep walking, to leave the store, head for the radio mast and not look back.

She wavered for a moment, and then . . .

"Fine!" She turned around, kicking out as she did so and sending a couple of unoffending tins of baked beans rolling across the floor. Pain flared in her toe and she limped for a moment, her ears burning. Muttering furiously, she headed out to the car park.

A pair of massive steel industrial bins had been pushed up close against the store's back wall, and on the rim of the right-most one, a little two-link strand of barbed wire perched almost coyly.

She took a breath to steady herself, clapped her hands over the metal lip and pulled herself up. "Up," she snapped. "Out."

Salt gawped up at her from the bottom of the bin. The black plastic bags he was cowering against had split open and were seeping milky fluids that smelled of spoiled fish and liquefying vegetables. Pen crouched on the edge; looking down she felt the familiar fury rise in her stomach. Yes, she still hated him, and there was still a tremor of anxiety in her knuckles and jaw. But at least looking at him didn't make her hate *herself* as much as it used to.

She wrinkled her nose. "Of all the places to hide, you couldn't pick one that didn't smell like a landfill site? I get enough of this with bloody Gutterglass—"

He gaped up at her.

She was babbling, covering for the old fear. Still, it was a small satisfaction—but satisfaction nonetheless—to see that fear reflected back in his face. She sucked her teeth and sat back on her haunches.

"To be honest, I'm surprised you're still here," she said. "I expected you to try and run for it."

"I . . . I tried, but—" His eyes darted to the little strand of wire sitting on the edge of the bin. She imagined the tiny thing inching gamely after him. He'd given up almost as soon as he'd begun.

"—I didn't know where else to go."

His voice shocked her. He didn't even sound like the Salt she remembered. He'd always been so harsh, so certain, as though the entire world stood behind his words and he *knew* it, but now . . .

"The city's so strange now. It's not safe."

Pen flashed him a humourless smile. "You don't know the half of it. You're making me late, Dr. Salt, so get up."

He went back to gaping at her, so she hissed impatiently and saw him flinch.

"Believe it or not—and I scarcely believe it myself—but I am trying to do you a favour. In a couple of hours this place will be a battleground. This is me saving your life."

He locked his jaw and looked her in the eye. "Why don't I do *you* a favour and just stay here and die then," he muttered.

"Don't be such a fucking child," Pen snapped scornfully. "If that's what I wanted, I'd kill you myself. You're going to do what you're told, and right now, I'm telling you to live. If I change my mind, trust me, you'll be the first to know."

He scuttled back on his arse, pressing his back to the metal. Pen rolled her eyes.

The wire whipped around his wrists in an eye-blink and he shrieked as it tightened, even though she kept the barbs out of his skin. With a light tug, she sent him flying out of the bin, screaming. He hit the tarmac with a hard, flat sound and lay there, wheezing and staring at her with panicked eyes.

"Get up," she snapped at him.

"I . . . I think you dislocated my arm." His skin was pale with the pain of it.

"Good thing you don't walk on your arms then, isn't it? Get up."

Gingerly, he pushed himself up, cradling his right elbow against his chest. He stared at her sullenly.

"Walk," Pen said flatly, "or I can drag you. Which will hurt, a lot. A fact which, I promise you, causes me no hesitation whatsoever."

He exhaled and his shoulders dropped. He wouldn't run for it, Pen realised. He was too scared of her. For some reason she couldn't put her finger on, she felt sick, deep in the pit of her stomach.

"Walk," she said anyway, and he walked.

CHAPTER THIRTY

"You have got to be kidding me. Him?"

Beth was standing under the radio tower, rubbing her face like she'd just woken up and staring suspiciously, first at Salt, then at Pen, then back to Salt again. A knot in Pen's stomach came apart at the sight of the city-skinned girl on her feet, even if she was leaning on the spear like it was a crutch. She threw her arms around Beth and gave her a tight, exhilarated hug, though the slate and asphalt of Beth's skin felt uncomfortably hot against hers.

It had taken them two hours to walk back, with Pen pacing behind Salt all the way. The shadow she cast across him grew slowly shorter as the sun rose. She could have snatched him up in her steel coils and covered the distance in a quarter of the time, but the Mistress was raging in her head about the delay and with the barbs that close to Salt's neck, Pen wasn't sure she trusted her control.

They'd struggled up the hill and found hundreds of people, those she'd warned, already here, and her heart leaped despite her exhaustion. A few of them were standing around gaping at the hulking metal forms of the Scaffwolves, but most were engaged in work of some kind—building fires, scraping the mould off potatoes, soaking clothes in scavenged washing-up tubs. Every few minutes another flock of pigeons flew in, struggling under the weight of a sack of rice or corn gripped in their collective claws. She looked around for Gutterglass and found him a few feet away, muttering to a young black kid who was skinning what looked like a fox with one of the trash-spirit's scalpels. When Glas saw Pen, he beetled over immediately.

"Wow," Pen murmured, "respect, Glas. You got them working fast."

"Indeed," Gutterglass said shortly. "They can't stay here."

"What are you talking about? This place is perfect—there's plenty of space, there's no concrete for the Masonry Men to come up through, and it's miles away from where the fighting's going to be."

"It *was* perfect," the trash-spirit murmured testily. "Now it's a death-trap. Some of them were keeling over from hunger so I'm organising a meal, but after that they're going to need to march straight away."

"I don't understand," Pen protested blankly.

Gutterglass lifted his cardboard chin in the direction of the kid he'd just been talking to. "Angelo," he called. "Come here."

The kid left his half-skinned fox carcase in the grass and ran over. He looked about ten. His face was neutral, his hands covered in blood. With a little jolt, Pen recognised him: he was one of the brothers of the girl with the cornrows, the one who'd begged her to guide them out of Liverpool Street.

"Tell Miss Khan what happened to your sister," Gutterglass told him.

"She got snatched," Angelo said woodenly. There was no emotion in his voice at all, and he didn't meet Pen's eyes. She wondered if the same thing had happened to his parents. "Grey man came up through the pavement and took her. We had to run."

It was all Pen could do not to scream.

Beth must have read her expression because she said, "*Thanks, Angelo. How 'bout you carry on getting that fox ready.*"

The kid kissed his teeth and glared at her for dismissing him like that, but he ran back to the corpse he was skinning.

"I . . ." Pen was stuttering, "she—she asked me . . ."

Beth took her hand. "*You did your best; you did really well.*"

"I could have taken longer. I could have taken the time. I could have . . ."

"*Those Fever Streets are almost at Birmingham, and Reach is champing at the bit as it is. His wolves have been prowling like they're caged. You did the right thing, Pen. It's not your fault it went bad. You did the right thing . . .*"

Pen met her gaze and felt tears fill her eyes. "How?" she asked. She knew Beth understood her: how on earth could she know that? How could either of them know that? For Heaven's sake, they were seventeen years old—how could they *do* this?

"*We do what we can,*" Beth said, her voice a soothing traffic purr. "*It's all we can do. And right now, that's finding somewhere new for these people to go.*"

Pen shook her head stolidly. "I met the girl—she was tough, and she has her family to think about. Maybe she won't give us up . . ."

"*You want to take that risk?*"

Pen sniffed back her tears and tried to gather herself. *Do our best*, she thought. Okay.

"Further southeast," she said. "Outside the M25, if they can get there, but as far out of the centre as possible, either . . ." But she tailed off, because Gutterglass was already shaking his head, an alarming motion that made rats' tails show in the gaps between the crushed cans of his neck.

"What?" Pen asked.

"That won't cut it any more, Miss Khan. They'd have nothing to protect them."

"Protect them from what?" she asked.

"From Mirror Mater."

"But as long as they're not with us, why would She *bother*?"

"*Because now She knows more than just where these people are,*" Beth cut in, her green eyes were full of sympathy. "*She knows we care about them.*"

A weight hit Pen's gut.

"*You trust Her not to try and use them against us?*"

Slowly, reluctantly, Pen shook her head. "So they don't just need evacuating," she said. "They need guarding."

"*Yes.*"

"And we don't have any guards."

"*No.*"

Pen tapped her fingers against the wire on the back of her palm as she thought about it. There had to be an answer; there *must* be. She glanced back up at Angelo, busy skinning his fox, and her nails latched into the skin on the back of her palm. There *had* to be.

Alarmingly, the idea that came to her wasn't any worse than most of the ones they'd put into action over the past few days.

"Maybe we don't send them out of the way of the city after all," she said. "Maybe we send them right into it."

Gutterglass' cardboard cheeks crinkled until he looked interested. "What do you mean?" he asked.

Pen blew out her cheeks. "St. Paul's."

"St. Paul's?" He sounded perplexed.

"Reach will fight to defend that place like nowhere else, and his cranes are better protection than anything we could give them."

Beth cocked her head to one side as she considered it. She winced. "*If we lose, it will be the first place She hits.*"

"If we lose, the fever will catch them anyway. Let's at least give them a chance of surviving the fight." Pen looked at Beth. "Like you said, we do all we can."

Beth hesitated, then she nodded curtly.

Gutterglass took his cue from his Goddess. From somewhere under his voluminous layers of black plastic he produced a battered megaphone. "Ladies and gentlemen," he called, "please finish your meals as quickly as you can. We will be departing in thirty minutes . . ."

They ladled soup hurriedly into mugs and ate it fast, burning their mouths. Pen didn't taste a drop. Over the edge of her cup, she watched Salt sitting on the grass on the other side of the tower, shovelling hot potato mush into his mouth.

Beth stumped over and sat down beside her. The green-lit gaze followed Pen's own. "*You let everyone else make their own way, but our dick of a maths teacher gets his own guard of honour? I never figured you had a soft spot for him.*" Even with the city-voice, Beth sounded worried. "*What's going on, Pen?*"

Pen hugged herself. Her thumb caught on a barb and she let the pain blossom through it slowly without moving it. "Let's go somewhere private," she said.

They walked away from the camp, down towards the woods. The day was already heating up and London was a smudge of reddish-grey in the distance. Beth walked with one arm around Pen's waist and used the spear to support her weight in the other. Oscar snored in little gusts inside her hood.

There was a fallen log just inside the treeline. Beth lowered herself onto it gratefully and Pen sat beside her, elbows on her knees, head bowed. A woodlouse wriggled on a blade of grass between her feet.

"B, do you remember the graffiti stunt we pulled, before"—she waved a hand to take in the three prowling Scaffwolves, the fussing trash-spirit and the statues smoking under the radio mast— "all of this?"

"*Sure.*"

"You remember I turned you in."

Beth looked at her sharply. "*Yeah. I was pretty pissed off about it at the time.*"

Pen took a deep breath. "I did it because Salt said he knew your dad hadn't been looking after you and that if I didn't cooperate, he'd call in Social Services and get you rehomed." She snorted. "I don't know if he really could have done it, but at the time, he sounded so sure . . ."

"*Pen, it was nothing—you really don't need to explain yourself to—*"

"B," Pen said sharply, and the sounds of cars and diesel trucks and electric generators beside her died down, "it wasn't the only thing. Turning you in wasn't the only thing he wanted me to cooperate with."

Beth didn't say anything. Pen couldn't tell if she'd already guessed what she was going to say.

"He put his hands on me." The air felt jagged in Pen's throat as she swallowed. "And he made me put my hands on him. He kissed me . . ."

She tailed off. Her neck felt like it was locked solid. Why was it this hard to look Beth in the face? Eventually she managed to turn.

Beth's expression was horrified. "*Did you—? Did he—?*"

"No," Pen said. "But I think what he did was more than enough, don't you?"

Beth's face set. Her eyes found Salt, moving amongst the distant crowd, and she snatched up her spear so fast that her tiled knuckles gouged sawdust from the log. She was halfway to her feet when Pen let a strand of wire uncurl in front of her face.

"If I wanted him dead, B, don't you think he would be?"

Beth sat back down. Slowly she turned away from Salt and looked at Pen. "*I'm so sorry, Pen.*"

"I hold the power of life and death over him. That's not the power I want . . ." Pen realised she was shaking.

Beth pulled her into a hug.

"*I'm so sorry.*" She murmured it into Pen's shoulder. "*What can I do? What do you want? We'll make it happen.*"

"I . . ." Pen faltered. It was the first time she'd ever put it into words, and for some reason it was hard to say. "I want him on trial. I want everyone who knew him and knew me to see. Does that sound stupid? It must do, after everything; it must seem so small. I mean, look at the world we're living in, look at what we're about to do, and yet . . ."

She put her palms on Beth's shoulders, and eased herself back so she could look Beth in the eyes. "It matters to me, B. I can't tell you why, but it does. He made me keep it a secret, and this . . . it feels like the only way to break that."

It was only when Beth reached up to her cheek to thumb a tear away that Pen realised she was crying.

"*Makes sense to me, Pencil Khan. I bet there are courts still running outside London. We'll get him there.*"

Neither of them felt the need to add *if we live* to that sentence.

"There's something else you need to know."

"*Okay.*"

"I could have sent Salt." Pen's heart felt like a lump of pig-iron in her chest as she said the words out loud. "Instead of your dad, I mean. I knew where he was—I could have made him do what I told him. I could have used *him*." Her expression was defiant, almost like she was daring Beth to hate her for that, but Beth just shook her head.

"*No, you couldn't.*"

"What—you wouldn't have let me?"

"*You kidding?*" Beth said. "*I would have let you in a heartbeat, but I don't think you could have. Not you. And even if you'd tried it, Dad would have begged you not to.*"

Pen looked up at her, puzzled. "He let me do it to *him*."

"*That's different, and you know it. You know what he told me, the night before he went? 'Finally, something I can do.'*" Her lip twisted in a bitter smile. "*He chose it, Pen, and that matters.*"

Pen turned the back of her hand, wrapped in wire, to face Beth. "Elizabeth Bradley, I am the last person who needs to be told that."

Beth put her hand on Pen's shoulder. "*You okay?*"

Pen sniffed. "Yeah, except my sinuses feel like they're full of wet cotton wool—you haven't got a tissue on you, have you?"

Beth shook her head. "*Couple of thousand streets of tarmac, some sodium lights, some tiny, tiny cars, but sorry, never a tissue when you need one. What kind of rubbish friend am I?*"

Pen laughed and wiped her face on the edge of her T-shirt.

"Nah, you've got all the major bases covered."

"*How're you feeling?*"

Pen stood and stretched and the muscles along her spine popped. "Warlike," she said.

"*Yeah?*" Beth sounded surprised.

"Not really, but I can fake it."

"*Just as well; I think we're about to get our call.*" She gestured up the hill: Gutterglass was hurrying down to meet them, arms held across his chest to keep the three deflated tyres of his torso in line with one another. When he reached them he was agitated, and his scavenged hands fidgeted.

"What is it, Glas?" Pen asked sharply.

"You won't believe this," he replied.

"*Not if you don't actually tell us, no,*" Beth observed, her voice underlined with a dry motor-purr.

"Lady Bradley, Miss Khan"—he beamed from molten candlewax ear to molten candlewax ear—"I have actual, *genuine* good news."

CHAPTER THIRTY-ONE

"*What is it with you and maps?*" Beth demanded.

Gutterglass didn't reply; he just stood there, arms folded, his eggshells set on a pair of pigeons wheeling overhead against the blue.

Beth looked down at the model; it was similar to the one they'd left behind at Selfridges, with cardboard streets and coathanger bridges over a silver-foil river. A single intact water bottle stood in the centre, surrounded by rat-runs of shredded plastic. Only the new districts were different: a few tendrils of housing snaked out to the west and the southeast, and most strikingly, the long sharp spike that stretched northwest into the grass, many times the length of the original city, as though London were a pendulum and this new bit of city its chain.

On the far side, a long column of people was already trailing down the hill. They carried their still warm saucepans and the unfinished supplies in the sacks over their shoulders. The head of the line was already lost to sight behind the curve of the hill. They were following one of Glas' rats. Three Scaffwolves slouched beside them, drawing shrieks from time to time when they snuffled the people in line. If all went well, the wolves would deliver the humans to the St. Paul's Demolition Field, and guard them there alongside Reach himself.

If all didn't go well . . .

Beth tried not to think about that.

"Glas?" Pen said. "What do you want to tell us? We don't have a lot of time here." She sounded pained, and the wires were twisting disquietedly in the air above her head.

Gutterglass craned his head upwards and held up a Biro index finger. The pigeons dropped like stones towards him, but he didn't flinch; ten feet from his head they flared their wings and slowed before alighting, one on each of his sharp cardboard shoulders. Beth half expected them to perch there like piratical parrots, but instead they each lifted a juice-carton from Glas' body and fluttered off to drop the little boxes on the map at the tip of the city's new northern spur.

Gutterglass gestured grandly. "See?"

Beth and Pen looked at each other.

"Er . . . no," Pen said.

Gutterglass looked a little crestfallen, but he rallied fast. "Only the new districts are growing," he said, his chewing-gum vocal chords twanging visibly through a tear in his newspaper throat. "Chelsea, Camberwell, Tower Hamlets—they're all still the same size they always were, don't you see?"

Pen shook her head slowly. "I'm not sure I—"

But Beth did. "*She doesn't have enough.*"

Gutterglass nodded vigorously.

"*The growth she's stolen—it's not enough for the whole city, so she's concentrating it on the outskirts. That's why the new spur out towards Birmingham's so narrow.*"

"I would surmise that she's trying to reach the next big population centre, so she can obtain more of the . . . the material that fuels the city's expansion." Gutterglass couldn't suppress a smile, and his bottle-cap teeth glinted in his mouth. "Which, admittedly, is moderately terrible news for the people of Birmingham—apologies, Miss Khan—but it's good news for us, because—"

"*—we don't have to kill off the whole city,*" Beth finished for him.

Glas' smile became a full-fledged grin. He pulled a fistful of drinking straws from his coat, planted them on the inner edges of the new districts and bent them over like cranes.

"Best of all, the Crane King is already in place. We can cut the new substance from the city like a tumour from a patient—"

"—and Reach will be the knife," Pen finished. She looked thoughtful.

"*Is that possible, Pen?*" Beth asked. "*Can you persuade Reach to limit himself to shredding the bits of London we tell him to?*"

Pen spread her hands. "I don't know," she said honestly. "I can tell him our help is conditional on it, but once he gets going I don't know if that'll stop him." She tilted her head at the wires crisscrossing her shoulder. "I can probably persuade him to start there, at least."

Gutterglass' smile shrank slightly, but he nodded. He'd take it.

"I hate to be the one to shit in your icing," Petris grunted, "but there's a hole in this plan you could run a Railwraith through."

"What?"

"The enemy," Petris said sourly. "Always a pisser when they get involved, I know, but can't be helped. The second old Rubble-Face gets stuck into Mirror Mater's precious new architecture, She'll bury him in claylings. We were relying on the Demolition Fields being spread through the city so She couldn't get to all of them. If Reach concentrates his attacks like this, he won't stand a chance."

Beth looked at the map and with a little inward shudder remembered the raw speed the Masonry Men showed under the earth. Petris was right. She ran her tongue over the church spires in her mouth, testing their sharpness.

"*What if Mater Viae was busy?*" she asked.

They all looked at her, Petris spraying granite dust as his neck ground around, but the only gaze Beth returned was Pen's.

"*You've read* Lord of the Rings, *right?*" she asked her.

"Nope."

"*Seriously? I watched you read the whole of* Anna-*bloody*-Karenina, *and you haven't read* The Lord of the Rings?"

"Couldn't get past the singing."

"*All these years, I thought I knew you.*" Beth shook her head in mock astonishment, and then began laying out her idea. As she spoke, she could feel the excitement building in her: this was a direction. After so long in hiding, this was action.

"*All through this, there's been one constant in the way Mater Viae's acted, and that's* over-*reaction. Sending a whole plague into the city just to come after me, the sheer number of Masonry Men She threw down on us at Selfridges: that all tells us something: She's smart and She's strong, but She doesn't do subtle. She over-commits. If we went for Her, right where She lives . . .*"

She reached out and toppled the upright water bottle. "*I think She'd hit us with everything She's got.*"

There was a long silence.

"Yay?" Pen said, nonplussed, but Petris got it.

"We keep Her busy horribly murdering us in Canary Wharf," he murmured thoughtfully. "Reach gets a free hand further north." He snorted. "It's simple, at least."

For five full seconds, Pen just stared at him. "You cannot possibly be considering this," she said at last.

"Diversion is a time-honoured military tactic, Miss Khan."

"If you're a hobbit! She's nicked this off a bloody fantasy novel."

"*I don't have a whole lot of field experience, Pen,*" Beth said drily. "*This is what I've got. If any of the actual soldiers here have anything better, I would be over-bloody-joyed to hear it.*"

She looked at Petris. The Pavement Priest stood silent for a minute before uttering the single syllable she'd both expected and dreaded. "No."

"Really?" Pen sounded incredulous. "*Really?* We're going with the strategy from the end of *The Return of the King*?"

"*I thought you hadn't read it.*"

"I've seen the films," she muttered.

"*I bet Glas has read the books,*" Beth said, pointing at the map, but Pen only glared at her.

"Fine," she said at last. "But if we're going to be this stupid, we'd better be this stupid fast. I don't know how much longer I can get Reach to hold off."

Beth shrugged. "*We're ready if you are.*"

Pen was still looking at her, and with an unpleasant prickle, Beth realised she recognised the expression on Pen's face. It was the way Beth had looked at Pen in the kitchen at Selfridges, just before she'd cast her out.

"*What?*"

"I don't think you should come, B."

"*What are you talking about?*"

"Glas?"

"You are *very* unwell, My Lady," Gutterglass said diplomatically.

"*And that means I can't help? Sod that. I don't want to sit this one out.*"

"You want us to win, though, right?" Pen asked.

"*Sure.*"

"Choose."

"*Ouch, Pen.*"

"Sorry."

"*It's okay, I'd rather have it straight.*"

Beth looked at them, and the sheer worry on their faces pushed her wounded pride back down into her chest. She thought about the ache in her muscles and the swelling in her joints; she thought about the prickling fever racing under her skin, and the way that the world blurred when she turned her head too fast. She thought about the slow, hollow ache in her stomach. She hissed in frustration. She was tempted, but her body wouldn't allow anything else.

And then she thought about her dad, dying, staring into space, on his back.

"*My decision?*" She was asking Pen.

Pen hesitated, but then nodded.

"*Then I'm coming.*"

"B—"

A little way up the hill, a small crowd had gathered, watching them: the seven remaining Pavement Priests, Ixia and Astral, their lights burning vaguely against the brightness of the day.

She lowered her voice and jerked a thumb in their direction. "*What does it say to them if I don't?*"

"Does it matter?" Pen said. "There are only nine of them."

Beth said slowly, "*And there's only one of me. And if you're going to go and tangle with a Street Goddess and Her concrete army, then that's where I am too. Even if it kills me.*" She tapped her chest, and then pointed at Pen. "*That's what this means, remember.*"

Pen's lip twisted and she looked down at her feet.

"*If you're there, I'm there.*"

Pen looked up. "Okay. Let's let the Crane King off the leash."

CHAPTER THIRTY-TWO

The jagged wall of the labyrinth reared in front of them. The thirteen of them stood, strung out in a line, eyeing their reflections in the glass.

They hadn't talked much on their trek through the silent city and now they were here, they didn't speak at all. Their heads were bowed, their breathing slow. Pen had a sense they were all putting things in order, moving around their minds like they were untidy houses, setting each thought in its right place. She bowed her head too, even though her own thoughts were anything but orderly. It had taken most of the day to walk here, and the wire's protests had grown fiercer with every step.

Now, the Mistress whispered eagerly, *now*.

Soon, Pen begged back, *very soon*.

The low sun burned in the reflection like the end of a giant cigarette. Beside it the Mistress' strands cast long shadows over Pen's face. The two Lampfolk raised their heads from whatever prayer they'd been saying and started warming up, their limbs growing brighter and brighter. When they'd finished, Ixia held her hand out to Astral and he held his palm above hers. There was an inch of clear air between them. White light mingled with orange. It was as close they'd get to holding hands.

Petris and his Pavement Priests, true to their nature, didn't move at all, but for the flickering of eyelids inside the eyeholes of their masks.

Gutterglass tossed a scalpel end over end, catching it easily in her palm. She'd switched to a female body for the walk without saying why. Now she started to whistle through her plastic lips, and the sound carried starkly in the dry spring air.

And then there was Beth. For once, Pen had no idea what her best friend was thinking. She checked her lead-flashed fingernails and then reversed her grip on the spear: "*Pen*," she asked, "*do you want to pray?*"

Pen shook her head. "I prayed Asr back at Crystal Palace."

"*Okay, then. Care to knock?*"

Pen felt the twitch at the base of her neck as she passed on the suggestion.

Wires lashed forward, hard. The silence shattered as the glass shrieked and dissolved into a glittering cloud. Everyone but Pen flinched and threw their arms across their eyes, but she just peered through the hail at the wire limbs flickering and darting, slashing the walls to tiny shards and bending back steel joists, taking the already broken buildings and tearing them further down. There was a hot taste in her mouth: dust and violence and thunderous noise. The Mistress' glee at the destruction flowed back into her.

And then it was over: the last of the broken glass tinkled as it settled on the ground, and then the silence returned. A path through the labyrinth gaped in front of them, fringed by fractured glass and twisted steel. At the end of it, hazed slightly by the distance, rose Canary Wharf.

Beth shot her a look, one eyebrow raised as if to say, *Yikes, Pen!*
Pen's fractional smile said, *I know.*

As one, they started forwards.

They walked steadily, their eyes fixed on the tower as it drew closer. Stone growled over stone as the Pavement Priests advanced. Pen's heart was slamming at the base of her throat. She wanted to scream, to run—forwards or back—or do *anything* but keep this maddening pace. But she couldn't. They had to give their enemy enough time.

The powdered glass crunched underfoot like snow. *Why is it always glass?* Pen asked herself, desperate to distract herself from her own fear. She remembered the cavernous chamber underneath the Shard in the mirror-city, with the broken bottles carpeting the floor and Mater Viae's green eyes shining through the dark.

She's the monster who burst through the mirror, she decided. *It kind of makes sense that glass is the trail She leaves in Her wake.*

Lost in her thoughts, she almost didn't react as the wire sprang off her palm towards the ruins. "No!" she hissed, jerking it frantically back. It snapped and hissed at her disconsolately. "Not yet."

The tower was close now. Pen couldn't see the tip of its pyramidal roof any more. The throne was on the far side and the growing sound of the waterfall suggested Mater Viae was still sitting atop it, but Pen knew She knew they were there.

The ground shuddered under them. Pen lurched, but recovered her balance.

The glass carpeting the floor sounded like wind chimes as it resettled.

"Beth," Pen said.

"*I see it.*"

Ahead of them, a single emaciated figure stood at the mouth of the passageway. Pen watched its clay-covered ribcage swell as it breathed. Two more Masonry Men breached behind it, landing in total silence, the liquid street dripping from their limbs.

"*Steady,*" Beth ordered.

With every step it became harder not to run. The ground shuddered again and again in waves. More and more grey figures burst from the asphalt ahead of them, rank upon rank of them, erupting from the road like they'd been grown from it. They blocked off all light from the end of the passage.

"What are they waiting for?" one of the Pavement Priests muttered.

"Us," Pen said. She was struck by how lonely the thirteen of them must have looked, delivering themselves up to an army. "They want to know what we're doing."

A single clayling stepped forward from the front rank. He moved his mouth and his ribs strained against his skin like he was shouting, but Pen heard no words. "B—"

"*Steady.*"

The Mistress raged in her mind. "Beth, I don't know how long I can—"

Motion rippled through the claylings. They arched their backs, put their hands flat forwards like blades.

"B—"

"*Now, Pen!*" Beth cried.

Pen didn't even feel herself ask the wire; it uncoiled from her hip and shot into a crevice in the ruins. Its barbs shrieked down to metal buried somewhere under the rubble, and then that rubble began to move.

Slabs of broken window slid to the ground as the metal beneath them shifted. Rust sprayed as bolts spun and locked and steel poles slid into place. Growling their hollow growls, Scaffwolves rose from their haunches and prowled forwards.

Rats chittered, beetles buzzed and Gutterglass' form sprouted a dozen more arms. She was armoured in wrecked car panels and scrap-metal, wielding blades of sheared-off girder.

A small dark shape flitted from Beth's hood. The air filled with an acrid scent and then Oscar ignited in a burst of heat so intense that Pen flinched away. Beth flung herself easily onto the Sewermander's broad neck. A Scaffwolf loped up beside Pen and she dragged herself onto it.

Ahead of them, the front rank of Masonry Men dived. The road swallowed them like water.

Go, go! Pen urged the Mistress. Her wolf surged forwards, metal paws ringing, and behind it, its brethren followed. They made it five bounds before the road in front of them began to ripple; six before the Masonry Men struck.

Dark grey figures burst from the ground a bare inch ahead, their fingers hooked. Pen felt their musty breath on her face and her own breath stalled, but the wire was ready. She was its host, its ally, its only refuge, and she could feel how determined it was to protect her. It whirled through the air, slicing down claylings like they were falling leaves. Her wolf snapped and snarled; its fangs punctured a grey torso. The creature's scream was all but silent.

The world was full of grasping limbs, concrete teeth and snapping wire. A hand clamped onto Pen's arm and she was dragged sideways from her mount. A skeletal grey face gaped to bite her; she screamed, and unloaded a palm full of barbs into its open mouth. The head exploded and blood like hot liquid clay coated her face. Pain tore through her leg. Her head swam and she looked down to see a Masonry Man had his fingers up to the knuckle in her calf. Blood was soaking through her jeans. The thing clung on grimly, bouncing and jerking in time with the wolf's bounds. She whipped the wire across its back and heard the crack as its spine snapped. It rolled away in the dust.

Waves of pain from her leg dizzied her. She felt sick. "Tour—" she gasped, then, "tourniquet."

The wire didn't need to be told; it was already lashing around her calf, cinching in tightly enough to make Pen hiss with pain. Her toes tingled into numbness. She dragged herself back into the saddle and pressed her face to the cold steel of the wolf's neck. The wire was a blizzard of metal above her, shielding her. Her lungs burned, her eyes were wide and the rushing air chilled their moist surface. Between the struts she spied Gutterglass, keeping pace on a constantly renewing conveyor belt of wriggling rats. Her trash arms windmilled and blurred, chopping at the grey bodies constantly springing at her.

Something flickered at the edge of her vision and a Pavement Priest appeared, his punishment skin stained with dark brown blood. His widespread arms took two Masonry Men around the waist and Pen heard the snapping of their bones as he crushed them. He stopped and dropped their bodies. Through a gash in his stone armour, Pen could see his chest heaving as he fought for breath. He sucked down two more lungfuls before clay hands ripped through the floor and dragged him under.

Don't stop, Pen thought, terrified, her nostrils full of her own blood, *whatever you do, don't stop.*

A wave of heat passed overhead: Beth swooped low into the mêlée in front of her, Oscar's wings spread wide in a wall of blue fire. In her wake she left blackened corpses, posed like statues.

An instant later Pen and the rest of the Scaffpack bounded through them, and they exploded into hot ash that blinded her and seared her skin. She choked and spat, trying to get it out of her mouth.

The labyrinth gave way around them and they burst out into Canada Square. Above the clatter of metal paws, Pen heard human screams and the roar of falling water. Oscar craned his burning head and shot upwards, Beth hunched forwards on his back, and Pen clawed ash from her eyes, peering after them. In the middle of the sky, four hazy, fiery shapes were beating their wings to intercept. Pen's heart shrank to a pinpoint in her chest, but she snarled at herself to focus.

Beth has to look after Beth.

Her wolf slowed under her: clay hands were clamped onto its steel struts. Grey bodies were using it to pull themselves out of the surface of the road. The other wolves were slowing too. They whirled and snapped, their progress halted, hemmed in by a sea of hands. Pen felt the boom of a shockwave, gaunt figures fell like cornstalks and she knew that somewhere one of the Lampies was still breathing—but still more claylings surged up from the ground between the corpses of their fallen comrades. There was no end to them.

Pen's stomach lurched sickeningly: her wolf was sinking. It howled its metal howl and snapped and struggled, but its legs were trapped in strong grey hands and the asphalt was seeping up its limbs like quick-mud.

Pen shoved herself from the wolf's back and hit the concrete hard. Wires hissed and struck like snakes as the Mistress shielded her. Her wolf was torso-deep in the ground. It bent its steel head back and bayed. Pen lashed wires to it and strained, desperately trying to pull it free, but it was stuck fast. Clayling arms grabbed its neck and twisted with obscene strength. Its howl cut off. Pen laid desperately about herself with the wire. Grey bodies filled her view from edge to edge.

"*Pen!*" Beth's voice echoed down, loud as a collapsing building. "*How are you doing?*"

"Like"—she gasped for breath—"like a rotten apple in a maggot farm!"

She had no idea how Beth heard her over the noise, but the answer came back sharp. "*Then I think it's time, don't you?*"

Pen bent her head, and a single wire leapt straight upwards from the back of her neck. It unwound fast, fifty, a hundred feet into the air, straight as an antenna. From the edge of the labyrinth, a dark line split the air as a second wire whipped in to meet it.

Pen shuddered as the two strands touched. The Wire Mistress' consciousness rippled through her body like an electric shock and then shot outwards. She raced with it, down the metal, leaping from wire to wire, across walls and fences and under foundations: all in a fraction of an eye-blink: a vast steel synapse firing.

In her mind's eye, she saw cranes rearing over building sites in the outskirts of the city like the skeletons of extinct giants. She felt the wire stretch for them, eager with news, and felt their battle cry, just as eager, humming back down the metal strand into her heart:

I will be.

I will be.

I WILL BE!

On a distant battlefield, the Crane King tore joyously into his work, and Pen was the first to know.

The first, but not by much.

Four seconds later, on Her throne on the top of Canada Tower, Mater Viae screamed.

CHAPTER THIRTY-THREE

It was a scream of shearing steel and tumbling brick, of steam searing through pipes and trains crashing into viaduct walls. It was a scream of the grief of a city, pouring from the roof of Canada Tower and filling the sky like smoke, and it all but threw Beth from Oscar's back.

She clung on grimly, winding her fingers into the rope-like currents of flowing gas in his neck. The wind shoved her hoodie into her mouth and she spat it out. Under and around her, Oscar's fire guttered as Mater Viae's Sewermanders hovered around him, hemming him in and flexing flame-etched claws as they strained to strip the methane from his back. "*Come on, buddy*," she whispered desperately to him. "*Come on, buddy, you got this.*"

But he didn't have it. He flapped his wings like a moth in a hurricane, but the other gas-drakes were too powerful and he couldn't escape. His wings were losing coherence, streaming away from him in traceries of blue flame, and he reared back, crackling and whispering in panic.

Beth stretched down through the fire and brushed his muddy-coloured back. *Trust me*, she sent the thought to him. *Now.*

Oscar went out.

They fell together, end over end, graceless as wounded birds, and past her flailing limbs Beth glimpsed the four other Sewermanders blundering into each other as the force that held them apart vanished. They baffled each other with their wings, tangled each other in their thermals. Beth spun in midair. Roaring filled her ears, blotting out even Mater Viae's shrieking. Oscar whipped his little brown tail in a frantic helix. A sour smell stung Beth's nostrils, but it was too late. She squeezed her eyes shut as the asphalt stormed up.

With a booming roar, blue flame ignited under her, scorching her clothes, but washing harmlessly over her tiled skin. Oscar swooped, skimming the earth and incinerating the weeds that peeped through the concrete.

She clenched a fist in jubilation. *Attaboy.*

She looked back over her shoulder. The gas dragons had already disentangled themselves and were beating their wings, hot in pursuit.

Fine, she thought. As long as they were on her, they weren't on Pen.

Faster now, Ozzie—come on.

They looped and slalomed around the hulks of ruined buildings. Another look back showed her two of the drakes were tracking them, chasing the burnt air they'd left in their wake, but the other two . . .

Beth's stomach plunged. The other two had banked off.

Up, she urged Oscar, *up. I need to see.*

He bent his neck and climbed, careless of the closing angle between him and his pursuers. The shattered city fell away before them. Beth clung to his neck with her hands and knees, desperately scanning the ground for the wire-wrapped girl.

There! A whirling cloud of glinting steel, tiny in the distance. The grey figures teeming around her couldn't get close, and . . .

Beth stared. They were bugging out.

Whorls like fingerprints marked the street where the claylings dived into it. Not all of them—Pen and the Scaffwolves bounding around her still had their hands full—but a lot. In the sky above them, two blue shapes were beating their wings frantically, disappearing to the north.

She's dividing Her forces, Beth thought. *They won't get there in time—they won't. They can't . . .* It was more hope than certainty. Reach had a few minutes at best; it would have to be enough.

A Sewermander scorched through the sky almost on top of them and Oscar wrenched himself into a spiral. Beth shot out an arm as the rival drake overshot and her outstretched fingers *just* tickled scaly skin.

In that instant she felt the little lizard's mind, muddied with methane and velocity and the hunt-and-kill instincts Mater Viae had instilled in it. She had less than half a second.

Go! She shoved the thought at it—and then it was past her and her fingers were smoking and trailing in empty air. The Sewermander beat its wings and surged onwards. She looked after it as it dwindled into the distance. It didn't try to turn.

One left.

She let Oscar bank and turn under her again as Canada Tower loomed into view, bright against the dark red clouds. The final Sewermander swooped down into their line of sight, burning jaws stretched wide, claws spread, heading right for them.

Oscar, Beth thought nervously, *you might want to turn . . . You might . . .*

Oscar smashed straight into the middle of his rival. Beth felt its fire blossom around her—an instant's furious heat—and then it went out. A dark shape that might have been a lizard shot out of view below them. Oscar crowed victoriously and Beth grinned wildly, even while she tried to beat out the flames guttering in her hoodie.

Aren't you the little badass?

He cackled in his quiet fire-crackle voice in response.

Movement snagged her eye: a figure in a bright green T-shirt was racing through the mêlée, dodging wolf and clayling alike. He made it less than a hundred yards before he fell—but no one had hit him. He was clutching at one bare foot. Beth traced his path backwards: bloody footprints led from a building on the east side of the square; broken glass was scattered in constellations on the asphalt outside it. She remembered her dad and the cut on his forehead that wouldn't close.

Beth hunkered down, hanging on to Oscar's neck, and flames guttered past her face as she urged him down. The building rushed up to meet them, and she saw shocked, pale faces through its broken windows: thousands of them. Beth glanced over her shoulder. The tower on the far side of the square looked empty.

Been busy, haven't you, Your Ladyship? she thought grimly.

Ten feet from the pavement she yanked Oscar back and he beat his wings furiously; the backdraught sent the shattered glass skittering and tinkling away up the street.

"*Run!*" she yelled, but they just gaped at her, smudgy and hollow-eyed, in the shadows of the building. "*There's a path: now get out!*"

The boy who moved first couldn't have been older than eight. He wore a Yankees cap on its smallest setting with his afro sticking out underneath it. He scrambled out through the doorway, dancing his naked toes into the spots between the remaining shards of glass, and then bolted headlong round the corner. A second later, everyone was surging for the exit; they boiled out of the gap frantically, eyeing the carnage in front of them with panicked eyes. One girl stumbled in the rush and fell, her hands jerked out instinctively to catch herself—

"*Don't*—" Beth started, but it was too late. Both the girl's hands grazed harshly over the concrete, and when she held them up they were shining, red with blood.

She scrambled to her feet, all the while gaping at her hands in horror. *She knows*, Beth realised with sickening certainty. They all knew—that was what had kept them quiescent in the dark. Beth slid off Oscar's back and all but collapsed. Her legs were jelly, but she stumbled forward, leaning heavily on her spear. She tore strips off the sleeve of her hoodie with her church-spire teeth, and the girl didn't resist when Beth took her hands and bound tight tourniquets around each wrist.

"*That should slow it . . .*" she murmured.

The girl was pale and trembling. Her lips moved like she was trying to speak, but she never made a noise; she just stared at Beth.

"*I . . . I can . . . I can try to*—" Beth's city-voice died away. She tried again. "*I can . . . We could*—"

Once again her voice failed her. She blinked and shook her head. She had nothing left. The girl looked baffled. She tottered away, her treacherous hands held out in front of her like they were poisonous.

"Greetingssss, *thief.*"

The voice was heavy with sibilants. It sounded close in her ear. Beth felt a weight settle into her stomach as she turned.

Canada Square was chaos, a flickering storm of steel-pipe jaws and dripping grey limbs, backed by the constant torrent of Estuary water down Canada Tower. Through the tempest, as calmly as if they were out for a Sunday afternoon stroll, walked five oil-soaked men.

Iron rang off concrete. Beth barely had time to hear the low metallic growl before the Scaffwolf raced out of the mêlée, jaws bared.

Johnny Naphtha didn't break step. A slick of crude oil flooded out from under his feet, like they were bleeding it. It spread in a wide puddle, right into the path of the wolf.

The Scaffwolf sank through the oil without a sound, barely disturbing the surface, but Johnny walked over the slick like it was solid ground, his grin still in place, his brothers flanking him. They paused at the pavement, their oil slick lapping the kerb. They straightened their ties and cricked their necks, moving as one.

Oscar circled and roared at them; as one they looked up. There were five synchronised snaps as each popped the cap of a Zippo lighter.

"Pleassse," Johnny Naphtha said dismissively.

The Chemical Synod lowered their gaze back to Beth and, despite herself, she fell back a step. She clung to her spear; it was all that was keeping her upright.

"We mussst have wordssss, little Goddesss, about your lack of ressspect for property rightsss." Johnny's voice never rose above a courteous hiss, but Beth heard it over the fracas like he was whispering right in her ear.

"*What . . . ?*" Beth started, but Fil's voice rang in her mind, clear and cold.

He means me.

"If there isss one thing above all othersss," Johnny said, "that we mussst not tolerate, it iss larssceny."

They stepped up onto the pavement, their oil slick flooding out before them, slow but inexorable. Beth backed away from it, terror pulling at her heart. She didn't know where she'd go if she fell through the shiny black surface, but she knew in her gut she'd never see the light again. Desperately, she opened her pores to the pavement, trying to summon *something* to fight them with, but the fever that bolted back up through the soles of her feet made her gag and she collapsed onto her knees, coughing. The oil swept around her in a circle, but it didn't touch her.

The synod advanced, hemming her in against the side of the building.

"Now, *Missss* Bradley . . ." Johnny said as they craned forward.

"BETH!"

The shout was so loud and so anguished that even the synod looked around. Beth struggled to see between their glistening black forms.

Pen was running towards them across the square, her face set in a grimace, blood running down it where the barbs bit. Wires slashed threateningly from her back. Two steps brought her to the edge of the oil slick; wire limbs planted themselves in the asphalt, coiled, ready to spring—

—and then went out from under her. Pen crumpled to her knees on the road. Her eyes wide in shock, she pressed her palms to her temples.

"I couldn't . . ." Beth was reading her lips more than hearing her. "I couldn't hold him . . . He's—"

Fil's voice sounded loud in her head. *He's coming.*

Engines growled; metal clanked on metal. Beth turned, and the Chemical Synod turned, and from the top of her skyscraper waterfall, Beth knew the Lady of the Streets was looking as well.

In the ruin at the edge of the labyrinth, the rubble was starting to move. Jagged slabs of concrete reared up on end, and then toppled over with a sound like the world collapsing. From beneath, slender, metal-strutted limbs reached up.

Beth gaped at the cranes as they unfolded as elegantly as mantislegs against the sky. The wolves yipped and bounded towards their master. The wire coiled and snapped over Pen's form. Mater Viae's concrete-skinned soldiers just stood and stared.

A motor whirred into motion, a crane spun on its base and a hook shot out, burying itself with a splintering crunch into the windows on the front of Canada Tower. A second crane lashed out at the building behind Beth and she cowered as fragments of it fell around them. Jackhammers reared up and began to pound the pavement. A bulldozer smashed through the wall of the labyrinth. Through its windscreen, Beth could see that it was driverless.

The voice carried in the engines of destruction was shatteringly loud.

I AM REACH.

Beth felt dizzy, buffeted by the noise. Her knees slid out from under her and her chin smacked into the floor, but the pain momentarily cleared her head. There was something she should have . . .

She pushed herself up onto her elbows and looked across the square. Reach's hook was still buried in the front of Canada Tower. The *front*, Beth thought muzzily. *I can see the front. When did the waterfall stop?*

A figure stepped out of the pool at the tower's foot. Water sluiced down the streets that armoured Her limbs and glinted on the towers that rose above Her brow. Her eyes were the green of traffic lights, and they blazed with fury and panic.

For an instant, Beth looked full into the eyes of the Goddess who had killed her father.

Mater Viae's mouth didn't move, but Beth heard Her city-voice, so like her own that they could have been sisters, as She said, "*No.*"

The Lady of the Streets extended her arms and her Estuary-water skirts became a torrent of orange flame. Fire raced across the surface of the square. Scaffwolves screamed as it caught them, their metal voices jarring the air. Masonry Men burned like effigies as the flame spread in a flawless circle around Mater Viae and went zigzagging up the floors of the broken tower blocks, leaving only Canada Tower itself untouched. Beth hastily scrambled back as it neared the oil slick in front of her. The crude caught with a muted *whoomph* and the synod vanished, swallowed by billowing flames that reached thirty feet into the air. The heat was like a wall. Squinting through the smoke, Beth could just make out Oscar, flailing in the updraught.

An instant later, the cranes caught, showing black against the fire like silhouetted skeletons. "*I Will . . .*"

Reach's voice ebbed into silence.

"Beth!"

"*Pen?*"

Her voice was coming from somewhere to the left; even over the roar of the flames, Beth could hear her panic.

"*Pen, are you there?*"

"Beth! Help!"

London's burning, London's burning. Fil's voice was sing-song in her head. *You know this fire; it can't hurt you. Go!*

Beth hauled herself to her feet and walked into the flame. She felt no pain, but the heat felt *solid*. She gritted her teeth and from *somewhere* she summoned up the physical strength to wade further in.

"*Pen!*" she called again.

"Beth!"

She barely heard Pen's call that time, the fire raged so loud around her. She couldn't tell where it was coming from. She was disoriented, dizzy with smoke. The ground under her was melting into blisteringly hot mud.

"*Pen! Get out—use the wire!*" she shouted.

Strands of barbed wire whipped through the air, striking out for the edge of the fire, but they recoiled like burned fingers, their tips glowing red-hot. The flames were too fierce. Beth stared at them helplessly. Pen was trapped.

"*Pen!*" She dragged herself through the fire in the direction the wires had come from. The flames raged taller, louder: a bright blindfold, eclipsing everything.

Almost everything: Beth glimpsed a dark shape through the flame, a four-limbed shape—a *human* shape.

"*Pen?*" she called out. The shape grew bigger, more solid, seeming to materialise out of the flame itself. "*Pen?*" Beth reached desperately out towards her—then she hesitated.

There's no way Pen could walk through . . .

Four more figures materialised, flanking the first as Johnny Naphtha erupted through the wall of fire, arms spread wide, suit burned to charcoal, ash flaking white from his grinning teeth.

His arms enveloped Beth and lifted her off her feet. He bore her backwards, her arms still extended over his shoulder like a yearning child. Cool air washed over the back of her neck as they burst back out of the fire bank. Eight other charcoal hands were reaching for her, liquid oil bleeding from the cracks in their hands. It was cold, and viscous and felt suffocating on her skin as it spread over her.

"*Get the fuck off me!*" She kicked and struggled, but the oil-slick fingers didn't slip an inch. "*Pen!*"

"Beth . . . help . . ." Pen's voice was weak; she was coughing and retching. The fire was everywhere. Oh God, she couldn't see Pen and the fire was *everywhere—*

"*Pen!*" Beth could barely hear her own voice now. The oil was racing up her torso, lapping at her jaw, the acid-scent of it stinging her nostrils. She gagged. Her teeth felt soft in her mouth. Her bones felt soft; she could feel them running down inside her, black liquid pooling to the floor.

"*Pen!*" she tried to shout once more, but this time no sound at all came out. All she heard around her was the crackle of flames as the world melted into black.

CHAPTER THIRTY-FOUR

"*Arissse, little Goddesss. Your city hasss need of You.*"

Beth's eyelids flickered: the world strobed brick-on-black. She was sprawled, her limbs flung out like a shipwreck victim. The floor beneath her fingers was rough-laid cellar brick. *Her fingers*—she curled them. They were solid again. She tried to focus; the shifting light revealed alcoves in the walls.

Fire—she closed her eyes and saw it, felt its heat on her face. There had been fire: giant billowing gouts of orange flame and—

Pen.

It was like a starting gun fired in her head. She struggled to push herself up. She had to get back—there was a fire—she had to get back—she had to help Pen, she had to—

Her muscles went slack. They were stringy and exhausted . . . There was a fire, a Great Fire, the flames hot enough to melt asphalt, and Pen's voice had been right in the middle of it.

Beth opened her mouth. No sound came out, and no air came in. There was a vacuum in the core of her, turning her inside out, and she couldn't spit it out.

Pen's gone.

She couldn't make sense of it—she couldn't make sense of anything. The thought was giant, clumsy; nonsensical. It went through her mind like a wrecking ball, destroying everything she understood.

She closed her eyes. She was back standing on a moon-washed rooftop, before all of this began, stretching out too late to catch Pen as she slipped on the rain-slicked tiles—

—she was back in the headmistress' office, burning with disbelief and anger at the sight of the headscarfed girl who'd turned her in, but never asking what that had cost her—

—she was crouching in an alleyway, putting the finishing touch to a breadcrumb trail of graffiti spiders at the end of Pen's street, above them: a written invitation: *meet me—*

Beth flopped onto her back to see five men standing over her, their oil-soaked skin reflecting the lights from the alcoves. She tried again to speak, but still no words came when she moved her mouth.

"Excussse usss?" Johnny Naphtha said politely.

She tried again, and this time she spoke with all of herself; even so, she only managed a tyre-hiss whisper. "*Meet me under broken lights . . .*"

She dragged her knees into her chest. All she could hear was Pen's voice, down in the labyrinth under St. Paul's: the plea she'd repeated over and over in those last few months: *No further, no further down the rabbit hole, B. Take me home.*

How many, Beth? she snarled at herself. *How many warnings did you ignore? How many times did the world have to tell you that you were going to get her killed before you fucking well listened?*

Five oil-covered index fingers tilted her chin up. "Dessspite our fondnesss for riddlesss, Misss Bradley," Johnny hissed, "there isss no time. Above usss, the Great Fire of your Adversssary burnsss unchecked through your metropolisss."

Beth opened her eyes and green light washed over their liquid tailoring. Her thoughts felt clumsy, confused. Why were they talking to her? Why did they think that mattered? Pen was gone.

"*So put it out,*" she snapped at them, willing them to leave her alone.

They sighed as one, their shoulders sliding down beneath their immortal grins. "Alasss, we lack the puisssance," Johnny admitted. "In the passt, it iss true, we have curtailed the Sstreet Goddesss' insscendiariess when they have been deployed, but only at presscisssley controlled scalesss and quantitiess." Five foreheads contracted in identical, courteous winces. "Under the presssure of your asssault, Mater Viae lacked that circumssssspection."

Beth's own voice carried back to her through her memory: *She doesn't do subtlety . . . She over-commits.*

She would have laughed if she could have remembered how. She would have beaten her own brains out on the bricks if she'd had the energy to lift her head.

Johnny was still talking. "There iss one force in the city that can exsstinguisssh the Great Fire in full flow, but as much as we wisssh it were otherwissse, we cannot accesss it." He tilted his head at her. "It requiress a Goddess' touch."

Beth stopped listening. Inside her head, Fil's voice sounded. *Stop, or carry on?*

Stop.

You can't stop, he said. *They have a name for that.*

I don't care. Pen's gone. Stop.

"Your city needsss you," Johnny Naphtha repeated. His voice was like a fly in the room, a hissing strung-out buzz.

Beth managed to pull herself into a sitting position against the wall and looked at them. Their smiles were in place as ever, but the stretch of the eyes above them, the cording of the necks below, suggested panic. The Chemical Synod were afraid. Their stores, their ingredients, their markets: soon all would be on fire.

The City burns.

Beth wanted to kill them. She wondered if she could; if there was enough left in her wasted cells to at least murder Johnny before the others put her down. If she could have, she would have, without hesitation, not because of anything they'd done, but because they were alive and in front of her and Pen wasn't.

Carry on, or stop? Fil asked again. *The City needs you. All those people Pen wanted to save—they need you.*

Beth clenched her jaw. *Don't you dare use her.*

I'm not, Beth, I'm only saying what she'd say if she were here, and you know it. You knew her better than I did.

"Misss Bradley, time isss of the esssenssce . . ."

All right! she thought back at Fil, *but then I stop. And I take you with me.* Everything *stops.* Her eyes moved from identical black grin to identical black grin—the same grins that had beamed down on Pen when they'd given her the means to enter the mirror. They were her accomplices in Pen's destruction and she hated them. She'd be damned if she was going to make it easy for them.

"*What do I get?*" she asked. Her mouth was full of the taste of burned concrete.

"Excussse me?" Johnny hissed.

"*Nothing for nothing: your equations always balance. That's what you say. So what do I get?*"

The five grins stretched a little wider. "Nothing," he said. "You ssstole. You owe."

Beth pursed her lips. She leaned back against the wall and closed her eyes.

"Misss Bradley?" Johnny said, after a moment.

"*Hmm?*"

"I sssaid, you owe."

"*I heard. You just didn't say anything that interested me, so I didn't answer.*"

Johnny's smile thinned. "This isssn't for usss," he hissed impatiently. "It isss *your* city. Your esssensce. Your home."

Beth opened her eyes. *You are home.* She remembered Pen saying that: *Home is with me.* Her tone stayed mild, but her hand clenched into a fist. "*I swear to God, Johnny, you have picked the very worst day in the world to try to tell me what to care about.*"

"You would bargain for your very esssence?" The synod's eyes were black on black: the eyes of sharks at the kill.

Beth met them without fear, or any other emotion she could identify.

"You *would*." It wasn't a question.

For a moment there was only dank silence.

"Very well, then we shall." Despite his anxiety, there was a note of eagerness in Johnny's hiss. This was what he lived for. As one, the Chemical Synod unbuttoned their jackets and lowered themselves to the floor. They sat cross-legged, meeting Beth on her level.

"A proposssition then," Johnny said. "One that might ssalve your sssolitude. We know what you sstole from usss; we can guesss where it now resssidess."

They each touched a finger to their temple.

"And we are well aware, alsso, of its incompletenesss. We could correct that."

Beth glared at them, mistrustful. "*What are you?*"

"We can ressstore the young prince to corporeality."

Corporeality . . . She held herself very still, trying not to visibly react. *A body.*

Fil's voice in her head was eager but uncertain. *Beth? Is he for real?*

Ten oil-covered pupils studied her and she felt the hope flare in her. Reality: Fil, alive, complete, back with her. Despite her wariness, the offer shone a little light into the future, and in doing so showed there was a future after all.

But when she looked again at those frightened, unsheddable smiles, she knew she couldn't take it, not for herself and not even for Fil—not when they were ready to give so much more. Their whole existence was at stake. This was a lowball bid. The equation had to balance.

And just like that Beth knew what she had to ask for.

I'm sorry, Fil, she thought.

Beth? Fil's voice was uncertain, a child wanting reassurance. *Beth? What are you doing?*

But it wasn't Fil, she reminded herself forcefully, not yet. It was only the sound of his memories rattling around in her head. The eagerness she'd heard in that voice was just her own eagerness reflected back at her.

Do you want this, Fil? she asked him, eager to be proved wrong. *'Cause Thames knows, I want it for you. Tell me honestly that you want it and I'll deal, right now.*

Of course I . . . Then he caught her meaning.

There was a long silence.

This is cruel, Beth.

Maybe, she thought, but by now she knew she was right. The brief hope of having him back guttered out in her heart. *Maybe not. You aren't hurt by it, are you?*

Beth—

Are you?

No, he admitted.

Do you want this, Fil?

I can't, he said at last, wretchedly. *I can't want. You know that. I only remember wanting, and that's . . .*

. . . not the same thing.

What Pen would do, if she were here—that was what she needed to do now. It wasn't enough, not nearly enough. But it was all there was.

"No deal." Beth's voice was the sound of heavy doors slamming shut.

The synod leaned back.

"Interesssting," Johnny murmured appreciatively. "What would you prefer?"

Beth thought of her dad, and of a girl with grazed palms.

"*You nicked the growth out of people*," she said. "*Put it back.*"

Five heads shook like whiplash. "Out of the quessstion."

Beth settled herself back against the bricks and closed her eyes.

"We have already usssed it!" There was a definite note of anguish in Johnny's voice now.

"*So get some more—scrape it out of your own carcases if you have to; what do I care?*" She smiled, utterly without humour. "*You stole. You owe.*"

For what felt like a very long time, no one moved and no one spoke. The delay told Beth the synod were agonising, though their expressions gave nothing away. They were struggling with it. Beth had a feeling they'd never before been offered a deal they couldn't weigh up in an instant. She laid a hand flat to the wall, brick on brick.

"*These are feeling pretty toasty*," she said, looking into the alcoves. "*All these precious little bottles—do you think the Great Fire will reach all the way down here?*"

"If it doesss," Johnny Naphtha snarled, "you will burn alongss-side uss."

"*Better people than me have gone that way*," she said, not having to fake her indifference. "*And much, much better people than you.*"

The synod breathed out slowly and oily bubbles popped over their lips. "We accept," said Johnny Naphtha.

The tunnel gave out onto empty space. Above and below and to the left and right of the opening there was nothing but darkness. A slow, rhythmic surging that was somehow familiar rose up from under her toes where they hung out over the edge of the bricks.

The only direction in which Beth could see anything was straight ahead. Across from the tunnel mouth, only a few dozen yards away, was a brick wall. Lights glimmered in its alcoves like constellations of bruised stars. Beth had seen them twice before; she knew what they were.

Every light was a bottle, and every bottle contained a memory, an emotion or an instinct. It was a vast artificial mind: the synod's pet masterpiece. The lights flared and dimmed, rippling with patterns of thought so complex that Beth could barely tell they were patterns at all.

They'd had to carry her. *Forget killing them*, she thought bitterly, *I can't even walk by myself.* She'd been half dragged through the brick warrens, a pair of oil-soaked shoulders under each arm, her toes trailing behind her in the dust. She was vaguely aware that once she would have felt embarrassed by that, but now it just felt like her legs were the smart ones, getting out ahead of the rush.

"*So what am I supposed to do with that?*" She gestured across the gap at the lights. The rancour had left her. She just wanted this done.

"With that? Nothing," Johnny Naphtha said. "That isss *our* contribution."

"*Contribution to what?*"

"The whisssspering giant we sseek to ssummon hass languished for sso long in itss chainsss, we fear itss sssentience may have eroded," Johnny replied. "Thisss iss a replacement. Our enterprissse will avail usss nothing if we cannot talk to our client."

"*Client? Whispering giant?*" Beth started. "*Chains? I thought we didn't have time for riddles. What are you . . . ?*"

She tailed off. The surging sound at the base of the chasm swelled again and her ears finally placed it: it was the slow hushing of the tide.

She had no idea whether it was her memory of Fil's voice or the voice of Fil's memories talking to her, but she heard it as clearly as she had that first night she'd sought him out behind the old railway footbridge, while Electra and her sisters sheltered from the rain.

My name is Filius Viae; it means the Son of the Streets. My Mother is their Goddess. She laid the foundations of the streets you walk on, and the bones of the roads buried under them. She stoked the Steamwraiths' engines and gave the lamps their first sparks . . .

. . . She forged the chains that hold old Father Thames in place.

"London'sss burning," Johnny Naphtha hissed quietly in her ear. "London'sss burning."

"*Pour on water,*" Beth finished, as she finally understood. She looked at him. "*How am I supposed to do this?*"

The synod spread their immaculate black hands. "That isss what we are employing you to disscover—and we ssuggesst you disscover fasst, Misss Bradley, or there will be no one left to ssave. Father Thamesss' resstraintss lie directly below usss. There iss very little time."

She turned back to the drop, looking down at the abyss below her in consternation. She had no idea where to start.

"Ssstill," Johnny murmured in her ear, "I ssuppose we can at leassst give you a pusssh in the right direction."

A cold hand shoved Beth hard in the back; her stomach tipped over a fraction of a second before she did, and then she was plummeting through empty space.

CHAPTER THIRTY-FIVE

Beth fell for six heartbeats, seared by rushing air, and then water hit her like a full-body punch. She shuddered hard with the impact, but though her descent slowed, it didn't stop. She thrashed, flailing her arms, trying and failing to kick her useless legs, but she just kept falling through the blackness, the beams of her eyes lighting two narrow green cones of nothing in front of her.

Stop flailing around, Fil told her. *You'll knacker yourself.*

Fil, I'm sinking!

Of course you're bloody sinking! What are you made of?

Her arm drifted in front of her eyes. Green light glinted off slate.

But . . . I can't breathe! The vacuum in her lungs felt like it was burning a hole in her. Her lips were pressed tight against the chill water that was trying to prise them open.

What makes you think you need to breathe?

I—

Open your mouth.

Beth hesitated, but that was enough; the water pressure levered at her jaw and suddenly freezing liquid was pouring past her teeth. She gagged and choked on it; a few desultory air bubbles ripped up out of her, and then . . .

Nothing.

Her lungs were swollen with water. She waited as she sank, but under her iron ribs the engine of her heart kept beating.

I don't need to breathe? Even after everything, she couldn't help but be astonished.

Last time you looked in a mirror, Fil asked, *did what looked back at you seem like it ran on oxygen?*

Beth's heels scudded through something soft, then her legs folded under her and she collapsed in a tangle of limbs. Black silt clogged the streets and pores on her arms, legs and chest; it slipped into her mouth and filled the gaps between her teeth. She tried to spit it out, but without air, it was hopeless.

Great, she thought. *I'm a human bloody anchor.*

Human? Fil's voice queried drily.

You're one to talk, Petrol-Sweat. The sarcasm was a reflex, driven by some reptilian part of her mind that was trying to just carry on as normal. *When the sun finally gutters out*, she thought, *snark will be the last thing to go.*

You're a lot less human than I ever was, Fil countered.

You're actually having fun, aren't you?

Who, me? His response was acid. *No, I'm only remembering fun. Completely different.*

She fought to get her hands under her. Without buoyancy, the water above and around her was just cold tonnage pressing her down. Her fingers slipped and sank into the silt. For a horrible instant she had an image of being swallowed by the mud underneath her, entombing her in the riverbed. Wrist-deep, though, she found a denser layer of mud beneath the surface. Her grip held.

Now what?

Well, you can't swim, and you can't walk, so I guess you'd better crawl.

Her muscles protested shrilly, but she managed to drag her right arm out of the mud and plant it a few inches further ahead of her, and then did the same with her left. Gradually, she began to make progress through the shifting murk.

Only forward, huh? A nervous note crept into Fil's voice. He was picking up on Beth's own anxiety. *You sure this is the right way?*

Nope.

Then how?

It's easier than turning around. I'm lost in the dark, Fil, and no one's coming to get me. I have no way of knowing which way I should go, but I've got something I need to find. Do you expect me to just sit here paralysed by too many choices, or pick a direction? What would you do?

He hesitated, but then said, *I'd do this.*

I know you would.

Johnny said the chains were right below them, and that meant they couldn't be too far away. Of course, it was possible that they were behind her and that every painful elbow-drag through the mud was taking her further and further away, but she tried not to think about that. Every time she put a hand forward, she stretched out her fingertips, groping for the feel of rusting iron. She cast about her with her eyes, all the while praying that their weak beams would reveal fat links of chain. But she saw only darkness and she felt only the tugging of the tide at her hair. She half expected to start hallucinating, to see Pen and her dad drifting down to her, pale white ghosts in the black. But her brain had no need of the oxygen it was starved of and she saw nothing that wasn't there. She was alone.

She pushed onwards, with no idea of how much time was passing.

Something slimy tickled the back of her neck and she jerked hard.

For Thames' sake, Beth! It's probably just a tadpole or seaweed or something.

She brushed her fingertips to the back of her neck. It wasn't a tadpole or seaweed; it was the slick, rubberised cable of her own hair, and something was pulling it, not back and forth with the tide, but off to the right, and now sharply *upwards*, yanking at the roots, almost to the point of pain.

Beth stopped. She was suddenly very aware of her heart thumping stolidly in her chest. She twisted to look in the direction her hair was floating, but her gaze just revealed more green water.

An idea struck her. She curled her fingers around a handful of silt and flung it upwards. Instead of drifting back down, the black particles ripped and twisted up through the water. They shot beyond the light of her gaze in an instant, but an instant was all she needed to see the shapes their paths marked out:

Chain links.

The chains are made of currents, Beth thought. *Of course—what else could a chain holding down a river be made of?* She remembered the flood of Mater Viae's skirts. Yes, the Street Goddess certainly had the power—the *puissance*, as Johnny had called it—to do this. She felt a little chill down the back of her neck at the implacability of the Goddess. The river had been Her rival so She'd tied it down with knots of its own substance.

How do I break them? she wondered.

Johnny said it required "the touch of a Goddess," Fil said. *So maybe you just touch them?*

You think She would have made it that easy?

Why would She have made it hard? As far as She knew, She was the only one who'd ever be able to do it.

Beth started to reach up through the murk to where she'd seen the chain, then she paused, stalled. The tide was slow and steady: the river's slumbering breath—a giant's breath—and she was right in the core of it. When she woke it, she had no idea what it would do.

But London was burning, and people were burning with it—people Pen had tried to save.

The current was strong; she could barely force her fingers into it, it was so fast. But she managed to slide her hand in sideways, and she felt the water ripple through all the streets on the back of her hand, racing through their corners and junctions, reading their topography.

The force of the current slacked suddenly—it was still flowing, but it was much weaker now. A lock had been sprung, but the bolt was still in place. Beth set her jaw and then twisted her wrist, blocking the flow of the water with her palm, and a moment later, the current subsided altogether.

Chain broken, she thought.

Nothing happened.

Okay, that's disappointing. She peered around her. The water was just as quiescent and cold as before; nothing had changed. *Maybe the synod miscalculated*, she thought. *Maybe the damn thing's dead, and it's a corpse that's been flowing through the middle of London for the last two thousand years.* But Beth's gut rejected that idea: she'd felt that tide, and heard it. It had been so very like the rhythm of a living thing.

Her head began to hurt, a squeezing ache in her temples. *Fil*, she thought, *I thought you said I didn't need to breathe.*

I don't think you do.

Well, this headache feels a lot like oxygen deprivation to me, she snapped irritably.

Only it wasn't just her head, she realised: her fingers and her arms and her chest hurt too. It was like they were being pressed from all sides, like the water was becoming denser, harder, more *concentrated*. As if it could hear her thoughts, the water squeezed her harder still; she could feel her metal bones creaking under the pressure. She forgot herself and opened her mouth to cry out, but nothing happened. The fluid in her lungs was pushing outwards, she realised, and without it, they'd collapse.

The world was quieter now—silent, in fact. She wondered if her eardrums had burst under the pressure—only there'd been no pain. And then she twigged: something *had* changed. The tide had stopped.

Like a half-drowned man drawing breath, the River shuddered. It started to rise.

Beth was flung upwards, and her stomach went plunging. Gritty mud sluiced between her fingers. Every beat of her heart felt like it would crack her open. She craned her head up and saw that she—*they*—were rising towards light. At last she spied the glowing alcoves, lit up like galaxies on a brick wall, rushing up to meet her; it felt like she was rocketing into space.

The water reached the first alcove and flooded into it. There was a soft explosion as the glass bottle inside shattered under the pressure; the light inside blossomed in the water like glowing ink and then faded as the substrate carrying it dissolved. There were more soft explosions, more swirling, more inky fireworks as the River raged through the synod's cavern, sucking it dry. There was a shift in the water and Beth felt it pause, like it was considering something. Purpose entered it where before there had been only instinct. It rippled over her, testing her shape.

After the first explosive shock of waking, old Father Thames was gathering himself.

Kicking helplessly, she was pulled above the level of the access tunnel. The Chemical Synod grinned at her from the other side of a wall of water. They were standing on dry land; the river hadn't entered their tunnel but was drawing itself up, holding itself back. Five pairs of oily hands were raised in identical, placating gestures and Beth could see Johnny's mouth moving as he made his pitch. Was Father Thames listening to them, considering their offer?

And then something changed: the eagerness left the synod's bodies. Their extended palms were no longer calming; now they were pleading, raised as hopeless shields. For the first time since Beth had known them, their smiles flickered.

The water hit them like a battering ram, and Beth flowed with it. Her head was ringing furiously as she surged up the tunnel like a bullet through a gun barrel. In front of her, the synod tumbled through the water. The invisible bonds of symmetry still held them and they whirled around Johnny in the centre, their fingers splayed, eyes and mouths stretched in panic. Bricks and glowing alcoves whipped past; more bottles shattered, more colours erupted and then dissolved in the water as the Thames gathered the synod's stores into itself. A low roar was building deep in the water; Beth could feel it rather than hear it. It jarred her bones.

Her skin began to itch, maddeningly. The water had changed: it felt like acid now, or some other fierce solvent. Tiles flaked off her and drifted away like sloughed scales. She glimpsed the dark figures as they whipped around her: the synod were dissipating, dissolving, threads of oil bleeding out from their bodies to be lost in the acidic wash. The outermost two figures were already skeletal and they grew longer and thinner, impossibly attenuated, more like midday shadows than men, before vanishing into the swirling River. Beth tasted oil and burning water in her mouth. The pain in her head was a searing white light, blanking the world out between pulses.

There was a loud *pop*, and sound rushed back into her ears. She could hear flames crackling, and for a moment she was back in Canada Square, watching wires recoil helplessly above her . . .

Then pain wrenched her back to the present.

Water drained from her face and air rushed into her mouth. She coughed reflexively and vomited water down her chin. She was angled so her head tipped back, gazing straight up. Above her, the clouds glowed with reflected fire. She kicked her legs in empty space and found a column of water was wrapped around her like a fat tentacle, holding her fifty feet in the air. She fought to lower her gaze, to look straight ahead, and despite her pain and her panic, she couldn't help but stare.

The Thames had left the riverbed and reared up before her like a molten iceberg, a rushing vertical torrent. Greedy in its freedom, it reached higher than the clouds and gathered their vapour into it.

An oil-black skeleton was spat out onto the shale bank below her. It was alone. The skeleton struggled to raise itself, its bony arms trembling under it. Its grin—Johnny's grin—was the same as always, only stripped of the flesh that had made it suave. It shuddered, and collapsed.

Beth gazed, stricken, into the vast, blank face of the River, and felt it gazing back. It *knew* her. She could feel its attention—a kind of half-recognition—and its frustration, like it was trying to match her to its memory and she wasn't quite *right*. And then she felt a wave of something else ripple through the water that held her: *hate.*

That was your mistake, she thought, eyeing the black skeleton below her. Father Thames' mind hadn't eroded, not completely. There were still some tattered remnants of memory left; and it remembered the Goddess who had entombed him.

With a dreadful inexorability, the column of water gripping Beth began to squeeze.

"No, please—I'm not h—"

But her protests were cut off as the water flooded the roads and railways and turbine halls that carried her voice. The River

squeezed her harder, and as her ribs cracked, an iron girder rup-
tured the skin of her chest. She stared at it dully through the
water that rushed around it. Her arms were pinned to her sides
and she couldn't even cradle the wound. She coughed, and liquid
filled her mouth; she tasted oil and blood.

She spat, and pain filled her up, wave upon mounting wave
of it, flooding from the compound fracture in her chest into her
stomach, her thighs, her throat—

Her eyes started to dim. Through the refracting wall of the
river, she saw her city. The synod hadn't lied; it really was burning. The towers rearing up from the skyline were silhouetted by
flames, like teeth in a dragon's mouth. The fire was only in the
centre for now, but she could see it was pushing outwards at a
frightening speed. Even as Beth watched, it reached the synod's
factory on the far bank and the building ignited like a paraffin-
soaked coal, its dark shape augmented by smoke. The Great Fire,
the insatiable fire, pressed on. A strand of it licked blindly out
towards the riverbank, melting shale as it went.

There was a faint hiss and a puff of steam as it met the River.
The pressure on Beth's chest slackened slightly and the world
came back into focus. That sense of vast attention had left her.
Old Father Thames was looking at something else.

The world blurred and Beth's stomach plunged as the River
dropped her. She crashed into the shale and the water drained
away from her. She curled up around her shattered chest,
instinctively flinching from the next blow, but it never came.
Rivulets of water were racing *away* from her, towards the factory. The River's tendrils groped over the burning building,
probing its doorways, its windows, its burning lintels, and a
roar emanated from the column of water above her, a sound of
terrible anger.

Then the River hurled itself down onto the factory.

The beach shuddered under the impact, making Beth's head jump and then smack back down into the rocks under it. Her vision clouded, but she kept looking until it cleared. The factory was rubble, completely crushed by the Thames. The flames died instantly, suffocated, but the water only hugged the wreckage for a moment before surging onwards, restless and eager, back up the path of the flame as though the fire itself was a fuse.

The River dragged every drop of itself with it, leaving the shattered factory bone-dry in its wake.

Beth tested her hoodie between numb fingers: it was dry too.

Impact after impact echoed off the sky and as Beth watched, the River surged across the city in a self-renewing tidal wave, extinguishing the fire and smashing the architecture which fuelled the flames. Dark fingers crept in at the edge of her vision, but she denied them with a shake of her head: she had to see this. She looked at the epicentre of the dwindling fire and something sparked low in her chest.

Underneath the fear that had dominated her for so long, she felt hope.

As the River entered Canada Square, it banked hard to the right, hugging the contours of the inside of the labyrinth, and swirled into a fast-flowing circle with Canada Tower at the centre. Even from where she watched, half dead on her hilltop, Beth could *feel* its eagerness.

Water poured into the square, more and more of it. It surged, faster and faster, its sides rising until it was a whirlpool, a rushing vortex with walls as high as the Skyscraper Throne itself. Looking down from her vantage on the hilltop, Beth glimpsed two green glints of light at the tower's apex.

With a titanic roar, the Thames fell on Canary Wharf from all sides, and the green lights vanished. Tearing steel and shattering glass were all swamped by the sound of the River's triumph. For a second, the torrent thinned enough for Beth to make out the tower, slumping as though exhausted. Every strut was buckled, every window shattered. At the apex, the throne was empty.

And then Canary Wharf fell.

It collapsed all at once, crashing inwards on itself. The glittering silver peak slid off it like a fallen crown. To Beth, her ears still ringing with the fury of the River, it sounded muted.

The River . . . she thought. Horror planted spider-feet in her heart as she watched. The River wasn't done yet.

The Thames gathered itself and hurled itself against the walls that surrounded it like a demented thing. Beth might have broken its chains, but the City was its prison and it still stood. The River threw itself on building after building, gurgling eagerly as each one collapsed beneath it.

Beth's brief-born hope drained out of her. The River had been imprisoned for millennia and it hated the City; she'd felt that. Perhaps it wouldn't stop until the whole place had been rendered down to flood-plain mud. She'd recognised that sentiment—she'd respected it too. After all, she wouldn't be satisfied with less in its place.

But . . .

Sorry, mate, I can't let you . . . She started to pull herself on her elbows over the slag, but collapsed on her face after three drags, her shoulders burning. There were still people alive down there, in the buildings below her hilltop. She tried to think of a way to warn them, but her mind felt clayish and her thoughts came slowly. *People* . . . She cast blearily over the landscape until her eyes landed on St. Paul's. Reach's cranes still clawed the sky around it. The dome was still standing. The fire had never reached it, but the water would. The thought was like an iron lump in the pit of her stomach: the water *she'd* unleashed . . . *All those people.* The refugees they'd sent there . . .

I have to . . . But the impulse was ragged and slipped away from her. She was too broken, too tired, too sick. She curled up on the shale. Her eyes began to close, but a sound reached her then that was so unexpected she snapped them back open again. Nearby, someone was sobbing.

Wincing, she struggled onto her other side so she could face where the sound was coming from. A few feet away, a black skeleton sat on the shale, elbows on rickety kneecaps, skull cupped between its bony fingers. Thick, oily tears ran from its eye sockets as its ribcage heaved.

Seriously? Beth thought. *You're crying? You. You don't even have eyes, let alone tear-ducts.*

But as so often in the past year, her disbelief didn't change anything: Johnny Naphtha, last git standing of the Chemical Synod, was bawling his eyes out.

It wasn't just to fight the fire, was it? Beth thought about asking it aloud, but it was too much effort, and anyway, she knew, with the muzzy self-confidence of the semi-conscious, that she was right. *You always planned to wake the River. That's why you built it a mind—a mind you thought you could negotiate with, a mind you thought you could manipulate.*

And then, with a clarity that startled her given how foggy the rest of the world was getting, *That was what Mater Viae was going to do for you. That was your price.*

She almost wanted to laugh.

The sky overhead began to bleach itself blue. The River's rage was a drumbeat in the distance. It grew slowly closer, but if even the ground beneath Beth had been falling away, she couldn't have moved.

"*Well,*" she said as she finally let her eyes close, "*we really bollocksed that up, didn't we?*"

CHAPTER THIRTY-SIX

Beth lay flat on the gravelled rooftop, staring up at the blank grey sky. There was a roaring on the horizon that she thought at first was the rhino, but on second listen sounded more like the sea. Somewhere, a city beyond this one was getting hammered.

Something white fluttered down beside her ear. Beth had precisely no desire to move, but she lifted her head by a few inches anyway and looked down. It was a letter.

"Dear Mr. and Mrs. Bradley," it began, and then continued, "We regret . . ."

"Want to explain that?" It was her dad's voice, impatient, tense. He'd stoked himself up for a row before he'd even clapped eyes on her. When she looked back up he was standing over her, his hairy forearms crossed over his stomach. "Beth, I've had it with you. You cannot keep getting into fights."

Beth cast her mind back over the last few months: cranes and wolves and wire and water . . . Hate to break it to you, Dad, she thought, but I really can.

"I was at work." The way he said "work" made it obvious it was miles more important than anything Beth would ever do. "I was covering the desk when I got the call. The letter's just for form—they didn't even post it. Your headmistress slapped it into my hand just before I left. Know who I have to ask to cover for me when you get me yanked out of the office for this rubbish? Allen—bloody Allen—I already owe him too many favours because of you."

Beth knew the speech off by heart, of course. She'd heard it in dozens of dreams like this one, and she knew her response just as well.

"Wow," she said, with the anvil-heavy sarcasm that her thirteen-year-old self had injected into everything, "you poor thing. Where were you when Shakespeare was doing tragedies? He'd have lapped this right up."

She'd been proud of that line at the time. It was versatile; she'd managed to trot it out about four times a week back then. She felt an echo of the old satisfaction, and the old anger, but both faded as she finally looked properly at her father.

There was something indistinct about him. His face was clear enough, but no matter how hard she looked, she couldn't work out what colour his shirt was. His expression flickered jerkily between the same hammy caricatures: anger, disgust and there, visible for just an instant in between the two, helplessness.

"You're making my life harder than it needs to be, and I'm not having it any more." He was yelling now, but his voice sounded brittle. The anger she could cope with, but the anger was a mask for the fact that he had absolutely no idea what to do with her, and that had terrified and enraged her.

"Well?" he demanded. "What have you got to say for yourself?" Clichés were all he had. He acted out parenthood the way he'd seen on telly.

Beth looked at him and just felt sad. This was how she remembered him. Had he ever really looked like this? His hands and forearms and elbows massive, like a gorilla's, his face red and his eyes lost while he bellowed things at her she couldn't remember? There was nothing in this memory to suggest this shouting man would ever make her tea, or hold her hand or go out to an abandoned factory armed only with two giant Toblerones and wait for alien hands to drag him through the floor. There was nothing that suggested to Beth she scared him enough for that kind of courage.

"What happened, honey?" It was her mother's voice. Her mum's face appeared above her, gentler than her dad's, and kinder, but just as brittle. Her face was set in an embarrassed smile, the same as in the photo Dad kept in the kitchen, but Beth couldn't work out what her hairstyle was. Was it a bun, or loose down the back of her neck, or cut short in a bob? Was it dark like Beth's, or greying like it had been in the years before she died?

Fil sat on the edge of the roof, legs pulled into his scrawny, grey-skinned chest, arms locked over them, head turned ostentatiously to look down into the street below. He kept his distance. They weren't like him, these sketchy remembrances. They were Beth's memories of her parents, not their memories of themselves, and Beth knew he felt like he was intruding, seeing her with them.

"What happened, Beth?" Mum asked again. "You're a smart girl; we take it as read that you know you're not allowed to hit people—"

"Not even Trudi Stahl?" Beth interjected. It had been a weak attempt at humour when she first uttered it and the years hadn't been kind to it since then.

"—not even her. So why did you?" Her mum's voice was patchy, like a bad radio signal. The closer she listened to it, the more it sounded like Beth's own voice. With a little twist of the heart she realised she couldn't remember what her mum sounded like any more.

"Something she said," Beth mumbled. The old truculence filled her mouth like a bad taste. "I just flipped."

Her mum sighed. "Beth, no matter what people say about you, you can't—"

"It wasn't about me," Beth protested. "It was about a friend of mine. Private stuff, serious stuff, you get me?" She didn't add that if anyone should know that sort of stuff about the friend in question, it should be her. "And if you think a couple of thrown punches is worse than that, then you really have been out of school too long. It takes a lot longer to come back *from those kind of rumours than a hundred bloody broken noses like I gave that little ginger cow." She sniffed, enjoying a vague sense of satisfaction. "Especially if you're . . . gentle like—"*

"Beth? What happened? Are you okay?" The new voice was urgent and scared. Something sat low in the pit of Beth's stomach. A familiar figure *was running across the gravel roof towards her.*

Pen dropped to her knees beside Beth. Her parents didn't react to her at all, but then, they hadn't reacted to each other. Pen's hand slipped in to cradle Beth's head. Her face was solid, clear in every detail. Of course it would be, *Beth thought.* I knew her better than I knew anyone.

"Are you okay? How on earth did you get here?" Pen asked.

"I hit Trudi Stahl," Beth confessed with a shrug that was more pride than embarrassment. The city around her echoed her voice.

Pen wrinkled her brow in confusion. Her face was latticed in wire and crisscrossed with scars. The hands that smoothed the hair out of Beth's eyes were striped in painful-looking black-red burns. Beth tried to remember when Pen had got those burns, but for the life of her she couldn't.

"Trudi Stahl?" she said. "What are you talking about, B?"

And then Beth was confused too, because she'd never told Pen about that fight, or the reason for it. Pen would have worried herself sick if she'd known about those rumours. Beth felt a swell of terrible shame as she looked at the scars that adorned her best friend's memory. Heat beat down from the sky. Behind Pen's head, it wasn't grey any more; it was a brilliant, burning blue.

"I tried." The shame twisting her gut was so strong it was hard to keep looking, but she managed. You have to look at the things you make, *she thought. "I tried but I screwed up."*

"It's okay, Beth. Just tell me what happened."

"We woke the River," Beth confessed. "It's destroying the City—everyone. Everything."

Pen's expression changed and she looked out towards the horizon. "Yeah, so I see. That was rash."

"Rash's where I excel."

"No doubt." Pen smiled, but she sounded scared.

Beth shook her head, trying with an act of will to remember Pen happy, not afraid. The way Pen would have wanted her to.

"Is there any way to stop it?" Pen asked.

Beth pushed herself up onto one elbow, and put a hand on Pen's shoulder. This wasn't exactly a secret, but if she confided it like one, it might feel like it.

"The River—Johnny made a mind for it," she said, "all across one wall of his stores. But it didn't react the way he thought it would."

Pen's expression changed. She gripped Beth's shoulder. "What did you say?"

"They made a mind," Beth started, but it was no good. She couldn't look any more. This memory of Pen was scarred and scared and she couldn't change it, couldn't seem to hold all the complexity of Pen in her mind at once. It felt like letting her down to remember her that way. She turned her head aside, and closed her eyes. "Mind made up," she mumbled. It almost made sense to her. "Made up mind."

"Beth!" Pen called to her, but Beth wouldn't open her eyes; she couldn't make herself open them.

"Beth!"

"Beth!" Pen shook Beth by the shoulders, but she just squirmed from side to side and dug herself further into the shale, her eyes screwed up close like a child's. Pen put a hand to her forehead and swore under her breath. The heat coming off Beth's street-laced skin was ferocious.

Oscar hissed and crackled, hovering anxiously overhead. Pen looked up at him. "I don't know, Oscar," she said. "I don't know." She felt oddly guilty when she admitted that, like she was welching on a bargain with him. She felt like the least she could do for him was wake Beth up—after all, the Sewermander *had* saved her life.

She thought back to Canada Square; the heat pressing in like suffocating cloth; the sweat soaking her headscarf. Again and again, she'd sent the wire's coils out, and again and again they'd sprung back in pain: the Great Fire burned hotter than anything, too hot for them to touch. But just when she'd given up, they'd gained purchase around Oscar's flaming claws and she'd been yanked above the battlefield, dangling by one wire from the Sewermander like a kid on a kite string; he burned hot enough to blacken the wire, but not to melt it.

Of course—she flexed her hands, wincing at the burns that crisscrossed the skin on them—wire was also an excellent conductor of heat.

Boom. To the west, the River levelled another building, hitting it like a solid shockwave. It was getting closer; the destruction was getting louder. She ran to the edge of the cliff and searched the city below for the source of the sound. *Boom.* The River surged into the side of the tilting Olympic stadium, glittering in the sun. Steel and concrete gave before it like cardboard and in its wake the Thames left only a fine-ground moraine, like a glacier's trail.

The River's destroying everything. Pen's mouth dried as she tracked its trajectory: the dome of St. Paul's was directly in its path, so massive and so intact it was almost taunting the River. She thought of the great mass of homeless people she'd sent into Reach's embrace; could they still be there? Might they, she dared to hope, have fled?

Fled where, Pen? The voice inside her was merciless. *You told them they'd be safe there, and it was true: the Fire never touched them. As far as they know, it's still a sanctuary. If you were them you'd cling to that place until the last possible moment, until the Apocalypse was right at the door. You'd keep your faith in the one person who seemed to understand what the hell had happened to your world.*

And by the time they worked out what a mistake that was, it would be too late.

Faith. Her lip twisted and she looked down at Beth. *You never understood it.*

"Johnny made it a mind?" She all but spat the words as she looked across at the pitch-black skeleton slumped on the shale a few yards away. He kept pushing himself back up the rock he was leaning against, only to slide back down it, smearing oil as the shingle under his hips subsided.

"Is that true? Is that what you did?"

Air hissed between Johnny Naphtha's teeth and bubbled the oil that covered them. It might have been the back end of a "*Yesss*" or it might have been nothing at all. Either way he didn't protest as the wire strand snaked under his arms, cinched in tight about his ribs and lifted him into the air.

Pen laid Beth's head carefully back down onto the beach. She was unconscious again, and Pen wasn't sure the last time she'd been otherwise. She felt like a corkscrew was being turned in her guts. She wanted to stay; even though she knew there was nothing she could do for Beth, she wanted to stay—just in case. Just so she wasn't alone.

"Oscar," she called upwards, "look after her." The Sewermander swooped and crackled. He probably didn't understand her, but she knew he would never have done anything else.

She faced St. Paul's, which loomed in front of her like a warhead, breaching London's shattered carcase. All that was left was to put one foot in front of the other.

"*They made it a mind.*"

Pen started to run.

CHAPTER THIRTY-SEVEN

She took the first two steps with her own feet and then wire tendrils planted themselves in front of her, flexing as they took her weight and she bounded down the dry riverbed on legs of coiled steel. Above her, on the end of the wire that bound him, the black skeleton that was Johnny Naphtha snapped and flailed in the air like some macabre flag.

Streets whipped past and air rushed over her face, freezing her lips. Pen could barely breathe. Everything was a blur but what lay dead ahead: St. Paul's. They scrambled over rooftops, the Mistress' barbs screeching on the tiles like cats' claws. The haste that thrummed through the wire matched Pen's own; the Mistress whined a frantic doggerel, over and over:

Master! Master!
Must go faster!

The cathedral was close now, and Pen could see the cranes around it were still moving. Reach—a part of him at least—had survived the Great Fire. The Crane King awaited them, or the flood, whichever got there first.

They careened to the base of Ludgate Hill. London's convulsions had dragged it up, making it taller than ever. They straddled a toppled tower block and sprang from there into the next road. One wire foot punctured the roof of a red phone box, another came down in the next street along.

Pen's stomach flipped as the wire leg slipped straight through the surface of the road like it was water and they tipped forward, their balance gone. The asphalt, surging slow as a tide, swept up to meet her face.

Wires shot out from her back; barbs latched onto cornices and gargoyles like grappling hooks. For a heart-stopping moment the Mistress wrestled against their momentum. Johnny skidded through the surface of the Tideway, throwing up sprays of liquid asphalt. Pen's guts compacted themselves in the lower reaches of her abdomen as they decelerated and then sprang clear.

Voices reached her ears as they scrambled into the cathedral square.

"Holy shit, it's *you*!"

"Are you okay?"

"What's going on?"

"Did you win? Are we safe now? Did you win?"

They all sounded worried, and relieved to see her: the girl they'd trusted. They sounded like friends, but Pen snarled at them to get back. The doors to the cathedral yawned open as they spilled out towards her, shouting greetings and questions Pen didn't dare stop to deal with. Three steel tentacles fired into the façade above the doorway and three more latched onto the roof. She crawled up the side of the building like a spider, Johnny bobbing behind her like her bound prey. The climb slowed them, and as the roar of the air died in Pen's ears, it was replaced by another: the roar of water.

The architecture under her blurred from white stone to grey. She was level with the crane jibs now, reaching over nearby rooftops. A wire tendril stroked them and Pen felt their fear.

As she crested the dome, she saw the Thames.

She stopped stock-still, throwing her arms around the cupola on instinct. Every cell in her jarred at the sight: a sheer cliff-face of water a thousand feet high, trampling the city as it stampeded onwards. Its shadow swamped everything she could see. It surged towards her, undulating like a vast inchworm. The wave front must have been half a mile across. It was too late to flee.

They made you a mind, she thought. Her thoughts flicked back to the brick warrens beneath the synod's factory and the price they'd exacted for her trip through the mirror—and the purpose they'd put it to. A sibilant whisper welled up from her memory: *A mind . . . to patch the perceptionss of a prissoner . . .* It had been missing only one thing:

A complete set of memoriesss of a child, rendered from the memoriesss of her parents.

Please, she thought, *please let me be right*. Deep inside the consciousness that drove that flowing edifice, she prayed, was every thought her mum and dad had ever had about her.

Pen sucked in her breath and screamed, "STOP!" She screamed her throat raw, throwing her arms wide.

But the River Thames didn't stop; it came on. It levelled the building in front of her.

Wires struck at it, coiling and snapping, but throwing up only spray. The memory of Beth's city-voice flashed into Pen's head.

. . . they misjudged how it would react.

And so had she. Her arms dropped to her sides. She wasn't afraid, just regretful. She could have stayed with Beth.

The wave arched over her like the end of the world, chilling the air. Its foam licked at her face and she hissed in sudden pain:

the wires were dragging at her skin, scrabbling through the air, clutching at the crane jibs, desperate to somehow protect Reach from the vengeful force of the River. The water fell towards her and she felt a twitch at the base of her neck. Underneath the shattering noise of the water, she heard the wire whisper something, but in that moment, she didn't understand it.

This steel guise blocks watery eyes.

Needles of pain rippled through her face, her arms, her chest like acid rain. The wire ripped itself free of her skin and tumbled from the rooftop like a sloughed skin. Johnny's skeleton rattled and bounced over the tiles towards the gutter. Pen closed her eyes; her pulse, in her ears, was indistinguishable from the tide.

Heartbeats thudded in her ears, measuring out one second, two seconds, three. Pen dragged in a breath and tasted cold river spray. Droplets tickled her eyes and they flickered back open.

The River had stopped. It held itself poised over her, still as a photograph. She could feel its awareness, its attention. The air between her and it thrummed with it.

You just didn't recognise me with the wire, Pen realised. She looked down, but there was no sign of the Mistress. The wire had sacrificed herself, not for her, but for the cranes—for Reach.

She tilted her head up towards the liquid cliff-face. The way the light hit it, she could just make out a reflection, a vaguely human shape in a headscarf. If she squinted, it looked as much like her mum as herself.

"You remember me, don't you?" she said.

The Thames made no move to show it understood, but then, she didn't know how it would if it wanted to. The wave was close enough to touch, and on impulse she put her hand out to it. Water bubbled out to meet her palm, sluicing between her fingers. She let it recognise the touch of her hand, the way it had recognised her face. It would remember that, she knew.

She turned her hand over, shivering as the water ran down her arm and soaked her sleeve.

You remember me, don't you? she thought. *You remember your daughter.*

A ripple like a sigh ran through the front of the wave and a stream of water came out from it and curled around behind Pen like a protective hand. She was suddenly, painfully aware of how tired she was, and it barely felt like a decision to let go of the cupola. The slates went from under her feet and she fell backwards, not caring. Water cushioned her, and she rested against it. Drops of blood fell from the wounds the wire had left and dissipated in the current. The sun, refracting through the water, was warm; its whispering soothed her. Pen let her eyes close and for a while she just lay there, cradled by the River.

She heard a clacking, like sticks smacking into one another, and she opened her eyes again. A few feet away, half immersed in the main wave-front, his bony knees knocking together in the current, was Johnny Naphtha. Pen could see the dark streaks running into the water where it was wearing him away.

"You want out of there?" she asked him. The skeleton grinned, the skull tilting forward and back in the current in a way that Pen decided to take as a nod.

"Then we need to talk."

CHAPTER THIRTY-EIGHT

Beth lay on the rooftop, staring up at the rhino. The rhino glowered back from the side of the next-door tower block. Footsteps rang on the metal fire escape and she heard Fil's delighted laughter.

"Where did you go?" *she asked, not taking her eyes from the rhino.*

"Racing Railwraiths," *he gasped, out of breath.* "Did you know you had Bahngeists in here?"

"I never really thought about it," *Beth replied.* "Glad to see you're making yourself useful."

He dropped to sit cross-legged onto the gravel beside her, close enough that she could hear the heave of his lungs. "Why? What have you been doing?"

"Having a staring match with Ricky here." *She gazed into the blank aerosol pools of the rhino's eyes. Her own eyes ached to blink.*

"You call it Ricky?" *Fil didn't sound impressed.*

"Phyllis was taken."

Fil made a tsking sound with his teeth. "Who's winning?"

"So far? The rhino."

"Well, it is painted on the wall, Beth. I reckon—as far as patience goes—that might give it the edge."

"Yeah, but I've got an ace in the hole."

"Which is?"

"It's only painted on the wall," Beth replied. She sighed and blinked away the itch in her eyes. "So it won't know if I chea—"

She broke off, wrinkling her nose.

"What is it?" Fil asked in sudden concern. "I don't smell anything."

"It's not that. Something's tickling my nose. I feel like I'm going to . . ."

But she couldn't finish the sentence, because the sneeze packing itself into her sinuses had seized control of every muscle in her face. On reflex, she inhaled sharply—

—and opened her eyes as the sneeze cannoned out of her. Something dark and fuzzy sprang away from her face. She sniffed back what felt like a ton of mucus and shifted. Her back grazed over thin shale, spread over the pavement. She was still by the factory. Her throat felt like it had been tarmacked. Her broken rib burned in her side.

She sneezed again, and flailed as the pain in her chest kicked. She struggled up onto her elbows, and something furry brushed the back of her arms. A plaintive meow sounded behind her.

A tabby cat bounded onto her chest and started to purr, kneading its paws into the front of her hoodie. A slender black shape raced past the soles of her feet. She heard a chorus of purrs behind her and twisted her head around to look: sinuous, furry bodies slinked past one another: tabbies, gingers, Siamese, calicoes. The riverbank was swarming with cats.

Beth turned back to the one on her chest. It met her green gaze with a green gaze of its own.

Fleet? she thought. She massaged the bridge of her nose with her thumb and forefinger, trying to clear the fog from her head. *What are you?*

Something sharp slammed into her side, right into her fractured rib, and she spasmed hard, gasping. Fleet sprang away and a fraction of second later a bare grey foot stamped down on her chest. She doubled up, coughing uselessly. Pain rippled outwards from the blow in shivering, fiery waves, into her stomach, her groin, her throat. She crossed her arms desperately over her torso, but that only earned her three more savage strikes to the ribs. She couldn't tell if what was hitting her was a foot or a fist or a steam piston. Thick, phlegmy liquid boiled into her mouth and she didn't even have time to spit it out before another blow crashed into her temple and the pain made the world go white

. . . flat on a rooftop, a grey sky flickering behind her eyelids . . .

and she collapsed flat to the ground. Oscar wheeled and snapped overhead, but there were two other Sewermanders keeping him at bay. Water gurgled beside Beth's ear and she felt the chill of it as it puddled against the side of her head. Slowly, the bleach drained out of her vision. A tall woman stood over her. The architecture of Her skin was clotted with river silt and weeds. Tower blocks rose from Her forehead like the spokes of a crown. Two of them were broken, ending in rubble-capped stubs.

Mater Viae's green eyes blazed bright with hatred.

Her lip curled, and for a moment Beth thought the Goddess was going to speak, but then Her foot burst through the front of Her waterfall skirts and drove down, down and down again onto Beth's solar plexus. Beth could hear the groaning inside her chest as her steel ribs sheared. Every muscle between her neck and her knees went into spasm. The pain filled her up.

Mater Viae knelt and drove a roof-knuckled fist into her pelvis with shattering force.

Beth threw her head back. Her mouth gaped and her throat burned with a scream that never emerged.

Mater Viae rose and spat, and oily film flecked Beth's right eye. The Goddess turned away. She stalked to the edge of the dry riverbed and looked out across the city. Her cats wove indolent figure-eights around Her ankles.

Agony washed through Beth like acid. Her thoughts were a mad gabble. She fought to wrestle herself back from the pain, and one idea came strong through the fog: *Not like this. Not by you.*

Panic and rage flared through the dullness in her brain and she seized onto them—anything to get her up, get her moving. Anything to beat the pain back.

You killed Pen. You killed Dad. If You want to kill me too, then You'd better at least fucking look at me.

She rolled onto her front and pushed herself up into a crouch. She launched forwards, her fingers crooked like claws.

Mater Viae didn't even look round; She just lifted one hand and curled it into a fist, and the earth under Beth trembled, shale rattling on shale. Five huge fingers burst upwards in a shower of pebbles. The hand was the height of a man, its skin the grey of river mud. Its wrist was warped and corded like a tree trunk where it fed back into the ground. It seized Beth around her chest, trapping her arms between its fingers. She was pinned, stranded and helpless as a scarecrow.

Tension entered Mater Viae's knuckles; the tiles on them paled from terracotta to sandstone. The Goddess turned and with a snarl on Her road-lipped-mouth, drove Her fist into Beth's temple.

. . . the world blurred. Beth clung to the gravel roof as the grey city shook around her . . .

She snapped back into wakefulness. Pain was an alarm bell ringing through her skull. Something was holding her hair. Her jaw hung horribly loose. Her vision cleared on Mater Viae's face, an inch from her own. The Goddess eyed her with the mix of wary respect and disgust you might give a tumour on your skin.

"*Imposter.*" The voice was a snarl of steam venting through sewers. "*Liar. Thief. What kind of Goddess are you now?*"

Beth dragged her head up. The air tasted like warm clay; her bones felt like water. She fought to dredge up enough sound from her body to make a voice. "*What kind of Goddess are You?*" she snapped back. With a tremendous effort, she managed to splay the fingers on her right hand. Tarmac was running liquid from the streets that edged her nails. "*What kind of Goddess deliberately gives Her city a disease?*"

Mater Viae's lip twisted as if She was considering Beth's words. Then She tipped Beth's chin up with Her fingers and pushed Her palm forward until it touched Beth's throat. Beth felt her pulse flickering against Mater Viae's skin. She felt the red-hot fever racing through the Goddess's own city's bricks. She flinched back hard.

"*Y-You're sick too?*" the voice, emerging from her own city, stammered in time with the jackhammers that formed it.

Mater Viae lifted Her foot and stamped forward hard. Beth's left kneecap exploded into a million fiery needles. She sagged against the stone fingers that held her, breathless and dizzy with the pain

. . . she tried to stand on the rooftop but her legs went from under her and she fell. The sky above her was as dark as a bruise . . .

then she shook her head hard and London came back into focus. Over Mater Viae's shoulder she saw the shattered skyline. The frozen Thames shone like a diamond over St. Paul's; it was motionless, becalmed somehow.

"*How?*" She managed at last to form the words. "*If you're sick too? How can you . . . ?*" She strained as hard as she could against the grey fingers that held her, trying to ignore the bruising pressure on her ribs. Mater Viae watched, coldly motionless, as Beth struggled. At last she sagged back, exhausted, Mater Viae unclenched Her fingers and the giant hand dropped Beth unceremoniously into the dirt. The Goddess wiped Her slate-scaled fingers through Her skirts as though they were contaminated.

"*By being better than you.*" The arrogance in the statement did nothing to change the truth of it.

Freezing Estuary water washed over Beth's stomach as Mater Viae knelt on it.

"*You caused the fever,*" she hissed. "*You sickened the streets. You. The City is in rejection—it's in shock. It can't survive with two of Us, any more than you could survive with a second heart or a second brain. You woke the cranes, you woke the River, and all you ever had to do if you wanted to cure the City was die.*"

Beth gazed past Mater Viae's shoulder at her empty, stricken city. She thought of the soldiers she'd watched drowning in the Tideways, and the kid's scream that had rung out from the Blank Street, and all the other hundreds of thousands of people she had never known who had perished by the fever. She thought of Timon. She thought about all the times in the past three months she'd fought and scrambled and killed to stay alive. *Hundreds of thousands*, she thought. If she'd only been a little slower, a little weaker, a little less determined, then some of those people would be alive instead of her.

Some, but not all.

Something set in her. She rolled her thumb over her forefinger and remembered how it had felt pressing down on a wound that wouldn't close.

"*You too,*" she hissed. The pain in her chest was a raging fire, like the fire that had killed Pen, and it devoured her. "*That's all You ever had to do too. You killed my dad. You killed my best friend.*"

Mater Viae looked at her for a moment, Her expression inscrutable. "*You killed My child,*" she said simply.

The hand that brushed Beth's hair back from her temple was almost gentle. Mater Viae pressed Her palm to Beth's cheek. Beth felt the heat in it, and the shape of the cranes that stretched under the skin like bones, and then . . . something else.

"*And you did it wearing my face.*"

Beth screamed: a cry of shattering windows and derailed trains and ruinous car crashes. She could feel Mater Viae's consciousness *in* her.

Just as Beth had once poured herself into the city around Her, the Urban Goddess poured herself into the city that was *Beth*. The power of the Lady of the Streets was a physical presence in her flesh. Beth shuddered as she felt it brush the foundations of the streets that crisscrossed her cheeks. She babbled and kicked.

And then, with a horror that drew the moment out like a teardrop, she felt her own body responding to Mater Viae's will.

The skin on her eyebrow and cheek bubbled like liquid clay and then closed over her left eye. Beth's breath came in panicked gasps. She shuddered, and hot and cold shivers raced over her skin.

Fil, she whispered into her mind. *Help.*

"*I can't.*" *The grey boy sounded dreadfully ashamed. His arms were around her chest and he was half curled around her, sheltering her from the wind that shrieked over the rooftop. She was slumped in his lap, her head nestled in the hollow of his shoulder, her useless legs splayed out in front of her. "There's nothing I can do."*

A storm swirled over them, as vast as the world. Towers of black cloud speared down towards them, cloud-streets and cloud-houses formed, mimicking and mocking Beth's home. The cloud architecture shifted suddenly, towers braiding themselves together, and the wind redoubled. It scoured the city, stripping paint from lintels and ripping asphalt up from the road. Walls buckled and tore under its power. Beth's ears throbbed.

The wind slackened as suddenly as a flicked switch and Beth climbed to her feet. She touched her ear and her finger came away tipped in bright red blood. She reeled to the edge of the roof and looked out past the dormant cranes she'd dreamed there to the tower blocks. Her stomach clenched. The buildings were warped, twisted together like crops after a tornado. They were dead hulks, their lights out. A perfect mirror of the city picked out in the clouds . . .

She blinked her one good eye. Tears and blue skies filled her vision again. She bared her church-spire teeth and scrabbled at Mater Viae's guts, trying to retaliate in kind, to concentrate on them, to *change* them. She didn't even care what to.

Mater Viae slapped her hand out of the way. "*Godhood is power,*" She said contemptuously. "*And you are a fake.*"

She grabbed Beth's hoodie in both fists and tore it. Beth kicked and flailed, but nothing could move the iron weight of the Goddess' knee in her guts.

A burning-hot palm and five splayed fingers pressed themselves to her stomach and Beth gritted her teeth and hissed as Mater Viae's power rippled through her again. Her abdominal muscles spasmed and she lurched up, vomiting oil. Everything seen through her one clear eye was close up and flat. Before she fell back, she glimpsed a handprint on her stomach the exact shape of Mater Viae's splayed fingers. There the architecture skin was blackened and ridged like a burn scar. There were no lights in the windows, no cars on the roads. It was dead.

Mater Viae laid Her hand on a neighbouring patch of skin. She was precise; Her fingers were tight against the edge of the wound She'd just made. Beth twisted and bucked and spat and made no difference as the skin there changed too.

Mater Viae was killing her from the skin inwards. The Goddess' face was set with a surgeon's grim concentration. Her accusatory voice echoed in Beth's head: "*Fake.*" With a dizzy horror, Beth understood why. In Mater Viae's eyes, her city-skin was a mockery, a lie, and She was venting Her fury on it.

Streets stretched like lifelines on Mater Viae's palm as She laid it over Beth's belly button, and she felt the energy humming into her skin as her enemy imposed Her will.

Pain flared, savage and electric: bone-deep, vein-deep, sub-basement deep. Beth could feel the voltage the Street Goddess had pumped into her body like knives. She panicked. She scraped up power from the joints of her knuckles and her toes, from the train-tracks in the whorls of her fingerprints and the air pressure inside her brick-cellar sinuses and *anywhere* she could find a spare scrap of energy. She channelled it instinctively, flexing a thousand tiny internal muscles, and hurled it at Mater Viae's palm where it touched her.

Beth jolted hard as the two forces met in her flesh. Mater Viae's energy broke in her like an electric shock and zigzagged, diverted from its purpose, racing through her streets and diffusing out into the ground beneath her.

Her head slammed back into the shale.

The storm whipped between the towers. Beth was sprawled face-down, the gravel grazing the soft skin below her eye socket. Rain hammered the back of her head. Fil lay next to her. She tried to look up. The world came slowly into focus, but there was an after-image burned on her retinas: an image of jibs and chains and metal arms. She blinked it clear and was left staring at a motionless horizon. The five cranes that had dominated the skyline of her dream for the past three days were gone.

Something invisible pushed down hard on her throat.

Her fingers flew to it, but couldn't get purchase . . .

She opened her eye. Mater Viae had her pinned to the ground by her neck. Beth thrashed and gurgled and blinked her intact eye, frantically trying to clear it as it watered. Her struggling shifted her half an inch to the left and for the first time she could see past Mater Viae's shoulder. She stopped suddenly, going limp and staring in incomprehension.

Five cranes loomed in silhouette against the dazzlingly blue sky. They were exactly as she'd dreamed them.

They *were* the ones she'd imagined, she was sure of it.

How? What had just happened? A millisecond earlier those cranes had been in her dreams—now they were out here in the real, broken, world.

Godhood is power, she thought, *and you are a fake.*

The idea that hit her then both appalled and elated her, a crazy hope born of pain and panic. She thought of all the times she'd tried to change the city, all the Masonry Men she'd tried and failed to raise that had afterwards lurked in the alleyways of her dreams. She'd made the shapes in her mind, but she hadn't had the *power* to make them real. She remembered Gutterglass' concerned face looking down at her in the Selfridges kitchen: *Pulling the claylings out of your mind requires considerable energy . . .*

Sick as Beth was, she hadn't been able to summon that energy for months—but Mater Viae had.

Beth. The memory of Pen's voice filled her head. *You* are *home.*

Mater Viae leaned over her, Her eyes burning with mad intent. Slate-scaled fingers covered Beth's mouth and nose; she could taste the sweat on the Goddess' hand.

Beth's face tingled for a moment, and then the pain came; and the power flooded with it. Beth felt her teeth soften even as she clenched them. She had to time this right. Her jaw hung sideways as the nerves died. Her skull fizzed with the urban energy Mater Viae was pouring into her.

Now! she thought. She scraped up the scraps of that energy and concentrated frantically on the idea of a Masonry Man.

Nothing happened.

The pain was too great. She couldn't focus. The shape and feel of the clayling's body slipped away from her. She ransacked her thoughts, but she couldn't find it again. There were too many streets, too many doorways in her mind to look behind. Her lips were dying; the nerves in her teeth and the back of her throat were dying. There was spit in her throat, but she couldn't swallow.

She couldn't hold on to her carefully balled-up energy; it was burning a hole in her. She had to use it or let it go. She could feel her concentration slipping. Random images flashed through her mind: her parents' faces, old adverts that had stuck with her, pictures she'd painted. The last image was a flamenco dancer, sprayed against a concrete wall, then consciousness slid away.

The hurricane raged over the rooftops. Beth was pressed flat to the gravel. She felt like the wind would rip the skin off her. Above her, the cloud-city was a horribly detailed ruin: broken metropolis, broken body. That intention was in every raindrop that fell from the sky. The air was charged with it; it prickled in her pores, conducted through her sweat.

The density of the air changed: a second wind was building. It poured out of manhole covers and windows and doorways and out of the pores in the bricks themselves, Beth could smell diesel on it, and hear the crackle of spiders' voices. It was hers and it rose up off the surface of the city like it was an ocean, and it howled a challenge to the storm.

The cloud-city eddied and the wounds in it lost definition, lost focus. Air-flows sheared at one another like continents, edged in heat and friction.

Lightning lit up the city, not leaping down from the clouds but up from the streets themselves. The bolt struck a tower block with a woman in Spanish flamenco skirts graffiti'd a hundred feet up on the side.

The shape of the tower and the shape of the woman burned white on Beth's retinas for a moment, then she blinked and they were gone. Nothing remained, not even dust.

That could be it, *Beth thought frantically.* That could be it. I have to wake up. I have to *see. She slammed her head back into the gravel and pain flashed through her scalp. Panic clawed its way up her throat, but she remained, stubbornly anchored to her dream. She slammed her head down again, and again, focusing on the pain, and she yelled aloud into the storm,* "I have to wake up."

"I have to wake—!"

"—*up*—!"

Beach and riverbed and burned factory blurred in front of her. Her chest was washed cold by Estuary waters. Mater Viae was snarling over her, Her palm grinding Beth's lips into her nerveless teeth. Beth thrashed, desperate to move her head just a fraction of an inch, desperate to *see*, but Mater Viae's grip was like an iron nail, pinning her to the dirt. She rolled her one good eye and peered out of the corner of it.

The last of her breath stalled in her lungs. Her vision was so blurry that she didn't know if she was seeing it because it was really there or because she really *wanted* it there.

Across the river, where moments before there had only been the ash of the synod's factory, a familiar tower block rose against the brilliant blue sky. A woman in flamenco skirts was picked out on the side of it in aerosol paints, a hundred feet high.

Beth, you are home. The thought circled deliriously inside her head. *She* was a city: she was streets and houses and sewers and Railwraiths and water and shelter. She *was* home.

All she'd lacked, just as she'd lacked with the stillborn Masonry Men, was the power to make that real.

Mater Viae slammed an elbow into Beth's ribs again; she tried to double up, but the knee in her guts held her down. The Goddess' expression was frantic with rage. Her eyes were unfocused; all concentration had gone from Her face. She started slapping and punching at Beth indiscriminately, determined just to rend and destroy, tearing at her with Her power like an angry wolf.

Beth closed her eye and let herself drift into the pain.

. . . Jags of lightning tore down to the pavement. The storm cloud above was a shapeless grey-black muddle, but still it poured its energy into the city below it. A lightning bolt yawed crazily and slammed into a row of houses, and the whole terrace exploded into nothingness. The wind screamed, its force like a boulder pressing Beth down onto the roof. The dirty gale that rose off the city hammered against it. Electricity crackled between the two air-currents and another lightning bolt arced. Beth felt it light up her agonized grin, even as another skyscraper vanished beneath it. Fil lay spreadeagled, unable to rise, his fingers stretched towards hers.

"Beth!" he hollered. "What are you doing?"

Beth hissed her reply through gritted teeth because she could feel the pain of her city around her. "Un-giving up."

Mater Viae's face twisted with effort. She kept moving Her hands, trying to get a better grip, but Beth's skin, Beth's whole *body . . .*

She could feel it receding like burning paper as the energy consumed her.

New shadows fell across the river shore, as though from towers that hadn't been there seconds before.

Beth couldn't move her neck; it hurt like she imagined electrocution must hurt, with a burning, spasming loss of control. She couldn't feel her hands. Her spine jumped and smacked into the floor. Her jaw clenched, and her teeth should have scraped together but the bottom row was missing; she probed the space where they should have been with her tongue. On the horizon, a clutch of new church spires reared up over London's shattered landscape, the brick and metalwork surging out of the ground as though the earth was liquid.

Mater Viae's lips peeled back in a snarl; She twisted, grinding Her palm down into Beth's mouth again.

Beth felt the energy ripple through her skull. *Come on*, she thought, desperately, giddily, *come* on. She raised her right hand in front of her face. All but two of the fingers were missing.

Her pulse hammered through her head like an express train. The stub of her tongue wagged in her mouth. Darkness encroached her vision, but she fought to stay conscious. She was weakening . . .

Come on . . .

Mater Viae howled in frustration and shoved at Beth with outstretched hands, like a child pounding on a locked door. Even in its petulance, Her rage was terrifying. She drew herself up, impossibly tall above Beth. Her body tensed, and Beth tensed with it.

Come on . . .

Mater Viae's green eyes went suddenly black, the power surging into Beth swelled like a tide and Beth gave way before it.

She didn't even *try* to focus the power any more. She couldn't—there was just too much. All she could do was will it to read the shape of her streets at it raced through them. Her thoughts were splintering under the pain.

Leaning over her, Mater Viae overbalanced, as if wrong-footed by the loss of resistance. Her power raged uncontrollably through Beth's streets and cellars and hallways, and Beth felt them dissolve under its force. She was disintegrating, her sewer-capillaries burning out like fuses. Her right shoulder blade vanished and her arm sagged suddenly and agonisingly at her side. More tower-block shadows fell across the riverbank.

You are home. She muttered it to herself inside her head in the broken moments where she could form a coherent thought. Maybe she was dying; maybe she was being born—she couldn't tell and she didn't care. *You are home.*

Above her, the fury on the Goddess' face ebbed to panic. Mater Viae's hand trembled and Beth felt Her trying to pull away. Beth clamped the stumps of her wrists over it, holding it down. Mater Viae struggled, but She no longer had the strength left to break Beth's fingerless grip.

Two words surfaced through the storm in Beth's mind: *She over-commits.*

The Goddess' free hand shook as She planted it on the earth beside Beth's head, desperately trying to summon power from the city to replace what she'd lost.

Now, Beth thought.

With a snarl in what was left of her throat, Beth opened herself up fully to the street. The poisoned urban energy slammed into her through her spine, her shoulders, her hips. She sucked it up greedily and it ripped through her, overwhelming her urbosynthetic cells: too much to take, too much to control, too much to survive, but Beth was dying anyway. She didn't want to live, she wanted to *win.*

Mater Viae's hand pattered desperately over the ground, but She was coming up empty; Beth had drained this district dry. Dim green sparks flickered in the Goddess' eyes, but they didn't reignite.

And then, with a suddenness and quietness that shocked Beth, the empty Goddess collapsed sideways onto the beach.

Beth tilted her head forward and looked at herself. Her legs were gone. Her hoodie was a ripped and ragged mess and beneath it skin, bones and wires were all searing away to nothingness. Her body was undone; it was too late to stop it, even if she'd wanted to. The blood dripping from her pipe-veins vanished in midair, dissolving under the power racing through it. As the world dimmed and blurred, Beth lifted her gaze. She looked out across the empty riverbed at the place where London had lain in ruins.

A new skyline blotted out the horizon: a skyline she knew more intimately than any other city. And it was all there, in the real world. On top of a hill directly ahead of her, sixteen church spires reared up, the iron crosses that capped them glinting in the sun. They were arranged in a rough semicircle as though lining a jaw.

The muscles in her neck burned away and vanished. Her head fell back.

The storm raged on, pummelling Beth's body, dragging at her hair. Freezing rain pounded her skin. With one hand, she clung to her tower, the only building left. All else was flat grey earth and uncanny light.

Lightning danced around her. Her body was pulled taut by the wind, her toes splayed out over empty air. Her arms burned all along their length. One hand was clamped to the edge of the roof and her fingers and knuckles were numb with the cold. The other was dragged out behind her; the skinny grey boy who clung to it flapped in the wind like a flag.

"Beth—" She saw her name on his lips, but she couldn't hear it. "Help—I don't—"

His fingers slipped and he was lost in an instant, spinning head over heel, weightless as a winter leaf, until he merged with the grey.

The clouds gathered in close around Beth. Lightning flashed again, scorching the air she breathed. Concrete grazed her fingertips as they slipped an inch. There was nothing left to do. She closed her eyes and thought of home.

She let go.

IV

THE END OF THE DAY

CHAPTER THIRTY-NINE

A steam-whistle echoed gleefully over the rooftops and the Rail-wraith clattered between the housing terraces, bearing its passengers north.

Pen watched England whip by through the window. In between the red blocks of houses she glimpsed patches of green. The fabric city was thin here: only a single row of terraced houses on either side separated the tracks from open countryside. Every few miles, holes gaped in the terraces, lined with rubble. Fire-blackened cranes lay at the top of the railway embankment like dug-up animal bones: signs that the battle had stretched even this far north.

On the far side of the carriage, Gutterglass gazed out the opposite window, her Biro-fingers twisting restlessly through the torn plastic of her hair. The proximity of the open fields made her nervous; for Glas, there was only City and un-City. The latter was a desert, barren and impossible to survive. Pen was grateful she was here. Even after everything, she wouldn't have wanted to be in here with the carriage's third passenger by herself.

Dr. Salt slumped against a chair three rows away, one wrist tied to the handrail with blue nylon rope. He didn't struggle. His eyes, shockingly wide and pale above the filthy thatch of his beard, flicked continually from the garbage-built woman to Pen and back again.

He hadn't given them any trouble. They'd found him crouched on a bench in a dark alcove at the back of the cathedral. The little two-barb sentinel Pen had set to watch him lay on the wood like a dead insect. When she'd ordered him to get on the train, he'd obeyed without a word. He saw no difference between Pen with the wire and Pen without; he was simply terrified of her. If she'd opened the doors of the carriage and told him to jump down under the wraith's clattering wheels, he'd probably do it. He was, in a way, her creature now.

Pen felt a shiver of disgust at that thought. Her fear of him was a small hard thing lodged in her chest and she couldn't shift it. Anger boiled up in her and she wondered if it would ever leave her. She remembered Beth's city-voice: "*You never could have done that to him.*"

"You were wrong, B," she muttered under her breath. "You knew me better than anyone, but you were wrong."

She could have killed Salt, and she knew it. On a different day, in a fractionally different frame of mind, if she'd made the decision a minute sooner or a minute later, on one of the million moments when her anger had burned so bright in her that she couldn't tell the difference between it and her desire to be free of him, then it would have been him and not Paul Bradley that she sent to bleed out on Crystal Palace Hill.

Right now, she wished it had been. Tomorrow she might feel differently. Or not.

She looked down at the notebook open in front of her. The page was blank except for one word.

Beth.

She stared at the white space beneath it. A few times she lowered her pen to the paper, and then pulled it back. She pressed the tip into the page and pushed harder and harder until with a loud *snap* it broke. Salt started at the sound and pushed himself back into the mouldering fabric of his seat. Pen ignored him.

Without looking around from the window, Gutterglass pulled a Bic from her right hand and passed it over.

"Thanks," Pen said.

"It'll come," the trash-spirit said.

Maybe Glas was right. She remembered returning to the factory, not understanding, fleeing from the strange new architecture that had materialised amongst the ruins of the city. She'd been sure, deep down, it had to be something to do with Beth; it *had* to be. That certainty had turned into a cold clamp around her heart when she had seen the architecture-skinned body lying face-down and motionless on the beach.

She remembered pulling that prone figure over by the shoulder, horrified by her stillness, her dead weight. She'd tried to set herself, to draw on all the little mental preparations she'd been making for this moment, but they were completely inadequate. What she'd felt as that face had come around to face her was sheer, unreasoning panic . . .

A panic that had subsided in a welter of confusion and relief, because she knew that face, and it wasn't Beth's.

"Glas, are—?" she started, but she'd already asked the question dozens of times and the answer hadn't changed.

"Yes, Parva," she said. "I'm sure." Her voice had an off musicality; her guitar-string vocal chords were visible through a tear in her paper neck. "No pigeon, rat, beetle or worm anywhere in the city has seen her. But it's more than that, we'd just *know*: if there was an Urban Goddess alive anywhere, we'd *feel* it."

Pen set the pen to the paper again, then she bit her lip. She was only trying to do what she'd always done, write out how she felt, but when she tried to tune into that part of her that should have been grieving, she got only static. *There was no body*, she told herself. *So maybe . . .* She couldn't accept it; she couldn't *feel* the truth of it. Perhaps her emotions had shut down to protect her: an induced coma of the heart. Or maybe she was just being stubborn and this way it would hurt more in the long run. But then—and she even managed a harsh little smile—that's exactly how Beth would have done it.

She closed the book. *Not yet*, she told herself. *Not yet.*

The Railwraith slowed under them, its swaying becoming more pronounced. They were almost there.

Pen tapped her fingertips on the hard cover of her notebook. A wordless anxiety rose in her. She jumped to her feet and paced up and down the aisle, ducking to peer out of the windows. She glanced back into the next carriage down and glimpsed the vague shapes of passengers that only the wraith remembered. Blue electricity danced on their teeth as they ignored one another.

The Railwraith screeched to a halt and the doors beeped and hissed open, letting in a shaft of noon sunshine. Pen jumped out and her feet crunched coarse gravel. She squinted in the brightness, looking around anxiously.

It was a tiny station: one track, one red-painted bench under a metal awning, one ticket booth, and one ticket machine covered in looping black graffiti, even though Pen doubted any other human had ever set foot here. The sun's glare had turned the window on the ticket booth into a perfect mirror. Pen checked her watch. It was one minute to midday.

There were three glass phials in the back pocket of her jeans. She pulled out the left-hand one, almost fumbling it in her haste, and eagerly unscrewed the lid, then hurled the contents against the window. As the clear liquid ran down the surface, it erased the glass and revealed tangled blonde hair and a beaming, seam-split face.

"Countess!" Espel jumped up onto the reflected countertop, ducked under the window frame and dive-bombed Pen. They fell in a tangle onto the train platform.

"Ow!" Pen muttered. "Knee—"

"Sorry."

They both laughed and shifted until their limbs settled into a more comfortable position. The sun-warmed pavement felt good on Pen's back. She tilted her head; Espel's lips found hers and opened over them. For a little while the world disappeared.

"Ahem."

Gutterglass didn't even bother to make the throat-clearing noise, she just said the word. Without breaking the kiss, Espel extended first an arm and then a middle finger.

"There's no need to be rude," the trash-spirit murmured. "I simply wanted to indicate that we had company."

Pen felt a little flutter behind her ribs and pulled away from the kiss. Espel rolled off her and she sat up. About fifty yards from where the railway gave out, a road shimmered in the heat. It twisted past the buffers at the end of the tracks and then bore straight on, vanishing into the low skyline of Birmingham, where England's makeshift new capital bulked on the horizon. Pen heard a buzz that might have been a distant engine or a nearby insect. Steadily the sound grew louder, until a white car with yellow hi-vis markings on its bonnet came into view over a rise.

The fluttering behind Pen's ribs grew stronger.

"How long can you stay, Es?" Even as Pen asked the question, she was playing the answer the steeplejill was bound to give in her head and trying not to be disappointed.

A few days at most. The claylings may have all dropped back into the floor but there are still plenty of officer-class dickheads to keep me occupied. Plus, Case is nowhere to be found . . .

"How long do you think?" Espel said, cutting across her thoughts. Intriguingly, it was her right eyebrow that was arched. "As long as you fragging well want me to."

Pen blinked. "But Case—and the Resistance—"

"We'll find Case," Espel said patiently, "and the rest of the Faceless aren't going keel over and die if they have to be without me for a few days. We don't really have figureheads, Countess. That's kind of the point of us."

She shaded her eyes with one hand, and then whistled. "*Mago*," she breathed in an awestruck voice.

"What?"

"There's just so much *green* stuff."

The police car pulled up at the side of the road, as close as it could get to the train tracks. The driver's door opened. A stocky woman in a leather coat got out and then immediately ducked as a disgruntled pigeon flapped out of the car after her, soared briefly over Pen and Espel's heads and lighted on Gutterglass' shoulder.

The woman in the leather coat squinted at Pen for a moment and then hurried over, her heavy boots crunching the gravel as she crossed the tracks. "Parva," she said.

"Detective Ellis." Pen was startled. "I didn't expect it to be you."

"To be honest, I didn't really expect it to be you either, despite what your note said. But then, I didn't expect the first message we've had out of London in months to come by carrier-pigeon, so what do I know?"

Pen frowned. "Why did they send you?"

"They put your name through the computer and came up with mine, so they called me."

"No, I mean . . ." Pen listened and craned her neck to look, but no more cars were coming down the road. "Why just you?"

Ellis winced slightly, but didn't say anything.

"Because if the letter was a fake and this was a trap, they'd only lose you, right?" Pen surmised.

"I wasn't ecstatic about it to begin with, either," she admitted. "But I've seen the mess those blue dragons made of the army, so I figured any protection they could offer me wouldn't be worth much anyway."

"But you came."

"Yes, I came."

Pen smiled at her. "Sewermanders," she said.

"I'm sorry?"

"Those blue dragon things, they're called Sewermanders, and they're not all bad when you get to know them." Pen leaned forward and looked past her case officer's shoulder at the car. "What I asked in my note—did you bring them?"

Ellis nodded. "I told them to stay in the car until I'd checked it out."

"Okay," Pen said. The fluttering behind her ribs became a drumming. "There's a present waiting for you on the train."

"A nice sort of present?" Ellis asked. "Or the sort of shitbag present you promised in your note?"

"The latter, I'm afraid."

"All right."

Pen started past her, but Detective Ellis put a hand on her arm.

"Parva, I . . ." she started, then hesitated before trying again, "I don't know quite how to say this, maybe it's . . ." She broke off again, clearly not understanding. "I don't think they remember you."

"I know."

Ellis gaped at her. "Their own *daughter*? How—? What did that to them?"

"I did," Pen said gently. She pushed the policewoman's arm away and started walking. Footsteps crunched beside her: Espel was keeping pace. Warm fingers, callused by years of scrambling over bricks, threaded through hers and she squeezed them tight.

When they were about ten feet from the car the passenger doors opened and a man and a woman got out. The man was short and wiry, slightly stooped around his pot belly. His black hair had been gelled back from his brow and his skin was a deep teak-brown. The woman was tinier even than her husband; everyone always said it was a miracle they'd had a daughter so tall. Pen's mother wore a sky-blue hijab and a dress that looked brand-new. Her dad wore a suit and a striped shirt. Pen's heart gave a little lurch. This was how they'd dress to meet an important stranger.

And then, all at once, she was right in front of them. She stopped walking, unsure how close she could get. They eyed her uncertainly. She could see recognition in their eyes, but no warmth. They knew her from the photos in her aunt's house, but nowhere else.

"I'm sorry," her dad said. His voice was hurt and confused. "I'm not sure what we're supposed to do."

"It's okay," Pen said. She didn't try to touch them. She pulled the two remaining phials from her back pocket. Each had been labelled in a careful copperplate hand, "*Mr. Khan*" and "*Mrs. Khan*." The writing was impossibly neat. Being wasted down to a skeleton didn't seem to have damaged Johnny Naphtha's handwriting.

Inside the phials, the liquid was silver as mercury. It clung to the glass.

She took one in each hand and offered them to them, like treats for children. They took them, regarding them mistrustfully.

"It's okay," Pen said. "They're safe." With a bitter tang of panic in her throat she realised she didn't know what she'd do if they didn't believe her.

They looked up at her, the child they didn't remember. Her mum unscrewed the cap first, her dad an instant later, then they looked to each other. Her mum gave her dad a reassuring smile and they linked hands, a mirror to Pen and Espel. Pen saw her mouthing, "*One, two, three!*" to him.

"Mum, Dad," Pen said as the phials touched their lips. She squeezed Espel's hand tight. "There's someone I want you to meet."

CHAPTER FORTY

The sun sets low over Battersea, or at least over the streets where Battersea once was. Perhaps they will need new names now, these nests of alleys and overpasses; then again, perhaps not. Cities often cling to their names when they slough off everything else. Either way, it's not up to me; these streets aren't mine any more.

I haul myself over the edge of a gable and the roof tiles clink as I scramble onto them. I can smell the sharp oil in my sweat and feel it running down between my shoulder blades to cool in the evening air. I race along the length of the terrace, my bare feet sure on the tiles. A steel bridge looms up in front of me and I race under its shadow. A wraith clatters overhead. It sounds its steam-whistle, challenging me, but I have no time to race. I look down into the road below me, peering into shadows and around corners. I sniff the wind, but all I smell is petrol and rain.

I need a higher vantage. A sheer grey tower rises on the far side of the road and I pick up my pace. The wind rushes in my ears as I leap for it.

I scrabble, and a window ledge catches my fingertips. I climb, winkling my toes into tiny crevices, scrambling crabwise upwards.

It's a long way up, and night settles around the city's shoulders while I ascend. The tower's windows become burning slabs of orange light. A woman dances towards me beneath its concrete skin, her flamenco dress picked out in aerosol paint. Her every step is graceful, for this is far more her element than mine.

She pauses beside me and I feel the brush of her painted hand as it slides beneath my fingers. She whispers her name and invites me to dance, to take my hand from its hold and place it on the smooth surface where her palm waits. I can feel the warmth rising from the wall where her skin is painted. One of her eyes is a diamond, the other a black swirling galaxy, flinted with stars. I realise that she is blind.

I don't think I would fall, but I don't pause to indulge her. I make my apologies and scramble higher, for there is no time, and there are deadlier things than her on the walls of this painted city. In the distance I hear a rhino snort.

With an exhilarated shout, I gain the roof. Lungs heaving, I race to the far side and look down. Streetlamps are igniting across the city, etching it in shadow and orange light, but how many of the spirits dancing in their bulbs are refugees from the old city, and how many were dreamed into existence with the new, I cannot say.

The towers are taller in this new London, the architecture stranger. The railings lining its parks are jagged-edged and sharp. Its shadows whisper promises and threats. Ahead, beyond the old burned-black apartment blocks and the new ring of church spires that rise up from the city like teeth, I see the river glint.

It's awake, I think. *In her name, it's awake.*

The sentient water zigzags between the new buildings, it arcs gracefully over bridges and then dips to crash through tunnels hidden far under the street. The Thames' course changes according to its mood now; this new city is its playground. Rediscovering its freedom has made it a fickle thing, and the humans beginning to recolonise the city will have to work hard to stay on the River's good side.

I see them occasionally, tiny figures moving in the windows of abandoned houses. Perhaps soon they'll be dancing with the Lampfolk or bartering octaves of their voices to hungry spiders in exchange for a message carried to their families. Perhaps they'll seek counsel from the veterans, the survivors, the ones who sit on doorsteps still marvelling at the freshly closed cuts in their hands and feet. I wish them all the luck they'll need, but they're not my concern. I scour the streets below me but find no sign of my quarry. I heave out a breath, and run on.

My muscles are burning. I've been running for four nights now, my bare feet sucking up energy from the street to keep me fresh. During the daylight hours I sleep fitfully in the shadows of the high-rises. My own dreams are full of her. I glance down at the tower-block tattoo on my wrist.

It's four nights since I woke in an empty alley, my skin leaching colour from the asphalt, the light from a single dancing Sodium-ite drawing my shadow across the floor. Four nights—my flagging heart trips faster at the thought—and perhaps she can say the same.

I remember my own voice: *Your body is a city now. Your mind is a citizen. Mine is a refugee.*

It's a desperate hope: if the city is real now, out in the world, shouldn't the citizen be too?

Four nights, I wonder. Who knows what she might have seen in four nights in this city she once wore as a skin, where her dreams and her nightmares were born into brick? Would she be helpless before it, paralysed by recognition? Or does she navigate these streets more expertly than I ever could?

Is she, even now, stalking *me*?

I cannot know. Nothing is certain now. She was the blueprint of this city. She was its essence and its source; these streets were her body and her brain. I remember the hooded girl who walked beside me while she slept, a girl who never forgot her human skin. All I can do is hope that, like me, that girl is restored to sight and smell and blood and bone and breath—that when this city was born out into the world, she was born with it. And so for her, the only one who has ever frightened me enough to make me brave, for my scarred, scared brave girl of a conscience,

I'm hunting.

ACKNOWLEDGMENTS

Well, we made it.

Enormous thanks to Jo Fletcher and to Nicola Budd, Andrew Turner, Tim Kershaw and the whole team at Quercus for shepherding these stories out of my head and onto the page. Extra special gratitude to my agent Amy Boggs for being a rock, and helping me bring this home.

Thanks also to Den Patrick, James Smythe, Emily Richards, Helen Callaghan, Sam Miles and Glen Mehn, who were invaluable to this final volume, and to Kim Eyre and Marek Kochanowski, the teachers who helped set me on this path in the first place.

I'm hugely grateful to Sarah Pollock, Barbara Pollock, David Pollock, Sally Simpson, Barbara Barrett, Robin Barrett, Moira Barrett, Olivia Simpson, Aislinn Laing, Hugo Laing and the rest of my extended family for their tolerance, love and advice. That goes quintuple for my wife, Lizzie Barrett, who has to live with me every day.

I cited a lot of authors in this section of the first two books, and I felt their influence no less when writing the third. There is one name still to add though: Jon Courtenay Grimwood, who sets the gold standard for writing voices in people's heads (among other things).

And the final thanks goes to you, for reading this far, for lending your imagination to the creation of Scaffwolves and slatestorms, and also for reading the acknowledgements, and knowing that no story is ever made by one person alone.

ABOUT THE TYPE

Typeset in Swift EF, 10/15 pt.

Named for an acrobatic city bird native to Holland,
Swift was designed by Gerard Unger in 1985 to meet the
need for a typeface that could remain crisp and clear
after coming off the high-speed newspaper presses of the day.
For its original distribution as a PostScript font, it was
leased to German foundry Elsner+Flake.

Typeset by Scribe Inc., Philadelphia, Pennsylvania

The City's Son
Book One of the Skyscraper Throne Trilogy

TOM POLLOCK

"An impeccably dark parable, endlessly inventive
and utterly compelling."
—MIKE CAREY, bestselling author of *The Girl with All the Gifts*

The Glass Republic
Book Two of the Skyscraper Throne Trilogy

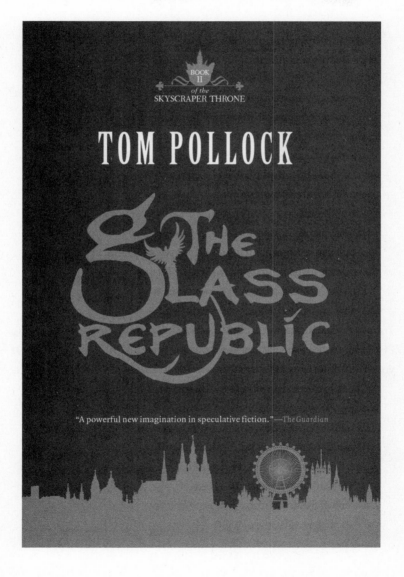

BOOK
II
of the
SKYSCRAPER THRONE

TOM POLLOCK

THE GLASS REPUBLIC

"A powerful new imagination in speculative fiction."—*The Guardian*

Tom Pollock is a graduate of the Sussex University Creative Writing Program. In 2013, *The Guardian* named him one of the twenty best young novelists in science fiction. He lives and writes in London.